2/95
BT

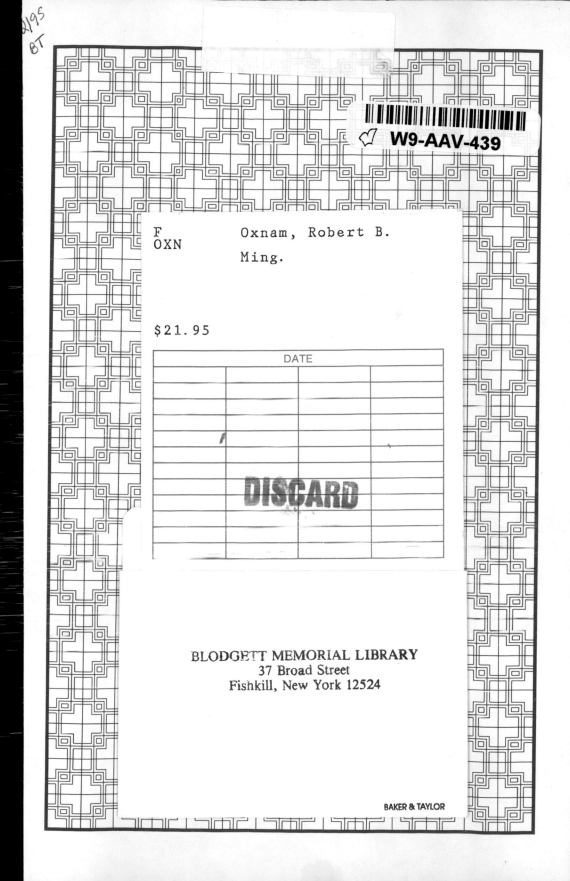

W9-AAV-439

F
OXN

Oxnam, Robert B.

Ming.

$21.95

MING

明

ALSO BY ROBERT B. OXNAM

Cinnabar

MING

明

A Novel of Seventeenth-Century China

ROBERT B. OXNAM

ST. MARTIN'S PRESS
New York

The author and the publisher are grateful to Columbia University Press for permission to reprint the Chinese character for *Ming* from *Self and Society in Ming Thought* by William Theodore de Bary.

Design by Sara Stemen

Maps by Frank Riccio

LIBRARY OF CONGRESS CATALOGING–IN–PUBLICATION DATA

Oxnam, Robert b.
    Ming : a novel of seventeenth century China / Robert B. Oxnam.
      p.   cm.
    "A Thomas Dunne book."
    ISBN 0-312-11315-3
    I. Title.
    PS3565.X36M56   1995   94-36361
813'.54—dc20   CIP

First Edition: January 1995

10 9 8 7 6 5 4 3 2 1

To Vishakha N. Desai,

esteemed colleague and wonderful wife

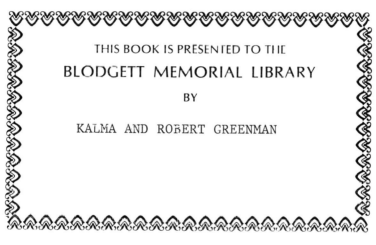

Acknowledgments

明

IN THE RESEARCH, writing, and revisions of this novel, I have been helped immeasurably by an extended family of friends and colleagues.

They include Nancy Blume, Peggy Blumenthal, Vishakha Desai, Inger McCabe Elliott, Karen Kenyon, Daisy Kwoh, Douglas Murray, Father Joseph O'Hare, Geoffrey Oxnam, Cynthia Polsky, Jonathan Spence, John Bryan Starr, Gary Stephens, Linda Sweet, Ross Terrill, Lady Judith Ogden Thomson, and Madeleine Zelin.

All of them have kindly diverted time and talent to helping me shape this work of fiction. I am indebted to each of them, but bear full responsibility for the final product.

Introduction

明

IN SEVENTEENTH-CENTURY CHINA—the late Ming and early Qing dynasties—literacy was the special preserve of elites, perhaps 20 million of a total population of 150 million people. Knowledge was power, quite literally, in a society where access to high officialdom required passing rigorous civil service examinations based on the Confucian classics.

For upper-class young men, the examination life required plodding preparation for a precarious test. Tutors schooled aspiring examination candidates from childhood through their twenties and even thirties, until they were ready to take the local, then the provincial, the national, and, for the most successful, the palace examinations. The examinations required that students memorize every word of the Confucian classics, absorb all of the stylized criticisms of those works of philosophy and literature, and then write answers to questions in an archaic form known as an eight-legged essay. It was as if all Western applicants for high office had to memorize every word of Shakespeare and Milton and then write examinations in Petrarchan sonnet form. Errors in calligraphy were evaluated harshly; all writing was done with brushes so there was no chance for erasures or corrections.

Most histories of the period have been written about the tiny minority of men who succeeded in the examinations, the few thousands who made it to the pinnacle of power. Those who failed, who lacked the ability or discipline to stay the course, have slipped from the pages of history. What anguish it must have been to confront parents after returning from the examination cubicles with bad news. And what greater pain it must have been to have been deemed a bad student, someone who couldn't even sit for the examinations, someone who was called stupid or a wastrel. There were no terms like "learning disability" or "dyslexia" in imperial China, so one can only imagine the excruciating lives of such students confronting an uncompromising Confucian education.

But what about women? The Chinese passion and pain for education applied almost exclusively to men. Most women were kept illiterate, following the ancient notion that females should be homemakers and baby-producers. Elite women were supposed to focus their attention on running mansions, managing servants, preparing parties, and playing politics in the "red chamber," the traditional term for women's quarters. The typical male view, echoed by many women, was that elite females had no time for reading and writing. After all, women were supposed to engage in "thrice obeying"—obeying fathers when young, husbands in marriage, and sons after their husbands were dead.

Nevertheless, it is now known that many women engaged in self-education, sometimes with the help of moonlighting tutors, but the numbers are most uncertain since it was not a statistic most men wanted to celebrate. Recent scholarship has suggested that the sixteenth and seventeenth centuries brought substantial increases in female literacy, including some well-known poets, calligraphers, and painters. A literate life may have been more acceptable for widows seeking diversion since tradition frowned on remarriage.

But most men adhered to the cliché that literate women were meddlesome and untrustworthy, not at all attractive as daughters, as mothers, or as mates. So there were surely many women who, having become secretly literate, sought to hide their abilities from the men in their own families, from eligible bachelors in other elite clans, and from the matchmakers who crafted suitable unions.

Early seventeenth-century China thus perpetuated a great double standard. The many men who struggled with classical education often pretended they were highly literate, while the fewer women who pursued secret educations often conveyed the image of total illiteracy. Not until later in the century did the famous male writer, Li Yu, openly advocate women's education. Not until the turn of the eighteenth century did the great woman painter, Chen Shu, achieve popular acceptance among elite connoisseurs. And while some literate female courtesans gained popularity with male intelligentsia seeking temporary companionship, most "women of standing" avoided such comparisons.

But Chinese dynastic transitions often provided opportunities to reshape society and revise values. The seventeenth century was such a time as the last native Chinese dynasty, the Ming (1368–1644), collapsed through corruption and rebellion, setting the stage for the northern Manchus to invade China and set up their Qing dynasty (1644–1912). It was a topsy-turvy epoch in which less literate sons could pursue unconventional options, a time in which secretly literate daughters could put their skills to new uses.

In Suzhou, the magnificent city of canals in the Yangtze River delta region, the biggest issue was Ming loyalism. The question was whether leading families would stay true to the outgoing Ming dynasty, resisting pressure to serve the incoming Qing, or whether they would shift loyalties to the Manchu invaders. With life in turmoil, loyalism could overshadow everything, including time-worn views of literacy as well as Confucian images of proper male and female behavior.

The Manchu conquerors offered an enticing alternative to Chinese men in the form of service in the new Qing dynasty military structure known as the banner system. Chinese bannermen—that is, Chinese who turned their backs on the Ming dynasty and joined the Qing military structure—often rose to very high civilian positions after the Manchus took power in 1644. These bannermen sometimes achieved remarkable success in the Qing bureaucracy, whether in Beijing or in the provinces, in spite of earlier failures in the examination system.

Women faced much more limited alternatives. Unable to serve in the bureaucracy themselves, most elite women followed their husbands, whether they remained aloof from service as loyalists or joined the new dynasty as collaborators. Many diaries and biographies recount the terrors that women faced in the 1640s as the Manchus swept into the lower Yangtze region. Rape, pillage, torture, and executions were commonplace as the Manchus, having toppled the Ming militarily, now sought to root out loyalism that supported various Ming pretenders to the throne.

While historical records often detail, and possibly exaggerate, the heroic behavior of male Ming loyalists, information is much more sparse about female Ming loyalists. We do know that women rose quite prominently in the courts of Ming princes who sought unsuccessfully to establish strongholds in southern China. We do know about some courageous women who opposed the invading Manchus—including one whose anti-Qing boldness was so great that it impressed a Manchu prince sufficiently to make her his princess.

But how far did female Ming loyalism go? Here this novel takes a calculated guess that bridges the gap between history and fiction. It suggests that secretly literate women might have banded together in a time of turmoil. Their literacy might well have become not only a reassuring psychological defense, but also indeed a weapon against the invaders. Men wrote illegal pro-Ming tracts after the conquest—why not women as well?

Elite men formed private armies, often involving their own families as officers and their servants as rank-and-file. Is it not possible that women might have done the same thing? Would it not have been natural for women to have developed self-protection techniques, perhaps even using the firearms that the Europeans had recently introduced to China?

The tradition of female rebels has great weight in the annals of Chinese history and mythology—as powerfully conveyed by Maxine Hong Kingston's novel, *Woman Warrior*. In the early Ming period a rebellion led by "demonic women" was reported. In the late eighteenth century, women actively participated in the White Lotus Rebellion. Women soldiers flourished in the great Taiping Rebellion of the mid-nineteenth century. Women revolutionaries, such as the famous Qiu Jin, fought valiantly against the Qing dynasty in its waning years of the early twentieth century. Women soldiers and officers played prominent roles in the Chinese Communist movement in the 1930s and 1940s.

During the Ming-Qing transition, which spanned the seventeenth century, we also find hints of women fighters. The rebel Li Zicheng was reported as having "three or four women among every ten bandits." Qing military reports describe militant anti-Manchu societies that trained both men and women to fight. A priestess in northwestern China was seen inciting troops to oppose the invaders; she was quickly captured and executed by the Qing banner forces.

These tempting seventeenth-century suggestions, along with strong evidence of women warriors from other eras, prompt us to wander the enticing ground between fact and speculation in imperial China over three centuries ago.

MING

明

Dragon Eye Hill

Tiger Hill

Shantang River

Wenhua Bridge

Grand Canal

North Temple Pagoda

Wu family Mansion

Lin Family Mansion

Lion Grove

Daoist Temple of Mystery

Han Shan Temple

Garden of Harmony

Twin Pagodas

Shou Yuan Teahouse

Surging Wave Pavilion

Garden of the Master of the Nets

N

Suzhou

fr.

CHAPTER ONE

Fate

明

Suzhou, 1618

"I WON'T WEAR it. I won't! It looks stupid!"

Concubine Wang, strings of red beads clacking against ebony combs in her elegantly puffy hairstyle, shuffled quickly toward her little son's screaming protests.

"Why today?" she muttered to herself, the black horn soles on her miniature silk slippers clip-clopping along the gray slate floor. "Longyan, why today of all days?"

Pausing momentarily at the bedroom door, she dabbed a handkerchief at sweat beads that seeped through her white makeup, dripped from the delicate arches of eyebrow mascara, and threatened to smudge her lipstick's perfect-pucker shape. Longyan, squirming in the grasp of one servant girl, kicked out at another girl who was trying to force his arms into a miniature blue scholar's robe with red dragons on the hem.

"It's stupid! I'm stupid!"

Glowering at Longyan, Concubine Wang snapped open her fan; her lavender gown fluttered rhythmically with her wrist. Longyan, red-faced with fury, clenched his fists defiantly at his sides. Concubine Wang tightened her lips, trying to maintain her stern demeanor and stifle a stab of amusement. How could you punish a three-year-old, looking so impish in his underwear, a tiny rascal who charmed all the ladies in the red chamber? Besides, time was too short for a real scolding. She had less than ten minutes to make Longyan polite and presentable.

Concubine Wang melted as Longyan's tantrum softened into a contrite pout, teary eyes opened wide, pleading for a gentle reproach rather than a spanking. "Little Dragon Eyes," she said, ruffling his hair, "you're not stupid. And it's not stupid. You've got to wear it. I had it made special. Just for today. Now hold this writing brush while we make you pretty for the Patriarch. Come now, hold the brush, just like I taught you."

She put a simple bamboo writing brush in his chubby hands, bristles crumpled from countless hours of practice. Still sullen, Longyan let his mother dress him in the robe, button the tiny frogs, adjust the matching slippers, brush back his unkempt hair, and fidget with the bowl-shaped cap until it seemed almost right.

"There now. The perfect little scholar. Ready now? You go ahead. Don't forget to bow when you see him. Don't forget anything. Understand? Just relax. *Don't forget anything.*"

Concubine Wang tugged the writing brush from his hand and pushed Longyan gently toward the Patriarch's quarters. Longyan waddled ahead like a caricature of a pompous Ming magistrate.

Concubine Wang's smile vanished. A shudder shot through her spine. She rubbed the chain of pale green jade beads on her waist-cord. "Oh, beloved Guanyin," she whispered, "please, oh please, let this happen the way it's supposed to."

Longyan edged into a dark-paneled room filled with the sweet smoke of incense and the acrid aroma of garlic breath and body odor. Head hung low and biting his lip, like a brave criminal confronting execution, Longyan trudged across the rugs, halting in a semicircle of adults, the men seated on ornately carved chairs, the women on smallish drum-shaped stools.

Chattering ceased, and the room fell silent except for a muffled cough and soft whispering. Longyan, fidgeting with his gown sleeves, tried to look at faces, but it was all too frightening. So he stared at feet: men's feet in colored embroidered slippers; women's bound ones, as small as Longyan's, with green or yellow silk shoes; servant girls' ugly "big feet" so they wouldn't trip when bringing tea to those fortunate women with "lotus petals."

Longyan glanced at his mother, praying he might be spared this misery. She smiled, but shook her head. Longyan sighed, tugged off his cap, knelt before the man seated in the center chair, and bowed deeply with his hands on the floor.

"Your unworthy second son . . . uh . . . born of the Concubine Wang," Longyan's trembling voice recited his mother's catechism, "dares to speak. It is a supreme . . . a real supreme . . ." Longyan, head still bowed, started to shake. He looked at his mother, who mouthed the words "supreme pleasure," but Longyan couldn't understand.

Tearfully, Longyan lifted his head and blurted, "It is a supreme punishment . . . unworthy Patriarch."

Everyone gasped. Longyan cocked his head at the funny sound—were they happy or angry? One look at the Matriarch, the Taitai, provided a swift answer. Her thin, bony face exaggerated the stony glare in her black eyes; a metallic hiss came through clenched teeth. She leaned toward the Patriarch, cupped her fingers over her mouth, and stage-whispered, "I told you so. He got her bad blood. Peasant seeds, peasant weeds."

The Patriarch raised both hands in a royal gesture to cut off the Taitai's diatribe while regaining his composure. The Patriarch was soft-spoken, leaving others to try to read his mood. Was he angry at Longyan? At the Taitai? At Concubine Wang? His roundish face gave no clues. Even after a lifetime of tension, the Patriarch of the Wu family preserved a façade of genteel serenity. Only skilled Patriarch-watchers knew to look at his eyes, grayish eyes with flecks of black, which sometimes reflected gently inward and other times shot fiercely outward. Today his eyes radiated softness with just a flickering of annoyance.

Concubine Wang, quivering in terror behind her still-prone son, wished she could snatch up Longyan and run back to her village ten miles outside Suzhou. How could it be any worse? Oh please, let him be forgiving, she begged silently.

A wrinkled grin spread across the Patriarch's face, outlined by his black mustache and chinbeard. Chuckling softly, the Patriarch stood up, smoothed the folds in his blue and white at-home gown, flipped the two long ribbons of his scholar's cap over his shoulders. He shuffled in his blue silk slippers softly toward Longyan. Cradling the child in one arm, the Patriarch brushed back Longyan's hair and wiped his tears, fending off servants who tried to help.

"Don't be scared, little one," the Patriarch said, sitting down with Longyan on his lap. "You just said aloud what the censors whispered about me in Beijing. 'Grand Secretary Wu. He's unworthy. Deserves the supreme punishment.' That's why I'm home now. Of course, I also came to see my Dragon Eyes. A nice name we gave you, Longyan. You were born in the Year of the Dragon. The element was fire. Oh, I'll bet you're a terror. Don't worry. So was I. Right, Amah Zhou?"

The Patriarch laughed, but everyone knew his concealed pain: a first in the 1597 palace examinations, board president at age thirty-five, grand secretary at forty-two, and now booted out before his fiftieth birthday, victim of Beijing's relentless factionalism.

Longyan didn't understand a word, but he knew the Patriarch wasn't angry. He stared into the Patriarch's eyes just to make sure. No, not angry. Just like the red chamber, Longyan thought, smiling, nobody's mad anymore, now I can play again. Puffing himself up, Longyan mimicked the Patriarch's gestures, mouthing words without saying anything, waving his arms to make unspoken points.

"Ah, a real scholar," the Patriarch chortled, and put his own cap on his son's head. "A Daoist. 'He who sees but does not speak is a true sage.'"

Concubine Wang relaxed as she saw the Patriarch's eyes fix fiercely on the Taitai. The matchmaker had called it "the perfect marriage"—the Taitai stemmed from a rich merchant "almost gentry" family, contributed a Suzhou record for a dowry, and later produced a firstborn son. Xinping, now six, sat ramrod straight, duplicating the Taitai's haughty expression right down to the smug smile. The Patriarch knew the Taitai's game: make sure *her* son inherits everything and undercut all pretenders to the throne. The perfect marriage? The Patriarch shook his head, knowing why he hadn't left Beijing for almost two years. Except for the gentle sensuality of Concubine Wang, political exile in Suzhou was indeed an awful punishment. Concubine Wang infuriated the Taitai; after all, the Patriarch still had the right to change his mind about matriarchs.

Another gasp went through the room. Longyan had grabbed the Patriarch's right hand and was staring at it. "Whatever you do," his mother had counseled him, "don't look at your father's hands!" Longyan, curiosity aroused, seemed compelled to do the opposite.

The Patriarch withdrew his hand into his sleeve, quickly regaining his composure. "Don't worry, Dragon Eyes," the Patriarch said soothingly. "Everyone knows about my accident long ago.

Trying to use a cleaver. Lost both my thumb and forefinger. You must be more careful. Promise?''

Longyan held up ten fingers and nodded.

"All right, Now it's time for a different game. We're going to tell your future. Want to play?''

The Patriarch's left hand snapped a clacker. A servant brought forth a black lacquer tray, bowed sharply, and placed it on the red-and-white-patterned rug linking all the chairs.

"Now, Longyan. This is why we're here today. It's usually done when you're a baby. But, you see, I've been away. So we waited until you reached the ripe old age of three. Go ahead. Take a look.''

The Patriarch plopped Longyan on the rug. The crowd of over twenty—the Patriarch's two wives, brothers and sisters, his mother, aunts and uncles, several cousins, and the senior servants—craned their necks to watch. The Taitai looked on disdainfully, pretending she didn't care. Concubine Wang clasped her hands together prayerfully and squinted her eyes, barely able to look at all.

As Longyan crawled to the tray, face close to the objects on it, hindquarters in the air, relatives started to giggle. Concubine Wang noticed that Longyan's gown had caught around his waist; his pink bottom was showing through the "convenience hole" cut in his underwear. Slipping swiftly through the onlookers, she straightened out his gown, leaving Longyan sitting before the tray.

Totally absorbed in the game, Longyan ignored the adults hovering over him. First he wriggled the tray around until it was placed symmetrically dead center in the rug. His fingers traced the rug's woven geometric patterns radiating from four corners of the lacquer rectangle.

"He's so stupid he doesn't even know he's supposed to look on top of the tray.''

"Shhh,'' the Patriarch hushed the Taitai.

Longyan wiggled his bottom until he sat next to the tray, legs straddling it. He stared for a moment, then picked up a circular red lacquer box.

"The rouge!'' Someone laughed. "A real ladies' man.''

"Is that the one?'' the Patriarch asked. "Do you want that one?''

Longyan shook his head and placed the little box carefully at the edge of the tray, exactly halfway down the right side. Then he lifted a string of silver coins and jingled them.

"A merchant. Maybe not smart. But rich."

"Is it true?" Xinping asked his mother in wonderment. "Are all merchants stupid?"

"No, it's not true," the Taitai snapped, recalling her own roots. "But it looks like your half-brother may be moving that way."

Longyan positioned the coins on the left side of the tray, carefully making them into an arrowhead aimed at the red rouge box. Then he picked up a small hemp sack of sorghum seeds.

"A peasant! At least he won't go hungry."

"Like mother, like son," the Taitai quipped.

"Stop it," the Patriarch whispered. "You're only two generations away from the rice paddies yourself."

Longyan placed the seed bag at the apex of the silver-coin arrowhead. Concubine Wang was relieved that only two objects remained: a writing brush and a small dagger. Suddenly she gulped. The writing brush was black ebony inlaid with silver, not at all like the bamboo one back in the bedroom. The dagger, both the hilt and the scabbard, was of dark-stained bamboo; round and thin, the dagger had the feel of an oversized writing brush.

Longyan hesitated, then selected the brush. Oh, would he keep it? Oh please, would he be a scholar? Concubine Wang touched her beads and shut her eyes. When she opened them, Longyan had already laid the brush lengthwise in the tray, linking the arrowhead and the hemp seeds to the rouge box. His mother watched helplessly as Longyan lifted the dagger carefully, so as not to destroy the pattern on the tray. His hands ran over it and he rubbed it against his face. It felt just right. He licked it. Just like the one mother had given him. It was the one she wanted. She'd be so happy.

"So that's it, Longyan. That one?" Longyan didn't understand why the Patriarch's voice was stern and distant. Not like before.

Longyan looked up meekly, biting his lip uncertainly. He nodded, just a little, then a little more. The Patriarch stared back grimly. But surely Mother would know he'd done just right, like she taught him. Twisting around, he held up the dagger in both hands and showed it to her. But what was wrong? She stood frozen, both hands on her beads, tears streaming down her face.

"A soldier!" the Taitai exclaimed. "I knew it! The absolute worst. No brains. No money. Not even a good match."

"The worst iron for nails," someone droned out the old saying. "The worst men for soldiers."

"Have we ever had a soldier? In the whole history of the Wu family?"

"He's not a Wu. He's a peasant Wang. Not even a real peasant."

"Stop it! Stop it!" The Patriarch stood up, towering over everyone at his height of five and a half feet. "He's just a child. It's just a game. It doesn't really mean anything."

Shaking his head but smiling forgivingly, the Patriarch walked toward Longyan. Longyan knew the look. No punishment. But he'd been bad again. He was always bad.

Longyan threw down the dagger and scrambled out of the Patriarch's grasp. Glancing furiously around the room, he lifted the tray over his head and slammed it to the rug. Enveloped in a great puff of red rouge and sorghum seeds, he tore off his scholar's robe and shouted, "It's stupid! I'm stupid!" Then he ran out of the room in his underwear.

CHAPTER TWO

Dragon Boat Festival

明

Seven Years Later: Suzhou, 1625

THE MIDDAY SUN warmed the grassy, rock-strewn hillock overlooking the city of Suzhou. A soft breeze teased the meadow wildflowers; fluffy clouds floated serenely overhead. Too high for constructing a temple or a mansion, the hillock was a daytime playground for children, a nighttime rendezvous for lovers.

Suzhou stretched out in miniature below: diminutive white houses around inner courtyards, boulevards with tiny pedestrians, bullock carts, and sedan chairs, scholars' gardens of gray, misshapen boulders and carp pools, red pagodas and green and red temples. Upturned gray dragon- and snake-shaped roofs slithered in sharp shadows below. The greatest tourist attraction, the great Tang dynasty pagoda, leaned asymmetrically but majestically on Tiger Hill just a mile away.

Glittering reflections shimmered off the choppy water in Suzhou's maze of canals and arched white marble bridges. Maritime peddlers poled tiny junks along water streets and alleys. Weighty brown barges, the pride of the city's merchants, were slowly pulled by armies of straining coolies along the Grand Canal leading all the way northward to Beijing, eight hundred miles away.

The Grand Canal was the premier north-south thoroughfare in Ming China. First-class tickets on the great passenger barges were reserved for scholars traveling north to try their luck on the examinations and officials going south to visit their families. Second-class tickets were usually held by merchants, cutting deals with each other and hoping for influence with the elites who meandered on the top decks. Third-class was a mélange of artisans, servants, hawkers, gamblers, priests, and adventurers. And when the barges stopped at night, all of local humanity descended on the floating city, trying to sell goods and buy influence.

Sometimes imperial barges meandered southward, up to twenty yellow-festooned craft in a convoy, carrying members of the royal family, high-ranking concubines, or top eunuchs. Not since the late sixteenth century had the Emperor himself taken the trip; everyone agreed that was unfortunate because the Son of Heaven might have seen that his empire confronted massive financial and military threats. Southern tours, while very costly since the Emperor might haul along ten thousand or more retainers, fostered the personal rulership favored by early Ming sovereigns. In the absence of imperial supervision, the Grand Canal also became famous as a waterway of corruption.

Suzhou and Hangzhou were always the culmination of barge voyages because they had the reputation of the best food, the best music, the best intellectuals, and the prettiest women in China. The old saying captured it: "Up above, there is heaven; down below, there are Suzhou and Hangzhou."

"Come on, Meihua, you can make it." Longyan was already standing on top of the hill, hands proudly on his hips, blue gown ruffling in the breeze.

Lin Meihua, age twelve, two years older than Longyan, struggled near the summit. After every few tentative steps, Meihua stopped to lean against a boulder and scrutinize the path ahead, before venturing off again like a fledgling little bird. Her clothing—flowing pink silk, ankle-length dress, and white short jacket embroidered with butterflies and birds—was no obstacle. And she was only mildly troubled by the fact that wisps of her long hair, so carefully bound with a pink comb and matching hairsticks, required constant fussing.

It was Meihua's feet that hurt, aching and cramping from unaccustomed exercise. For three years, age six to eight, she had screamed daily as her amah wrapped her feet in wet bandages very tightly, contracting as they dried, so that the arches stretched downward and backward. Eventually her feet became half the normal size, the toes touching the heels underneath, like a little songbird grasping a twig.

Meihua was thus rendered a cripple from childhood. But her

feet already had the perfect look of a real Ming lady: white, round, no bumps or breaks. When it didn't hurt too much, she walked daintily, like a ballerina on pointes. Of course, ladies didn't climb hills, but at age twelve on a holiday, she had made an exception— especially since she had been prodded by her neighbor, Longyan, whom she'd described to her sister as "still a child, of course, but not bad looking."

"Longyan, I told you we shouldn't be doing this," Meihua said breathlessly. "I hope mother doesn't find out. We mustn't tell anyone. Next year, you know, I can't see any men without matchmakers. Not even little boys. Oh, look, what a mess I am! Now turn around. I've got to rest my . . . just turn around and don't look. Promise?" Meihua sat on a rock, checked to be sure Longyan wasn't peeking, took off her shoelets and stockings, and rubbed her swollen, elongated arches, the part of the bound foot that absorbed the weight.

"Can I look now?"

"No! Not yet." Meihua quickly pulled down her dress, designed so it just revealed a hint of her feet. She'd been warned that you could never trust men—they always want to peek. Was Longyan old enough for that? Well, it paid to be careful.

"All right, now you can look." Even at ten, Longyan knew he should look first at a lady's face, for it got more personal as you looked farther and farther down. It was a pretty face, without heavy cosmetics like older girls, an oval with almond-shaped dark eyes, small pert nose, and expressive lips that Meihua licked with the point of her tongue when reflective or bit gently when animated. Longyan liked the little tufts sneaking out of Meihua's satiny black hair.

"This is my special hideout," Longyan announced. "Dragon Eye Hill. I named it myself. See, there's your mansion. And just over there is the Wu family mansion, my father's house."

"But you're Wang Longyan? Not Wu Longyan?"

"Wang's my mother's family name. My father—Wu Jinglun— already has two wives. My mother's just a concubine." Longyan paused wistfully. "But she's the number one concubine," he added quickly.

"Why not the number three wife?"

"The Taitai's against it. She hates my mother. And she hates me."

How could she hate him, Meihua wondered, suddenly feeling motherly toward Longyan, who sat cross-legged on the grass in front of her, twisting together the stems of several early spring daisies. He glanced up, cocked his head, a grin on his angular face, and held out the bouquet.

"For you. Flowers from Dragon Eye Hill."

"They're really nice, Longyan. Thank you. I'll keep them. Amah Ding will dry them."

"What's it like, Meihua?"

"What's what like?"

"What's it like . . . you know, being a girl?"

She looked at him in astonishment. How could he have read her mind? She was just thinking how nice it was to be a girl. Her mother had asked, "Why don't you like Xinping, the older Wu boy?" Meihua knew why. Xinping teased her—"Just a girl . . . little feet, little brains"—and the other boys laughed.

"Being a girl? It's nice, mainly. You learn all kinds of things. Women say things to each other they'd never say to a man—about people, about money, about houses. About other things, too."

"But don't you want to run and play? Didn't it hurt?"

"Of course it hurt," Meihua replied in a patiently maternal tone. "No one likes the pain. But that's a girl's lot. It gets us ready for being women. Good things never come without some suffering." Meihua, now a bound-foot veteran, was already an expert in consoling her younger sisters.

"Is it true that girls are better at pain than boys?"

"Yes. Better at handling outside pain. Not as good at inside pain."

"What's inside pain?"

"Oh, you know, like when you're angry or sad. Boys get over it faster, I think."

"Not me. I sometimes yell. Even cry, a little. But then it doesn't go away. I just do hurt-smile."

"What's hurt-smile, Longyan?"

"The more it hurts, the more I smile. Then everyone thinks I'm happy. It's funny what happens. Everyone starts talking about *their* problems. I guess they wonder why they're not happy like me."

Meihua cast him a tender glance. "Longyan, you're really different, you know. Different from the other boys."

"I'm sorry," he replied, feeling scolded.

"Don't be sorry. It's good. Don't change it."

Longyan toyed pensively with a blade of grass. "You've got one thing even better than boys."

"What?"

"You don't have school. You don't have to read and write."

"I know something I won't tell," Meihua sang coquettishly.

"What? Please tell," Longyan implored, his wide eyes begging her.

"Well. Promise you won't tell anybody else. Not anybody. Not ever."

"I promise. I promise." Longyan opened both hands, the ancient gesture proving that nothing was concealed.

"I can read. Even write, a little." Meihua licked her lips through a proud smile.

"What?"

"Sometimes, when Tutor Qian comes, I listen to the lessons. In my secret place. Behind the bookcases. Please don't tell. My parents are real old-style. You know, things like 'Women who read are women who try to lead. . . .' "

"I don't believe you anyway."

"Oh no? Try me. Name a word from Confucius, a complicated one."

"*Yi*—art."

Meihua picked up a stick and drew the character in the shade of a boulder.

"Wow. That's great!"

"Okay," Meihua intervened. "Now you draw one. Even more complicated. And I'll tell you what it means."

"Oh, not now," Longyan replied nervously, "it's time to go. We can't miss the dragon boat races."

"Just one character. It'll just take a second."

"No! Really we don't have time. Do you want your mother to be furious?"

"Oh. I guess you're right. But it sounds like you're afraid to write something. What's the matter? Are you a bad student?"

"No! That's not true! I just want to be a good son."

Squeezed into the cramped space between two carved marble pillars on the Wenhua Bridge over the Grand Canal, Longyan and Meihua hung on for dear life against the pressure of the crowds. The din was deafening. The world was a stream of feet, knees, and hips, a rainbow of silk and cotton clothes, a torrent of shouts and swear words.

"Do you know all the secret places? All the hideouts?" Meihua yelled, grabbing Longyan's arm to keep from falling as she peered over the bridge.

"Lots of them." He grinned back. "Oh, look!"

Kneeling side by side, Meihua and Longyan surveyed the scene in joyful amazement. Spectators by the tens of thousands swarmed the canal's massive rectangular stone embankments, which had been constructed by corvée labor in the Mongol dynasty three hundred years earlier. Red, yellow, and blue banners floated above the viewing stands for rich merchant and scholar-official families on the East Bank, the affluent side of Suzhou. Spotting the Lin and Wu family banners, Longyan and Meihua shared a delinquent smirk, knowing that servants were surely combing the streets to find them.

The usually clogged canal had been cleared of all maritime traffic for a distance of two miles, its murky water strangely serene by contrast to the commotion on the banks and bridges. A drunken workman, wearing tattered pants and muddy jacket, balanced precariously on a piling at river's edge, shrieking a song about a lost lover, probably not "Suzhou's most precious phoenix," as his lyrics claimed, before passing out into the canal with a great splash. As his friends fished him out, the crowd on the bridge roared with laughter, especially when a bulbous woman fishmonger deemed him the "ghost of Qu Yuan."

Meihua nudged Longyan, hand over her mouth to keep from snickering at such profanity. They had been taught that Qu Yuan, the fourth-century B.C. scholar who had drowned himself after being rebuffed by his king, was a true saint. The Dragon Boat

Festival was held annually in his memory, always on Double Fifth, the fifth day of the fifth month. Tradition had it that the people of Qu Yuan's time, so moved by his sacrifice, rowed out into the river in dragon-shaped boats, throwing rice cakes into the water so that the spirits, or perhaps the fish, would spare his body. Meihua pulled a small triangular package from her sleeve, a green leaf–wrapped sticky *zhongzi* rice cake, and offered half to Longyan, both of them licking their fingers of the sugary residue.

A crescendo of shouts surged up the canal. Two long, thin boats, dragon's heads on their prows, were furiously paddled by fifty men as the coxswains beat rapid strokes on large red drums in the sterns. The two vessels, red and yellow, churned the canal. Dragons' heads vied neck and neck, water frothing from fiercely opened mouths, foam pluming from imposing tails. Agile men climbed out to the dragons' snouts, reaching desperately for flags on poles at the finish line. To a raucous chorus of cheers and boos, the red flagman snatched his prize a split second before the yellow.

"Ha," Meihua gloated, "a Lin boat. The Wus lose again."

"So what?" Longyan shrugged his shoulders. "It's only the first heat. They're saving it for the finals."

"Your father's going to the poorhouse," Meihua taunted. "Come down the street if you need a loan."

The word *father* startled them back to reality. It wasn't that there was any danger to the children—who would dare harm the offspring of Suzhou's most powerful families? But both of them had clearly violated parental orders to return before the races began. Stumbling and giggling, Longyan pulled Meihua by the hand through the crowds to the East Bank, pretending not to be worried.

As they neared the viewing stands where their families sat in rigid rank order as if posing for a portrait, the children hid behind vendors' carts and clusters of shopkeepers gambling on the races. For a few seconds, they melted into a throng watching a street circus performed by monkeys dressed as clowns. One monkey, a mimic, pointed at Meihua, threw his head back haughtily and walked on tiptoes, then sat down and bit his fingers anxiously.

"It's you!" Longyan laughed, then mellowed as he recognized that Meihua was truly upset at the prospect of her parents' scolding. "Don't worry," he said confidently. "Just hide under the viewing stand for a few minutes. Then when you come out, tell them you were there all the time. They'll believe it and be mad at the servants for not looking there first."

"But that's a lie," replied Meihua.

"So what? You were planning to tell the real truth? 'Esteemed Father, I was playing with Longyan, thus disobeying honorable Mother's instructions. I had so much fun I came back late.' "

"I wouldn't say that! I was going to make up something else. Maybe just a little lie."

"All lies are lies. So isn't it better to tell a good lie than a bad one?"

"I guess so." She walked off as stealthily as bound feet would permit.

"Oh, Longyan," she called back, "I really did have fun."

Longyan crouched under the scaffolding, awaiting an opportune moment to make his appearance. Above him the boards creaked from the weight of the whole Wu clan: the Patriarch and his male relatives in the first row, the Matriarch and the womenfolk in the second. Another pair of dragon boats was approaching. Longyan covered his ears as the deafening stomping of feet and bouncing of chairs rattled the planking.

Glancing down the bleachers, he saw Meihua in the arms of her tearful amah; Meihua pointed under the stands and the amah threw back her head in an "oh-that's-where-you-were" gesture. As her amah apologized profusely to her parents for failing to look in the most obvious place, Meihua shot Longyan a triumphant grin.

"Damn the Lin family!" the Patriarch exclaimed above Longyan, whose eyes opened wide at his father's uncommon vulgarity. "May locusts eat their crops and donkeys mate with their daughters!"

"Don't be a bad loser," his older brother counseled. "It's just the second heat."

"It's not just the race. I don't care about a couple thousand taels. The whole world's falling apart. We play in Suzhou while Beijing rots. The August Imperial Wand explores ten thousand Virgin Moonhills. Doubling taxes so he can enshrine that ugly bitch—oh, excuse me, we must call her the 'Exalted Sage Empress and Her Divine Progenitors.' That neutered idiot, Wei Zhongxian, whose only skill is twaddling the emperor's nurse, is running the whole place."

"Keep your voice down! You don't usually talk like that."

"I don't usually drink like this! I don't usually bet like this! I didn't used to feel like Qu Yuan!"

"You're just angry because you're here and not there."

"Why shouldn't I be angry!? Twenty years of my life to the Ming dynasty. And now I'm *former* grand secretary on home leave. A polite term for political exile. You advocate reform? You want to save the dynasty? And you get a kick in your backside."

"But everybody says there'll be a new emperor soon. The Emperor's son? Won't—"

"The Emperor's son! You want a rosewood table? That's what he does—carpentry. He cuts wood while fathers cut off their sons' balls. Twenty thousand eunuchs in the Forbidden City."

"Okay. Forget it, then. Just stay here. Be a leader in your own family."

"The family? That's a mess, too. You can't believe . . . oh, excuse me, elder brother. See what I mean? This woman wants a word."

Longyan, peering through a thin crack in the board, saw that the Matriarch had interrupted by whispering in the Patriarch's ear. He could only hear his father's half of the conversation.

"So what if Longyan's off playing someplace? What's so important about that?"

The Matriarch whispered again. Longyan, eyes open fearfully, struggled in vain to hear what she was saying.

"No I haven't made my final decision," the Patriarch replied firmly. "So what if you hear that Xinping's the better student? I think the little one has lots of hidden talent. And I could still make his mother a wife. If you keep bothering me, I could make her the Taitai, the first wife."

More Taitai whispering and shuffling of chairs, but Longyan still couldn't make out her words.

"You wouldn't!" the Patriarch barely concealed his shock. "I told you that as a complete secret. You said you'd never tell. It would cost me everything. I couldn't be appointed again."

Barely muffled whispering. Longyan, heart beating rapidly, tried to pull himself up the bamboo supports to eavesdrop, but only succeeded in losing his grip and flopping on his back as family members jumped on the boards to encourage their oarsmen.

"Oh, all right," the Patriarch whispered loudly. Longyan was just able to make out the sounds. "You don't give me any choice. I'll tell her. But not the little one. He stays. Is that clear?"

Longyan picked himself up, dusted off his robe, shaking fearfully at words he didn't understand but that sounded ominous. He knew he couldn't wait any longer. Mustering a frozen smile, he scampered up the scaffolding and slunk into a beat in the back row. "Just playing under the stands," he explained to Concubine Wang, who was scowling at him from the row ahead. The Taitai glared at Longyan; no one could miss the gloat of victory on her face.

The crowd roared again. "Damn," the Patriarch shouted, "lost the finals, too!"

Red Chamber Reminiscence

明

The Next Few Weeks: Suzhou, 1625

MEIHUA FRETTED THAT she might literally outgrow her chance for education. Huddled in a fetal position, she barely fit into her tiny hiding place adjacent to the study. Just a year earlier, before she turned twelve and shot up six inches, she had squeezed snugly into the gap between inner and outer walls, an architect's clever effort at insulation. Now, pressed between rough-hewn beams and almost suffocated from the stale air and dust, she couldn't move a muscle for four hours, not until Tutor Qian snapped the book shut and dismissed her three brothers. Her cramped position rivaled foot-binding for pain, but the goal was to open vistas unknown to most women, pleasures of the mind rather than sensual servitude.

The tutor spoke precisely. "Our initial exercise is completion and identification. Jingdao, you're first."

Meihua's youngest brother, seated but a foot from her, cringed as his name was mentioned. Through the crack where two walls met, she could see the eight-year-old bite his lips. The tutor continued. "In the *Book of Poetry*, it is said, 'A peach tree is so delicate. And its foliage so elegant. A girl goes to her husband's house. . . .' Now Jingdao, where's it from? And what's the rest?"

"It's from the *Book of Poetry*."

"What?" The tutor gasped and the brothers laughed. "Of course, the original quotation is from the *Book of Poetry*, that's in the text. But we're not studying the *Book of Poetry* now! What's it from?"

Jingdao put one hand to his head, as if seeking inspiration, and the other fell to his side, fist clenched, knocking quietly against the wall. Meihua sighed. Not again. *"Great Learning,"* she whispered, "the final line is 'She will rightly order her household.' "

Jingdao, not an adept student, did have the makings of a great actor. "I've got it," he exclaimed, patting his head as if a heavenly oracle had spoken to him. "Let's see. It has the feeling of the *Great Learning*. Yes indeed, very wise. Definitely from the *Great Learning*. I think it goes something like this:

> *"A peach tree is so delicate*
> *"And its foliage so elegant.*
> *"A girl goes to her husband's house.*
> *"She will rightly order her household."*

Tutor Qian was speechless. Jingdao's two older brothers stifled their guffaws, knowing precisely what had happened. Luckily, the elderly tutor was partially deaf and, even more luckily, he always insisted on the youngest boy sitting off in the corner. So every Lin youngster benefited from Meihua's divine intervention. And, in the process, Meihua had become a rising Confucian scholar in a society where most women remained illiterate.

The book snapped shut. Tutor Qian knew he'd been tricked, but he never figured out how. He always thought it was whispering from an older brother or perhaps crib notes of some sort. The boys bowed as they exited, jostling each other with giggles. Mei hua grinned smugly as she squirmed between the walls, then popped through a hole into her dressing room, a bit like a disheveled mouse who had just stolen some cheese. She sat limply, sucking in the fresh air, wiping smudges from her cheeks and making sure her hands had no cuts or splinters (faces and hands were all that women exposed in public). Perhaps, she thought to herself, it was the right time to outgrow Tutor Qian's classes, but how then to pursue more advanced education? Too bad her brothers were all younger; otherwise an afternoon tutor would offer instruction in Neo-Confucian texts and interpretation, and a calligraphy instructor would refine handwriting. Could she disguise herself as a boy and go to the Confucian School?

No, quit it, Meihua scolded herself. Remember what is also written in the *Book of Poetry*:

Bears are for boys.
Snakes are for girls.
Boys should have beds to sleep on, and play with scepters,
Wear red leather shoes,
Scream out when they want to,
Wear fine embroidered coats,
Prepare for rulership.
Small girls should sleep on floors and play with tiles,
Wear simple clothes and never act improperly,
Cook, brew, and behave just right,
Bring peace to the household.

But those words were written over 2,000 years ago. Couldn't I just be a little different? Meihua wondered to herself. It's not that I don't want to be a wife. I do. I really do. I want to be a taitai. Not so I can lord it over everybody, but so I can raise children. But couldn't I raise better children if I knew more about the world of boys as well as girls? Shouldn't education continue outside the library? And wouldn't—

"Where were you?" A sharp female voice interrupted Meihua's musings.

Meihua jumped to her feet, brushing the dusty cobwebs from her loose, off-white house gown, hastily pushing back the right side of her piled hairstyle that threatened to fall down altogether. She was relieved that the voice belonged to Peach Blossom, her senior servant, and not to someone of an older generation. Peach Blossom was older—all of sixteen years—and the daughter of Meihua's childhood amah. Peach Blossom did menial jobs, but she was also an authority figure of a sort, hired by parents to make certain their daughter matured with the right female virtues. So Peach Blossom, like many elite servants, was a combination of mentor, confidante, friend. And, when circumstances demanded it, she was supposed to be a prickly conscience. Today the circumstances demanded it.

"Okay. Answer me. Where were you?"

"You know where. Listening to the class. I go there almost every day. Why are you so upset? Nobody saw me. Nobody ever sees me. Besides I have lots of girlfriends—*real good families*—who are learning to read and write. Some better than their brothers. Why just last week—"

"Hush! Stop it!" Peach Blossom intervened before her mistress implicated others. "You know I can't approve of such things. I don't care who else does it. Just imagine if your parents found out. Just imagine if your future husband found out. But that's not what I'm upset about. Now tell me. Where were you? Yesterday. During the first part of the dragon boat races?"

"Under the scaffolding. Just playing." Meihua gave her best open-eyed how-could-you-doubt-me look.

Peach Blossom knew her mistress was lying. It made her furious. It was clearly time for the ultimate threat—she'd only used it once before. "Mistress, you give me no choice. I must resign. I will inform your parents this evening."

"Don't be silly. This isn't a resigning matter. You're overreacting. You're just upset because you couldn't find me for a while." Meihua was hoping she could change Peach Blossom's mood, ideally without confessing, but she knew she might have to tell the truth. In a society that allowed little privacy, having someone you could trust was enormously valuable. Peach Blossom would not break that trust by snitching to Meihua's parents, but she could sever the relationship altogether, forcing Meihua to the most horrible fate confronting any young adolescent: loss of one's best friend. That was clearly worse than changing her story.

"Quit it!" Peach Blossom snapped. "Last chance. Tell the truth or I am no longer in your family's service."

"Oh, all right," Meihua blurted. "I was with Longyan. You know, the little Wu boy. We weren't doing anything bad. Just sitting on a hill."

"You *climbed* a hill? With a *boy*? Without a *chaperone*?"

"Yes," Meihua replied meekly.

"Besides," Peach Blossom summoned all the righteousness she could muster, "he's not the *Wu* boy. He goes by a common name—I forget—one of the old hundred names. He's the son of a concubine. Just a commoner in a gentry household."

"Well, what about you?" Meihua retorted.

"Me?" Peach Blossom's eyes flashed. "Everyone knows I'm just a servant. A stupid servant. You can beat me. You can fire me. But at least I don't pretend to be an aristocrat.''

Meihua pulled Peach Blossom into her arms. "Oh, I'm sorry. I didn't mean to insult you. It's just that Longyan seems so different. He's, well, sort of sensitive. Maybe it's because he's not so sure of himself. Not cocky, like so many high-born boys. Yes, you're right, his real name's Wang. We just had fun. I didn't mean to make you angry. I hope it didn't get you into trouble."

"Of course it got me in trouble," Peach Blossom whimpered. "It's the only time your father has ever asked me where you were. And I had to say I didn't know. I looked like a fool."

"I'm sorry. I really am. I'll talk to Father. I'll make sure he doesn't blame you."

"That's not good enough," Peach Blossom spoke sharply, pushing herself away from the embrace. "You are not to be alone with any boy again. Not until you are married. And you are not to see that Wang boy. Never again. Not even to talk to him. Understand?"

"Yes," Meihua said slowly.

"Oh, I hope you didn't tell him you can read and write. That would be a disaster. You didn't do something stupid like that, did you?"

"Of course not," Meihua said with that extra dose of firmness that seeks to conceal a lie.

Peach Blossom scrutinized Meihua's face, dubious about her assertion, but not wanting to provoke another confrontation. "There's talk, you know, about your marriage one day. Some have even suggested a union with the Wu family. Probably with the older child. What's his name? Xinping? Yes, that's it. It's a powerful family. Your father has great respect for the Wu patriarch. But, if anyone ever thought you might settle for the son of a concubine . . . oh, just imagine. . . . Now, do we have an agreement?"

"Yes."

"Okay. Then I will not leave. And I, a stupid maid, ask your forgiveness for speaking so directly. Please beat me." Peach Blossom knelt before her mistress.

"All right," Meihua said, tapping Peach Blossom gently on her cheek. "That's your beating." They hugged warmly and Peach Blossom left her alone.

Oh no, not Xinping, Meihua fretted. Maybe such marriages are great for the families, but for me? And to be in the same house with Longyan? Oh, please let it not be so. Oh, did I ruin everything by confiding my studies to Longyan? Oh, how can I fix it? I'm so foolish! Oh, I didn't ruin my life, did I? Please, oh please, don't let my parents know. I'm just so completely stupid!

One night every year in mid-May the Lin matriarch dispensed a bit of magic when the family invited relatives and friends to celebrate the Night of the Phoenix (this year it was just three weeks after the Dragon Boat Festival). The Night of the Phoenix celebration was over two hundred years old, stemming from the creation of the Lin garden, a constellation of gray, misshapen rocks, greenish pools, meandering paths, and miniature pavilions. Smaller than most Suzhou gardens, the Lin garden offered drama on a human scale, interest for the eyes, and intimacy for the heart. A profusion of *wutong* trees enhanced the warm, welcoming feeling, and in the spring sprouts of broad, shiny green leaves filled the air with life, a contrast to the more imposing monochromatic gardens elsewhere in Suzhou. Indeed it was the *wutong* tree that had inspired the first such Lin festival in the early Ming, to celebrate the myth that its beautiful leaves attracted the powerful phoenix, the source of energy and joy, and the symbol of the coming summer.

The romance of the Night of the Phoenix depended on the weather, of course, and that's where the Matriarch's magic worked its charm. The Lin taitai always picked the date. It was said that some taitais in the fifteenth century became infamous for picking a rainy night every time, others like Meihua's grandmother had managed mixed records, but Meihua's mother was the only one to produce a perfect forecast, seventeen years of clear nights. And tonight was glorious—mild, cloudless, with a bright, almost-full moon and a touch of breeze.

"Welcome. Family, friends, everyone. Welcome," the Lin patriarch, a handsome figure in his mid-forties, his hair still without a trace of gray, spoke with easy grace. The dozens of guests cast their eyes toward him, but remained in their seats in neat semicircular rows on a large island in the midst of the biggest pond in the garden, connected to the shore by an elegant arched bridge. Hundreds of conical red lanterns hanging in the *wutong* trees cast a roseate glow over the island; the flickering lights offered a mute counter-point to the burping frogs and chirping crickets.

"I know it violates modesty to speak positively of one's wife in public, but it's nearly two decades now of perfect weather. The astrologers in Beijing must be envious. How do you do it?"

The Lin taitai, a tiny woman whose face radiated a quiet gentle-ness, cast her head around the throng, acknowledging their ap-plause without eclipsing her husband. "Just silly luck," she said softly, knowing that it was mainly that, plus the fact that she relied on the suggestions of three fortune-tellers and consulted an alma-nac reported to have come from the famous Jesuit Matteo Ricci. She also consulted her physician, who suggested finding a date in the second week after her menstrual period—she wasn't sure whether this was for good weather or good feelings. Anyway, ev-eryone seemed to love the Lin taitai, so why shouldn't the weather gods feel the same way?

Meihua, sitting next to her mother as was proper for the eldest daughter, watched the Matriarch's every move as a guide to future taitai behavior. She was certain that her mother could predict the weather. So, Meihua lectured herself, remember to say "just silly luck" when you are brilliant, otherwise the men will feel threat-ened and perhaps the women will be jealous. Ah, see how Mother nods her head to each of the other taitais, sort of like a toast at banquets. Her mother stopped her nodding briefly, puzzled that the Wu taitai seemed too absorbed with making her own children presentable to acknowledge the greetings of the hostess. Longyan caught Meihua's eye, grinning and clandestinely waving his hands near his chest and, when his mother lightly slapped his wrist, put his hand over his mouth. Meihua quickly cast her eyes downward, hopeful that no one saw Longyan looking at her, wondering what his hand-over-mouth gesture really meant. Finally the Lin taitai caught the Wu taitai's attention, nods were exchanged, and the ritual was completed.

"A toast"—the Patriarch raised his cup high with both hands—"to all of you, to the enduring virtue of friendship, bottoms up, *ganbei*." After draining it, he lifted his cup over his head upside down to show that it really was empty, the other men following suit, women by custom only taking little sips. "Tonight we wish to do what men have always done in difficult times. We must revive the past. Rekindle it, quite literally. After dark of winter, and the uncertainty of spring, the glorious summer is surely ahead. . . ."

Meihua listened intently, unlike most other women, who dozed during "men talk," and realized for the first time that her father was speaking forthrightly, and dangerously, about politics. "Like Zi Gong, we often ask about government by day, but tonight we will forget. . . ." Meihua gasped along with the other adult men, knowing that the passage from the Confucian Analects admonished rulers to nurture the people's affection above all, above even food and military security, for "if the people have no faith in their rulers, there is no standing for the state." Her father continued, "We know that the sun rises in the east, so shall the phoenix rise with it, and so give new life to the forest, whose energy comes from the same direction. . . ."

Meihua knew immediately what he was saying, for her father, and several others in the room, belonged to the Donglin ("Eastern Forest") Society, which sought honest government in an era dominated by corrupt eunuchs, led by the infamous Wei Zhongxian. Recently Wei had counterattacked his accusers in the Donglin Society, executing six of them and dismissing hundreds of others—the Wu patriarch was among the disgraced figures. Annoyed that the other women were chatting, Meihua felt grateful that her self-education suddenly had a use beyond clandestinely coaching her brothers.

For most guests, the highlights of the Night of the Phoenix celebration were the performing ensembles—red-garbed women dancers, *erhu* and *qin* string players, a brass and drum percussion group, acrobats and clowns for the children—each occupying a different stage across the moat from the island and lit by large white lanterns during its performance. Servants brought food and wine between performances; youngsters gorged themselves as if it was new year, and adults tipped cups toward one another in the ancient alcohol bonding ritual.

But Meihua ate almost nothing and drank little of the grape juice given to children. Instead she stared into the sparkling night sky, wrapping herself in a light cotton shawl as the air grew chilly, wondering over the events that flowed around her. Not until dawn did the festival end, a brilliant red sun heralding a new day. Each guest was given a small potted *wutong* tree to be planted at their own

25

homes, by the Lin patriarch's instructions, "to the east, all family members together to make a little forest, to beckon the phoenix every day of the year."

As the last guest departed, Meihua went up to her father, bowed politely, and spoke softly. "Your silly daughter has a request. I would like to meet with you and Mother. Privately. Would that be possible?"

"What's it about, little one?" The Patriarch was puzzled at such an odd request. Children, especially female ones, never met alone with their parents. The other children and relatives would wonder what rumors were being spread. The quest for privacy always conveyed something surreptitious.

"Please? It's important. I won't ask again. Please?"

"All right. Tomorrow morning at ten. In my study. Whatever it is, be sure it's quick. We won't have but a few minutes."

"You're crazy," Peach Blossom said as she dressed Meihua in her dark blue gown, which, but for the delicate embroidery around the lapels and sleeves, had the look of a scholar's robe. "It won't work, you know. You'll probably make your parents mad at you. Maybe at me, too. Who knows?" She rolled Meihua's hair carefully, fastening it only with blackwood combs, no sign of the usual flowers that enhanced femininity. "But maybe you'll get lucky," she said as she turned Meihua around twice, making sure that the gown flowed properly, covering her feet and thus causing her mistress to look as if she was hovering over the ground. "You were lucky with that boy. What's his name? You know, the Wang boy . . ."

"Longyan?"

"Yes. Him. I heard from his servant. He won't reveal anything. Nothing. Not even about 'art.' Whatever that means. What *did* you do with him?"

"Nothing. I told you. Nothing at all. Oh, you're right. I *am* so lucky! Now wish me more luck." So that's what he had meant when he'd put his hand over his mouth, Meihua thought, not a word about the fact that I can read and write.

Meihua floated out of the women's quarters, across two flagstoned courtyards, and into her father's study, a detached building adjacent to the garden. Her father and mother, seated across from one another, each on a darkwood couch, waited expectantly as their daughter bowed and composed herself on a ceramic stool. Nothing was said for a moment. Indeed, no one quite knew who should speak. Children never spoke first. But then again female children never requested such meetings.

"You wished to see us?" her father inquired, a hint of irritation in his voice.

"Yes, Father. And Mother. You see, I have an unusual idea. Sort of a request. But you have to understand something first. . . ." This wasn't going the way she expected. It had sounded so convincing in the red chamber when she tried it out on Peach Blossom. Now she felt like an awkward little girl, precisely the opposite of what she intended. "You see, I would like to help our family. Father, I heard what you said last night. I mean the part from Confucius—Book Twelve, Chapter Seven—where Zi Gong asks of government. Maybe I could help you here at home, sort of as an assistant. . . ."

"Meihua. What are you talking about? How do you know these things? How do you know about the Confucian texts?"

She felt like a butterfly skewered by her father's sharp eyes. "Because, Father, because . . . It's because I . . . Well—"

"Out with it!"

"Because I know how to read. And write." She waited for a response, but only received blank stares. "I listen to Tutor Qian every day, through a little hole in the wall, next to the library. I've been doing it for seven years now. I hope it's okay. It's said that many families are actually encouraging girls to read. I know at least five girls who are studying. So it's not really unusual. . . ."

"Not unusual perhaps for *merchant* families. Sometimes they want literate daughters so they can do business. But you're a *scholar's* daughter."

"I wasn't talking about merchants' daughters. I'm referring to daughters of some of the highest families. Surely you have heard the rumors too. We aren't hurting anyone, you know."

"Not hurting anyone? I'll be the judge of that. Now what did you think you would do with such talents?"

"I thought that maybe . . . maybe you'd want someone to keep notes for you. Someone totally trustworthy. Someone that outsiders would never think of as a secretary. Imagine—*a woman secretary*—nobody would ever think of that. Then you could have all sorts of secrets. You know, the Donglin kind—"

"Hush, daughter. Don't ever speak those words. What unspeakable terrors they have led to. 'Donglin' must be said only by men prepared to die. Not by women who don't know what they're talking about."

"I am prepared to die," Meihua said quietly, surprising herself with the firmness of her conviction. "For what you believe in. For what the family stands for."

"Quiet. You really don't even know what I stand for. How do you know it's a good cause?"

"Because I know you. It's all I need to know."

"That's a most generous thought," her father said gently, realizing she was serious. "Loyalty at its most pure." He paused with a mischievous smile. "Which, my daughter, would you rather have—fish or bear's paws?"

"Bear's paws," she answered without hesitation.

"Excellent!" her father exclaimed, causing Meihua to smile and her mother to stare in bafflement. The great classical philosopher Mencius had once said that he liked both fish and bear's paws, that he also liked both life and righteousness, but if one had to be chosen over the other, he would take bear's paws and he would take righteousness.

Her father paused, shook his head a little, and said what he felt had to be said. "And in the five relationships, does any of them involve women?"

"Yes, Father."

"Which one?"

"Husband and wife."

"And which is dominant?"

"Husband," she said glumly. She should have known it. Why assume that a bold reformer at court would also be an advocate of change at home?

"So your duty is?"

"To be a good wife to my husband, a good daughter-in-law to his mother, and a good mother to his children."

"And where does reading and writing fit into all of that?"

"Well, perhaps I could help him with his correspondence,"

Meihua answered, giving it one last attempt. "And assist in the education of the children. And maybe—"

"Where will you find the time for all that? Don't the other duties constitute full-time jobs? What does your mother say to all this?"

"It's *definitely* a full-time job," the Lin matriarch said with conviction. "I really didn't know that Meihua was studying. I heard whispers about other families, of course. But lots of girls pick up a few characters, a few phrases. *My* worry is what this would mean in finding a husband. Meihua's beautiful and devoted, but surely most families would have doubts about a girl whose mind is in the books. Who else knows about this, Meihua?"

"Only my brothers and Peach Blossom," Meihua left out Longyan because he'd promised not to tell.

"Meihua, you must give us your word," her father interjected. "We'll talk to the boys and to Peach Blossom. Don't breathe about this to anyone else."

"Yes, Father."

"And stop the studying right now," her mother continued. "I understand. I really do. But you can't jeopardize your future. Nor our future. Henceforth you will spend the mornings with me, learning more of how to manage a household."

"Yes, Mother." Meihua bowed, spun about, and sped out the door, trying to hold back the tears.

After Meihua retired, the Matriarch said, "I'm mortified. I had no idea. I should be punished as a bad mother. I apologize from the bottom of my—"

"Don't apologize. I had to be harsh with her. After all, it would be terrible for everyone, including her, if people knew we were training our girls to be literate. But you've got to admire her. What remarkable imagination! What a spark! We should both be a little proud, secretly of course, that she should show such devotion. Maybe, in another life, she would have the good fortune to come back as a man."

Back in the red chamber, Peach Blossom added insult to injury. "I told you so. Maybe it's best that your parents know. Now, at least, you won't play all these silly games. And if you do, I will have the authority to tell your parents."

Meihua wanted only to die, but knew it was unfilial to take her own life. All right. That was that. She would be the best bride, wife, mother, daughter-in-law imaginable. But they couldn't lock up her brain.

CHAPTER FOUR

Mencius

明

One Week Later: Suzhou, 1625

"NONWRITING, NONREADING, NONTHINKING. Long-yan, you're an expert in those. No one's better."

Longyan hated Tutor Lu's constant scoldings in the library. Sitting rigidly in an unforgiving straight-backed chair before a heavy oak desk, hands folded in his black robe, Longyan stared at the formidable "Four Books" anthology opened to a passage from Mencius, the fourth-century B.C. Confucian sage.

It was all so boring. He still was preoccupied with the Dragon Boat Festival, though it was already a month back. If only Xinping knew he'd played with Meihua. But he'd given his promise not to tell. How different she was! Not just houses, babies, and food. She liked ideas and games and other things. And she was one of those bold girls who was secretly studying. Longyan couldn't figure out why some girls would want to open books when most boys couldn't wait to close them. He wasn't sure whether it was that girls were really different, or maybe that it was just natural to want things you weren't allowed to have.

But the Dragon Boat Festival also left another, more ominous memory. What was the Matriarch whispering to the Patriarch? And why did the Patriarch, such a forceful father, seem such a weak husband in her presence? Why did the Matriarch hate Longyan so much? Longyan was used to reprimands and switches, short bursts of pain, but the whispering was worse—who knew what was in store?

Tap. Tap. Tap. It was Tutor Lu bouncing his onyx paperweight on the desk. Longyan privately called him "carpface" for his unchanging expression and ever-opening mouth. Thank heavens, he was pointing to Xinping who sat opposite Longyan in identical posture.

"Mencius said," Xinping recited mechanically, "when left to follow natural feelings, human beings will do good." Xinping weighted each character equally as if it was a totally separate thought, smiling all the while because he knew he wasn't making mistakes. "This is why I say human nature is good. . . ."

Tutor Lu glanced at Longyan to make sure his eyes were riveted to the page, his head nodding in tempo with his elder half-brother's recitation. In fact, Longyan had perfected the art of "pretend reading" because, much as he tried, Longyan couldn't begin to follow the passage. The two characters that comprised "human nature" came unstuck before his eyes, first blurring, then fracturing into three smaller ideographic components. "Human nature" became a man, a heart, and a newborn child dancing up and down the page, stopping momentarily when they found similar shapes, then spinning in place. He'd told his mother about the "jumping words" problem, and she had counseled him to concentrate harder by rubbing his temples and eyes. She would have liked to show him how, but, of course, Concubine Wang could not read or write.

"If human nature becomes evil, it is not the fault of man's original capability." Xinping droned on. "The sense of mercy is found in all men. The sense of shame is found in all men. The sense of respect is found—"

"Stop, Xinping, that's fine," Tutor Lu said firmly. "Now, Longyan, quit rubbing your eyes. How many times do I have to tell you? Now, what is Mencius saying?"

"About what, Teacher?"

"About human nature."

"It's good."

"Yes, and . . . ?"

"And what, Teacher?"

"Why is human nature good?"

"I don't know."

"Oh, Longyan, what are we going to do with you? All right, Longyan, continue reading. Start with 'The sense of respect is found in . . .'"

"The sense of respect is found in all men. The sense of right and wrong constitutes . . . uh . . . two men."

"Two men? What are two men together?"

"Brothers?"

"No! May the beloved Buddha spare you! It's one word. The number two plus men means 'humanity.' In forty years of teaching, I've never had to instruct peasants. You're the single most impossible—"

Tutor Lu stopped short as he noticed that the Wu patriarch had walked in quietly and was standing just behind him.

"The single most impossible what?" the Patriarch asked gruffly.

"Oh, it's of no consequence. Longyan was just having a little problem with Mencius."

The Patriarch placed his hands firmly on Tutor Lu's shoulders, keeping him from standing up. "Let's continue the lesson, tutor. Please tell your students what Confucius said to Yu about knowledge."

"When you know a thing," Tutor Lu sucked in his breath to keep control, "say that you know it. And when you do not know a thing, say that you do not know it."

"And what did he say about social background?"

"In education . . . there are no class distinctions."

"And Yen Hui? What did he say about Confucius's teaching methods?"

"You look up and it seems so high," Tutor Lu looked blankly at the oil lamp spluttering overhead, his fists clenched under the desk. "You try to drill and it seems so hard. You look in front and it appears behind you. The master is skilled at teaching by gently leading his students."

"So perhaps," the Patriarch continued, glaring at Tutor Lu, "we have all learned something today."

Releasing his grip, the Patriarch walked to the opposite side of the table, his sons now beside him, the tutor facing him sheepishly. "Perhaps you could show me what you have gently taught your pupils. Some calligraphy?"

"Gentlemen," the tutor responded, "please prepare your paper, ink, and brushes. We shall write the four characters, 'Human nature is good.' "

Xinping, delighted at the fact that all the characters were simple ones, quickly dipped his brush and wrote.

"That's perfect, Xinping," Tutor Lu exclaimed.

"That's not perfect," the Patriarch objected.

"No, I guess it's not perfect," the tutor corrected himself. "But he's only twelve. What do you expect? Begging the Patriarch's pardon, but aren't you asking too much? You yourself, sire, were among the greatest calligraphers. But even you, if I recall, did not achieve brilliance until you were fifteen or sixteen. That was, of course, before—"

"You remember it well, tutor. Before I lost my fingers. Why doesn't anyone dare say it? No, I don't expect genius from a twelve-year-old. But I do expect his tutor to explain that individual characters are not islands in a sea of silk. They must be linked together. Like a road. A path to discipline, knowledge, art. Now Longyan, how about you?"

Longyan ran his fingers through his shock of black hair, pressing his eyes and temples as hard as he could. Then he rolled the brush tip in the jet black ink pool in the gray schist inkstone. Pondering the blank paper held in place by marbled green paperweights engraved with *filiality* and *knowledge,* his hand trembled, almost splattering ink. Four characters, right in a vertical line, that was what the lesson demanded. But again the words danced in his mind, breaking apart into six components; Longyan's brush drew radical cursive shapes, characters on different angles, all in a strange circular pattern:

ALSO

MAN WOMAN

HEART BIRTH

SON

"Oh no," Tutor Lu exclaimed.

"That's certainly unusual, Longyan." The Patriarch squinted his eyes and puzzled over the paper. "What does it mean?"

"I don't know. But there are paths and roads."

"Where?"

"You can link them in threes. Triangle roads. Each three has its own meaning."

"I'm sorry, sire," Tutor Lu said mournfully. "I've tried everything."

34

"Everything," the Patriarch replied, "but trying to see what's in your student's mind. Not just trying to impose what's in your own." He gazed at each son in turn. "Xinping, please look beyond characters, see the big picture. And Longyan, please keep trying to study the standard way, Tutor Lu's way. You'll never lose the—"

"What, Father?" Longyan asked.

"No matter." The Patriarch's eyes were still on the circular calligraphy. He muttered to himself, "The blood, it must be in the blood. Bloody genius. And a bloody pity."

"What is it, Mother? What's wrong?" Longyan could tell that Concubine Wang had been crying. Stoic posture and swollen eyes always meant crying. It was rare to be called to his mother's bedroom late at night. It wasn't going to be good news.

"Sit down, Dragon Eyes," Concubine Wang patted the empty space next to her on the yellow-cushioned dressing-table bench.

What had he done wrong this time? Was it the Dragon Boat Festival—had Meihua told her mother? Was it Tutor Lu—had the Patriarch decided he was really stupid?

"Dragon Eyes, what have you learned about Confucianism?"

"I'm sorry," Longyan blurted involuntarily. "Tutor Lu told you about the reading and writing? I really try. Honest, I do. But it's the jumping words."

"Hush, now. I'm not talking about the written words. I'm talking about the ideas."

"Oh, I know the ideas. They're easy. I know them all by heart."

"What's the first obligation of a son?"

"Filiality. To his parents."

"To the father or the mother?"

"Both."

"And if there's a choice?"

"To the father. But why? Is there a choice?"

"I'm afraid so. Your father has reached a decision. The Taitai will always be the Taitai. Her son will be the first son. And I . . ." She paused to steady herself, putting her hand on his knee.

"What?"

"I must return to my parents in Pingdao. I can't live in the Wu mansion anymore."

"Why?" Longyan cried, clinging to his mother. "It's because I'm stupid. I'll try harder. I know I can do it. I'm not really dumb. . . ."

"That's not it. I know you're not dumb. In fact . . . he told me not to tell . . . but it doesn't make any difference anymore. The Patriarch thinks you have great talent. That's what he said. He knows you're much brighter than your brother. He liked your calligraphy. A lot."

"Really?"

"Really. I wouldn't lie to you."

"Then why doesn't he want me here?"

"He does want you here. You're going to stay. It's only I who must leave."

"Oh no! I can't be here without you. I'm going with you. I can't stay here alone. It's awful. Please take me."

"No, little Dragon Eyes. I've got to go. You've got to stay. That's it."

"Is it because he doesn't like you anymore?"

"No. He says he likes me a lot. That I'll always be in his heart."

"I don't understand."

"I don't either. Just politics, I guess. Winners and losers. I lost. But I've still got you. If you come to Pingdao, I can see you on holidays sometimes. It won't be so bad."

"It'll be awful."

"It's not that bad. You'll be the second son. It means wealth, a good life. I'll be well cared for. So will my family. And you can use the name Wu. Not Wang."

"I don't want to be a Wu! How could he do this? Why? I can never trust him again."

"You must. It's required. It's filiality. Now you listen. Listen and never forget. Everything depends on you. If you rebel, everyone gets hurt. Not just you, but me, too. Be a good son. Be a good student."

"But I can't believe in my father."

"Try to understand him. He's having trouble, too. He can't believe in himself. Maybe you can help. If you can't believe in him, at least believe in what he believes in. Look for hope. Look for success. Understand, little Dragon Eyes?"

Longyan shook his head. "I'm a loser, too."

CHAPTER FIVE

Roots

明

Eight Years Later: Suzhou, Winter 1633

A FIERCE WINTER gale pounded the Shou Yuan ("Longevity Garden") Teahouse. Hissing winds snaked through paper wads stuffed under windowsills; thick rain droplets plopped from cracks in ancient roof tiles; angry gusts battered peeling stucco walls. The rickety teahouse trembled ominously over a windswept canal where vicious waves toyed with moored junks. Jagged bursts of lightning etched instant images in black and white: a gang of coolies struggling to haul a wayward barge back to its mooring, a lady screaming at her servants from a sedan chair whose top had blown away, a street performer climbing a signpost to retrieve his frightened monkey, and a dark-robed monk sitting on a marble bridge playing his bamboo flute as if enjoying a sunny afternoon.

Longyan smirked as he peeked through the shutters, taking perverse pleasure in the chaos outside. "What a lovely day!" he chortled, then commented, sotto voce, "Sort of a weather forecast for the dynasty, don't you think?"

"Shhh," replied a friend, "even joking can get you into real trouble. And if you don't care about yourself, how about the rest of us?"

"Relax," Longyan responded, "everyone knows it. Besides, who's listening?"

Longyan, a lean young man of eighteen years, poured hefty doses of rice wine for four teenage colleagues sitting on heavy ceramic stools around a dark oak circular corner table. It was their table, headquarters for the self-styled Five Sages of the Bamboo Cup (after the famous third-century drinking poets, the Seven Sages of the Bamboo Grove). Sons of influential scholars and merchants, none had the fortune to be the first son. All had opted out of the rigorous Confucian schooling for the all-important civil service examinations. The Five Sages sported shabby robes, originally from elite tailors, sloppily opened to expose undershirts in front in a style of affluent arrogance.

Every night, from five o'clock until closing time, the Sages gossiped, sang bawdy songs, roughhoused, teased waitresses, and ridiculed other customers. Teahouse life was expensive, even for rich children's allowances, so mainly they drank cheap rice wine, occasionally nibbling at higher-priced food.

A year earlier, despairing as the rascals drove away other business, the proprietor made the mistake of chasing them out. The next morning, orders came from the district Magistrate: "Close down the Shou Yuan Teahouse for one month for the offense of insulting high officials." The fathers of the Five Sages, all close confidants of the Magistrate, much preferred wayward sons away from home at night, relinquishing both their care and their commotion to someone else.

"It's poetry time!" a pockmarked young man shouted. "Oh waitress, thou whose three larges exceed thy three smalls, bring the dice and another round."

The Sages guffawed. On the positive side, she did have uncommonly large breasts and dreamy eyes, and on the negative side, she did not have bound feet and her mouth was too big to call pretty; one could only guess about the rest. The waitress scowled and took her own time tossing soft coal into a cast-iron heater, eventually bringing a tray with wine and a bamboo cup with long, thin ivory sticks imprinted with characters.

The pockmarked fellow snatched the long ivory sticks from her tray, clattered them in a cup, and scattered them on the table. "Damn it, four!" he fretted. Four (si) was the most unlucky number of all because it rhymed with death (si). Pockmark would surely have to go first. The other boys, aged thirteen to seventeen, clacked the dice with deep earnestness, vying to see who would have the honor of reciting last in the game. But when it came time for his turn, Longyan adamantly refused to shake the cup.

"You never play," Pockmark complained. "That's not fair. You have to take a chance."

"No, I don't. You know the rules. The oldest Sage is always the judge."

"Those are your rules."

"Right. It's my group, my game, my rules."

Pockmark sighed, chugged his bamboo mug, then stood unsteadily on his stool. "Theme poem is:

> "Toward evening, the weather turns cold
> "and I moor my boat for the night by the shore.
> "Lying on my pillow, I can't fall asleep:
> "rain at night, on the roof of my lonely cabin."

"Well done," Longyan cheered. "It's 'Night Rain Beneath the City Walls of Pizhou' by Yang Shiqi. Excellent theme. Everyone drinks a half cup." Longyan sat cross-legged on a stool, leaning against a soot-blackened beam in the wall, slightly apart from the group. He smiled smugly and straightened his soggy brown robe, enjoying his role as acknowledged leader of Suzhou's most annoying delinquents.

A sallow-faced chap took his turn, improvising on the theme poem:

> "Clouded peaks, muddy roads,
> "the dangers ever mount.
> "The scholar sits on craggy rock,
> "better to think than to act."

Everyone turned to Longyan for his verdict. "Stunning!" Longyan announced. It was indeed a great effort, a word landscape, but more deeply a satire of the great Confucian debate about linking thought and action. Longyan felt a special kinship to the young man, who clearly would have been a fine scholar had fate not made him the third son. "A full cup for everyone!"

A nervous fellow stood up and stuttered:

> "D-d-drowning man with w-w-water to his n-n-neck,
> "C-cries to the w-waitress,
> "Q-quickly pour the wine,
> "T-this other stuff could k-k-kill you."

Longyan doubled over in laughter. "Right spirit. Wrong style. Penalty cup for the poet. Sympathy half-cup for the others."

A red-faced young man stood up, drunken legs shaking as if on a tightwire. He opened his sash and held out his arms to make the robe look like wings.

> *"Quack, quack goes the duck,*
> *"Happily sloshing in the cold rain.*
> *"Water merrily splashing off his back,*
> *"But that's not what comes out the front!"*

The Sages all jumped on their stools and mimicked ducks, making sure the other patrons saw their underwear.

"The worst poem. Two cups for the poet. The best joke. Two cups for everyone."

Energy spent, reeling with wine, the Sages slumped around the table, each endeavoring not to be the first to pass out. The penalty for passing out was severe—the other Sages showered their colleague's clothes with the remaining wine so that his amah would scold him and then tell his parents.

"Hear the one about the seamstress?" Pockmark nudged Longyan, who was almost slumbering, head on the table but fingers prying his eyes open. "She makes red sheets as well as red dresses. Won't have to wash them after Meihua's wedding."

Longyan's arms tightened and fists clenched. "You bastard!" he screamed, pushing himself upright. "You fucking bastard!"

Pockmark dodged a swipe from Longyan's arm. "The truth hurts, eh? I fear you're the bastard. And you won't be fucking. At least not Meihua. Unless you want to stand behind Xinping. I hear the astrologer has set the date. This year, July. It's perfect. Summer, red phoenix, and . . . red sheets."

Longyan lunged at Pockmark, throwing him on the table, pummeling him with his fists.

"Q-q-quit, s-s-stop!" The boy grabbed Longyan's shoulders, pulling him away from Pockmark. "R-r-remember your r-r-rules. Always t-t-truth among S-Sages. Always lies to p-p-parents."

Longyan scowled at Pockmark, then pulled himself erect, straightening his disheveled robe. "You're r-r-right," Longyan mimicked, "the t-t-truth. Even when it comes from someone whose face looks like an orange p-p-peel."

The teahouse door exploded open with a blast of wind and a spray of rain. The Sages stared in disbelief as a fearsome creature entered. A giant, he stood over six feet in his curious black leather boots. He removed a rain-drenched black woolen cape and a floppy circular hat, both of strange foreign manufacture. The Sages gaped at his oversized Buddhist robe, dark crimson from some southern sect, its clean cut indicating a recent purchase. Head shaved and beardless, the giant's skin was strangely pink, his face fleshy and full, his nose long and pointed, and his round eyes steely blue.

"Esteemed proprietor," the giant intoned, "might a wayward traveler have some food and drink?"

The Sages glanced at one another in wide-eyed astonishment, then broke into hysterical laughter, pounding the table and grabbing their ribs. "Methinks the monk emanates from distant lands," Pockmark chortled, imitating the giant's use of archaic early Ming expressions 200 hundred years out of date.

"Shhh," the proprietor scolded, delighted that he could seat the giant next to the Sages, cloistering his problem customers together. "What will you have, sir?"

"A bowl of your best noodles and a flacon of distilled rice spirits."

"Yes, yes," Pockmark shouted, "distilled spirits for us as well."

"In a d-d-distinguished f-f-flacon. If you p-p-please."

The giant smiled forgivingly at the torrent of insults. Brushing water droplets from a small black satchel, he drew out a silk-bound dictionary called the *Sea of Words,* pulled apart the ivory catches, selected a thread-stitched paperback, and studied a passage. The Sages could see his lips move, practicing words from the dictionary.

"Oh, many thanks," the giant said, setting aside his book as the proprietor brought his meal. "And special thanks for what seems a nice bottle of wine."

"Of course," the proprietor replied curiously, wondering how the guest suddenly managed to speak colloquially, albeit with a heavy accent.

The Sages stared as the giant paused, shut his eyes, folded his hands, and murmured words over the food. After touching his forehead, chest, and both shoulders, he ate heartily, chopsticks in one hand, book in the other. For a while, Pockmark kept the Sages entertained, slouching over his wine, babbling from a pretend book, touching various parts of his body as if they were holy.

"L-l-looks like L-L-Longyan l-l-loses," the stutterer chortled, pointing to the body slumped against the wall, arms splayed as if Longyan were a battlefield casualty.

"These peasants," Pockmark remarked snidely, "just don't know how to drink."

The giant gaped open-mouthed at the bizarre ritual that followed. Four boys entwined arms, standing around their fallen comrade. Pockmark chanted an excerpt from Xi Kang, one of the original Seven Sages:

"He whose physical faculties are clear and whose mental faculties are enlightened does not allow his feelings to be bound by desires. Since his mind is not occupied with attachments, he is able to overcome established doctrines and let nature take its course.

"Pure talk reveals the true man," Pockmark concluded, "and pure drink reveals all."

Each boy took a deep swig from his bottle before drenching Longyan with the residue. Then they swaggered off, singing a boisterous song to ward off the bitter black night, leaving Longyan soaked and stenchful.

"Sorry, sir," the proprietor said to the big foreigner, "it's nine o'clock. Closing time."

"Nine o'clock closing time?" the giant replied with surprise. "Where I come from, establishments don't close until after midnight. Oh, no matter, I was leaving anyway."

"Where do you come from?"

"It's far, far away," the giant mused, dropping the book into the satchel and placing a few copper coins on the table. "Across the sea. Then by land from Macao. It's a long story. I just arrived in Suzhou last week."

"But why are you here?"

"Because," the giant said hesitatingly, "because I like to meet different kinds of people. I love travel."

The proprietor wrinkled his brow skeptically, but did not challenge his customer. The giant wished he could tell the truth because no one ever seemed to accept his wanderlust story. He had tried the shipwrecked-on-the-way-to-the-Philippines tale, but that also elicited dubious frowns. Maybe it would be easier to explain what he was *not* trying to do in China. He was *not* what many people feared—*not* a subversive nor a demon. He was *not* a merchant trying to undercut local producers and suppliers. He was *not* a Buddhist, though he looked like one. But the giant concluded that the negative approach was another bad idea; listeners would surely become more suspicious as he tried to convince them he was not a threat.

The proprietor shrugged his shoulders as the giant wrapped himself in his cape, tugging his cap snugly against the weather. "Sorry about the noise, sir. Those boys are always causing trouble. Too rich for me to kick them out. Too poor to pay their bills."

"What happens to him?" The giant nodded at Longyan, asleep in the corner, cuddled in his reeking robe, like a stray cat.

"After closing time, I have no obligations to anyone. I just throw him out."

"On the street? On a night like this?"

"Of course. He'll crawl home or maybe huddle in an alley somewhere. Sleep it off so he can be back here tomorrow."

"You can't just toss him into a storm."

"Oh no? Watch this! Rich bastard!" The proprietor lugged the lifeless Longyan by the arms. "It's such a pity! His father is a great scholar. Once a great calligrapher. And formerly a very high official in Beijing. To have a son like this, it must kill him. Wu Longyan, you're a rotter!" He deposited Longyan unceremoniously outside the door, holding it open for the giant to leave as well.

"A high official? Really?"

"Formerly. Now he's out of favor. Too straitlaced for what's going on in the court these days."

"That's a pity," the giant said as the door closed. He shook his head at the snoring body and walked into the darkness. Then he stopped, thought a second, and returned. The giant lifted the boy into his arms, cradling him with his satchel resting atop his wine-soaked robe, enshrouding the whole package with his cape as he trudged against biting wind and rain.

"Women can enjoy sex, too," the Lin matriarch said with eyes twinkling.

"Mother!" Meihua was shocked. "You're not supposed to talk like that."

"Why not? No one's here to hear. It's just only the two of us." The Matriarch had indeed arranged a brief moment of privacy in her own dressing room, deep in the red chamber. Mother and daughter sat on gnarled-wood stools, a matching tea table between them, both wearing pastel morning gowns, looser and less formal than the stiffer afternoon and evening silks they wore when visitors were expected. The Matriarch had a bittersweet purpose in mind—a farewell chat with her eldest daughter on the brink of marriage.

"But Mother, you embarrass me."

"It's time you overcame your embarrassment. Otherwise in sex you will be just a willing vessel for your husband. It's better if you are actively involved. It's a rare moment when you can be equal, even dominant. It sets the context for many other things, including how much time he spends with other women." The Matriarch blessed her own mother for conveying the same message twenty years earlier. Why, she wondered, are we so reticent to tell the truth? Especially when it comes to bodies, feelings, marriage—the most basic things in life?

"But . . . I don't know how to talk about . . . you know, sex. . . . I don't even know what to ask."

"It's not so complicated. Just know if you feel something, then do it. If you feel he wants something, then try it. If you want something from him, then ask for it. And, hardest of all, if you think he wants something, but is afraid to ask for it, find a way to bring him out of his shell."

"How do you do that?"

"By overcoming his embarrassment. It's best when you are both mirrors. Getting the other to understand innermost feelings. I'm speaking figuratively about the mirrors. Though you can use real ones. Do you understand?"

"Not really." But Meihua sensed that her mother was saying something important. She would store the words in her head until the feelings came and the time was right to understand. Meihua did know how rare was her mother's revelation; sex was usually talked about by sisters or servants, and intimate sentiments were seldom discussed at all, by anyone.

"You're not confident about your marriage, are you, dear?"

"Why do you say that?" Meihua knew it would be unfilial to question her parents' decision.

"Don't try to fool me. You fear he may be too conventional, too insensitive. It's a natural fear. Yet marriages have a way of working out. You may not think so, but parents really have a sense of what works. Besides, families are a powerful inducement to make marriages work. So give it your best."

"I will. I promise."

"I know you will." The Matriarch rose, walked a few little steps, and opened the bright brass clasp on a small black lacquer chest. "But it's always important to keep your sense of self. Always remember who you are. That you have your own essence." She handed Meihua a jade *bi* disk, buttery white, perhaps two inches in diameter, hanging from a simple hemp cord. "From my mother at my wedding. So it's right to give it to you. It symbolizes the *you* that must always be preserved. A *you* that I helped fashion. I'm proud of you. Be proud of yourself."

"Thank you, Mother." Meihua bowed her head.

"By the way, I know about your secret."

"What secret?"

"Your candlelight studying. Between the walls. Every night for an hour or two. Reading. Practicing calligraphy."

"I'm sorry, Mother. I disobeyed you."

"It's true. And I'm not angry. My worry was that it would impede your marriage. It didn't. So now I'm not angry. Maybe just a little envious."

"Really? I could show you how. Guess what I heard about Widow Gu? Both daughters are teaching their mother how to read and write. So why not you? It wouldn't take that long."

"Now that's a laugh. Teach an old cow how to sing? No. But don't lose the ability yourself. Hide it. But nurture it. It might serve you well."

A deep emotion welled up in Meihua. "Mother. Oh, I'm going to miss you terribly. It's not that I'm so scared about the marriage.

It's that I'm scared to leave. But at least you'll be nearby. I can see you whenever I want. I can always get your advice. I can—"

"No, you can't," she replied firmly. "Your new obligations are to your husband and his parents. You must not seek advice from me. You must never look to me for solace. That is the way it is. The way it must be."

"I understand." Meihua sighed.

"You'll only really understand when you have your own male child. Your job is to nurture that child and, when he's an adult, make sure his family supports him fully. His wife must obey you. Not her mother. Any other way and the whole system breaks down."

"So what more is there to say?"

"We must both say what must be said." The Matriarch put the jade pendant around Meihua's neck. "Good-bye, my daughter."

"But we still have many weeks before the wedding."

"Yes. But it's right that you prepare for your new life. We cannot speak like this anymore. Good-bye, my daughter."

"Good-bye, Mother." Meihua threw herself into the Matriarch's arms and cried.

Longyan, accustomed to waking up hungover and sweaty, rolled over on the floor and groaned. "Amah Yang, Amah Yang, bring me hot water and a towel." He surveyed the strange surroundings through groggy eyes: tiny, white-walled room, rough-hewn bed, simple desk with a rock supporting a broken leg, small barrel for a chair. He jumped up when he saw the giant, silhouetted by the brilliant morning sun, holding a shiny brass instrument.

"Sorry, my son, I'm not Amah Yang. The water basin is by the bed. Only one towel, but you're welcome to use it."

"Who are you? Where have you taken me?"

The giant, still in crimson robes, walked barefoot to the barrel, sat on it, gesturing Longyan to sit on the bed while he washed. "Let's just say I'm the Good Samaritan." The giant rested the instrument in its red-lacquered case on the tabletop.

"You're the Good what?"

"Never mind. My Chinese name is Gao. Here I'm usually called Father Gao. Some call me old Gao. My real name is Wolfgang Gutkinder. Gao was the closest they could find when I arrived in

Macao two years ago. I apologize for my spoken Chinese, but it's a difficult language. I often rub characters—"

"Mistake characters," Longyan corrected Father Gao's misspoken Mandarin dialect, offering the accurate tone for the right meaning, still staring at the giant disbelievingly. "Are you one of those kidnappers? Have you taken me for money? If so, you took the wrong son. I don't think my father will pay a copper piece to get me back."

"No, no, no! You've got it all wrong. I haven't stolen you. I couldn't leave you sleeping in the rain. I brought you back here. You can leave anytime you want. It's just a rooming house. Owned by a Mr. Deng."

"Crazy Deng? The spirit freak?"

"I don't know what you call him. He's a Christian. Looks kindly on foreign Jesuits like myself." Father Gao showed Longyan the heavy silver crucifix suspended from his robe cord.

"I know about that! The Japanese dwarf barbarians nail up the big-nosed barbarians. Takes a long time to die."

"That's right." Father Gao sighed. He too had heard recent reports of mass crucifixions of European Christians by the Tokugawa shoguns fearing foreign subversion. Thank God the Ming emperors hadn't done the same.

The Jesuits, who had only arrived in Asia a scant fifty years earlier, saw themselves as the elite among European missionaries. Unlike the Dominicans and Franciscans, who greatly outnumbered them, the Jesuit followers of Ignatius Loyola sought converts from the top down rather than from the bottom up. Jesuits tried to become fluent in the languages and sensitive to the cultures of the countries where they worked.

China became the ultimate testing ground for Jesuit tactics. The brilliant Father Matteo Ricci had paved the way, astonishing Ming scholars with his ability in the Chinese language (applying Western mnemonics to Chinese pictographs and ideographs) and impressing the Ming court with his skill in astronomy (important because accurate astronomical predictions were crucial to court ritual). A few hundred Jesuits thrived in China because, like Confucian scholar-officials, they lived a life of the mind, wrestled with serious moral issues, and brought a touch of arrogance to their humanistic philosophy.

47

Father Gao felt doubly blessed. The China mission was the dream of any young Jesuit, a chance to show his skill and faith in the most cultured traditional society on earth. And what could be better than Suzhou, a glorious city in the heartland of China's intelligentsia?

Father Gao's initial task was clear-cut: make contact with influential families, seek to build friendships and confidence, and constantly study Chinese language and civilization. The longer-range goal—creating a network of elite converts in the society at large and eventually in the court—could wait. Western critics would say that Jesuits put loving heathens above loving God; Jesuits usually ignored the criticisms, especially those from less sophisticated religious orders. Chinese critics, furious because officials and even emperors often took a liking to several Jesuits, sometimes tried to diminish their influence by implicating the famous Jesuit fathers in factional conspiracies.

"I'm not a Buddhist," Father Gao continued, wondering whether this disheveled wastrel really came from prominent parents. "I'm a follower of someone who was killed like that. A long time ago. Accused of being a criminal."

"You're part of a criminal gang?"

"No. He wasn't a real criminal. You see, they killed a good man because he was . . . no matter, it's too complicated to explain now. I wear these Buddhist robes so that people will know I'm like a priest. I'm certainly not a criminal."

Father Gao thought about speaking truthfully: young man, you need help, maybe I can provide it, and then perhaps I can get to know your parents. Not a promising strategy, the priest had to admit. Momentarily he considered creating a bond by describing his own history: an orphaned child, raised by Jesuit fathers, top honors in seminary, finally winning the right to come to China. But he imagined how that would read in China: lower-class birth, parents threw him out, grew up with chanting priests, studied religious tracts, not secular philosophy, and then turned his back on his native country. No, the priest concluded, the boy couldn't possibly comprehend.

"Now, how about some tea?" asked Father Gao. "I've got some special tea for pilfering pain."

"For head pain?" Longyan corrected another misspoken tone. Father Gao nodded his appreciation and rang a bell for hot water.

"Careful of that." Father Gao saw Longyan tinkering with the brass instrument, a flat disk with a pivoting dial hand, its lustrous surface meticulously engraved with numbers and images of stars. "It's a special device. It uses the Sun to tell where you are on the Earth, even what time it is. I made it myself back in Germany. You use this book to make calculations. It's from Rome. Clavius, fifteen ninety-three."

Longyan sat on the bed, sipping tea and flipping through the strange leather-bound book. Unable to comprehend the Western numbers and words, he stopped at a line drawing describing the functions of the astrolabe. Engrossed, Longyan gulped down the tea and used his finger to trace images and angles on the drawing. "I see," he said finally, after five minutes of absorbed silence, "if you know the time, then you can use the Sun to find your location. If you know your location, you can use the Sun to find the time. It's all angles. You guess first, then correct the guesses after you've made measurements."

Father Gao stared in open-mouthed astonishment. "You've studied this before. Right?"

Longyan snapped the book shut. "I'm not a student. I hate books."

"Why?"

"Because it's all boring. That's why."

"What do you like?"

"I like my friends."

"You mean the ones at the teahouse."

"Of course."

"Drinking and fighting all the time?"

"That's not true. We usually just talk. You couldn't understand, anyway."

"Oh, I think I understand. I was once a student. At a university. München."

"And I'll bet you were a good student. A book-lover type."

"Not true. I was better drinking with my friends. It wasn't until later I started to like books. When I found a reason."

"Well," Longyan retorted, "I never found any reason. Books are

like chains. Ways for stupid tutors to torture students for money."
He started inching toward the door, seeking to escape an uncomfortable conversation.

"I think you're right."

"You do?" Longyan replied in astonishment, halting his retreat.

"Of course. Where I come from, this is the most important book." He unwrapped purple velvet to reveal a well-worn leather-bound Bible. "Sort of like the Four Books. Lots of people have used this book to torture others. Not just by boring lessons from dull tutors. This book has offered an excuse to use knives, fire, whips against other human beings."

"So why do you keep the book?"

"Because it's not the book's fault. It's the fault of people who use—and misuse—the book."

"Okay. Okay. I get it. Enough. No lectures, please."

"Is that how it sounded? Sorry! I'm not here to lecture. I'm here to learn." Father Gao privately chided himself for violating the number one rule of the Jesuits: Don't try for conversions, try for communication.

"I was just impressed," the priest tried to ease the tension. "I've never seen anyone grasp aspects of star watching—what do you call it?"

"Astronomy."

"Oh, yes . . . never seen anyone grasp some aspects of astronomy so quickly. Especially using a book in a foreign language. I meant it as a compliment."

"Sometimes intended compliments result in unintended insults. I would think it important to learn the difference." Longyan crossed his arms and smiled smugly, knowing he'd scored a point against the barbarian. Father Gao smiled back, acknowledging the uncommon quickness of his companion, but not saying anything to give Longyan further cause to gloat.

A moment of weighty silence passed between them. Will I ever understand these people? the priest wondered. You try to be a friend and they mock you.

What a terrible fate to be a barbarian, the Chinese concluded. They are so earnest but so obvious.

"Would you like to help me with a little astronomical observation?" Father Gao asked. "We can still see the planet Venus at this time of the morning. How about it?"

"I wish I had the time. It's late. My family's probably looking for me."

"Before you go, here's a spare robe Mr. Deng gave me for you. He'll have your other one washed. You can pick it up anytime. And here's a little packet of powder. Put two pinches in your wine cup. It'll keep you from getting drunk."

Longyan swiftly changed robes, unconcerned that the foreigner saw him in his underwear. "I will bring back the robe. And thank you, old Gao."

"For what?"

"The tea worked. My headache's gone."

As soon as Longyan glimpsed the white crepe paper over the Wu mansion doorway, he broke into a run and stumbled into the household. "Who? Who died?" he asked breathlessly. "Not Father? It wasn't Father, was it?"

Xinping shook his head and put his arm around Longyan. "No. Not Father."

"But who? The Matriarch? No? No one else ranks high enough to have white drapery outside the house."

"It's the Patriarch's orders. Highly unusual. You know how close she was to him. It's been ten years, but he's never forgotten her—"

"Oh no! Not my mother!"

"I'm really sorry. What can I say?" Xinping helped Longyan to a chair, beckoning servants to bring tea.

No one, least of all Longyan, was truly surprised at his mother's death, but he hadn't expected it so soon with no warning. Shortly after she had left the Wu mansion a decade back, Concubine Wang had fallen ill in her native village, suffering coughs and chills, her weight dropping until she was almost a skeleton.

"Don't try to visit me," she had admonished him on his only trip to Pingdao two years earlier, "it's just too far." Pingdao was scarcely ten miles from Suzhou, but it was worlds away from cultured society. Longyan was shocked to find his mother, emaciated and clothed in rough cotton, amongst huts of pounded earth and thatch, scantily clothed children begging for food, unrestrained cows and pigs dropping manure on doorsteps.

"No," she had said when he had suggested moving her to a relative's house on the edge of Suzhou. "This is where I was born and it's where I belong. Please don't come anymore. It hurts me too much to remember. I can't stand saying good-bye."

"When did she die? When did you hear she was dying?" Longyan had to know. He'd heeded her wish. He hadn't visited her again. While it filled him with guilt, it was also easier not to be reminded of her pain and his own humble roots. But he'd always promised himself to be with her in her waning moments, to comfort her as she died.

"When?" he asked urgently.

"She died just before midday, today. Lao Li was with her at Father's request. It was peaceful. Without pain. That's what he said."

"And *when* did you know she was dying?"

"Yesterday evening. We sent for you at the teahouse. But it was already shut. We didn't know where to reach you. We tried, believe me, but imagine the difficulty in the storm."

Longyan slumped forward in his chair, holding his head in his hands, caught between grief and guilt. Why couldn't he have heard during the day? Why couldn't he have still been at the teahouse? Why couldn't he have sobered up as usual? Why did that stupid barbarian hide him away? Why?

"Here. Your mother told Lao Li to give this to you." Xinping handed Longyan a square wooden box wrapped in white silk. Longyan opened the box and withdrew two objects, a brown writing brush with worn bristles and a thin dagger with wooden handle and sheath.

"What does it mean?"

Longyan grimaced, holding each object in a separate hand, as if weighing them. "She's saying that she thinks the verdict is still out. Scholar or soldier. She's saying she still has faith in me. Whatever I choose. She never gave up."

He shook his head, dropped the brush and dagger into the box, snapping its lid shut as tightly as a coffin. "She should have," he mumbled.

CHAPTER SIX

Lost Loves

明

A Few Months Later: Suzhou, Summer 1633

NESTLED DEEPLY IN the Wu estate, behind the main house and even behind the rock garden, was a shabby, rough wood toolshed. The shed, unused in the half century since a larger stucco toolhouse had been constructed, contained battered wooden rakes and pitchforks, boxes of broken roof tiles, packages of hardened whitewash, and an assortment of rotting barrels. A slender shaft of sunlight slivered through an open cobweb-covered window. The door hung outward from a single lower hinge, its orange-rusted iron creaking in the lightest of dawn breezes.

The toolshed had a close, musty feeling. Longyan sat meditatively on an empty hemp sack spread over the earthen floor, opening his light blue robe for a bit of air, wiping back the sweat beads gathering on his forehead. Sunlight illuminated his face; early morning steamy fog rendered a haze over everything else.

He smiled contentedly, as he always did, when he visited the old shed—the Ben Tang, "Idiot's Palace," as he called it. The Ben Tang was his zealously guarded secret; he'd bribed several servants to keep it that way. He usually came here at daybreak after jarring himself awake with a cold-water bath to repel the aches of alcohol.

Pasted calligraphy—large-brush black ink on white rice paper—covered the stucco walls. It was his own writing, strange and vibrant, depicting fragments of characters, in various sizes and angles, often in serpentine cursive script. He delighted in the fact that every character was rendered backwards, as if viewed in a mirror. Conventional scholars would have been appalled. Only a hermit philosopher or artist might have understood. The viewer was *inside* the scroll looking out, examining the world through the calligraphy, the scholar's ultimate conceit.

Longyan shut his eyes for a moment of peace. Then he lifted a white silk cloth, revealing a lustrously lacquered *qin,* the lute of the Chinese elite class, resting splendidly on a black squat table. Gently touching each string with his fingertips and nails, he adjusted the bridge and tuning nuts until the harmonics resonated perfectly.

Hands hovering just above the gut strings, Longyan breathed out slowly and gazed into murky space. Then he dropped his right hand and softly plucked a single bass string, his left hand rocking in slow vibrato as the note wavered its way from fullness to thinness, as if pulling a single thread from a strong rope. His thumb and three fingers plucked rapidly, recalling a lady with bound feet bouncing down a pathway. After a melancholy interlude, the *qin*'s tempo increased imperceptibly as Longyan's left hand moved to the higher strings, releasing sprays of brighter sounds, finally a sustained tremolo like a hummingbird's wings. Suddenly it all stopped with a pause that seemed to last forever; finally the original bass note was played three times, the last one seeming to resonate forever, fading to infinity. His hands motionless just above the strings, Longyan's head fell to his chest, as if it had been someone else, some larger force, moving his fingers.

"Stunning," said a chunky man standing in the doorway. "Absolutely stunning. And I had no idea you played."

"I didn't know you were there," Longyan gulped, quickly throwing the white cloth back over the instrument. "I told you to meet me in the garden. Not here. Not now. Later. No one knows I play. It's only for scholars. I'm not a scholar."

"Well, now someone knows your little secret. You should play for others. Maybe the family will want to hear you after I tell them." Cao Laozi, the Patriarch's chief secretary, had a smug look on his round face. He liked being privy to confidential information; he'd played that role for thirty years of service to Longyan's father. Most secrets he couldn't reveal, but this one was different.

"You *won't* tell them," Longyan ordered.

"And why not?"

"Because then I'd have to pass along another little secret."

"What?"

"Oh, nothing much. It's just something about Xiao Ma. You

know. The one who drowned her baby in the well. Unmarried Xiao Ma. I know who the father was."

"I don't know what you're talking about."

"Perhaps the Patriarch would like to visit the little closet behind the laundry room. I often walk that way. Coming back at night. Say, about eleven o'clock?"

"That's enough! All right. Both our secrets are safe. Right?"

"Right. Totally safe. I won't tell anyone. I won't make sure you're out of a job. If you'll agree to a favor. A simple one."

"Yes?"

"You'll write confidential letters for me. Not often. Just every once in a while. Definitely not in your usual penmanship. I want a distinctive style. And no one, absolutely no one, must know. Not ever."

"All right. But I hope you're writing outside the family. Everyone here knows what a poor scholar you are. They wouldn't believe a letter from you."

"It's outside the family. And we begin today. You take notes. This one's to Lin Meihua."

"But she's engaged to your brother! This is most irregular!"

"Yes, irregular. But not illegal. Not even immoral. You'll see. Just write it and make sure it gets to her."

Secretary Cao sat on a barrel, spreading his paper on a crate, taking his brush and ink from his portable wooden scholar's case. "I'm ready. Proceed."

Longyan began his dictation:

> " 'To the noblewoman, Lin Meihua, this humble letter is written to inadequately express my deep and enduring respect.
>
> 'I am well aware that you are about to be married to my esteemed older brother. It is a marriage that brings great happiness to the Wu patriarch and taitai. I assume that happiness is shared by your parents. Marriage is, above all, a union between families. Indeed that also brings me happiness, for I shall soon be your brother-in-law.
>
> 'We have not spoken since the Dragon Boat Festival in the last years of the Wanli reign. As I have grown older, I have thought often of that wonderful day. It was highly

improper of both of us to speak, but I cannot suppress the joy I felt at our meeting.

'A most unworthy idea has come to me. Would it be improper for us to write from time to time, as brother to sister? I know you can read these words. And that you can write back . . .' ''

"What? She's not going to have someone read and write for her?" exclaimed Secretary Cao, shock on his pudgy face. "A lady who can write? Your brother's in for a hard time. Next thing *she'll* be wanting to be a secretary. Ha! Can't wait to see her ugly scrawl."

"Hush. Just write. You better not tell anyone she can read and write. You reveal anything and I'll make sure Xiao Ma sees the Patriarch."

"Okay. It's just all so irregular."

Longyan continued to dictate.

" ' . . . that you can write back. I have some inner thoughts that I would humbly like to express to you.

"How about 'Some humble thoughts to convey to your noble mind'? It sounds better. Yes?"

"You pretty it all up later. Make it nice. Now stop interrupting."

" ' . . . some humble thoughts to convey to your noble mind, I dare not pass them along to anyone else. I thought you might want to do likewise. If so, I will treasure your letters. If not, do not respond at all.

'If you agree, then my father's loyal secretary, a man of great propriety and thus of great loyalty, will arrange exchanges of letters. His noble name is Cao.

'Please forgive my inadequate calligraphy. I only hope my ideas are clearer than my hand.

'Your dutiful friend and future brother.' ''

"What's that about 'inadequate calligraphy'?"

"Make a couple of minor mistakes so it looks real. I cannot appear perfect."

"Don't worry, young master. No one would make that mistake."

Longyan scowled at Secretary Cao. "Just get it to her. Don't change a word. As soon as possible. And not a word about my playing the *qin*."

Longyan walked briskly out of the shed. It was getting late. No one dared miss the morning family gathering in the garden.

The Wu matriarch loved mornings, even steamy ones in early July. Mornings belonged to ladies, and she adored being the first lady of the Wu mansion, especially in the summer, when the family gathered outside, with everyone in her sight.

"The air's so thick the cicadas can't breathe," she said brightly, watching a hunchbacked old woman servant sweep the brown insect carcasses from a raised stone pavilion into a murky green carp pond. With sharp snaps of her tasseled fan, the Matriarch directed male servants as they shoved a heavy wooden table and four matching chairs into a shady spot near a round red pillar supporting the pavilion's dark green tile roof.

"Wedding weather, don't you think?" she said, sitting down and nodding for a female servant to begin sweeping the big pole fan over her head. The Matriarch rested her hand on a portable manicure table so another servant could polish her nails with an elkhide buffer.

"Wedding weather, don't you think?" she repeated more loudly, the long nails of her left hand tapping the red-lacquered table for attention.

"Yes, yes, of course, wedding weather, indeed," replied the Patriarch, deeply engrossed in a game of *weiqi*, the Chinese version of Go, with his son, Xinping. Longyan lounged in a chair beside the game table, mildly interested in the contest, more bemused by two carp barely escaping collision as they gobbled dead cicadas.

"Feint to the corners, but move to the center," the Patriarch counseled Xinping.

Longyan glanced at the board, shook his head, and beckoned Xinping to lean in his direction. "Noble Father always takes the classic approach," Longyan whispered. "Fake a move to the center and keep strength in the corners. Always three corners at least. Then you can pick off his pieces."

Xinping grinned and made a quick move.

The Patriarch puzzled over the board, then swiftly jumped over two pieces. "Bad advice you're taking, my son."

Xinping frowned. But Longyan held down his palms quietly, gesturing Xinping to remain calm, to keep to the strategy.

Ten minutes and five moves later, the Patriarch stared at the board in amazement. "How did you do that?" he exclaimed. "I should have won this easily. I've got all the power. But . . . I'm the hawk caught in a spider's web."

"Give up?" Xinping asked.

"That's something I'm good at. Knowing when to give up. You win. You *both* win." The Patriarch smiled at his sons.

"Good, the game's over. It's time," the Matriarch announced.

"Time for what?"

"Time for our talk."

"Please," the Patriarch pleaded, "just one more game. It's my turn to play Longyan. I think I know his strategy. It won't take long. Can't you wait an hour?"

"Now," she ordered. "This is important. And you promised we'd talk this morning."

The Patriarch shared a grumbling shrug of shoulders with his sons. Unenthusiastically, they left the game and took chairs around the Matriarch's table. The Patriarch knew what was coming—an hour in which the Matriarch would take charge—but he never knew how to stop her. In Beijing, when he gave orders, thousands had obeyed fearfully. But in Suzhou, he was powerless in his own household. He could always reassert his authority, so he consoled himself, but it was such a bother to negotiate with the Matriarch that he seldom tried. He remained oblivious to difficult domestic situations, pretending he did not have a clue about what was happening.

"Now let us speak of weddings," the Matriarch declared, "for 'tis weddings that chart the course of families." Longyan found it embarrassing when the Taitai employed formal speech patterns at home. It showed her lowly roots, like *nouveaux riches* wearing imperial regalia.

"Everything ready for the wedding?" the Patriarch asked just to make conversation.

"Everything ready! How could you ask that? Only two weeks to go and it's chaos. The caterers. Housing for *your* relatives. My gowns still not back from the tailors. And those Lins—it's a wonder they figured out how to have children at all. They've got no sense of organization. Xinping, your Meihua is so lucky, getting out of that household. I'll turn a spoiled child into a good wife. You just watch. She's a lucky girl. Right, Xinping?"

"How could anyone be more lucky?" Xinping replied.

Longyan admired the fact that Xinping's face remained expressionless. Xinping's learned a lot, mused Longyan, from the old days when he used to ape the Taitai's every expression. Ironically, as the two brothers went different ways, Longyan found it easier to like Xinping and to appreciate the subtle ways he preserved his self-respect.

"Well. Too bad not everyone can be lucky." The Taitai glowered at Longyan. "But you could at least try to make the most of limited talents. Longyan, what do you say to that?"

"I have much to learn from you," Longyan replied quietly.

The Taitai wrinkled her brow, sensing that she'd been insulted, but not quite sure. "Well . . . yes, of course. Now, do you think we'll ever have the pleasure of your wedding?"

Longyan shrugged and slouched in his chair, avoiding eye contact.

"Can you imagine the matchmaker's response if I asked about a marriage for Longyan? She'd bring back some gangly clodhopper from an obscure village. Who else would marry a wastrel with no talent?"

"Mother. Please. That's not fair." Xinping was provoked enough to break his usual filiality. "Longyan has lots of talent."

"Sure. At *weiqi*. At drinking. At causing trouble."

"Please," interceded the Patriarch, "give him his due. He's got fine abilities, maybe not fully developed, but really great potential." The Patriarch, realizing it was futile to try to change her mind, was simply consoling Longyan with his words. The Matriarch had a potent weapon at her disposal: if provoked, she could reveal a devastating truth about the Patriarch. The Matriarch knew his ultimate vulnerability, the secret that could destroy what remained of his reputation, and she had threatened to use it. Mild protests were his only defense.

The Matriarch shook her head. "Can you imagine what the Lins would have said if we'd suggested Longyan rather than Xinping? The parents would have become hysterical. And the poor girl, she would have cried herself to death. . . ."

Longyan raised his eyes, stared at the Taitai, and gave her his strongest dose of hurt–smile. In his gown sleeve was a letter he'd committed to memory. Recalling it was his best weapon against maternal tirades:

> *My Dear Brother-in-Law-to-Be:*
> *I have reflected these many months on your proposal and, unusual as it is, have decided to accept it. I too have fond memories of that May afternoon so long ago and have regretted no chance to talk since then. Of course, it was most inappropriate that we met at all, without a chaperone, but no harm seems to have come of it. I appreciate your maintaining confidentiality. I have done the same.*
> *I would also like to have an opportunity to write letters secretly so that no one will see me practicing calligraphy. And when I come to your household, it may be best to communicate this way, lest anyone think we are talking too much and come to improper conclusions.*
> *Of course, the wedding gives my family great pleasure. The Wus are a fine family. I believe you now go by the Wu name, yes? And my father says your noble elder brother is a fine scholar. So I too am pleased. Everyone says your mother is an excellent house-keeper so I shall look forward to learning much.*
> *Forgive my handwriting, but what can you expect from a silly woman. Yours was so elegant. And thank you for tossing in a few mistakes to make me feel less insignificant.*
> *Your Devoted Future Sister-in-Law*

". . . right, Longyan? Longyan? Right?"

"What?"

"Oh, Longyan, were you listening at all?" the Matriarch nagged. "What will we do with you? Anyway, your father has some gifts to give both of you."

"Now?" the Patriarch asked.

"Now," she replied, nodding sharply to a manservant who brought a bundle to the table. "First comes Xinping."

The Patriarch stood up, unwrapped the burlap, and with his left good hand pulled the ivory pins from a long green box, gently lifting a scroll and opening it on the table. "Ah, a genuine Song Taizu," he intoned, "maybe the greatest imperial calligrapher of all time. It's yours, Xinping."

"Father, I don't know what to say. I'll treasure it."

"Don't just treasure it! Study it, Xinping. See the essence of characters, not just their outer form."

"He's already very good at that," the Taitai announced proudly.

"Hush. You don't know what you're talking about. No, he's not very good at that. I'll listen to a lot of what you say, but I won't accept your views on calligraphy."

Seemingly unaffected, the Taitai prattled on. "Now it's Longyan's turn. Show him what he gets."

The Patriarch opened two doors on a large embroidered presentation box, cautiously lifting out a blue and white porcelain vase. "One of the earliest, and the very best, from our own dynasty."

Longyan held the vase and turned it slowly, letting the light play off its luminous surface. "Father, why me? I don't deserve this. . . ."

"Right," interrupted the Taitai, "tell him the rest."

"Oh, if I must. . . . Your mother insists I tell you. Longyan, the real value comes from the fact that this is a matched set of two vases. The only such set in existence. I'm only giving you one vase now. The other will come when we feel you've earned it."

"And when might that be?" Longyan wondered.

"When you show some talent." The Taitai grinned. "And some filiality. And some common sense. And some decency. And——"

"Enough, woman. I, and I alone, will determine when he receives the other vase. Longyan knows his faults as well as I do. He and I shall discuss this matter over time. Among men." The Patriarch left no room for argument.

The Matriarch shrugged her shoulders and rocked her head saucily, a gesture that conveyed much more than words. If she had her way, Longyan would never get the other vase. And she usually had her way.

Meihua found it appropriate that her last duty before becoming a bride, her full entry to womanhood, was to comfort her youngest sister during her initiation to foot-binding, the first step into womanhood. Normally such an event would have waited until after a wedding—who needs more stress and commotion? But five-year-old Jingjing desperately wanted her Dajie, Elder Sister Meihua, present during the ordeal. Besides, it was the only time that the woman known as the Foot Lady—whose scruffy clothes and frizzy gray hair had frightened several generations of Suzhou girls—was available. Many mothers swore by the Foot Lady, who knew the right amount of pressure to apply and how to prevent infection.

Foot-binding initiations brought together every woman and girl in the household, gathered in a large circle around a chair with a footstool, all in the heart of the red chamber, the courtyard in front of the Matriarch's bedroom. The Foot Lady was already seated on the ground, legs straddling the footstool, busily checking her long, wrapped bandages and the temperature of the water in the ceramic basin. Little Jingjing, white and speechless with fear, was led in by the Matriarch and Meihua and placed in the chair.

"Are you ready, my child?" the Foot Lady asked, a gentleness in her voice that defied her gruff looks.

Jingjing looked at the Matriarch, eyes filling with tears, and shook her head. Still too frightened to cry, she pulled her legs up from the footstool and tucked them under her. Compressing herself into a little ball, Jingjing silently shook like a leaf. The Foot Lady threw up her hands, announcing that, while she was sympathetic, she would have to leave soon for her next appointment.

Meihua quieted the Foot Lady and, sitting on the chair's edge, put her arms around Jingjing. "Little One. Remember we talked about this. It's never easy. But you're getting to be a big girl now. Besides, you wanted me here. Now, how about you sit on my lap? Then it will be much easier. And if you're good, I have a big surprise for you."

Jingjing peeked up. "What surprise?"

"I can't tell until later. It depends on whether you're good now. Will you be good?"

Jingjing scrambled into Meihua's lap and hugged her sister. "Will you be good?" Meihua asked again. Jingjing nodded and slowly lowered her feet, facing forward but with her arms still clinging Meihua's neck. "I've got you," said Meihua, wrapping her arms around Jingjing's waist. "Now you just look at me. Everything will be okay."

The Foot Lady thrust Jingjing's feet into the tepid water basin, firmly massaging them to loosen the tendons and relax the muscles. Then the Foot Lady looked up at Meihua, nodding that the time had come. Meihua tightened her grasp around Jingjing. The Foot Lady grabbed one foot and, wrapping a bandage twice around the arch and toes, compressed it firmly in one strong hand, toes moving sharply toward the heel, the wet bandage holding the contorted foot in place.

Jingjing's mouth opened as if she'd been stabbed, but Meihua pinned her arms so that the child couldn't move. Jingjing screamed from pain and terror. "Hush, hush," said Meihua, "the worst is over. It really is." Meihua knew that the first wave of pain was the most intense—so it would be every day for the next three or four years. The slow tightening of the bandages as they dried simply transformed the first knifelike stab into a pounding throb. Jingjing would learn that womanhood was associated with pain: foot-binding, menstrual cramps, first sex, childbirth. Meihua feared that the worst pain of all might be the loss of one's first family.

"Dajie, Dajie," Jingjing whimpered, bandages drying ever tighter. They were alone now, everyone including the Foot Lady having left.

"Yes, I'm still here." Meihua stroked the child's wet forehead. "What is it, Little One?"

"What's my surprise?"

"Tomorrow. In the wedding procession. You can ride with me. Hidden in the sedan chair. Until we're almost to the Wu mansion. Would you like that?"

Jingjing nodded through her pain, snuggling up to her elder sister. Meihua remained motionless, cradling Jingjing, until the child was finally asleep.

Dozens of servants of the Lin and Wu families lined the arched marble dock in front of the Wu mansion. A parade of red gondolas floated slowly along the narrow residential canal, announcing the coming wedding procession. The wedding ceremony itself had already been conducted a day earlier, a short and simple ritual at a nearby temple, the priest picking the precise moment for the most auspicious union. But it was the bridal procession, a public display of wealth and power, that attracted the most attention. Musicians celebrated with a deafening clamor of horns, drums, cymbals, and gongs. Strings of fireworks exploded rapid fire, finishing with concussive bangs, echoing sharply against the whitewashed walls lining the waterway.

Lao Li, senior servant of the Wu family, ducked behind the glistening marble spirit screen with carved dragons and banged his fist on the iron-strapped heavy wood front door. Red bunting decorated the walls and windows; white calligraphy on red paper rustled in the wind, promising eternal health, happiness, fortune, and fertility.

"My lords. My ladies," Lao Li proclaimed to a buzzing cluster of humanity just inside the doorway. "It is time. She is coming."

Pushed from behind, the Patriarch popped out of the doorway, dressed in a rust silk gown with pale blue fringes, matching shoes with upturned toes, and a black scholar cap trailing two black ribbons. Just behind, in mute red symbolizing a great celebration and the auspicious summer phoenix, Xinping fidgeted in his father's shadow. Longyan, definitely a background figure in the festivities, chose a solemn dark blue with a touch of crimson at the sleeves and robe opening. The Matriarch, in a puffy pink gown to disguise her slight frame, fussed about, making certain Xinping's two sisters and several female cousins stood in proper rank order.

A narrow, flower-festooned barge bobbed along its way, red silk encasing the bridal cabin, propelled by eight polemen. Ahead in their own private gondola were the Lin patriarch and his four sons. Following behind as far as the eye could see was a profusion of gondolas: a boatload of Buddhist monks robed in orange, another clanging-banging percussion band, four clowns with monkeys screaming in terror of the fireworks, the bride's personal attendants, the Lin family retinue, and guests by the hundreds.

Suddenly the wedding barge stopped just a few hundred yards before the Wu mansion. A little girl was plucked out of the draperies by a servant. A delicate hand reached through the red drapery; it gave Jingjing a beautiful bride doll garbed in red, patted the child gently on the head before she was handed to other servants ashore, then motioned for the procession to continue.

As the barge settled at the Wu dock, mothers shooshed their children, hands over mouths, and a hush settled over the crowd.

The Lin patriarch, flanked by his sons, bowed slightly and smiled formally; the Wu patriarch responded in kind and gestured for Lin sons to join their father in a row, thus forming a channel from barge to doorway, the two families constituting the channel banks. As the polemen secured their craft and readied a gangplank, four female servants flittered at the cabin companionway, readying the occupant for public viewing. The servants tittered for a moment, then peeled back like a ripe bud revealing a flower.

Lin Meihua stood demurely on the deck, pausing to collect herself, then delicately walked ashore with the confidence of a Suzhou woman used to gondola transportation. She bowed her head respectfully before her father and father-in-law, her brothers and brothers-in-law, and her new husband. As she raised her head, Longyan felt a deep stab in his chest. Beads of pinkish jadeite quivered from her hairstyle of flowers and pearls, slightly veiling her soft oval face and properly downcast eyes, but not hiding the fact she was biting her lower lip anxiously. The bright red bridal gown, embroidered with a phoenix-and-bird pattern, flowed gently over her body, the wafting breeze pressing it enough to offer a hint of her form. Her red slippers showed slightly as she daintily tripped through the cordon of family and servants, nodding to her new husband while avoiding Longyan's guarded stare.

Longyan had already anticipated this moment in his last letter:

> Do not worry, my sister-in-law, I shall do nothing, absolutely nothing, to compromise your arrival in our household. Not my expressions, nor my words, nor the sending and receiving of letters shall cause you any concern.

Meihua had read his letter in her boudoir scarcely a week before the wedding. Her deeper worries centered on the next moment:

> *Your words allay anxiety, dear brother. But this fretful woman cannot overcome fear. Though my life has been wholly focused on this great event—marriage and good wifeliness—I shiver awaiting what my aunt calls the Great Confrontation. She says that for a woman marriage has nothing to do with the husband and everything to do with the mother-in-law. I know it would be*

*inappropriate for you to comment on this matter. It just makes me
feel a little better—strangely perhaps—to know that you know
I'm afraid.*

Longyan heard Meihua's jadeite beads rattle as she bowed before
the Wu matriarch. "A foolish child of the Lin family," she said
whisperingly, "seeks the noble counsel of the Matriarch of the Wu
family."

The Lin patriarch hid his cough in a gown sleeve, recalling when
his father had refused to buy porcelain from the former family of
the Wu taitai; "Their dishes and their daughters are the same," he
had said many years back, "surface glitter, but cheap clay underneath." The Lin matriarch, a woman of uncommon persuasive-
ness, had prevailed over her husband's doubts: "Yes, I'm sure it will
be trying for little Meihua, at least for a while. But remember, good
jade lights the darkest caves. The trials of the daughter-in-law will
be the triumphs of a future taitai." The Lin patriarch was much
more persuaded by the scholarship and statemanship of her future
father-in-law than by much hope for the future mother-in-law.

The Wu matriarch had rehearsed carefully, for the receiving of
the daughter-in-law was a chance to radiate goodness in public.
"My dear child," she said, lifting Meihua's chin with a touch of her
finger, "welcome to our home and to our family. We cannot hope
to match your noble upbringing, but we shall try to offer some
modest nourishment and care." The Matriarch squeezed Meihua
softly by the shoulders, turning her head so that all could see her
gentle smile.

Meihua's new sisters clustered around with hugs and giggles.
Only Longyan saw Meihua's little glance toward him through her
veil of beads. The Matriarch's polite greeting reinforced the cautious optimism of Longyan's last letter: "Could it be that the
snake's greatest power is not its venom, but its ability to arouse
fear?" Maybe it would be tolerable, Meihua thought as she was
whisked inside to cascades of laughter from sisters and servants
alike. The Matriarch bowed to both Patriarchs and withdrew
through the doorway. Xinping looked longingly inside, knowing
he was basically irrelevant to all the proceedings.

The Patriarchs shared a knowing "these women" look, then
waited outside to view the dowry. A small army of servants con-

veyed hundreds of packages from an armada of gondolas, large characters proclaiming the contents: 30 BOLTS GRADE AAA SILK; 2000-PIECE SILVER BANQUET SERVICE; PAINTINGS, SONG AND YUAN PERIODS; LACQUERWARE FOR LADIES; DRESSING TABLE; 1000 BOTTLES GANSU COOKING OIL. Crowds of neighbors oohed and aahed, nudging one another with impressed glances; this was clearly one of the best dowries in recent years and everyone knew that it showed the Wu matriarch's tough-bargaining tradition. The Lin majordomo had orchestrated it well—the finale consisted of five magnificent blackwood tables, each topped with golden Buddhist sculptures, borne by ten male servants, who were also part of the deal.

The Wu patriarch nodded his appreciation, but restrained any smiles that might have made him look like a greedy merchant rather than a scholar who was above materialism. As the two disappeared inside the mansion, the crowds milled by the canal banks, knowing that there was one last act. Private security guards mingled outside, bearing pikes and clubs, waiting for the job ahead. It was a sign of the times—brigands even had the audacity to prey on weddings.

An hour or so later, the Lin patriarch would return home, polemen groaning as they ferried the "bride price," roughly a ton of silver in rectangular ingots. Two teams of hired merchants had negotiated for over a month before settling on the precise composition of the dowry and the exact amount of the bride price. In this respect, the wedding was an exchange of high-quality goods for the purest rare metal; it was a good business deal in which the market prices of commodities were tallied against the latest currency exchange rates.

Two families were thus linked, not just by ceremony and symbolism, but also by an important commercial transaction. Now that the Lins and the Wus were joined together, surely the bride and groom would do their part.

Late in the afternoon, when it was all over, Longyan strolled out of the house, hailing a gondola. As the oarsman pushed off, Longyan glanced back at the abandoned doorway, long shadows darkening the red bunting, strong breezes tearing at the red calligraphy.

Longyan smiled tightly. Suzhou gossips would long talk of the great Lin-Wu wedding, uniting two of the top twenty families in

China's most affluent, most cultured region. Everyone had triumphed: both families, the merchants and craftsmen who served them, the inflation-battered economy of Suzhou.

Everyone is a winner, thought Longyan, clenching his fist and urging the oarsman to make haste toward the Shou Yuan Teahouse.

CHAPTER SEVEN

Crossed Lives

明

A Year Later: Suzhou, 1634

It is so kind of you, dear brother, to ask after my welfare. Please rest assured that I am very well. Your esteemed mother treats me quite properly, correcting my many faults so that I may be a better wife to your good brother. I have no complaints, only gratitude.

Meihua sobbed in Peach Blossom's arms, her tears trickling down her cascading black hair, soaking her white night robe, and eroding her facial makeup to reveal dark eyes and hollow cheeks.

"Please, my lady, please," Peach Blossom protested. "You've got to eat. You've got to sleep. You're killing yourself."

"I'm not hungry. I can't sleep. Who wants to live?"

"Hush! Please hush!" Peach Blossom knew that someone was always listening in a world of thin wood and stiff paper walls, a haven for eavesdroppers and Peeping Toms.

"I don't care if someone hears. Everyone knows, anyway."

"This really isn't normal, you know. Being a new daughter-in-law is supposed to be difficult. But not torture. That's what I told my mother."

"Oh no," Meihua pushed back her servant in shock. "You told your mother? She'll tell *my* mother!" Peach Blossom's family had been in the Lin household for generations—no Lin child could suffer without the Matriarch and Patriarch hearing about it. "You *must* tell your mother you were exaggerating. Tell her everything's getting better."

"But . . . my lady . . . Why lie?"

"Have I taught you nothing? My parents can't do anything about it. Nothing except worry. My father wouldn't think of saying anything to Xinping's father. I'm his daughter, but now I'm somebody else's wife and somebody else's daughter-in-law. Besides I'm only a woman. It's my duty to keep my parents from suffering."

Meihua rubbed the tears from her face and held Peach Blossom firmly by the shoulders. "When I cry, it's your role to ease my pain. It's *not* your role to tell others. Is that absolutely clear?"

"Oh, my lady, I didn't mean any harm. I was just trying to . . ." Peach Blossom broke into tears.

Meihua pulled Peach Blossom to her breast, cradling her as a small child. Comforting her servant was strangely comforting to Meihua herself. But no one could hide the sorrow. Chambermaids always knew an evening's mood by the next morning's bed linen. The bed told the story—silk sheets stained with tears, mascara and rouge seeping into the fabric covering wooden neck rests designed to protect ladies' hairstyles.

One might have suspected that Meihua's misery stemmed from her new husband rather than her new mother. But not so. In the year since the wedding, Meihua had evolved an awkward relationship with Xinping, featuring genteel deference in public and unsatisfying sexual service in private. Since Xinping found intimate conversation difficult, he often visited her briefly late at night, then retired to his own bedroom. Meihua found it difficult to implement her own mother's advice about relations with her husband. But that seemed a pretty minor problem. Meihua wouldn't have considered complaining to Xinping about the Matriarch—that would have violated her ethics and, besides, what could he do anyway? Why should she mar a relationship that had some potential? Meihua remembered their wedding night: Xinping had been inept, but gentle, calling her his "little taitai."

Meihua's greatest fear about Xinping was his cautious, retiring personality. In her experience, neither scholars nor officials could get very far without being direct and aggressive. She knew Xinping was a very conventional student who prepared his lessons diligently, but never did much reading or thinking when not prompted by tutors. Twice he had postponed his lower-level civil service examinations, always claiming that he had a bad case of the flu. Meihua knew better. Xinping was so overwrought at the thought of the examinations that he literally became sick with fever and vomiting. How could she make him stronger? She didn't know. Why was he so weak? She attributed that to the pressure of the Taitai's impossibly high expectations.

"But can't you tell anyone?" Peach Blossom blurted through her tears. "Someone who might do something? Someone who has influence over the Taitai?"

"Hush now," Meihua enveloped her again. "No. It doesn't matter. Just don't fret. No, I can't tell anyone. What's to tell, anyway?"

What she couldn't tell could have filled a book. The Matriarch never asked her to do anything; she gave orders—"Check the vegetable list. . . . I mean now, not next week," "Make sure the oil is strained, not with your usual little lumps and bubbles," "You make sure the tailor is here . . . at three o'clock exactly." Frequently the orders were transmitted curtly through servants. And when things didn't go properly, Meihua was the universal excuse: "Since you've come, meals are never on time," "Dark blue silk? For a fall robe? That may be Lin taste, it's not *Wu* taste," "Meihua, you're such a silly idealist. . . . Do all Lins gaze at the heavens when Earth is falling around them?"

But on winter mornings, when the entire family gathered in the ornate carved wood receiving room heated by soft coal whose thick smoke infused the still air, the Matriarch invariably took the high ground when asked about her daughter-in-law. "Meihua?" she'd say with a smile in the girl's direction, "what a pleasure to have her in our family. A few things we do differently. But she's such a fast learner. Right, my dear?"

Meihua nodded demurely, keeping her bloodshot eyes to the ground, lest anyone detect she'd been up two hours before dawn trying to make sure that the servants produced a mistakeless breakfast. She'd failed, of course, as the Matriarch had reminded her at seven o'clock, "We Wus *never* chop winter cabbage. It must be grated, quite finely. I suppose you want to ruin the Patriarch's teeth."

Meihua was a good actress, the product of a perfect red chamber education—inferiors never expressed feelings in public. The new bride, no matter how elite her parents, was always at the bottom of a family. Daughter-in-law jokes always brought chuckles, except when the reality was too painful for humor. Longyan might have

71

been fooled by Meihua's uncomplaining demeanor, but no one could silence the rumors that bounced through kitchens, bedrooms, and gardens. Xinping knew, too, but feigned ignorance to avoid confronting his parents.

The Patriarch, having heard stories, once confronted the Matriarch. "Mistreating her? Who's telling such lies?" the Matriarch huffed. "I'll bet it's that silly Lin girl herself. I'll have a word with her!" It was the last time any male dared raise the issue. Meihua was beaten so hard that the cane raised welts, everywhere but on her face and hands, which might be noticed in public. The servant who beat her—one of the Matriarch's own—was publically chastised for such temerity, then privately rewarded with a string of copper coins.

But why, Longyan wondered, does Meihua pretend everything's all right, even in her letters?

"Hss. Master. *Hss.* Over here." Peach Blossom stood across the frozen carp pond, green wool shawl wrapped around body and head, looking about anxiously to be sure she wasn't seen. "It's from my lady," she said, handing Longyan an oblong package wrapped in red silk. "Now that she's in the Wu household, she worries about your Mr. Cao. What if he tells somebody? Shows somebody the letters? From now on she'll write formal letters through him. You know, the kind no one could get upset about. But she says one day later, at sunrise, I'm supposed to give you another letter. More private. And she says—read the tenth line of her letter through Mr. Cao—it will tell you where I'll be the next day. You know, like a code."

"But how is she? Is she all right?"

"I can't say. I can't say anything. Just read." Peach Blossom vanished through the frost-covered, soft gray rock garden. Peach Blossom's heart would take hours to return to its normal beat. Imagine the punishments if the Taitai ever discovered that Meihua could read and write. What was discouraged in the Lin family would surely be seen as the ultimate put-down of the Taitai.

"Just read?" Longyan fretted to himself, sitting at his bedroom dressing table, afternoon light filtering through translucent glass framed with elaborately curved wood. Without Mr. Cao to help, absorbing each word of Meihua's letter was a struggle. Slowly, character by character, he committed it to memory; then he recited it by sound alone, bypassing the written words, finally understanding her message. Finally, just as the sun was setting, Longyan came to the end, closed the letter in its silk packet, and hid it behind a brick in the wall. Donning black fur boots and a heavy black shawl, Longyan began to walk the inner perimeter of the Wu estate, chanting the letter to himself like a monk at evening vespers. Meihua had written:

> *I try, dear brother, so hard to do her bidding. I do it not just for me, but for my family. I want to show everybody that the Lins have style and grace. I want to show her that we respect current position, even if from less cultured backgrounds.*
>
> *But I can do nothing to please her. It's as if she derives no satisfaction from tasks done well, only from correcting tasks which fail to meet her standards. Her servants mock me. Your sisters stand back from me. I dare not tell my family, for it would cause them such discomfort. Your brother will hear nothing of my complaints. I have only Peach Blossom. And my letters to you.*
>
> *Tell me, dear brother. Is this the way of the Wu family? Will it ever be different? Can I, not born of Wu parents, ever be treated as a Wu daughter?*
>
> *Is this just prattle from a whiny woman? If so, forgive me. Is there any justice in my complaints? If not, chide me. Is there any hope? If so, show me.*

A blast of cold air invaded the reception room as Longyan, still shrouded in black, ripped open the doors and slammed them behind him. A dozen pairs of eyes stared as he stood, arms folded defiantly, face reddened in speechless fury.

"Yes, my son?" the Patriarch asked, noting Longyan's eyes fixed furiously on the Matriarch. "Something we can talk about?"

Longyan never took his eyes off the Matriarch, even as she instinctively cowed behind the Patriarch. He walked slowly around the room, prompting the Matriarch to cringe in the opposite direction, in her husband's protective shadow. Wood-and-tissue oil lanterns projected eerie silhouettes of the unjoined battle against the white walls. Like a black cat stalking a chattering parrot, Longyan crept along, unblinking eyes never leaving his prey. When his back was opposite Meihua, who sat wide-eyed in amazement, Longyan stopped for a second, clenching his teeth and staring fiercely as if to kill the Taitai. He hovered ominously, leaning side to side, prompting the Taitai to cower, dodging possible attacks. Suddenly Longyan spun around and strode off, slamming the doors once again.

"What was that about?" The Patriarch scanned shocked faces for an answer.

"He's crazy," exclaimed the Matriarch, recovering quickly. "I've told you that before. Absolutely crazy. You should kick him out."

"Woman," he said, staring at her, "what caused him to do that? What did you do?"

"Nothing. How can you suggest it? He's crazy. I told you. A lunatic."

"Won't someone tell the truth around here?" the Patriarch pleaded. "Someone must know what caused him to do that."

Someone did know. But she couldn't say anything. She knew that what Longyan did was shocking. An unforgivable breach of Confucian etiquette. But she didn't feel shocked. She felt vindicated. And protected. Then a dart of fear shot into her heart. She hid in the shadows so her face wouldn't reveal her feelings. Would Longyan have to leave? Would she be left with only Peach Blossom? Would the Matriarch punish her for Longyan's act?

"Careful!" Father Gao's voice boomed. "It's the King's cavalry. Right behind the door!"

Longyan nudged open the door, stuck his head through tentatively, then slipped into the room. Finding no place to stand, Longyan balanced gingerly on the balls of his feet and stared in disbelief. Dozens of wooden soldiers, meticulously painted in vivid blues, reds, and greens, marched and clashed around Father Gao's little room. Officers brandished swords from the backs of prancing horses. Artillery units, replete with brass cannons, supplemented the foot soldiers, who clashed with spears, bows, and muskets. Beyond the Jesuit's bed, Longyan saw strange detachments of black-faced troops ominously dressed in black and yellow.

"Ah, good," the Father said, "you've come at a difficult moment. Sit down and give me some advice. The good King will surely need all the help you can give him."

"But Father Gao. I've come for *your* advice. I really can't wait very long."

Father Gao, eyes fixed on his little soldiers, correctly read tone in Longyan's voice. The young man was desperate. But he was also used to having his own way, what he wanted when he wanted it. Longyan surely spoke the same way when asking a special favor from a senior servant. Father Gao wanted to help, not just because Longyan needed it, but also because helping elites was the Jesuit way. Making contacts and winning confidence were essential to the long-term goal of promoting conversions. But Father Gao knew he had to work slowly, as in a chess game, never moving rashly. So he adopted a tactic that had worked quite effectively on pushy parishioners in Köln.

"Is that right? A matter of life and death? You're seriously ill?"

"No, it's not that. It's just that . . ."

"Not life and death? No one else about to die?"

"No, but . . ."

"Then it can wait. *This* is a matter of life and death."

"Toy soldiers?"

"Is that what you think? A game? Not at all. This is a replica of the tragic battle of Alcazarquivir. Year of Our Lord fifteen seventy-eight—Wanli Fifth Year by your reckoning—North Africa, Morocco. The great Christian King Sebastian of Portugal against the Moors under Abd al-Malik. The Moors are the ones with the black faces. Rather nice job old Ding the carpenter did, don't you think? Poor fellow didn't believe the Blacks. Thought they were ghosts or something—"

"Father Gao. Please?"

"Oh, yes. Yes, of course. How I do go on. Your request. Something quite important. Right away. But first, see that horseman by your foot? Now move him this way a bit. Whoa! Not so much. Yes, much better. Right there next to the blue scarf. It's the river, of course. At least the good King's horses will be watered. Terrible desert heat, you know. Water is more important than weapons. If I'd only been there to advise the King. Oh, I suppose you're wondering what all this is about. I'll give you the short version. . . ."

Longyan listened impatiently as Father Gao explained that King Sebastian, a great patron of the Jesuits, had sallied forth with eight hundred vessels to bring Morocco back under Portuguese dominion. Sadly, the King misjudged his adversary. Abd al-Malik had the advantages of more troops and knowledge of his home territory. Worse yet, King Sebastian did not know how to travel light—his entourage carried portable pavilions and chapels, massive coaches, and thousands of slaves, musicians, priests, and prostitutes. Furthermore, the King and his noble followers fought in good European style girded in metal armor, not exactly desert fighting gear. The result? The King and twenty thousand troops and followers were slaughtered, left to rot in the sun.

"So?" Longyan asked.

"So, we're fighting the battle again."

"Why?"

"To show that King Sebastian might have won."

"Why?"

"To demonstrate that while God was on the King's side, God helps those who help themselves."

"Who's God?"

"Sort of a Great Force. Not here. Up there."

"Like Heaven?"

"Sort of like Heaven. Now quit asking questions. I'm going to make a great concession."

"Yes?"

"You can play King Sebastian."

"Sure. And get chopped to pieces?"

"No. And show how he could have won. Look here. Here's the battle map."

Just as Father Gao surmised, less than ten minutes after Longyan glanced at the map, he was totally engrossed in the cause of King Sebastian. He stepped back from the map, thought carefully for a minute or two, then sounded a massive retreat, all troops moving to the low ground along the river, sentry units guarding the hills on either side. New orders came from the King, now under Longyan's supervision: "Move all noncombatant retainers back twenty miles toward the sea. Place the armor on dummies on horseback so that the enemy will be fooled. The real soldiers will fight in light clothing protected not by armor, but by shields. Rest and wait. Let the enemy attack through the gap in the high ground, thinner ranks being more vulnerable to attack. Confuse the enemy with campfires lit in several locations on the hills. Divide attack forces into

76

smaller units, hidden strategically in the hills, ready to swoop down when the Moors attempt frontal assaults."

As darkness fell over Suzhou, Father Gao's candles and oil lamps replicated the Moroccan campfires. Over a simple dinner of steamed fish, brought by the dumbfounded innkeeper, Mr. Deng, Father Gao explained to Longyan his mathematical formula for determining the firepower of various military units based on types of weapons and mobility, modified by position, geography, and climate. Longyan dropped his chopsticks and jumped up several times, adjusting his troops here and there, maximizing his positions by Gao's formula.

"Ready to fight?" Longyan asked, candlelight sparkling in his eyes.

"Yes. If you wish."

"Good," Longyan said gleefully. "It's over. You lost."

"What?" Father Gao exclaimed. "We haven't even begun to fight. How do you figure that?"

"Just add it all up."

"That'll take hours. Even on an abacus."

"Try it. Four hundred and sixteen skirmishes. I win two hundred and eighty-four. You win one hundred and ten. The rest are draws. I had a two-to-one disadvantage in troops. And I win decisively in spite of it. Give up?"

"Not at all. I think you're making it up." Father Gao pulled out brush and paper, then walked from battle to battle, dashing back to his desk to record the scores before he forgot them.

"I'll be back in a while." Longyan smiled as he weaved his way through the battle of Alcazarquivir and on to the Shou Yuan Teahouse. Three hours later, Longyan returned in his crisp gown, looking remarkably refreshed for almost bedtime after an evening with his friends.

"What, no drinking?" asked Father Gao.

"Sure, I drank," Longyan laughed, holding up the packet of anti-inebriation potion the Father had given him on their previous visit, "but this powder works. My friends, you know the Five Sages, they all think I'm some sort of god now. I can drink them dead."

"Well, you may be a god, but you're not perfect," the Father interceded triumphantly. "I've added it up. You're wrong."

"What? That can't be."

"You don't win two hundred and eighty-four. You win two hundred eighty-five. You forgot the detachment of musketeers under the bed! So we proved it! King Sebastian could have won." The Jesuit wrinkled his brow in puzzlement. "Now how did you calculate all that? What's the trick?"

Longyan grinned. "No trick. I just have that kind of head. Maps. Charts. Diagrams. Objects. Whatever. I just look and they stick up there."

"A memory palace."

"A what?"

"Memory palace. It's what the great Father Matteo Ricci brought from Europe to China half a century ago. You create an image in your head. An image of a palace with many rooms. Then you put your information in various sections, various rooms, various places. Easy to remember. Especially for tricky things like Chinese characters. It's what you do. Right?"

Longyan shook his head.

"No? You're too modest. I'll wager you have some system for the language. Like a room for all the characters with the 'heart' radical, for instance. How about it? How about naming all 'heart' radical characters with thirteen strokes?"

It was as if Longyan suddenly wove a cocoon around himself. He looked away from Father Gao and stared through the open window at the crystalline winter sky.

"I'm sorry," Father Gao said contritely, draping his crimson-sleeved arm over Longyan's blue-gowned shoulder. Nothing was said for a moment. They stared into the cold, moonless night lit by shimmering starlight alone. Father Gao began to feel a rising instinct; the desire to help Longyan, to reach out to a troubled young man, was outweighing his hope for a conversion. "It's something deeper, isn't it? Want to tell me about it?"

Longyan shook his head.

"Well then, how about the help you wanted earlier? What's it you want?"

"Oh, nothing. Except maybe . . ."

"Yes?"

"A place to stay for a few days. So no one will know where I am.

You see, I could never stay with my friends. Everyone would know immediately. Is there a place?"

Within minutes Longyan was deeply asleep in Crazy Deng's tiny loft bedroom. Father Gao sensed that Longyan had held back the real truth, something painful and personal. No longer did he see the Chinese boy as a useful tool, a sort of key to unlock a room filled with influential connections; rather he started caring about Longyan as a pained young man. The religious side of Father Gao's title was being eclipsed by a repressed paternal side. He wished he could call Longyan "my son," in good Western tradition, but was certain that it would cause consternation in a Confucian society. Father Gao pulled the comforter around Longyan's shoulders and patted him on the forehead before quietly shutting the door and retiring for the night.

Meihua couldn't sleep. Meihua couldn't cry. Less than a week had passed since what was now called "Longyan's Madness." Longyan had been seen at the teahouse, but no one knew where he was living, when and whether he'd return.

The Matriarch, always adept in adversity, thrived in the aftermath of Longyan's Madness. The story became more and more vivid with retelling. "Did you see his eyes? Killer eyes. He would have killed me. And why? Why, oh why? I've allowed him to stay here even though his mother was a peasant."

But the main object of the Matriarch's vengeance was Meihua. Was it just spite? A substitute for Longyan, who was nowhere to be found? Did she suspect something? The letters? Maybe she should stop writing them. But she couldn't. The letters were her only link to expressing feelings. She felt she'd die if she couldn't write.

> *I never would have told you about my problems if I'd known you would do something crazy like that. I know you meant well, but you can't believe how awful it's been. She's taking it out on me. Lies, screams, accusations, rumors. Yesterday she lost her mother-of-pearl inlaid hair comb and blamed me for stealing it. She told the Patriarch. I said I didn't do it. I don't need a hair comb. But everyone thinks maybe I did it. I think one of the servants did it. They laugh when I am giving my explanation.*

Where are you, anyway? I've heard about your capers. Drinking all night. And they say you've given up on your studies. Is that true?

Longyan, is it possible I have misjudged you? I thought you were very sensitive. What's the matter? Please tell me. Maybe I can help.

And please don't try to help me anymore. I'll be all right.

Oh, I hope this letter reaches you. Of course, it wouldn't make any difference if it didn't. Oh yes, I guess it would. I worry about you.

"Young man. Wake up, young man," Father Gao spoke gently. "You have a lady caller."

"A lady? At this hour?"

"This hour is almost noon. Seems you always sleep late here. Quick, put on that gown. Push back your hair. She's downstairs."

Peach Blossom stared at Longyan through the doorway. Her lady's worst fears were confirmed. Disheveled, unkempt, red-eyed—clearly a wastrel, another rich kid gone bad. And living in Crazy Deng's little boardinghouse? With a giant Buddhist with round eyes and a big nose?

"I can see you're shocked," Longyan said, secreting her letter into his gown sleeve.

"Oh no, sir."

"Of course you're shocked. How did you find me?"

"I just followed you, last night, coming here from the tea-house."

"Does anyone else know?"

"None but my mistress."

"You won't tell anyone. No one. Understand?"

"Yes, sir."

"Just tell your lady it's not what it appears. Your lady? How is she?"

"Just read. You'll see."

"No! Don't go. I need to send a message back to her."

"If you wish." Peach Blossom smiled demurely. "She told me I could wait up to an hour for a return message. Please write it quickly."

"Quickly?"

"Yes. She sent me on several errands. I can't wait too long. I apologize. An hour's all I've got."

"Then I won't be able to do it."

"No?"

"Not today. You see, uh . . . I'm busy for the next hour or so."

"Tomorrow?" Oh no, thought Longyan, he couldn't let Mr. Cao know where he was staying. He couldn't write it himself. What to do? "Okay. Come back tomorrow. I'll see if I've had time. If not, I'll tell you when I'll have a letter ready."

"Is it so complicated, sir?"

"Not complicated, but . . . It's just that . . . Well, I want to be in the right mood to write your lady."

"I see," said Peach Blossom, not seeing at all. "Tomorrow, then. At noon."

Longyan stumbled down the hallway, brain swirling from fear. Bad student, drunkard—he could live with those allegations. But an illiterate elite? That was unforgivable! Knowledge—total recall of the Confucian classics, both reading and writing—that was the only way to power and prestige. Illiteracy was the dreaded scourge of the masses. Oh, how he wished there was another word to describe his problem, something other than *illiteracy*.

Never forget the fundamental Confucian axiom: "Those who work with their hands serve those who work with their minds," Longyan reminded himself. Most people had no chances, no choices; peasants and laborers rarely received any education. But illiteracy for a scholar's son was unthinkable. Illiteracy for a grand secretary's son was unprecedented. Longyan knew that he couldn't sustain the illusion. Meihua would know what everyone else knew. She had been shielded from the truth, shielded by the Wu family, who didn't want the Lin family to know. Now it would be obvious. He was stupid. Just plain stupid.

It wasn't fair, Longyan fumed, he wasn't really stupid, not really illiterate. But that was how it looked to others. Who would possibly believe that words wouldn't stay put, whether on a page before his eyes or on a brush in his hands?

Suddenly Longyan brightened. Maybe, just maybe, there was a way out. "Father Gao," he said, pushing the door open, "I hate to trouble you. But I really need your help."

"Of course. Sit down. Let's talk." Was Longyan actually ready to seek his help? Father Gao prayed he was—not just so he could minister to his soul in the best tradition of Saint Ignatius, but so he could help someone who was reaching out, someone he really cared about. Father Gao remembered how lonely were his first ten years, in the Catholic orphanage before the Jesuits took him under their wing, when he began praying to the Virgin Mary as the mother he never had. Back then he'd invoked religious figures— "Holy Father, Holy Mother"—as if they were his own family, never daring to confess his sense of informal proximity to deities. The "Son" was not some distant Christ, but rather he himself was the son, nourished by the ultimate caring parents. He yearned to extend to Longyan the same familial care.

"I don't know if you could possibly understand."

"Understand what?" Please don't back off, Father Gao prayed. It was the first time, after more than a year in China, that a Chinese had spoken to him without veils of distance. It was the first time in many years that he wanted to be a friend more than he wanted to be a priest.

"Understand how much it hurts to fail . . . How painful to study and not succeed . . ." Longyan hadn't felt so inadequate since the days of Tutor Lu. Why was he telling any of this to an ugly, giant barbarian who was so stupid that he wore Buddhist robes? What elite Chinese would ever talk to a big-nosed Buddhist wearing a huge necklace depicting a criminal being executed? But whom else could he talk to? Nobody in the family, for sure. And nobody on the streets, for they would surely inform his family about his whereabouts. At least the barbarian seemed smart. And he wanted to help. What was the alternative?

"I do understand your pain, more than you can imagine," said the giant imploringly. "And I won't tell anyone. I promise. Think about it. You're stronger than I am. If you told anyone I was keeping you here against your will, they'd surely execute me. Come on, please, tell me the honest truth."

The honest truth? I'm the master of the partial truth. Longyan smirked to himself, a whole new approach occurring to him. "I need to have someone write a letter for me," he said with renewed confidence. "A very private letter. That servant, Peach Blossom, she wants to pick it up tomorrow."

"Why don't you write it yourself?"

"Because . . . well . . . You see, I want it to be anonymous. If anyone intercepted the letter, they would surely recognize my calligraphy. It's very distinctive, you know. So could you help?"

"Me? Write a letter for you?"

"No. Of course not *you!* I'll dictate a letter to you. You could then pay a letter writer to render it in fine calligraphy. Then you could bring it back to me. Of course I'll pay for everything. How about it?"

"Well. I guess there's no problem. You'll have to help me with some characters." This is crazy, Father Gao thought to himself. Why is he doing this? Surely he could fake someone else's handwriting. What's he hiding? Well, at least it keeps us talking. What's the harm of going along with him? Nothing illegal, nothing immoral. Just bizarre, but, of course, I specialize in the bizarre. Why else would I be in China?

"Now here's how it goes: 'My dear sister-in-law . . .' "

"You have a relationship with your brother's wife?" Oh, please, the Jesuit pleaded privately, don't let this involve a sin of the flesh.

"No! There's nothing improper. Just write this down . . ." Four hours later, Father Gao had produced a draft in scrawled calligraphy. Longyan refused to read it himself on the grounds that bad calligraphy ruined the eyes of the reader; so he approved it only after it was read to him. By noon the following day, Father Gao had done his duty. Longyan had a neat version ready for Peach Blossom, written in a businesslike calligraphy that might have been rendered by a scholar seeking to communicate with someone who needed simplicity to understand. Just right for a lady who'd engaged in a bit of self-study:

> My Dear Sister-in-Law:
> What can I possibly say? I did not go crazy. But I was motivated by anger. Anger for you. I thought it totally wrong for no one to hear your complaints. It never occurred to me that you might be hurt even more because of my silly act. I deeply apologize. I shall try to make amends.
> I am now in hiding, trying to decide what to do next. Your servant knows where I am. The place is strange enough that probably no one will think to look here. Do not come to improper conclusions. I am not turning my

back on my values. I am dealing with this barbarian solely
for short-term practical goals.

Father Gao had dutifully written the word *barbarian,* choosing
not to protest the insult. After all, he knew that was the Chinese
term for "foreigner." Longyan, sensing the priest's discomfiture,
softened his prose:

Some barbarians have hearts more civilized than their faces
and their clothes.

Father Gao, stifling bemusement, offered a nod of gratitude for
the intended compliment, then wrote rapidly as Longyan started to
open his heart:

You may not believe it, but I understand the terrible anguish you must feel. I, too, came from outside the family.
Oh, please do not think that I am comparing myself to
your noble birth. But I know what it is to live under the
Wu roof bearing another surname. I cannot tell you today
what I suffered at the hands of your tormentor who, also
not born a Wu, now flaunts the family name to punish
others.
I have thought many days of your plight. There is, I fear,
no easy solution. Time is the only cure I can think of. If
something else occurs to me, I shall surely tell you. I promise I will tell you before I do anything again. . . .

"What," asked Father Gao, "is this all about? Anything I can
do?"

Longyan sighed. Certainly there was no problem telling the barbarian what everyone in Suzhou seemed to know, but how ridiculous to think he might do something. "Well, it's the oldest problem
in China," Longyan said hesitantly, "the agony of the daughter-in-
law." Curiously, after a shaky start, the story flooded out. Longyan
found it cathartic to talk to Father Gao, to tell him the story of Lin
Meihua, even to tell about his irate confrontation of the Matriarch.
Longyan didn't expect much help. It was like telling a tale to a
monkey who listened, made noises at the right times, but who
surely couldn't understand.

"Do you wish this woman was your wife?" Father Gao asked quietly, knowing full well that one of the Ten Commandments was at stake.

"Of course not," Longyan replied indignantly, believing his own lie but not fooling Father Gao for a moment.

"I see. You couldn't marry her because you're not firstborn. Because, as you say, your mother was not your father's first wife. So it wasn't a possibility for you. Correct?"

"Why, yes," Longyan replied, "that's precisely right." Longyan was astonished. Father Gao did understand, both the social relationships and the inner rationale that kept Longyan from even considering a relationship with Meihua. What a strange priest! His bulbous, ugly eyes somehow penetrated into forbidden feelings.

"So you want to help this woman? This wife of your brother whom you could never marry? This woman who reads and writes?"

"Yes. But only because she needs help. I'm the only one who understands. But I can't do anything."

"Don't come to such quick conclusions!" Father Gao admonished him while a deliciously evil thought welled up. Vengeance may belong to the Lord, but saving souls occasionally required liberal interpretation of the Gospel. "Do tell me a little about the Matriarch's background." As Father Gao listened, an impish smile filtered through his mustache and beard.

"Now here's what I'd do," the Father said when Longyan was finished. "Clearly some research is in order." Longyan listened carefully as Father Gao outlined a plan of action. Longyan thought for a moment, then concluded his letter with great excitement:

> Maybe, dear sister, there is some hope after all. Don't do anything. But don't despair. It will take me some time, but perhaps I can help.
>
> I cannot deny the rumors. I have strayed a bit from my studies. I do occasionally drink a bit of wine. But now I'm studying with a new teacher. I have new insights, new ideas.
>
> Don't give up. Someone cares.

"A fine letter," Father Gao commented, having reread the final draft. "I'm so glad you found my idea useful. I do hope it works. And what good news for you! Who's your new teacher?"

Longyan shook his head. Just like a barbarian, he thought smugly, always missing the obvious. An hour later, Peach Blossom having taken the letter, Longyan's gondola rocked him back home where he planned to apologize for his failings to both the Patriarch and the Matriarch. Then, once at home when his emotions were more at ease, he could put the priest's plan into action.

As soon as Longyan left, Father Gao fell to his knees in prayer. He begged the Holy Father to help the young Wu man through his ordeal. He beseeched the Virgin Mother to offer solace to the Lin woman who was suffering. And he asked forgiveness from Saint Ignatius—forgiveness for his hope about the identity of Longyan's new teacher. And then the priest took off his robes, removed his crucifix, and cried as a lonely man who had found solace in consoling another lonely man.

CHAPTER EIGHT

Decisions

明

A Month Later: Suzhou, Winter 1634

THE WHOLE FAMILY watched as Longyan, neatly dressed in a dark green gown and sporting a scholar's fan with stylish cursive calligraphy, rendered his humble apology. Bowing before his parents, head touching the ground, Longyan spoke convincingly, tears streaming down his face: "I have disgraced myself before you and our ancestors. Madness crazed me. Evil spirits invaded me. Rice wine ran through my blood. I have committed the sin of unfiliality. I wish the most severe punishment."

"Hush," said the Patriarch, stifling the Matriarch's attempt to speak and trying to suppress his own smile. "This is better. Finally a little hope for Longyan. Of course, what he did was unthinkable. But it's my duty, and my duty alone, to decide the punishment. Now let's see. . . . Yes. Two things. Number one, Longyan must agree not to drink. Not a drop. For a whole year. Longyan, do you promise not to visit the teahouse? Not to drink? Do you swear it?"

"Yes, Father, I so swear." He cringed at the thought, but what choice was there? Oh please, he prayed, let the next penalty be the right one. Everything depended on it. Let his father make a good, tough Confucian decision.

"And, number two . . . Longyan must spend four hours a day in the library, studying with Tutor Lu. He may study what he likes. There's no chance he'll ever sit for the examinations. But he must show discipline. Longyan, do you swear it?"

"Yes, Father, I so swear." Perfect. Fantastic, Longyan thought smugly, so far it was going flawlessly. Don't grin, he counseled himself. Look contrite. Wince a little. "And Father?" Longyan asked deferentially.

"Yes?"

"If I have to study . . . could I study local history? Could I study about our family?"

The Patriarch beamed. "You mean it, my son? Oh, nothing could make me happier. It's a great family. But no one has ever written our history. If you could only gather some notes, I myself might oversee the actual writing of our family history someday."

Relatives murmured and grunted approval. Xinping was left jealous, wishing he'd come up with Longyan's inspired scheme. How brilliant, thought Xinping, Longyan's project neatly highlighted all Confucian virtues: ancestor worship, history, education, proper social relationships, and, above all, the family.

The Matriarch glared at Longyan. What was he up to? Longyan the perfect disciple of his father? Impossible! Her skepticism turned to raw astonishment at what happened next.

Longyan settled cross-legged on the double-woven red-and-black silk rug, facing the Patriarch as he had on the day the tray was presented on his third birthday so many years ago, nodding to a servant, who brought forth his *qin*. A calmness infused him, so different from his usual nervous reticence in social settings. He tuned the instrument and waited for his family's startled surprise to subside.

Meihua watched in disbelief, fluttering her sandalwood fan to hide her face and her fears. Oh, please don't let him make a fool of himself again, she prayed. Why do I even care? Oh please, not some silly stunt, something that would embarrass everyone. Oh, so what? The only reason I care is so he won't anger the Matriarch— she'll take it out on me. Oh, Longyan, please don't.

Ting. The sound was so light it could barely be heard. Then *ting, ting, ting,* the same sound, as if echoing. As Longyan's fingernails touched the strings, unleashing soft splashes of sound against the persistent rhythmic ting, hushed incredulity faded into whispered admiration. No one, save Mr. Cao, had even known that Longyan played. Certainly no one could have imagined a virtuoso performance on a scholar's instrument by one who had rejected the classics. But why he was playing before such an unconventional audience, one that included *women* as well as men? Didn't he know any better?

Meihua knew differently. Her fan fluttered feverishly, concealing traces of tears. She heard a message in Longyan's mournful melody. Don't give up on me, it said. Listen. My feelings are deep. Watch. My fingers are sensitive. I'm not worthless. And see, this doesn't cause trouble. No embarrassment. No pain.

Meihua peeked over her fan and watched Longyan, his eyes shut and head canted toward heaven, his finger wobbling softly to bring roundness to a deep note. Oh, she wondered, was there something else he was trying to say? Something he couldn't say in his letters? Something he could never convey in person? Of course not, she said firmly to herself, fluttering her way back to concealment.

The Patriarch heard a different message. Father, Longyan was saying, I know I've been a disappointment. I've tried, but I just can't make it the usual way. I can't be what you are. I can't be a calligrapher, a writer, an administrator. But I haven't thrown away all your hopes. See. This takes discipline and feeling. It's something I can do. A link to the past. And, oh yes, Father, do you hear something else? Another message only you will understand. Listen. Remember this theme? The loyal scholar, outside the walls when he overhears the enemy approaching, decides to sound the warning, to strike bells and drums, even though it means his death. I'm faithful to you, Father, but oh, please be alert for another enemy. The enemy has hurt me, hurt others, too, but don't let the enemy destroy you, destroy our family.

All of this escaped the Matriarch. But as Longyan's fingers sounded the last notes, a sad tolling of bells, she heard an ominous warning. Watch out, Longyan was saying, I'm no fool. Not a buffoon for your laughter. Beware. I'm a wily adversary. Keep your eyes peeled. And ha! How does it feel not to be the center of attention?

Scarcely three hours later, Longyan sat on Father Gao's bed, gesturing and laughing as he told his story, profusely expressing his thanks.

"Don't mention it." Father Gao smiled, daring to put his hand on Longyan's arm. "I'm glad you think it's working. But don't thank me until it's really succeeded. What is it you say about seeds?"

"A handful of seeds does not make an orchard."

"Quite right. You've just planted them. Wait for the harvest."

"No. I insist. You helped me. I must help you. Some money perhaps?"

Father Gao needed money desperately. A winter storm on the South China Sea had destroyed four oceangoing junks whose holds were filled with Jesuit silk destined for textile-hungry European merchants and noblemen. Without the silk trade, the tiny Jesuit colonies along the China coast had to live on small stipends supplemented by occasional gifts from Chinese friends. The Jesuits were in fine shape until the shipwreck, indeed Jesuits were thriving in Manila, where they could trade with Spaniards from the Americas using Mexican silver. Foreign silver made anybody rich in China since it was the preferred medium of exchange in the dual silver-copper currency system. But without commerce, there was no regular income. Father Gao, like most Jesuits, did not pride himself on vows of poverty; but he shook his head and said to himself, I will not beg.

Longyan measured the moods flittering across the Jesuit's face. Too proud to accept help from strangers? And no family to fill an empty bowl? A classic Chinese tragedy. What do you give to someone who is proud and obstinate? "All right," Longyan said eventually, "have it your way. But there's one thing I must give you."

"No. I don't need anything. Nothing at all."

"It's not a thing. It's a suggestion. Those robes you're wearing . . ."

"Yes?" said Father Gao, looking at the faded crimson cotton covering his huge frame. "Too worn? Too dirty?"

"No. Too Buddhist. I know what you want. You'd like to know Chinese gentry and officials. You'd like to talk to them and use their influence. You're like all monks. You want new believers. Don't shake your head. You know it's true. Well, you aren't going to get anyplace looking like some overgrown Buddhist with a begging bowl. Now here. Take these. Wear them."

Father Gao paused for a moment, then removed his crumpled crimson robe, revealing the largest loincloth and the hairiest body Longyan had ever seen, and quickly donned one of the three new black scholar's gowns. "Better?"

"Much better," replied Longyan, trying to forget the apelike body underneath and the fact that the robe seemed big enough to

house an army on maneuvers. "And could you perhaps wear that
. . . that thing . . . inside the robe?"

Father Gao hesitated, then pushed the crucifix through the collar
opening and out of sight. Slowly, as Longyan smiled infectiously,
the significance of the new robes fully dawned on the priest.
"You've given me a great gift. Not just clothes. But honesty. How
can I thank you?"

"It's too early to thank me."

"What do you mean, 'too early'?"

"Too early to harvest your orchard." Longyan laughed.

"Young man, you have remarkable talents," said Father Gao,
parrying the laughter with a serious comment. "No. Don't shake
your head. You've got great abilities—diagrams, charts, battles.
More than that. Instinctive knowledge of things and of people.
Stop shaking your head. I know you've got a problem."

"What problem?" Longyan asked sharply.

"I've thought long and hard about this. About all our meetings.
I finally figured it out. You have a terrible time reading and writing. Right?"

Longyan pursed his lips, wanting to walk out in a huff but concluding that that would be cowardly. He sighed and offered a little
nod.

"And everybody calls you stupid? Even *you* think you're stupid?"

Longyan's low-hung head and deep sigh told the whole story.

"Well, you're *not* stupid. It just that you have Father Jerome's
problem."

"Father Jerome?"

"Another priest like me. An extraordinary man. Remembers everything he hears. Often knows what people want before they
know themselves. Sound familiar? Ah, I thought so. And his problem? When he tried to read, the words run together. When he tries
to write, the words fall apart."

"Dancing words," Longyan uttered in astonishment, his mouth
open.

"Yes. Exactly. 'Dancing on the page.' That's what Father
Jerome said. What honesty he showed! And now what courage!"

"What's he doing?"

"He wanted so badly to come to China, but now he stays behind in India. He's the genius who keeps us alive. He runs the shipping business between Jesuit centers in Europe and our outposts across India, the Malay Peninsula, China, and Japan. Schedules, order forms, trade maps, ships and crews—his mind is like a machine. He's involved in constant negotiations—Arabs, Indians, Persians, Africans, Asians—and they're all wary of him. You can't beat him. *Xinyan waiguoren*—'foreigner who sees into hearts'—that's what the Chinese junk captains call him. Yes, we'd be dead without Father Jerome. Yet, even now, when he prays, he often confesses that he's a failure. Failure? Ha! He's a genius. An unconventional genius."

"Unconventional genius," Longyan softly mouthed the words. "Will he ever come to China?"

"Maybe yes, maybe no. Certainly not in the typical Jesuit way. But enough about Father Jerome. Here. I've got a little present for you."

Strange Scribbles was the title on the silk book binder Father Gao gave Longyan. Inside Longyan opened thread-stitched rice paper booklets to reveal a collection of charts, maps, and diagrams. They were perfect copies, surely done by some incredulous Chinese calligrapher, from Father Gao's collection of astronomy, navigation, military science, engineering. A library without words. Longyan flipped slowly through the pages, enraptured by what he saw, disbelieving it was his.

Then, for a fraction of a second, Longyan and Father Gao shared a rare glance of friendship. The Jesuit, now in upper-class tailored garb, had finally realized a dream—a direct connection to an elite Chinese, albeit a rather unusual young man. And the young Chinese, now with a glimpse of hope about his malady, held in his hands the essence of the European Renaissance, albeit in a most unusual form. But both sensed something else, a deeper potential, a caring and a need, that could infuse their relationship.

"I'm truly grateful," Longyan said sincerely. "I suppose you're telling me what I should do? Right? What I should do with my life?"

"No." The priest shook his head. "Not what you should do. What you *could* do. You could be a remarkable success if you chose a military career. It would use all your talents and . . ." Father Gao decided not to say that it would bypass Longyan's weaker points in reading and writing. "And . . . at a time of troubles, perhaps the dynasty could use great soldiers as much as great scholars."

Longyan listened as calmly as he could. The priest was right, of course. Scholarship was out of the question. The merchant life was unappealing. His skills were unconventional. Maybe an officer-ship would be a different way to serve. But—Longyan's heart jumped—how would his father react? Could he possibly under-stand? Could he realize that true loyalism—to the family and to the throne—might take a different form?

Father Gao watched as Longyan breathed slowly, trying to slow his racing heart and mind, trying to steel himself for a tough deci-sion. Longyan said nothing, but the priest was almost certain the die was cast. As they bid farewell, Father Gao and Wu Longyan both sensed it was a special moment. But who might have known they were building a remarkable bridge between cultures, chang-ing the course of seventeenth-century history? And who might have known it would be several years before they saw each other again?

The early morning air was cold and still, not yet posing a threat to the paper-thin white ice enshrouding the carp pond. Lin Meihua, her yellow wool shawl tightly drawn over her shoulders and head, sat motionless except for little puffs of breath. She stared at a tiny sparrow jumping about on the ice, picking at brown stalks at the pond's edge.

Hang on, she said to herself, knowing just the slightest move-ment would break her control. Longyan was surely waiting for her letter. She had to write something. But what? All she felt was a torrent of conflicting emotions. How to start? Keep calm, she said to herself, just try to keep calm.

In the month since Longyan's return, an eerie quiet had settled on the Wu household. Longyan had kept to his word, spending every day in the library, studying history and genealogy with Tutor Lu in the mornings, trying to produce legible calligraphy with a specially hired instructor in the afternoons. A new Longyan seemed to have been born, a quietly disciplined student. Only Meihua, in daily correspondence with Longyan, knew the frenzy beneath the surface.

She recalled fondly the softness of their letters in recent weeks, wondering fearfully what and whether they would write in the future:

> *My dear brother, I knew it, I knew you had depth and feeling. Oh, what music! The gods must have cried. I surely did. I shall harbor the secret wish that you were playing for me. I know that's probably wrong.*

> Please, kind sister, don't exaggerate. If you weren't a woman, you surely would have heard much finer music. Of course, it was for you. It was an apology.

> *Only an apology?*

> Also a way to make peace. To curtail your pain. Did it work?

"Yes." Meihua had lied. Longyan's filiality had enraged the Matriarch, but why bother Longyan with that? These letters were the only fun in her life. *"There is new hope,"* she wrote, *"but weren't you saying something more? Didn't I hear something else in your music?"*

Oh, what to say? Longyan had wondered, deriving titillating delight from her letters, enough fantasies for a year of nights with Suzhou prostitutes. "Yes indeed, there was something more in my music. It was a tribute to the loveliest lady of our family?" That would be getting too serious. How to deflect it? "What a joy to have you among us! What joy it must be for my honorable brother!" he wrote instead. That should do it, he had thought regretfully, hoping she would know he wasn't squelching the emotion, only being proper. "But, please, enough of my music, I must focus my attention on other matters. I have a great decision to make. I must decide my life's direction."

"It is too bad I am not a man, a scholar," Meihua had replied, *"for then I could advise you. What might I say then? Would I not say that you should consider fully immersing yourself in your studies? Preparing for the examinations?"* Meihua sensed that would never happen, but it was important to suggest it, to show that she thought Longyan really had the option. She had heard that he was a terrible student, but surely that was due to nothing more than bad habits. Or was it? She had a funny inkling, maybe something about his calligraphy:

How clever of you to disguise your calligraphy these days. I trea-
sured your earlier fluid style, but understand why you now use
standard formal characters. No one would ever guess it was you.

Longyan ached to tell her the truth. But what to say? "It's absolutely impossible for me to be a scholar?" He couldn't imagine
himself saying, "Dear Meihua, I can't read and write. But don't
worry, I'm not really stupid. A barbarian tells me that another
barbarian, a really smart one, also has my problem. The letters?
Of course, I didn't write them. No, don't worry, nobody will
tell. . . . At least I don't think so. . . ." Instead he had written:

> Dear sister, you are kind to suggest it, but I have decided to
> forgo the life of a scholar. I lack the patience. I must seek a
> more active life. I must find new challenges. I must throw
> off the restraints of my present life.

Restraints of *your* present life? Meihua thought when she read
this. You who can run around Suzhou at will? You who can make
a fool of yourself and then bring peace with a little apology? You
who can *decide* what to do with your life? She replied:

> *Of course, dear brother, it must be your decision. Many will be*
> *disappointed that your talents will not serve scholarship. But what*
> *are the alternatives?*

Good question, Longyan thought. If not a scholar, what? A
dilettante? A gadfly? A dabbler? Certainly not a merchant! No.
There had to be more than that. But Longyan had paused before
writing the obvious conclusion:

> In Suzhou there are no alternatives. There's no choice. I
> must leave. I must go north, perhaps to Beijing. I shall miss
> some things here, of course, you yourself most of all
> among those things.

Is that it? Meihua wondered, a steamy sigh seeping through her
shawl. Am I just the most valuable among the things he's leaving
behind? How could he even think of leaving? It's the only thing

that makes life tolerable. How can he toy with me, touch my heart, then cut it out with a knife?

Meihua tossed off the shawl, threw back her head, and breathed deeply. The first rays of sunlight were slightly heating the air. She distracted herself by flicking a few seeds over the pond, watching the little brown sparrow skitter to and fro across the ice, trying unsuccessfully to skate to a stop. Meihua laughed as it bounced up and down, tiny legs collapsing so it flopped on its breast. Suddenly she heard a hiss, then a crack. The sparrow flapped its wings frantically as the ice collapsed around it, frigid water sucking at its feathers. Meihua jumped up and shouted for someone to help, but the house was shuttered too tightly for anyone to hear. She threw her shawl toward the sparrow, but missed by a few inches, watching helplessly as shawl and sparrow sank before her eyes. There was only one thing to do.

Scarcely an hour later, Meihua stirred slightly in her bed, shivering in spite of the blankets enshrouding her body and the hot compresses on her head.

"My lady," Peach Blossom blurted excitedly, "what were you doing? You would have frozen to death in that pond if it hadn't been for all the noise."

"What noise?" she asked weakly.

"A little bird. Chirping away. Banging its wings against the door."

"It's all right?"

"The bird? Of course it's all right. It flew away. It's you I worry about."

"Don't worry about me," Meihua said before fading back to sleep. "I'll be all right, too. It's knowing someone cares that keeps you alive. And Peach Blossom?"

"Yes, my lady?"

"Don't breathe a word of this. Not to anyone. I was *not* trying to kill myself. But they won't understand that. So you keep totally quiet. Do you understand me?"

"Yes, my lady," Peach Blossom responded dutifully, not understanding at all.

★   ★   ★

"No!" shouted the Patriarch. "A thousand times no! We've *never* had a soldier in the family. Even our poorest relatives chose farming over fighting. I will not hear of it. The answer is no."

Longyan remained calm in the face of his father's fury. He had rightly assumed that the Patriarch would object, but had underestimated the strength of his reaction. Everyone in the reception hall—twenty or so immediate relatives and several servants—watched the Patriarch pace the floor, silk slippers scuffling across on smooth stones, black gown swishing to his steps.

"May this silly woman speak?" The Taitai's voice had a trace of genuine timidity, which was not alleviated by the Patriarch's annoyed nod of assent. "We, all of us here, know how angry you are," she said. "It's an awful disappointment. But please remember, it's not the first time he's upset you. He's always been trouble. Remember what you said: 'Can't keep anything in his hand but a wine cup, nothing in his head but a drinking riddle.' "

"But that was before he came back. Before he began studying. Started to reform."

"Reform? A month of good behavior. For what? So that he can decide to run off to the army? A lot of good that did!"

"I intend to talk him out of that decision."

"You can't do it. I guarantee you can't change his mind."

"Longyan, please," the Patriarch pleaded. "Please show me she's wrong. Please tell me you'll see reason. That you won't leave for the army."

Longyan stood face to face with his father. The Patriarch had just uttered the ultimate Confucian request for filial obedience. No son who expected any future as a son could possibly refuse. Longyan's eyes locked on his father's eyes. The feelings poured out speechlessly: sorrow that it had come to this, a hope for forgiveness, and a hint that Longyan had come upon some long-hidden secret.

The Patriarch saw it all. Then he waited for the signal he knew had to come. Yes or no? What would it be?

Longyan shut his eyes momentarily, looking inside himself for conviction and courage. Then he shook his head firmly. "I'm sorry, Father. It's what I must do. It hurts terribly to disappoint you. But I have no choice."

The Patriarch spun away from Longyan and stared at the Taitai.

"How did you know, woman?" It made it worse that the Matriarch had predicted a dire future for Longyan. "How could you possibly know?"

"The dagger. He picked the dagger in this very room."

"Ah, yes, the dagger," he muttered, rubbing his hands against the sharp pain in his forehead. Moods flashed across the Patriarch's face like that of a madman. Anguish, despair, fury. "Bring me the vase!" he screamed.

"The vase, sire?" asked Lao Li.

"Yes, you fool, the vase. The remaining one from the set I presented to Longyan."

After a minute of excruciating silence, the Patriarch held the gleaming blue and white vase in his hands. "What, my son, does this represent to you? What does this stand for?"

Longyan was puzzled, but knew he had to answer his father. "Perfection. The finest tradition of craftsmanship. The best in connoisseurship." Was the Patriarch going to forgive him? A farewell present?

"And?"

"The greatest art of our dynasty. Ming at its best." What was the Patriarch trying to say? Maybe that Longyan would still be serving the dynasty as an officer?

"And?"

"And what, Father?"

"And why are there two vases?"

"Perhaps to symbolize reciprocity? The five relationships?"

"And what's the most important relationship within the family?"

"That between father and son," Longyan completed the catechism mechanically.

"Correct," the Patriarch replied coldly. He looked at the vase for a moment, then walked off the rug onto the cold stone floor. Holding the vase away from his body at shoulder height, the Patriarch stared fiercely at Longyan, then let his hand go limp. The vase hit with a loud report, decomposing into shards of clay and glaze, just another broken bowl like the thousands tossed out by Suzhou restaurants every day.

"Longyan, you are no longer my son. I disinherit you. I should have listened to the Matriarch long ago. I'm angry. But I'm not cruel. I will give you sufficient funds for food, shelter, clothing, and a manservant. But you will leave this house as your mother entered it. Your name is not Wu. Your name is Wang."

"So be it, Father," Longyan responded, resignation overcoming shock. "I had hoped it wouldn't come to this. But it must be your decision. Before I leave, I would like to offer you my deepest apologies and a small gift." Longyan would not expose his true feelings, his utter dismay, until he was alone, until he could cry. For now, he had to finish the scenario as he had planned it.

"A gift! One does not offer gifts on occasions of sadness. Why should I want your gift?"

"It's not much." Longyan beckoned two servants to bring several silk-bound sheafs of paper. "Just the scattered notes of a failed scholar. I have traced your honorable Wu family through several generations. What extraordinary traditions! Artists, calligraphers, poets in so many generations. My calligraphy teacher copied the notes so you could read them clearly. And there's something very strange as well."

"Strange?" the Patriarch asked in startled voice.

"Talent and accidents both seem to run in the family. I never knew your father. He died so young. But he lost his eyesight?"

"Yes. It was terrible. A flash fire with cooking oil."

"And your great grandfather. Lost his arm?"

"Oh, yes. I guess I was told that. Robbers tried to kidnap him from his palanquin. Slashed him with a sword as he ran off. The doctors had to amputate."

"Well. It will make an interesting story. Accidents just like your fingers."

"Longyan, thank you for the gift," the Patriarch burst in to stop his son's flow of historical recollections. "I just wish it wasn't under these circumstances. I so wanted you to be a scholar. To use your abilities to create. Not to waste yourself on the arts of war."

"Yes, Father, I know your views. Oh, there's just one last little thing."

"Yes?"

Longyan took three identical scroll boxes from a servant. "I would never have the temerity to develop a full genealogy of your esteemed family, Father. But genealogies fascinate me so much, I couldn't resist trying one. So I did one for the honorable family of the Matriarch. I thought you would like it, Father."

The Patriarch opened the scroll and studied it, his emotions ranging from irritation to bemusement. It was accurate, complete, and devastating. The Taitai's roots were clear—merchants and peasants on her mother's side, and worse yet, wandering performers on her father's side. And there it was, just three generations back—her great-grandfather had married a prostitute who remained in the profession long after the marriage. One could only guess what sweaty peddler was actually the Taitai's progenitor thrice removed. Longyan left the Patriarch surprised again with another display of unconventional brilliance. The genealogy, the product of bribery and thefts, was a devastating weapon. But what did Longyan intend to do with it?

"Take it, Father, it's yours. So precious that I thought you'd want to keep it hidden."

The Taitai couldn't read a word, but knew instantly what the document conveyed. Longyan had discovered what her family had concealed from the matchmaker. If the genealogy was ever made public, a terrible scandal would ensue, probably requiring a formal declaration of divorce by the Patriarch. It was his right, of course, to choose and dismiss mates as he saw fit, but it was also his duty to avoid public embarrassment to himself and his ancestors.

"Yes," gulped the Patriarch. "Precious indeed. Don't worry. I'll keep it hidden. But what's in the other two boxes?"

"Identical copies."

"What for?"

"Oh. I'll keep one. Just as a reminder of my first effort at a genealogy. It'll be safe."

"And the other?"

Longyan smiled and carried the box across the room. To everyone's astonishment, he handed it to Lin Meihua. "Just a symbol for the daughter-in-law," Longyan said matter-of-factly. "To symbolize deference to the Matriarch and her family. And, should other copies of this precious genealogy be destroyed, it would be the duty of the daughter-in-law to preserve her copy. Under such circumstances, she might even share it with her own honorable father so that everyone might know the noble lineage of her new family."

With that, Longyan bowed respectfully to the Patriarch and the Taitai, and walked out of the room.

CHAPTER NINE

Lady
明

The Next Three Years: Suzhou, 1635–1637

A WEEK LATER, Longyan departed the Wu mansion, porters ferrying his eight brass-buckled camphor trunks of clothing and belongings to the barge pier on the Grand Canal, his manservant gently carrying his *qin* case. Wang Longyan was one of four first-class passengers traveling all the way to Beijing, more than a month to the north. At dawn, dozens of coolies strained at the two-inch-diameter hemp ropes linking the massive 500-ton vessel to the barge path, slowly hauling it northward at the average pace of less than a mile an hour. The coolies chanted softly to a drumbeat in the barge's bow while the polemen pushed the gunwales off the gray stone embankments.

By midmorning the barge groaned its way past the Wu mansion on a hill overlooking the Grand Canal. Boulders in the rock garden thrust up like mountains in a monochrome ink landscape against the gray winter sky. Undulating roof tiles slithered like a dragon's back on the horizon.

A bonfire crackled in the midst of the mansion, shooting off red and yellow flames, and spewing a plume of black smoke across Suzhou. Longyan, leaning against the carved guardrail on the promenade deck, knew that a loyal servant had fulfilled a last request from a departing master. It wasn't anything serious. No one would miss the old toolshed. No one would ever see its strange interior decoration of calligraphy written backwards. No one would ever suspect the charred remains once had the name "Idiot's Palace."

Hands tightening around the weathered teak railing, Longyan sucked in gulps of cold air, held back tears, and reminded himself why he was doing this. It's over, he convinced himself, the first volume of my life is over. He watched a melon hawker toss his rotting unsold fruits into the river; orange, green, and yellow spheres caught in the barge's bow wave, rolling over and over, until they were finally split apart and spit aside as garbage. For twenty-three years I've been a bit player in an itinerant street tragedy, he mused, always bowing to other directors, always being upstaged by other actors. Whatever happens next, he vowed, I will be in charge—my successes, my mistakes.

Father Gao, observing the barge's ponderous progress from the shadows beneath a white marble bridge spanning the canal, prayed for Longyan's life ahead and that he had offered the correct advice. He sensed the young man's spinning emotions and knew he had been right not to see Longyan off—ultimately it had to be Longyan's decision.

As the barge passed by, Father Gao secretly watched the young man's face and, as if viewing a mirror, saw himself scarcely ten years earlier. He too had left Köln by riverboat, determined to take control of his life, to go to Asia and serve in the China mission. It had taken the better part of those ten years—Paris, Rome, Cape Horn, Goa, Manila, Macao, Suzhou—to discover that the most difficult journey was inside himself, to know what he wanted and how to get it. He concluded that a priest had two options: either defining himself as a servant of God, a passive actor who did His will and offered His sacraments; or seeing himself as a confidant of God, an active agent who had to rely on his own wit to pilot a moral course across a foggy sea. Option two, the tougher but more rewarding, had guided Father Gao for the past ten of his almost forty years. The same choice lay ahead for Longyan. Father Gao sighed as the barge slowly slipped around the bend and out of sight.

Meanwhile, Meihua, drawn by the fire at the Wu mansion, arrived as the rickety shack imploded from the heat, charging the cold air with showers of white-hot sparks. A charred piece of white paper fell to her feet, tiny character fragments danced around its edges, a sort of nonsense poetry from some madman: "mind," "winter," "fire," "earth," "ice," "tears"—every character written backwards. She picked it up, puzzled a moment, then, not recognizing the calligraphy and, not wanting anyone to suspect that she could read, crumpled it and tossed it into the flames. She glanced toward the canal, briefly glimpsing Longyan as the black barge slipped behind a hill, hoping that his last wave was for her, wondering when she would ever see him again.

Would it have made a difference if Meihua had known that it would be over five years before she saw Longyan again face to face? Would she have acted differently if she'd been told that over two years would pass before she received a letter? Would she have given up on her strange brother-in-law? In her old age, she would often ponder those curious "what ifs," shuddering as she recalled the terrible trials—for herself, her family, her city, her country—in the last decade of the Ming dynasty.

At first, she pretended she didn't care about such things. He was gone. That was that. Life went on. In fact, life improved dramatically in one respect.

It was a pretty May morning when the Taitai announced her intention to take a "southern tour" and invited Meihua to join her. The term came from imperial parlance, referring to the Emperor's great voyages down the Grand Canal to his southern provinces, replete with thousands of retainers. The Taitai's tours were more modest, a few hours in a rented party barge, accompanied by a couple of friends or family and an assortment of servants. What was rare about this tour was that Meihua was the one and only guest.

The two ladies sat sedately at the barge's bow, properly covered by a white awning, sipping Fujian green tea and nibbling at "taitai treats," dishes of cold and hot dumplings filled with figs, plums, pork, or colored sugar paste, always four to a plate, enough for munching, but not so much as to leave you stuffed. Peach Blossom and Winter Plum, the Taitai's maid, stood behind their mistresses, directing the waiters, making absolutely certain that not a shaft of sunlight fell on their ladies. Everyone knew that ladies' skin darkened and wrinkled if exposed to bright sun, making them look like working women at best, threatening an early death at worst. Ladies' skin was always treated with exceptional care: light sponge baths, followed by immediate drying, then heavy application of skin oils to the body, and cream bases which soaked the face before applying four or five layers of makeup.

"Shoo," said the Taitai, waving her hand toward the maids but keeping her head facing forward so as not to ruffle her hairstyle or to catch a bead or an earring on her stiff green gown.

"Milady?" Winter Plum inquired softly.

"Shoo, shoo, shoo," repeated the Taitai, snapping her wrist at her servant. "We won't be needing the likes of you for the next half hour. Now, shoo. I mean it."

Winter Plum beckoned Peach Blossom to withdraw to the stern. Both fretted that their charges might need some fanning or a bit of tea. Servants rose to the top by anticipating the needs of masters and mistresses; those who always waited for orders generally found themselves performing menial tasks. But when the Taitai "shooed," you left or you were out of a job.

"My dearest daughter," the Taitai began, looking not at Meihua but staring instead directly over the barge's bow, pausing for a moment with a tiny smile. Actually the main purpose of the conversation was already over. She had called Meihua "dearest daughter," not "newest daughter" or "outside daughter."

"Oh, honorable Niang," replied Meihua quickly, using the formal term for mother, but breaking etiquette by snapping her head and staring in surprise, "you cannot call me that. I don't deserve it." Meihua was right in the sense that mothers-in-law almost never spoke so affectionately about daughters-in-law. What was going on?

"Nonsense, dearest daughter." The Taitai turned toward Meihua and softly touched her hand. "It's entirely correct. Even more, I owe you an apology. I have often treated you cruelly."

"How can you say that? You have treated me too gently. I'm only a collection of faults." It *was* unheard of. A taitai apologizing to a daughter-in-law? Why was she doing this?

"Faults? Not at all! You are from noble birth. You know I am from lower levels. You have the genealogy. Merchant. Before that peasant. Even lower. How can you let me sit next to you?"

Meihua was speechless. One *never* acknowledged such things personally, even though everyone knew them to be true. This wasn't the planned dialogue at all. "Please don't talk that way. You're the mother of my noble husband. It is one's current position, not one's roots, that count."

"Current position, not roots? Is that what Master Confucius said?"

"How could I know?" Meihua stared in puzzlement. "I'm only a woman."

"Only a woman? Really? Not a scholar? Not an expert on the classics?"

Oh no, thought Meihua, she knows! Somebody revealed the secret about my reading! Meihua tried to keep from fainting. Surges of emotion shot through her brain and limbs. Did the Taitai know about her correspondence with Longyan, letters, too?

"Dearest daughter, what is ever the matter?" asked the Taitai, beckoning the servants to fan Meihua and offer her tea. "How marvelous to be so accomplished. We shall, of course, keep this a secret between us. How nice to each have little secrets."

Meihua felt both relief and resignation. It wouldn't be public. But now their relationship was radically altered. She and the Taitai would be forever entangled through mutual secrets. Like the cobra and the mongoose—each could kill the other, so maybe neither would use its lethal power. But were the secrets—Meihua's literacy and the Taitai's lineage—equally devastating? Did the Taitai have the edge? What of the Longyan letters?

"Shoo," the Taitai said again with a glint in her eyes, waiting to speak until the servants had retired. "I'll bet you'd like to know how we found out. It wasn't very hard. A servant saw you reading by candlelight one night. Then again another night."

"I should have been more discreet."

"I suppose so. But I hear other women of your generation are doing the same. Rumors float all over Suzhou. But *never* in the Wu family. At least not until now. Tell me, is reading hard?" the Taitai asked, dropping her conspiratorial voice, genuinely wondering about the question since she had never encountered a literate woman.

"Very hard. I really can't read easily. I forget the characters. Too bad I'm not smart, like a man."

"Too bad. Then you could learn to write as well."

Meihua stared at the Taitai, whose face had become placid again, eyes staring off across the canal. It was clear that she meant what she had said. The gloating was gone. Meihua thanked the spirits for the blessed ignorance of women, for the total insularity of the red chamber. The Taitai honestly thought that reading and writing were totally separate acts, one requiring books, the other requiring brushes. It never dawned on her that if a woman learned to read, she also might have learned to write. Thank goodness Meihua did her writing in a hidden chamber, behind closed doors and away from snooping eyes. Half her secret—the devastating half—remained confidential.

The two women sat side by side, faces emptily perusing the greenish water ahead. The barge rocked softly from side to side, gently lifting and dipping each lady in turn, as if some giant scale now deemed them equal.

As the emotional surge subsided, Meihua felt spent, exhausted from the mortal combat that had ended in a draw. But, shifting her eyes toward the Taitai, she felt something else, something she hadn't expected. What was it? As the Taitai whispered orders for the barge to return, Meihua glimpsed the pained sadness in the Taitai's lined eyes, knifelike etchings in the skin that no cosmetic could hide. The Taitai, having exercised her power for the day, was already pondering her next moves, over dinner perhaps, maybe in the kitchen, or perhaps with the servants. The Taitai was always running, always maneuvering, trying to escape the ghosts of her past. Suddenly Meihua saw her for what she really was: a low-grade actress whose roles and masks blinded everyone, including the Taitai herself, to the real personality underneath. What was down there? Meihua wondered.

"Now, wasn't that fun?" the Taitai asked Meihua as servants helped them to the marble wharf, umbrellas shifting overhead and fans fluttering. "Just a touch muggy. But then, successful southern tours are always a bit arduous. Yes?"

"Yes. Thank you, honorable Niang."

"And I thank you. Dearest daughter."

Scarcely six months later, a miracle happened to Meihua, suddenly giving her life direction and meaning. It had been a strange invitation, to the first meeting of the Ladies' Filial Piety Society at the Zhang residence, on a Saturday afternoon in chilly January. There was an even stranger collection of delicate women's palanquins on the street, showing winter curtains of maroon, green, blue, and pink, all pulled down to protect the occupants and then opening up to allow many of the elite daughters to enter the Zhang portals, each accompanied by servants who fussed to make them pretty.

But inside, in the Zhang reception hall where the fifteen young women gathered, was the strangest scene of all. The Zhang taitai, a tallish, serious woman in her mid-twenties who had assumed her position because of the premature death of her mother-in-law, presided over the meeting. She sat in front of her colleagues, slowly opening a hand scroll on a table in front of her. "Dear sisters, this is why I asked you together. My late father has willed me this incredible present. It's Song dynasty. Twelfth century. Ma Hezhi's remarkable work. It's the illustrations to accompany the *Ladies' Classic of Filial Piety*. Come here. Come now. Don't hang back. Take a look."

Meihua moved slowly to peek. Women *never* gathered to look at artworks. Art, especially in the form of didactic Confucian paintings, was the private world of men. Meihua inched closer, glancing down as the Zhang taitai slowly rolled the hand scroll, revealing scene after scene of elegant paintings of virtuous women, tending to their husbands, spinning and weaving, respecting older people, revering established customs. The Zhang taitai's hands moved expertly, rolling and unrolling, giving the scroll the feeling that the images moved with precision and rhythm.

After a few minutes, when the women had all huddled together and the initial nervousness had faded, the Zhang taitai spoke softly, never lifting her eyes from the table. "Of course you are all aware of these lessons. We all know them. This great *classic* states the ideal: we women are subordinate and we must never try to change our roles. It is our duty to pay homage to elders and to men, especially to our fathers and husbands, and to nourish our children, especially our sons. But . . ."

The Zhang taitai paused for effect, smoothly rolling back to the beginning of the hand scroll, pausing at the initial calligraphic text. "But sometimes one must be slightly more active in pursuing our subordinate roles. Now let's look at the beautiful writing. It's the text of the *Ladies' Classic of Filial Piety*. The calligraphy is attributed to the Empress Yang, Yang Meizi, thirteenth century. A woman of great filiality. But also great ability . . ."

Again the Zhang taitai paused. "Yes, the Empress Yang could read and write. So could the great Ban Zhao of the Eastern Han.

And so can . . . many of you. . . ." A hush swept through the huddle of women. Eyes stayed riveted downward to avoid suspicion. "So can I . . ." the Zhang spoke barely audibly. "It says, 'First Chapter, The Starting Point and Basic Principles.' Now who will continue our reading? Meihua, perhaps?"

Meihua gulped, her hands and head sweated; she thought about bolting, but that wouldn't solve anything. Could she lie? Pretend she couldn't read? No, that would make her weak among women. "It says," she stuttered, "it says. 'Cao Dagu asked a group of seated women whether they know about the way of filiality handed down from the Sage Emperor Yu.' "

"Precisely. A brave show, dear Meihua," said the Zhang taitai. "And who is Cao Dagu?"

"It's the literary name of Ban Zhao, the great scholar."

"So you've done some secret homework, too. Just like me." The other women laughed a little. "Now how about you, Dingyu?"

And around the room they went, several women reading a line or two, some quickly and some hesitatingly, more than half with some degree of literacy. Each of them read deeply orthodox words like "filiality broadens heaven and earth, deepens human relationships, moves ghosts and spirits, affects birds and beasts." But the very act of reading together was radically unorthodox, a show of literacy among women.

So the oft-rumored secret was finally revealed—not to men, of course, but among women who had spent years beautifying bodies while concealing brains. Meihua glanced at her friends' faces; most shyly cast eyes downward, but a few smiled excitedly. They were sensing China's ultimate truth: While education in solitude might offer some solace, shared knowledge opened the real path to power. But, Meihua wondered privately, where would this lead? What could literate ladies possibly do in a society that frowned on their very existence?

After the women finished their reading of the first chapter, Meihua asked the Zhang taitai softly, "You're the one who's brave—how dare you do this?"

"Not brave. Just filial. My late father knew I could read. He scolded me, of course. But then, just before he died, he gave me this treasure. He said to open it when I became twenty-five. Then the eunuchs had him executed. Crushed to death with huge stones. I was only fourteen then. Now I'm twenty-five. I know it's what he would have wanted me to do. So it's just filiality. Besides, I'm not alone. Most of you have relatives who are true patriots. Real Ming loyalists. But they've lost out to corrupt elements. That's what happened to your father, Meihua. And especially your father-in-law. Both alive but without influence.''

"So what do we do now?''

"I'd suggest we continue our meetings. The Ladies' Filial Piety Society. Once a month. Right here. Who could be against that? Yes?''

Murmurings of assent buzzed around the room.

"Good. But maybe we could also share a little information. You know, about what's happening around the empire. All I get are little rumors. Maybe we could compare what we're heard. Creative eavesdropping.''

A fortnight later, her mind still spinning with excitement, Meihua had her first chance at creative eavesdropping. Maybe I have a cripple's feet, Meihua mused, but I have developed a monkey's arms. Pulling herself up on a pillar bracket, she hovered momentarily, then dropped soundlessly into a giant blue and white floor vase at the doorway of the Wu family receiving room. Now if she could stay still for a couple of hours, she would become the first woman to overhear a meeting of the Fushe or "Restoration Society" which Suzhon elite men had organized to replace the now-banned Donglin movement. She waited, frozen in place, until she heard the rustling of shoes and the murmuring of male voices.

"No ceremonies, no poetry, no allegories," the Wu patriarch was saying. "Not today. No time for luxuries. Just facts.''

"As you say, Doctor. Unroll the map, the big one, covering all of China." Meihua smiled to herself. So that's why Dr. Long carried the scroll case with him. Everyone thought he collected only antique maps. "Yes," said the Wu patriarch, "hold it down with these stone paperweights. Yes, quite nice, I agree, carved in the Yuan period. Now, no more distractions. What do we know?''

"I've got a report from the coast. From Fujian, where my son's a district magistrate." Old man Liao was speaking, Meihua knew the voice instantly. He was a rich wine merchant, invested everything in his son's education; the boy was brilliant, but brash, like his father, so he was sent off to the remote south. "He says Japanese and Taiwanese pirates control a thousand miles of coastline—south Zhejiang, Fujian, Guangdong, even Hainan Island. Take anything and everything they want. *But* he says, and this is important, they only want loot, not power. No one talks of a new dynasty."

"Right, right, right. That's what I've been saying. . . ." Who was talking? Maybe the elder Hu. Smart fellow. Once chief secretary to governor of Henan, back in the late Wanli years. "I still get regular reports. Not just Henan, but also Hunan, Hubei, even Sichuan. The post routes go directly through Zhengzhou, after all, and I spent twenty years in that town. Twenty years in purgatory . . . but that's not the point. . . ."

"What *is* the point?"

"I was getting to it. Provincial memorials to the throne are hardly secrets, you know, so I get almost everything. The plain fact is that dynasty has lost over half of its territory to the rebels. We live in a small pocket, a protected coastal cocoon. But Ming forces have total control only over parts of Hebei, fortunately including Beijing, and most of Shandong and Jiangsu, fortunately including Su- zhou. The rest of the empire is in rebel hands. Unless a miracle happens . . ."

". . . it's all over." Someone else—was it Lao Chen, the artist?— finished the sentence. Meihua stretched a little, pushing her head up in the vase, straining to hear his soft words. "My brother is married into the Bai family, you know, *the* Bais, the ones with the huge collection in Beijing. He hears from his sister-in-law that no- body's in charge in the capital. It's one huge battle for money and power. It's crazy. Like a condemned criminal fighting for his win- nings at the gaming table."

"Well I hear slightly more optimistic reports," the Wu patriarch interjected, "from my son in the army, captain in the Beijing garri- son." Meihua held her breath. Had she heard it right? Longyan was a captain? Was there a note of affection in the Patriarch's voice? Had he accepted the inevitable? "He thinks the army can hold off the Manchus to the north, corralling them behind the Great Wall, then sending crack troops to cope with the rebels."

"Begging the scholar's pardon," Magistrate Hai interrupted, "but your son is a junior officer, young and new to his post. Isn't it possible that he's letting his patriotism—laudable as that might be—cloud his judgment? Now, as for me, there's nothing I'd like better than some optimism. My job depends on the health of the dynasty. . . ."

"But what can *we* do?" someone asked. "We can't just sit here and wait. Can we?"

"That is precisely what we should do," said Meihua's father with his usual quiet authority. "I'm not sure who will win. Maybe the Ming will prevail. Or maybe they'll fall to the barbarians. Or perhaps to the rebels. We've got to wait. We don't have the power to make a difference."

"So we're like reeds? Blowing with whatever wind comes along?"

"No," the Lin patriarch replied sharply. "Like hawks. We keep a watchful eye and wait."

"And if the Ming should fall . . ."

"To me," the Lin Patriarch spoke without hesitation, "there's no question about my loyalties. I am a servant of the Ming dynasty. I do not shift my allegiance to rebels or barbarians just to suit the fashion of the times. If Beijing is lost, then it is our duty to rally around the ousted Ming sovereign, name a new capital, rebuild the dynasty, revitalize the army. Should the Emperor be lost, then a new emperor will ascend, a Ming emperor."

"But, without troops, what can we do? The young men have all been conscripted. The local militias are jokes. We don't even have weapons. How could we possibly resist?"

"That," the Wu patriarch said, "is the subject for our next meeting. *Long life to the Ming emperor.*"

"*Wan Sui,*" everyone shouted, "*Ming Huangdi Wan Sui.*"

The cheer rang loudly through the ceramic vase. Meihua waited until the footsteps disappeared, then reached up to the rim, pulling herself up as if on parallel bars, vaulting delicately to the floor with a balanced landing on her tiny feet. Meihua stood shakily for a moment, her body still trembling from the ordeal of stillness, her mind racing to answer a terrible question. What could they do? What could anyone do to protect themselves? Protect their families? Protect their dynasty? What can I possibly do? she wondered. Maybe—

Meihua froze as her mother-in-law suddenly entered the room, the Matriarch's eyes scrutinizing Meihua suspiciously. "I see the men have left. But why are you here? You surely didn't intrude. I hope you weren't—"

"Oh, noble Niang," Meihua said deferentially, trying to make herself sound sincere. "I just got here. It's four o'clock, you know. I just wanted to help oversee the table setting."

"Is that why you're here? Yes, yes, of course. Yes, dearest daughter. How very kind of you to offer to help."

CHAPTER TEN

Soldiers

明

Two to Three Years Later: Beijing and Suzhou, 1638–1640

A STRANGE MOOD hung over the Qianmen, Beijing's Front Gate, the entryway from the outer residential city to the inner administrative city, just a mile south of the Tiananmen, the Gate of Heavenly Peace. What caused the creeping sense of foreboding? Was it the eerie gray dawn, a touch of drizzle in the air? Or perhaps the season, not quite spring, trees starkly leafless, branches clawing like spiderlegs into the mist? Or maybe the prison wagon rumbling its way over damp cobblestones conveying three sobbing condemned prisoners to the execution grounds outside the city. White placards behind their necks explained that two were to be beheaded for murder, one to be slowly sliced to death for treason. Did that explain the ominous atmosphere?

To Capt. Wang Longyan, commander of the Qianmen guard detachment, none of this seemed strange at all. It appeared a typical dreary March morning. He brushed the water droplets from his uniform: embroidered blue belted jacket, black cotton pants tapering into heavy leather boots, small, flat-topped green hat with peacock feather to indicate his rank.

Resting his hands against the balustrade, carefully so as not to muss his crisp uniform, Captain Wang peered southward. He knew that most people, condemned criminals aside, liked the Qianmen. The gate was spectacular: over 100 feet high, 150 feet wide, and more than 80 feet deep, with a huge tunneled passageway below. Guard towers loomed above, composed of massive timbers that were intricately painted in blues, reds, and yellows and topped with splendid yellow imperial tiles from the kilns at Jingdezhen;

ceramic roof ends featured processions of tiny horsedrawn carts and dragons.

First-time visitors, like the Korean tribute mission wandering through the misty morning to an imperial audience, stood open-mouthed in awe, water dripping off black top hats onto stiff silk robes. Old-timers thrived on the traffic moving through Beijing's most popular chokepoint: a scruffy juggler trying to win a few copper coins by balancing a heavy mason jar on his head, a rag-garbed leper child with a long-poled box for contributions without endangering the donor, and a fortune-teller already clacking his box filled with little sticks that, for a price, he shook out to reveal your future. Even in the murky halflight, merchant shops were beginning to open; the merchants included a cotton-shoe cobbler, leather bootmaker, silversmith, gold-jewelry dealer, bird-cage maker, calligrapher (and sometimes forger), candymaker, herbal medicine dispenser, dentist, wine merchant, acupuncturist cum moxabustionist, bookseller, five tea-shop owners, and no fewer than seven money changers, each setting up the scales to transfer value from copper to silver (rates shifted hourly and were posted by the doorway).

Suddenly, seemingly out of nowhere, a weighty gong sounded, then cymbals clashed, creating raucous reverberations dampened by the clinging water vapor. Even before Captain Wang could shout his "Clear the streets!" command, most pedestrians did precisely that, cowing in corners and kneeling by the roadside. Slowly the sounds became brighter, thumping drums and crashing brass. Now the reason for the morning's odd mood became obvious: the Emperor was approaching.

"Down! Knees, hands, and heads! That means you! Yes, you!" Captain Wang shouted his orders to a demented teenage girl who was dancing in the street to the percussive rhythm; fortunately some friends pulled her to the ground, stifling her singing with hands over her mouth, watching fearfully until the guard captain looked away, apparently satisfied. After all, disrupting an imperial procession was a capital offense.

Given his special duty as a "shield of the throne," the term for ranking guardsmen, Captain Wang was among the very few permitted to stand and gaze on the proceedings. The gray mist filtered the images before him, transforming the usually brilliant imperial colors, vermilion and yellow, into soft, wet pastels. Sharply pressed silks wilted into soggy uniforms of the guards, palanquin bearers, and band. The familiar crisp *pat-pat-pat* of cotton shoes on pavement became a sloshy slapping sound. The retinue of saffron-robbed Buddhist and ruby-clad Daoist priests, dragon-breasted imperial household officers, blue-and-green-garbed chief servants and physicians, and black-capped court officials slogged through puddles at a plodding pace.

It seemed a funeral rather than a divine procession of the One Who Linked Heaven, Earth, and Man. But for Captain Wang, it was a rare moment, the first time he had seen an imperial procession, though he had been in Beijing for a year and a half and had served in the gate guard detachment most of that time. The Emperor almost never left the confines of the Forbidden City. But this morning the Holy One was returning from the first light ceremony at the Temple of Heaven, where he had appealed to the spirits for a fertile spring and a good crop (the soothsayers would later tell him that the wet morning was a good omen for the rains to come, hoping that His Majesty would have forgotten last year, when a sunny day was interpreted as the shining face of heaven itself).

There he is! Captain Wang thought to himself, watching intently as the yellow-draped imperial palanquin lumbered into view, supported by black lacquer poles borne aloft by more than twenty footmen. The band erupted in a clanging racket, to attract the blessings of good spirits, while fireworks exploded alongside, to ward off unkind demons. Flagbearers waved their yellow dragon banners. But the focal point of the procession—the Emperor himself—was hidden as always behind the draperies. None could see the Exalted One, certainly not the scraggly roadside commoners, not even the ranking officials who were always denied a direct view (even when talking with him during audiences there was always a golden lacquer screen with fine filigree carving to permit sound but not sight).

The imperial charade, as some critics privately described court ceremony, almost always worked its magic. Captain Wang had heard the Beijing gossipers' prattle. The twenty-three-year-old Emperor, son of a syphilitic philanderer who loved carpentry more than administration, tried his best to surpass his late father. A dullard in the classroom, the young Emperor still learned to parrot a few Confucian passages and took the time to read an occasional memorial from a provincial governor. Unlike his grandfather, the young Chongzhen emperor, as he was called, did meet with his senior ministers, but imperial audiences were formalistic gatherings, given to ministerial pontificating and simplistic imperial responses. Earlier in the dynasty, some noble officials might have found the Emperor a useful front for reforms in taxation, local governance, education, and military forces. But not today, not when China was run by eunuchs at the top and very conventional officials at the bottom.

Ah, the eunuchs, there they are, thought Longyan, looking at the twenty pudgy, red-robed figures, plodding ponderously under weighty umbrellas emblazoned with golden dragons. At the head of the procession was Wei Nan, who claimed to be the adopted "son" of the infamous late eunuch Wei Zhongxian, whose rotund face conveyed an imperious annoyance as if those in the streets were causing his damp discomfiture. In one hand, Wei Nan carried a yellow towel to dab his moist bald head, and in the other, like all eunuchs, he held his emblem of power, a lacquer box that contained a sealed bottle, which, in turn, preserved the remains of his sexual organs, which had been severed when he was a child. The castration ceremony, usually ordered by a father seeking greater influence in high places, was a bloody affair, removing the entire scrotum and sometimes the penis as well, often performed by local surgeons without any experience in the operation. Those who survived could indeed make it to positions of enormous prominence. And eunuchs always carried their lost organs so that they would always remain intact at least symbolically; one could not become a potent posthumous ancestor unless all body parts were together at death.

The eunuchs didn't look so imposing—they seemed soft, genderless, older men—but Longyan knew they ruled China with impunity. Eunuchs levied taxes, made appointments, fired officials, decided on public projects, and, above all, meted out justice. Eunuchs specialized in torture and agonizing deaths (slicing, cracking bones, burning, boiling); harsh judgments were levied every few days, sometimes against their critics, but frequently against innocent officials simply to display eunuch power. Originally selected because of their presumed absolute loyalty to the throne—eunuchs could not, after all, begin new families and new dynasties—the eunuchs assumed tyrannical power with the advent of weak emperors in the last century of Ming rule. They often amassed astonishing fortunes, sharing it with their original families, sometimes adopting children so as to have rich heirs (thereby undercutting the original purpose for castration).

"All clear!" Captain Wang shouted as the procession passed through the gate and northward toward the Forbidden City. "You have been blessed by the Imperial Presence. Good fortune for all. All clear. All is well."

But was all really well? he wondered, observing the streets coming back to life, only the demented child still kowtowing to an unseen authority, fireworks pop-popping in the distant mist. Rumors spoke of impending dynastic collapse, and not simply because of eunuch corruption and soft sovereigns.

Everyone spoke of the "three terribles." A shift in international trade toward Southeast Asia and the Americas led to a rapid decline in silver, prompting a truly *terrible* fiscal crisis. Longyan knew only too well that today's silver exchange value for a string of Ming copper currency was only one-third of its value when he was born. While the rich hoarded their silver, congratulating themselves on how quickly one can become richer with no work, peasants were forced to pay their taxes in silver, protesting that all they had were strings of copper, which they lugged to market, slung over their bodies, where the coins bought less and less.

And what was it that caused the *terrible* sicknesses across China? In Zhejiang it was said that illness afflicted eight or nine of every ten households. From Henan came a report that there was so little human life that "all one heard was the buzzing of flies." The diseases, which sounded suspiciously like the plague, included swollen glands, diarrhea, pustules, scabs, boils, cramps, and fever.

While the first two disasters were frightfully evident in Qianmen Square, right beneath Captain Wang's eyes, his special training was to cope with the *terrible* military threats confronting the Ming empire. A noose was slowly being tightened around Beijing's neck, a militant garroting that was squeezing the life from the dynasty that had ruled China for almost three hundred years. To the south and east, pirates ravaged the rich coastal provinces of Shandong,

Jiangsu, Fujian, and Guangdong, stripping towns of their wealth, then stealing off to hidden island fortresses in swift, low-draft, lateen-rigged vessels. To the south and west, the most fearsome rebels in hundreds of years, most notably Li Zicheng and Zhang Xianzhong, controlled massive areas in the heart of the Middle Kingdom, their armies mobilizing tens of thousands of peasants and lower-class troops, including both men and women soldiers. The rebels set up their own dynasties, replete with reign titles and civil administrations, thus terrorizing emperors and peasants alike. It was rumored that the rebels enjoyed killing scholars and that Zhang specialized in such odious practices as cutting off the bound feet of gentry women and burning the severed appendages in huge bonfires.

Captain Wang strode slowly across the walkway, gazing through the mist to the north, imagining the shrouded red Tiananmen, the glorious yellow-roofed Forbidden City, the spectacular marble animals guarding the tombs of the early Ming emperors, and even the Great Wall itself. He had seen the Great Wall, on maneuvers, less than a year earlier, and was astonished by its gargantuan dimensions, a defensive audacity stretching across thousands of miles, a history that dated back to Qin Shihuang over fifteen hundred years earlier. Wang Longyan had also been shocked to find the wall in terrible disrepair, large sections crumbling away, grass growing from its sides and top, long expanses apparently unguarded.

Today Longyan shook his head, knowing the greatest military threat might come not from pirates or domestic rebels, but rather from the north, from the Manchu barbarians who had organized themselves into a new dynasty as well. *Qing* ("pure") it was called, with the clear-cut intention to cleanse China of Ming corruption. Already the Manchus had broken through the wall on several occasions, burning and pillaging before retreating to their large encampments along the Bohai Gulf coast. Ever since the turn of the sixteenth century, the great Manchu leaders, Nurhaci, and his son, Abahai, consolidated their power in southern Manchuria, organizing their Manchu and Mongol followers into eight banner units, each with its special flags (plain or bordered yellow, red, blue, and white). Chinese residents of Manchuria had but few choices: those who resisted were imprisoned and executed, those who cooperated were enslaved, and the lucky ones were mobilized into their own

Chinese banner forces. All Chinese were forced to wear the "queue," a Manchu practice whereby the front of the scalp was shaved and the rear hair allowed to grow long and braided.

Longyan shuddered. How humiliating to lose your hair to some smelly barbarian. He'd rather die than submit to Manchu rule. Besides, he had been told that Manchus were stupid, uneducated, mainly herdsmen and peasants. So, like most Ming soldiers, Longyan assumed the Manchus couldn't topple the dynasty. They couldn't run an empire. They didn't have either the brainpower or the firepower. Maybe they would win a few lucky victories, but the Manchus would ultimately fail in their audacious desire to take the Middle Kingdom. Defending China against the barbarians was a primary task of the Ming Green Standard Army, of which Longyan was part. He was sure the Ming could hold the wall against the barbarians. Of course we will prevail, Longyan said to himself, how can we lose?

A frosty breeze prickled his face as he stared northward into the grayness. The north was the Chinese symbol for cold, winter, darkness, and evil; the north was frightening enough so that all imperial buildings were constructed facing southward. Even the Chinese maritime compass was oriented toward the south ("south-pointing implement" it was called). The north—Captain Wang couldn't suppress his private fears—would it bring his own end? The end of the Ming? Maybe the end of civilization?

Of course not, how silly, Longyan answered himself. He spun in place and marched smartly to the doorway, passing the guard's baton to his replacement with the curt comment, "All is well."

In Europe, Father Gao had enjoyed being tall, for it conveyed bearing, gravitas, even manliness—all desirable attributes given some contrary stereotypes about the priesthood. But in China, he hated his height. Every doorway seemed to have a malevolent interest in cutting his balding head; every room appeared designed for midgets; all clothing cost twice as much. And, worst of all, everyone gawked at the "Big-Nosed, Black-Gowned, Looks-Like-a-Scholar-but-Is-Actually-a-Priest Tall-as-a-Pagoda Barbarian," as he was called in gossip parlance.

So to minimize embarrassment, Father Gao became a nocturnal

animal, buying supplies and foods at dusk just before the shops closed, then roaming Suzhou's labyrinthian streets and alleyways. Over time he came to know central Suzhou by heart, whooshing about barely visible in his black cape covering his black gown. In the mornings people often chattered about "Big-nosed-barbarian sightings," as if they had encountered the elusive Tibetan Yeti the night before.

Tonight was different. It was late March, just a few days before the Grave-Sweeping Festival that marked the true beginning of spring. Tonight he crept softly along walls, trying to avoid being spotted. Tonight he prayed more than ever that no one would see him. Without the map he'd memorized, no one, except possibly a veteran barge-poler, could have known where he was going—over tiny bridges, along edges of small canals, through shantytowns in the outskirts of Suzhou.

He knew it was dangerous to stray so far from the inner city, especially at night when Suzhou's seamier realities poked through its daytime gentility. Suzhou was a city of glittering richness by day, but of dark plots and gnawing rats by night. Armies of night watchmen were Father Gao's biggest dangers, employed by rich families, artisan guilds, and even government officials (since the regular security was woefully corrupt). Bands of homeless marauders, forced from farms and small towns by a ravished economy, lived on Suzhou's outskirts, often venturing forth at night. Someone creeping about them was either about to commit a crime or a criminal fleeing from the scene. Either way, night watchmen tended to act on instinct, using a club or knife first, then disposing of the body in a watery grave rather than answering questions later.

"Who goes there?" came the gruff cry from the shadows just across a bridge barely illuminated by diffuse moonlight through the gray black mist. The harsh banging of a nightstick, staff at one end and glistening blade at the other, accompanied the heavy *flip flop* of padded feet. "Who is it?" the voice bellowed from bridge.

Father Gao cringed behind a stack of barrels in front of a pottery store at the near end of the bridge. The stocky watchman kept coming, right toward the barrels. Father Gao pressed against the wall, his hands groping to find someplace to hide. Suddenly he touched something soft and warm, human skin. His hand recoiled and the stack of barrels came crashing down. A naked woman and a half-naked man jumped up and ran down a nearby alley, dragging their clothes and trying to cover themselves as well as possible.

"Get out of here!" shouted the watchman. "This isn't a brothel!" The watchman shook his head, trudged back over the bridge, chuckling to himself. Everyone knew that privacy was impossible inside tiny Chinese houses, so darkened street corners often had to suffice.

Heart beating wildly, Father Gao waited until the watchman retreated, then slipped quickly over the bridge. Then slowly, ever so slowly, he crept along dank, dark walls. *First door on right after bridge, knock slowly three times, say your name twice,* he remembered. He groped for the small, rough-hewn door, then did exactly as the instructions required. It had all come in a mysterious unsigned note, concluding with a harsh threat: *If you wish those who wear the cross to remain in Suzhou, you must come next Tuesday night.*

For a moment, nothing happened, so he leaned against the door, which opened at just that moment, popping the priest through it. Father Gao fell with a thud, his head hitting the hard, pounded-earth floor, sending a flash through his head and leaving sparks in his eyes. For a full minute, he lay there in stunned stupor; finally he groaned and lifted himself up to a huddled sitting position, hands kneading the throbbing pains in his eyes and brow.

"Barbarian priest," came the order from a softly firm female voice, "you will sit." Out of the darkness came two male servants who grabbed his arms and jostled the big foreigner into a heavy armchair.

"But what's this all about? . . . The message said that I would be meeting important people."

"Silence," said the voice. "You *are* meeting important people. You will not speak. Unless we speak first to you. Do you understand?"

Father Gao nodded his reluctant agreement, shaking his head to clear the headache and opening his eyes fully. He sat in the receiving room of a gentry home, which, by the musty feel, was not in regular service. The four walls were illuminated by frosted-globe oil lamps perched on chairs, projecting pools of diffuse light below eye level. Dust-covered furniture was scattered in lumpen piles about the room; rolled scrolls and folded screens supported glisten-

122

ing cobwebs in the corners. Four large armchairs faced one another in the middle of the room in a cramped space that the servants had obviously carved out by shoving the rest of the furniture aside.

The other three armchairs contained elegantly dressed women: soft-hued gowns of yellow, blue, and lavender, piled hair interlaced with combs and beads, hands delicately holding tasseled fans or resting demurely in laps, bound feet hidden behind the gowns and resting on little stools. It was astonishing enough for a barbarian to be received by three aristocratic women, but even more surprising was that he could not discern their identities. Each face was concealed by a lavishly painted mask—on the left, a round, white mask with blue lines radiating from the eyes and below the nose like an eerie cat; on the right, a longish, oval, yellow mask with baggy eyes and droopy ears like a whimpering puppy; and in the center, an elegant triangular mask, with red lips, small white nose, large almond eyes, all highlighted with gold paint as if to make the wearer an empress.

"Barbarian priest," the woman with the empress mask spoke in a clipped, direct fashion, as if informing a skilled craftsman that she intended to use his services if the price was right. "We are three women of standing. We have disguised our faces so that you will not know our names. You will not attempt to discover who we are. Do you understand?"

"Yes," he replied, knowing that it would be difficult, probably impossible, to ferret out the answer on his own. As a foreigner, he would almost never meet elite ladies. Furthermore, even if invited to a gentry home, he would never be involved in conversation with women. And even if he heard them speak, detecting female identities by voice recognition was quite beyond his linguistic competence.

"And you will never tell about meeting us. Just to make certain, we have prepared this little document." A servant handed him a stitched rice paper book. "It tells precisely what you are doing here in Suzhou. Trying to spread a new religion started by someone who claimed he was born as a supernatural spirit. Worshiping someone who rebelled against his government and his king. Praying to the image of a criminal who was nailed to a cross and left to die. We know that you and your other barbarian priests are trying to find influence in rich families. And we know you're using money from the textile and tea trade to pay for your insurrection."

"Not an insurrection at all. It's a noble cause. . . ."

"Silence!" Her voice sharpened and the two male servants moved to grab the priest. "No. Don't touch him. He will obey. Won't you, barbarian priest?"

Father Gao nodded glumly. Even by flickering oil-lamp light, he caught the gist of the text. Written in clear classical Chinese and illuminated by woodblocks, the book represented the Jesuits' greatest fear. Previous popular attacks had made ridiculous allegations, usually aimed at Franciscans, claiming that Christians worshiped pigs (since the word for "Lord" and the word for "pig" were pronounced the same, but with different tones) or the cutting out of children's eyes for sacrifices. Father Gao could easily refute those lies. But this booklet was much more devastating, telling the story of Christ in a basically accurate way, each episode seeming to add more fear to a Chinese heart. Christ did magic tricks to win popular support for a rebellion: walking on water, turning some bread and fish into a feast for a large crowd, healing sick people. And look how the rebels dressed like vagabonds. Their leader attacked honest businessmen exchanging money (a shocking thought in Ming China, where streetside bankers were central to the fluctuating silver and copper currency rates). Worse yet, the rebel was clearly in league with evil spirits, for how else could he be killed and come back as a ghost?

"Now, barbarian priest, I think we understand each other. One mistake and your entire corrupt movement, all the robed rebels in China, will be exposed."

Father Gao didn't protest. He knew he couldn't win if such a tract was released in a highly literate, gossip-loving society. "I understand. But what do you want from me?"

The three masked women leaned forward as if to make their own circle. Beads rattled and fans fluttered. A high-pitched child-like chatter ensued, a rapid-fire sequence of syllables wrapped in some strange chanted code. Cat nodded her head vehemently, rapping her folded fan against her hand, chirping away in staccato fashion. Puppy clearly disagreed, shaking her head and folding her arms, babbling her protests in a louder voice. Empress clicked her tongue rapidly, like a monkey demanding attention, and rapped her fan scepterlike against her chair. Then at a slower speed, Empress chanted more deliberately, in a lower voice. To Father Gao, all of it sounded like monkeys screeching. Finally Cat and Puppy nodded their heads, some strange agreement having been reached, and sat rigid once again.

Empress rested both hands on the chair arms and tittered at Father Gao's look of utter befuddlement. "Didn't understand a word, did you? That's why we use it. It's 'chamber chatter.' Girls of good breeding learn it when we're young. So we can talk without brothers or servants understanding. Now let me make it clear why we brought you here. You have something we want. Something no one else has."

"Really?"

"Yes, really. Firearms. Guns. Cannons. We want you to teach us how to make them. How to use them."

Father Gao's eyes opened wide. "Guns? I don't know a thing about them. I'm just a simple priest. A foolish barbarian priest, as you say." Surely it was a lie that Saint Ignatius would condone. How would it look to announce that Father Gao's band of criminals knew how to make the ultimate weapons that could topple the Dragon Throne?

"Do not lie to us. You do have this skill. We know it. Look at this!" A servant passed him an etching, slit carefully from one of Father Gao's books, depicting a small cannon being fired from a tripod by three Western soldiers, two aiming and supporting the contraption, while one lit the firing wick. Father Gao silently cursed the militancy of the Jesuit order—training in martial skills was supposed to protect the priesthood, not expose it to new violence. And how ironic that here in China, where gunpowder had been invented over five hundred years earlier, no one had exploited its military potential, content instead to perform the world's greatest peacetime fireworks displays.

"All right," he replied reluctantly. "I cannot deny it. I do know a little about firearms. But who wants to learn about them?"

"We do."

"You! Women?"

"Watch your tongue, barbarian. It's 'ladies.' Not just 'women.' Do you think we're so stupid that we couldn't learn such things?"

"No. No. Of course not. It's just that I thought that . . . that you ladies did not concern yourselves about such violent things as warfare." Were they rebels, Father Gao wondered, seeking to overthrow the government? That didn't make sense. They were indeed ladies. And it was their dynasty, the Ming, that thrived on the gentry life. Rebels would surely attack elites. So who were these strange ladies? What would they do with weapons more terrifying than any known in China's four millennia of recorded history?

"Well, barbarian, you're wrong. Wrong for now, anyway. Sometimes we have to leave our usual pursuits. Sometimes there are higher goals. . . ." Empress was cut short by a sharp hiss from Cat. Cat was clearly saying that the barbarian, and the servants, did not have to know the rationale for learning about firearms; they only had to fulfill their assigned roles.

"What is it exactly," Father Gao interceded, "that you wish me to do?" He looked closely at Empress, who had stiffened, ramrod-like, her head carried with regal certitude. She was trying to look so confident, so authoritative. It all seemed a sham to Father Gao, as if her forthright demeanor hid an inner uncertainty. Why had Empress wanted to reveal the cause? Ah, he surmised, it's the universal desire to show others that you're acting from noble motives, especially when your tactics seem suspect.

"Just as I said," continued Empress. "We wish you to teach us. How to make weapons. How to use weapons." She stared into his eyes, trying to ignore his heavy features and large nose, which distracted her. Eyes are mirrors to a man's soul, so her own mother had said. They were complex eyes, sometimes dark and piercing, sometimes softer and more consoling. Yes, she could feel it. Yes, he understood. They weren't rebels for selfish motives. They were fighters for a higher purpose. He did understand, didn't he?

"Teach you? You yourselves?" Stony silence answered his question. "Yes, yes, of course. Teach you. But how shall we do that? Where shall we do that?" Oh, dear Lord, he thought, for this I have given you my life? Teaching women how to kill? Western-style gunfire in the Celestial Kingdom? Introduced by peace-loving Jesuits? Oh Lord, please let there be some kernel of goodness in all this, he prayed silently.

"You will come every week, at a prescribed time and place, to instruct us in person. Meanwhile you will prepare lessons for us. Using diagrams as well as written materials. These you will give us a week in advance. . . ."

126

"In writing?"

"Yes," Empress replied hesitantly. "You must know our secret," she said with rising confidence bordering on pride. "We can all read and write. We all studied on our own. Sharing books and reading at night. Of course, you know what happens if you tell anyone. And they wouldn't believe you anyway."

"I understand." And so he did. Not only what she had said, but indeed even who she might be. She had no idea that her brother-in-law, now so long gone to the north, had revealed her most guarded secret, a secret that was coming perilously close to becoming common knowledge. Of course, Father Gao did not realize he was making a lucky guess since literate Chinese women were much more numerous than the Jesuits, whose contacts were primarily with elite men, ever imagined. Jesuits had accepted the female illiteracy stereotype as gospel truth, especially since it was true in many parts of Europe as well.

"Good," she said, beckoning the servants to help her down from her footstool and to stand on the floor. Cat and Puppy joined Empress in a shaky trio of footbound ladies. The flickering lamplight made them appear even less substantial, masked spirits who could be blown away by the slightest breeze.

"Come here." Empress beckoned and Father Gao complied, towering almost two feet above his diminutive hostesses. "Now give those materials to the servant." Father Gao handed over the anti-Jesuit tract and the snipped etching of artillery fire. "And take this." She handed him a silk *tao* binder containing a series of paperbacks. "And now, barbarian priest, next week this time. You may give the introductory class at that time. Please have the written materials for the following week as well. Total secrecy. Now you may leave."

As she nodded her dismissal, the two servants tugged Father Gao toward the door, opened it, and shoved him back into the street. By moonlight he could glimpse the bold characters on bound books—*A History of the Founding of the Illustrious Ming Dynasty*. He sighed in relief. It was a legitimate cause, the most legitimate cause of all. Loyalism was the highest Confucian virtue. Then he shuddered; had it really come to this? Was the Ming dynasty so near collapse that its women had to come to its rescue with the most unconventional weapons imaginable?

The Jesuit moved as stealthily as he could, cradling his unusual package, knowing that if he was caught, it would arouse enormous suspicion. Why would a barbarian be wandering about with a book that had near sacred significance? Was he on a dangerous mission? Why would anyone be slinking along darkened walls, a full hour after the curfew?

After he made it back safely, Father Gao sat for hours staring into the diffuse moonlight filtered through wet fog. He knew that when decaying dynasties fought for their lives against rising forces seeking to replace them, those were the times when Confucian principles were ultimately tested. Would you be loyal to the old rulers? Even as the cause seemed hopeless? Or would you switch sides, seeking to purify corrupt systems?

Father Gao suddenly knew that the time had come. These would be the questions testing Chinese elites in the mid-seventeenth century. The same questions would also test all Jesuits who sought access at the highest levels. Which side would the Jesuits choose? For Father Gao, there was no choice anymore. Some little ladies of Suzhou had made the decision for him. But could it be that they were doing the will of the Lord? Could guns possibly make for converts?

The Jesuits as a whole would probably treat the coming conflict like a horse race, Father Gao surmised, putting bets on several contenders. But he wondered what would happen to individual Jesuits, especially those who backed losing horses. For now, Father Gao was clearly linked with the Ming loyalists, an alliance that could cost his head if the Manchus won the empire. He would teach the ladies for now, but he would keep his eyes open, bolting if it looked like their cause was hopeless. Beijing—that's where he would go if he had to, that's where he could test the political winds far better than in the passionately loyalist Yangtze Delta region.

Beijing, Father Gao thought, and smiled, that was where Longyan had finally met with success. The Jesuit postal service, itinerant priests carrying letters, gave him regular reports. "An exemplary officer" was what the stolen Green Standard evaluation form had revealed about "Captain Wang." It *was* the right decision—Father Gao crossed himself—at least in the short run. But what if—the priest shuddered—Longyan is fighting on the wrong side, an excellent soldier in a futile mission? It was Father Gao's advice that had pushed him into the military and, if it ever became bad counsel, Father Gao vowed to do what he could to rectify the situation. After all, Longyan was almost like an adopted son, at least in the Jesuit's imagination. He had to care for him, not as priest but as father.

Black clouds seeped across the sky, obliterating all light, making it impossible to read even the title of the book that still lay on his lap. The darkness eclipsed the character "Ming," so no one could see its two components, the sun and the moon, together meaning "bright."

CHAPTER ELEVEN

Defeat

明

One Year Later:
Beijing, Shanhaiguan, and Suzhou, 1641

NOT UNTIL LATE 1641, after two momentous years in which threats to the Ming dynasty reached crisis proportions, did Longyan communicate with Meihua again. When he finally wrote, it unleashed a six-month correspondence burst with two letters on each side.

> My Dearest Sister-in-Law:
> It has been a while since I have written. You must be very angry with me. I have been exceptionally busy. Can you believe the progress I have made? I am already a captain in the Beijing Imperial Guards Detachment of the Green Standard Army.

"Be sure you give my proper military title," Longyan counseled the letter writer, who would be paid well for his services and for his confidence. Unemployed secretaries were even easier to find in Beijing than Suzhou; and they tended to be trustworthy when writing for military officers whose swords were sharp and tempers often quick.

Why hadn't he written before? He had been preoccupied, but, to be honest, not so busy as not to write at all. Maybe it was that he had to make sure the letter would go through Father Gao safely. But that was all arranged before he left Suzhou. The truthful answer was that he didn't quite know what to write. He had cut loose from Suzhou and all its associations. Reviving the flow of letters, at least before he was established in Beijing, seemed like backtracking. He had done what he could for Meihua as a caring brother-in-law, or so he argued to himself; any more might have seemed to court a more intimate relationship. What more to say?

Angry? How can you suggest it? I have been so busy myself, there's no time for anything. Certainly not anger. I am so happy for you. What progress you are making.

Angry? I'm irate! she really thought. For months, we are in constant contact. You show more care for me than for any other living being. Then nothing? You don't even wonder how I'm doing? And you don't even give me an address to write you? Longyan, I cursed you every day. You take the sun out of my life and then ask if I'm cold.

Dear sister, you probably wouldn't care to learn much about what I'm doing, but I really like being an officer. The officer training program at the academy is quite demanding—military history, tactics, battlefield command along with more practical training in horsemanship, archery, swordplay. I have a real knack for all this.

Knack? What an understatement! mused Longyan as he dictated. I was 1640 Cadet of the Year. I can't tell her that because she'll think I'm only a soldier. Maybe it's true, maybe this is my calling, maybe it's all I can do. Everything depends on memorizing visual things—charts, maps, organization lists—and then on making good decisions about people. It's mainly lectures, fieldwork, direct observation—very little reading and writing.

Actually most officers are failed scholars, he thought. A lot of these are really hopeless. Many have problems of motivation, some with limited intelligence, so I really am in a different situation. I work harder and use some skills that never worked with Tutor Lu.

Longyan longed to tell Meihua everything that had happened to him, everything he was thinking:

On our first border patrol, unbelievably, the major in command got us lost in the middle of the night, very close to a Manchu guerrilla area. We couldn't light a torch, of course, that's the best way to lose your life. But I had the entire map memorized. So it was simple to get us back to camp by dawn. Now they call me "picture-brain"—with respect, of course. Senior officers invite me to play *weiqi* with them, to sharpen their skills. No one believes that everything sticks up in my head. Sometimes I don't quite believe it either.

But I like thinking about tactics most of all. A fortnight ago, I commanded a small cavalry unit supported by foot soldiers, thirty men in all. We captured a Chinese rebel group of more than fifty, killing twenty in battle and imprisoning the rest. Know how I did it? Not by fighting a frontal battle, as some suggested. Instead I looked at a map of the area north of Beijing and south of the Great Wall. The whole area has hills and mountains, interspersed with farms, here and there a little stream or small pond. Water is the absolute necessity for soldiers, so I looked on the map where rebels might camp, close to water, but presumably protected. And I found it: a remote and concealed rocky canyon, a quarter mile from a stream. The rest was easy. We positioned ourselves around the rim of the canyon at night, shot fire-tipped arrows into their tents, and captured them as they tried to flee. The whole trick was to think about a map differently, to put myself in the rebel commander's mind. My commander called the tactic "brilliant" and gave me a commendation; it just seemed obvious to me.

Oh, Meihua, I wish I could tell you all this. I really miss you. Sometimes, late at night, I just chatter away to myself, pretending you're listening. I know it's silly, but it helps me anyway. And I can be completely honest. And you always understand. In my imagination, of course. Such were Longyan's thoughts as their correspondence continued.

Meihua wrote:

> *It's rumored that the Ming armies are collapsing. Surrendering to all of the rebels and barbarians. The court is said to be filled with corruption. Can it be true? Tell me it's not.*

It's not true! I've seen nothing of the sort! Ming soldiers are proud and loyal. Yes, we've had a few defeats. And, yes, maybe there is some corruption. But we are not collapsing.

These rumors! Longyan thought to himself. Maybe it's true about what happens inside the Forbidden City. Who can say? I hear the same things. Eunuchs, corrupt officials, graft, parties day and night. The Emperor is said never to tire of virgin women, so they're brought from every province. But it could just be a rumor. And maybe it's usually like this in the palace.

But it's not true in the army. At least not in my part of the army. We're proud troops in the great tradition of Gen. Yuan Chong-huan. Everyone knows he was falsely accused and executed ten years ago. But before he died, he showed the general staff how to defend the strategic passes, how to keep the barbarians bottled up.

We've won a lot of battles. In fact, I myself went north of the wall last year, he yearned to tell Meihua. We surprised three de-tachments, two Manchu and one Mongol, killing hundreds and imprisoning the rest. In fact, I used another trick based on the avail-ability of food and supplies. In a hundred-mile radius, I plotted the market towns on a map, then worked out the weekly cycle of markets so we knew when the farmers would be going to various locations. I knew that was just what the Manchus were thinking: go for easy food in large quantities. We attacked them just as they were sacking the foodstalls.

So we're holding our own. Why all these stupid rumors? Long-yan fumed silently. Well, I've got to admit it's not all lies about military weakness. Eunuchs eat up half the defense budget. Lots of defeats have occurred. The Manchus are right at the wall (they weren't anywhere near it a decade ago). Rebels control half the empire. And the Ming would lose a lot more battles if the troops actually fought, rather than retreating as soon as there's a skirmish.

Collapsing? That's an overstatement. But we've got to get things together. New leadership. A few fresh victories. Some bright re-cruits. We'll win. I'm sure of it.

Meihua had written:

> *My life is so much better. Your stratagem, like a good military plan, worked so well. Now I can devote myself to supporting our honorable Matriarch. I also try to provide help to your noble brother, Xinping. I'm sure he has a fine career ahead. But his*

health hasn't been perfect. We're hopeful he will improve as the weather becomes warmer.

Why worry Longyan? Meihua thought. Actually now it was Xinping who worried everybody. Six months ago he had failed the lower-level civil service examination for the third time. Everyone was devastated, particularly the Matriarch, who privately worried that her blood would be blamed for watering down a scholarly family. The Patriarch accused no one, but fretted about that old Chinese proverb about how families go from poverty to wealth and back in three generations.

Why did Xinping fail? I know why, thought Meihua. He's just not all that smart. He can't memorize all those passages. And then he panics in the examination. Which makes his calligraphy terrible. I wish I could take the tests for him.

Xinping is very sick. He's really sick this time. Not just faking to avoid the tests. Dr. Long isn't sure what it is. Terrible fevers, sweating, cramps. He hallucinates at night. And those awful sores on his arms and legs, red blotches that ooze white pus. The doctor sees him twice a day—acupuncture, moxabustion, herbal drugs—but no improvement.

It's "bad *qi*"—bad spiritual essence—the doctor says, "no known cure." I know twenty people—rich people, not commoners—who are deathly ill. I know at least five who have died, and their family members are sometimes too ill to attend the funeral. Is it those terrible Manchus? Or maybe the pirates? Do they bring sick spirits, bad *qi,* from abroad? Will it kill Xinping too?

Longyan wrote:

> I wish that father could understand. I hear so much good about him up here. All the reformers miss him terribly. I'm trying to do his bidding, defending the court as best I can. I'm not a scholar. But I'm also not a failure. Sometimes those who cannot serve in other ways must take up arms.

If only father could really understand how much I have learned from his old associates about the horrible situation he faced two decades back, Longyan wished to himself. "Your father was just this far," old Jin had told him while he held up two fingers, barely separated, "from becoming the ranking grand secretary, the most powerful official adviser to the throne. But all it took was a campaign of rumors started by the eunuchs. 'Corrupt, biased, disloyal.' And so he is but a footnote in history."

Old Jin, once his father's private secretary, was now unemployed and made a sparse income by advising incoming officials and foreign tributaries on how to use influence in Beijing. He had tracked Longyan down, both to hear about the Patriarch and to see if he could pry free some cash by arousing guilt and pity. "What a laugh." The old man had coughed out his words. "If I had any influence left I'd use it myself. I would have followed your father to the end of the earth. But when the Donglin purge began, it was almost just that. The end of values. The floodgates of corruption were opened."

Can't Father see it? Longyan wondered. The Green Standard Army is all that holds the rebels and barbarians at bay. You can't cleanse a dynasty that doesn't exist anymore. You can fret in Suzhou. But the only hope for the Ming is here in Beijing. I haven't compromised anything. You have to have control before you can rule. Please understand, he'd beg his father in his thoughts.

Old Jin had also said something strange. "Do you know the truth about your father?" he'd asked.

"What truth?" Longyan had wondered aloud.

"It's just that . . . well, your father gave everything to try to fulfill his father's dream. The dream of bringing back high-minded values to government. He did *everything* imaginable to make his father proud of him."

"What's *everything*?" Longyan asked.

"If you don't know, I cannot be the one to tell you. You'll probably find out some day."

Longyan, deeply puzzled, had pressed a sack of copper coins into the old man's hand as he left. Oh, Father, Longyan fretted, I wish I was there to ask you. What was the *everything* you sacrificed for your father? Tell me. And I'm ready to give still more. I'm not a loser. I don't lack courage. Really I don't. Maybe you'll see it someday. Longyan's yearning was nearly a torment.

Meihua had written: *"Whether your father understands or not, I do understand. The dynasty needs fighters."*

★ ★ ★

"This is the hardest part," Father Gao's words echoed in the damp cave, as he kneeled within a semicircle of more than fifty women. The cave was Meihua's idea. Once the hideout for Tang dynasty rebels, it was the perfect place for target practice, rocks and hay-bales at the cave mouth muffled the gunpowder explosions. No one wore masks anymore. Father Gao wasn't about to talk; his life and his church depended on silent obedience.

"Hold it still. Hold it firmly. Keep your aim. Light the fuse. Don't move. Don't—"

A blinding flash was followed by a deafening boom. The kick threw Meihua backwards, still holding the muzzle loader and its iron tripod, knocking over at least ten women as she flew. The lead ball smashed into the cave ceiling, dropping several stalactites to the stone floor. The women, who were splayed about like toppled dominoes, struggled to right themselves, no mean feat given their bound feet, which they sought to conceal from male observation.

"What's so funny?" Meihua spoke sharply to Father Gao, who was doubled over in laughter. She tried in vain to wipe the dirt from her gown, unaware that her face was covered with black gun-powder soot.

"I'm sorry, my lady," he chortled, "but it does appear that you're doing more damage to your own forces than to the enemy."

Meihua was not amused. "We shall try this again. Right now."

And so she did, until she could hit the straw effigy every time. So did every woman, twice a week, until a crack musket unit had emerged. The training also encompassed Western-style military drill using light foils rather than heavier sabers, and several women became quite adept at fencing in spite of their crippled state.

"That's stupid," Meihua retorted when Father Gao showed her books on fixed-position warfare. "It's easy to beat them. Just hide on the flanks. Shoot them like ducks. You could win with less than half their troops."

"But that's not what is accepted!"

"Accepted where? Surely not here. Our enemies do not wait for everyone to line up neatly!"

Since she deemed Father Gao useless on tactics in a Chinese setting, Meihua read Sun Zi's *Art of War* late into the nights. It was here that she learned of surprise attacks, of strategic retreats, of ex-ploiting weakness, of military intelligence, of safe combat odds.

How strange are these barbarians, Meihua thought. They invent the ultimate weapon, then they stand in rows to see if they can blow each other up. And they think us odd for using gunpowder solely for peaceful purposes.

It was also Meihua who designed the uniform: black cotton, loose-fitting shirt and trousers, matching booties to cover bound feet. The character *de* was embroidered in white on the back of the shirt, meaning both "virtue" and "achievement."

The women's detachment—fifty literate officers—would be known as the *Dejun,* the Virtuous Army. It was an army with two enormous strengths. First, its very existence was a total secret—it had to be because no Confucian father or husband would think of tolerating a woman in military service. None of the women could possibly reveal her new hobby. Males simply beamed when they found out how popular was the new Ladies' Filial Piety Society— how nice that the womenfolk had a new diversion at a stressful time. And, just as important, it was an army with great recruiting potential. No one knew how big the Virtuous Army might grow. The junior officers—sisters of the original recruits—could number in the hundreds. And the rank-and-file soldiers—trusted female servants of the elite families—might even reach to the thousands. So, unlike the other Ming armies, where attrition and desertion were decimating the ranks, the Virtuous Army had numbers on its side.

Longyan wrote to Meihua:

> I shall not be returning to Suzhou, not until we can guar-
> antee the fate of the dynasty. I'll be stationed in a location
> I cannot reveal. I am not sure if I'll be able to write.

Shanhaiguan, that's the location, the most crucial pass where the Great Wall meets the sea, Longyan mused. We're throwing our best troops against the Manchus at the wall, hoping to hold the dike against the barbarian pressure. I get to command—underscore *command*—an infantry company armed with bows, spears, and swords. It's a wonderful opportunity. I report directly to Gen. Wu Sangui, the Green Standard's most famous field commander.

If only we can do this right, what a coup for the Ming dynasty! What no one can do with a brush, I can do with a sword. The

Manchus will be bottled up in their own homeland. We'll first isolate them, then exterminate them. Beijing will be saved, then we can concentrate our efforts on the rebels and the pirates. Can you imagine the welcome-home celebration in Suzhou?

> *We women tremble in fright. We cannot know what men know,*
> *but we must feel the emotions that men repress. It is an awful fate*
> *to be helpless. Some must think for us. Others fight for us.*

Meihua smiled at the helpless image as she wrote. It would surely appeal to the Longyan the commander. And it was a deft way to deflect suspicion if the letter was discovered. But it was unlikely that anyone other than Longyan would read it. She knew that Father Gao would be especially careful to send the letter "Jesuit express," a trusted courier moving up the Grand Canal, under the care of priests each night, an armed guard offering protection at all times. That's the way Jesuits send all their messages, and all their income, Meihua reflected. If they lose my letter, they'll also starve. Besides, if someone reads my letter, they'll be more likely to target the Jesuits than the dainty daughters of Suzhou gentry families.

Almost miraculously, Meihua's letter arrived only two days before Longyan led his infantry company through Beijing's great Eastern Gate to begin the weeklong march of hundred and fifty miles to Shanhaiguan. He dissected the letter at night, under the flickering oil lights in camp, in the privacy of his circular white-canvas tent, sole occupancy of a tent being a right of rank.

Longyan preferred the long hours alone, struggling to memorize the letter, rather than seeking the distracting presence of a camp-following prostitute. While sleeping with whores was seen as a privilege of officership (or for common soldiers who had won enough gambling to purchase the pleasure), Longyan liked to set an example for his subordinates. He desisted not on moral grounds—indeed his exploits in the pleasure districts of both Suzhou and Beijing were legendary (at least as he told them). Rather he chose solitude on military grounds. Good soldiers, he'd been taught, were well rested, slightly on edge, and healthy, hardly the product of long bouts with women of the evening.

By day Captain Wang Longyan rode a stocky, smallish black

horse, one of the dwindling number of riding animals still available in Beijing, heading a column of 500 lesser officers and foot soldiers. Unlike the often ragtag Ming troops sent off to engage rebels and pirates in the south, Longyan's company represented the best of what was left to defend the throne, soldiers who had actually trained for several months, directed by sergeants who knew how to use swords, pikes, and bows.

The Twenty-eighth Infantry Company—of the famous Seventh Foot Battalion, which had been crucial to the fourteenth-century Ming consolidation of power—now trudged eastward on muddy, pockmarked country roads. When the path veered to the south, the soldiers threaded their way along tightly planted fields of wheat and sorghum, skirting the marshlands that marked the northern rim of China's great plain of arable land. When the road turned north, they groaned their way up and down the foothills of the great mountain ranges and plateaus, a great wrinkled uplifting of landscape that meandered from southern Manchuria all the way southwestward to the Himalayan chain. What looked so pristine on a map offered an endless chain of obstacles to the marching troops. "Fucking mosquitoes and lice to the right, crummy rocks and cliffs to the left," in the words of one sergeant.

Each day en route left its own deep impression of the disasters confronting the Ming dynasty. Scorching thousands of acres of earth, a ruthless effort to hold the Manchus at bay, proved fruitless because the invaders had massive farms just north of the Great Wall tilled by captured Chinese slave labor. A dozen severed heads, impaled on tall pikes at the edge of a village, grinned a fearsome warning of what might happen to those who resisted Manchu troops. Perhaps most chilling was the total absence of live people; everyone had been removed by imperial command, had fled before the advancing armies, or had been cut down by the weapons of war. The remaining contest was among the flies, jackals, and blackbirds devouring the remains of crops and corpses.

Would I have written so confidently to Meihua, Longyan wondered privately, if I'd visited this hellish scene earlier? Are we all that stands between a sick dynasty and a ruthless band of barbarians? Just our little company, and a few like us, throwing our puny shoulders against the floodgates?

Finally Captain Wang stopped his troops on a small hillock

where, in the late afternoon sun, they surveyed the sinewy path of the Great Wall as it snaked out of the sea and wound its way to the West. They were mesmerized by the heavy gray wall that had been built two thousand years earlier; a military barrier that had been breached hundreds of times by invading armies; a cultural barrier that was the ultimate symbol of Chinese arrogance, the dividing line between civilization and barbarism. In spite of its unimpressive military history, the Great Wall infused the little company of foot soldiers with new confidence. It looked impregnable.

"Wash up, now," Captain Wang gave his orders. "Dress uniforms. We're going to look like soldiers."

An hour later, Longyan proudly led his detachment into the encampment on the edge of Shanhaiguan, a small town that had sprouted around the gate controlling traffic between China proper and southern Manchuria. On the ramparts above the gate, fluttering in the early evening breeze, was a huge imperial banner, a wriggling, yellow, five-clawed dragon embroidered on gossamer red silk. The Ming emperor's most famous general, Wu Sangui, was on duty, protecting the vital organs of the Middle Kingdom, guarding the main artery that led to the Forbidden City.

"See, men," Captain Wang shouted, "there isn't anything to worry about. You think some bad-breath barbarian with pigtails could break through this?"

A fortnight later, Captain Wang was still beaming with confidence. And why not? He had suddenly entered the elite ranks of the Ming military. He was present when General Wu presided personally over the officers' mess, sharing anecdotes of campaigns across the empire, exuding conviction that he could crush the throne's enemies.

"Never forget," the General gestured with his chopsticks, a marinated "drunken prawn" between them, "the Manchu is illiterate and boorish, but he's not stupid. He'll attack precisely when you least expect it. Always distrust moments of utter calm, especially north of the wall. It's the eye of the typhoon. It's always deathly quiet just before the Manchu strikes. And if the barbarian captures you, you're better off dead."

Total silence spread across the regal dining room, which was usually occupied by Ming princes on holiday. The clicking of chopsticks and tinkling of glasses stopped totally as dozens of officers reflected on the General's chilling words.

"Oh, come now, what's all this quiet?" the General joked. "Are you testing my theory? Silence before the storm? Remember, you have the edge. You have fine troops and imperial training. You're fighting for the glory of civilization. And you have the total support of those beneath the wall. You'll do your duty. And we'll win."

The officers cheered loudly, raising glasses of clear sorghum liquor, a mass toast to their commander and to their dynasty. "Long life to the Emperor!" shouted General Wu.

"Long life to the Emperor!" they cheered in unison. "Long life, long life, long long life!"

"So you're Grand Secretary Wu's son?" General Wu asked Longyan as the mess was dismissed.

"Yes. Yes, sir," Longyan responded. Actually, Longyan had wondered whether he should tell the real truth, that he was the *disowned* son of *disgraced* former Grand Secretary Wu. Did the General know the truth anyway?

"He's a fine man, your father. We lost a lot when he left Beijing. And of course, I know what's going through your head," the General said smilingly.

"Sir?"

"Your father is both a model and a heavy burden. Yes? You want to do your father proud. You want to show him that you're a worthy son. Right?"

"Yes, sir." How did he know? Who had told him?

"And you want to show him that a soldier can do something as important as a scholar?" Look at the poor fellow's eyes, the General thought to himself, not smugly, just matter-of-factly. How do I know all of this? It's so easy. *Every* young officer has precisely the same story. I always get the same response. And they don't tell each other because I always add my little final plea. "Captain Wang," the General continued. "I do understand. Believe me, I really do. And I won't inform your fellow officers. We all have our weaknesses."

"Oh, thank you, sir. Really, sir. Thank you."

"And Captain, just one more thing. You will move out in the morning. At dawn. You'll support the blockade of the main road— the second section twenty miles north of the wall—against any enemy movement. We have other companies stationed every mile or so to a depth of a hundred miles. Like links in a chain. Don't let it break. Don't let us down. Make your father proud."

"Yes, sir."

It had been so easy. Two days' march northward on the Shanhaiguan-Shenyang highway and not even a glimpse of enemy soldiers. Heavily armed Ming guard posts sprouted every few hundred yards on both sides of the road. Small Ming detachments combed the surrounding countryside, sweeping the rocky, sandy ground down to the sea, searching the greener wheatfields to the west. Greener still were the Ming banners fluttering above a profusion of garrisons and campsites.

No one was trying to hide the Ming troops. In fact, Gen. Wu Sangui's orders had been clear: "A total show of force. We'll try to frighten them with our numbers. And it will bolster our boys' courage."

By the evening of the second day, as a soft mist cooled the day's bright sunshine, Captain Wang's company was encamped in a classic defensive posture, just under the top of a ridge. Guards screened the hillside above and below the camp; tents dotted a flat plateau, far enough apart not to make easy targets, close enough together so soldiers could rally quickly if attacked. Fires were kept burning so other detachments, camped less than a mile away, could see all was well; the hills flickered their flames like tiny fireflies in darkened bushes. The guards marched slowly, well away from the tents and from the flames that might have affected night vision, scanning the rocky granite slopes and the scrub-pine forests for any movement.

Even four hours after dark, Longyan couldn't sleep. He leaned against a whitish boulder at the perimeter of the camp, away from the fires, hiding his anxious insomnia. What was it? Why couldn't he sleep? The encampment was textbook perfect: a high vantage point, clear views on all sides, easy to protect. Besides, it was hardly a remote location; Ming troops were swimming the rippled south Manchurian plain.

So what was it, then? Loneliness? No, Longyan shook his head. He liked the aloofness of command. He felt he had finally come of age; he had a mission, he was responsible for others, and he was finally responsible for himself as well. Well, maybe a little loneliness, a little homesickness. Oh, if there was only someone he could tell, someone who would understand all this. If only Meihua were here. . . .

Longyan stopped his train of thought. He was sensing something else. Longyan felt a tingling on his skin as if the tiny hairs on his arms were suddenly antennae reaching into the low-hanging mist. He cocked his ear. Did he hear something? No, nothing. Nothing at all. Just a total silence that enveloped the camp. Utter stillness. A quiet so total that it was overwhelming.

But what was it that General Wu had said? What had he said about silence? A shudder shot through Longyan's limbs. He jumped up and, almost involuntarily, scrambled down the embankment toward the tents. He was about to shout a warning, but it was too late.

The camp exploded into a chaos of shouts, screams, and flames. Manchu horsemen thundered through the tents, trampling startled soldiers, clubbing those who tried to flee, cutting those who remained to pieces with broadswords. The tents burst into shooting flames as burning campfire logs were thrown into them, and several Ming soldiers ran like screaming fireballs in their ignited night clothing. From the ridgetop came a barrage of arrows, whining like a bevy of hummingbirds, impaling soldiers who tried to escape the fray. The iron-tipped willow arrows, driven with enormous power from hide-backed recurve bows, dropped men in their tracks, struggling to pull the shafts from their arms, legs, necks, and stomachs. It was easy for Manchu foot soldiers to rush in and hack away at the wounded figures writhing on the ground.

Longyan, still wearing his captain's uniform, instinctively pulled his sword and rushed into the fray. Somehow the Manchus sensed that he was in command, and they encircled him with their horses until several foot soldiers disarmed him, shoved a pole behind his back, and pinned his arms to it with heavy hemp rope. In total shock, Longyan was kicked and prodded away from the camp.

As dawn came, Longyan found himself in a deep forest, surrounded by foot soldiers, trudging behind a column of cavalry through a narrow path. It was difficult to navigate with the heavy pole, which hit trees and rocks, chafing at his arms. Longyan looked back and absorbed the dimensions of his defeat—only three officers and twenty or so soldiers were taken prisoner. Were the others all dead? Had some been taken for slaves?

Oh, how had this happened? Oh, heaven, was everything lost? After all the training, what had gone wrong? The Manchus pushed onward in a forced march, jabbing prisoners with the blunt ends of battle pikes. They didn't understand his Chinese, but they taunted him with Manchu invectives. The soldiers appeared fearsome in their tunics, with heavy belts, big boots over cotton pants, heads shaven except for a long pigtail hanging down in back. Their bodies were bigger than those of the Han Chinese, their faces more sharply angular, their muscles taut from a lifetime of nomadic military service.

"Quit shoving me. Don't you understand. I'm Captain Wang Longyan, company commander, Ming Green Standard Army. You stupid barbarians. You stupid barbarians!"

The more he protested, the more the Manchus mocked him, one of them standing at attention and whining in unison with Longyan's cries. Then, abruptly, his tormenters quieted and backed away, all of them looking at a powerful Manchu on a black horse. He wore a conical black hat with a jade ball at the top, a yellow and black silk coat with horsehoof-shaped sleeves that covered his hands, and highly polished leather boots. His face had nobility written all over it: tight, smooth flesh; sharp, clean bones; and coal black eyes that could have pierced iron. He stepped down from his horse and walked up to Longyan, their faces but a few inches from each other.

"Ah, Captain Wang," the Manchu said in fluent but accented Chinese. "So sorry we have had to treat you so, how to say, ungraciously? But then, we are at war, after all, and sadly it appears you have lost a skirmish. I trust you're not too uncomfortable."

"No," mumbled Longyan, blood dripping from raw sores on his arms and wrists.

"Ah, how discourteous of me not to introduce myself. I am known as Dorbo. Like you I command this detachment. I fear I outrank you—I'm a major in the Bordered Yellow Banner Forces—it's the highest unit you know, the Emperor's own banner."

"Emperor?"

144

"Of course, Emperor Taizong. Of the Qing dynasty. The *Pure* dynasty. The one that will soon replace your own."

"Never!"

"I see. You assume that—what is it you call us? ah yes, 'barbarians'—could never overrun your precious empire.'

"Right. Never!"

"But then, Captain Wang, your own little setback today hardly augurs well for the Ming cause. In any case, someday you'll join us. I know you will."

"Never!" Longyan drew himself up as well as he could and glared raw hatred at Major Dorbo.

"No? I'm going to give you a chance to join us right now. You and your officers. Just say the word we'll welcome your services. If not, it distresses me to tell you, but we are going to have to execute some of your troops."

"I spit on you, barbarian."

Major Dorbo pointed to a shivering private, whose eyes opened wide in panic as his feet were tied to a tree, his arms to a horse. As the horse was slowly prodded by its rider, the private's shoulders and hips dislocated from their sockets, his gagging screams drowning out the animal's whinnying. Suddenly the horse lunged forward, pulling the blood-spurting remainders of the victim's body, two legs left at the tree, only one arm still attached by a few shreds of sinew. The corpse lay still, mouth open in a silent scream of death.

"Now perhaps, my dear Captain, a different answer?"

"You sick, ugly pig. The answer is the same."

The Major gestured toward another soldier, who was grabbed as he tried to run off in terror. His arms were bound to a large tree, then his legs, so he faced the Manchus, struggling to free himself from the ropes. Several of the Manchu soldiers surrounded the tree and began a macabre dance, weaving around their captive, singing what seemed to be a boisterous drinking song. At the end of each verse, instead of drinking wine, the soldier who stopped directly in front of the Ming private was required to invent his own form of torture. The first teased him with a knife, pricking his arms, ears, and legs, prompting him to writhe and scream, causing the Manchu troops to laugh that he reacted to such slight injury. Subsequent soldiers became more and more vicious, eventually cutting off fingers at the joints, sticking knives into his armpits, knees, and groin, the torture continuing even after the victim passed out. One Manchu, seemingly inebriated from the delirious frenzy, swung his sword, slicing off the soldier's head, impaling it on the tip, and waving it about to cheering troops.

"And now, noble Captain, what is our answer?"

Longyan held back the bile rising from his stomach. "It's the same, you sick dog."

"I'm impressed by your fortitude. But also by your stupidity. Are all the sons of Han idiots?" Major Dorbo eyed Longyan for a moment. Realizing that his opponent was not about to change his mind, the Manchu snapped an order that Longyan couldn't understand. The soldiers laughed in unison, then grabbed at various of the Ming captives, making each think he was the next to be tortured. Only as the convoy pushed ahead on the path did the screams abate to whimpers, everyone relieved that their captors seemed sated for the moment.

For two days, Longyan was prodded up a narrowing trail, through dense forests, across boggy meadows, along rocky paths in the southern Manchurian foothills. Still up they went, scrambling over boulder-strewn meadows, through craggy passes, along precarious footholds carved into granite cliffs. Finally, Longyan limped into the Manchus' mountain headquarters on a high plateau guarded by black walls of rock. The grassy edges of the plateau were grazing lands for thousands of horses, cattle, and sheep. Across a cold, steel blue lake was the encampment—clusters of small *yurt* tents, rounded poles covered by hides, centered around three huge tents, half-barrel-shaped longhouses where the nobility and senior officers lived, ate, and governed.

Children ran alongside the convoy, greeting fathers and brothers, jeering at the Ming soldiers. Teenaged boys, garbed in dark cotton pants and tunics, ran back and forth in deerskin moccasins, pelting prisoners with sharp pebbles, cheering when a direct hit was scored on a head or face. Across soggy, spring-fed wetlands, well away from the tents, was a flat shelf of hard, yellow rock where, from a distance, it appeared that people were resting on their backs in the noonday sun. Only as the convoy came closer was the grisly truth revealed: the sunbathers were actually Ming soldiers, shackled to the rocks, left to be slowly picked apart by ants, birds, coyotes,

146

and mountain lions. Most of the bodies were already corpses, but some still moaned in agony, unable to see through sun-scorched eyes.

Longyan and his half-dead survivors were thrown into a large, rectangular pit, with walls thirty feet high, that was cut from the earth and granite and covered by a crosshatch of rawhide-tied poles to make an escape-proof prison. Scraggly bodies huddled on the floor of the pit, scarcely noticing the new arrivals, only groaning as their infested skins were bumped. The stench of excrement and rotting skin was overwhelming, causing the new prisoners to add their vomit to the fetid air.

"Oh, Captain," Major Dorbo called from horseback down to the pit. "Welcome to our little guest house. Sorry it's not up to your standards. No one escapes from here. And everyone dies. Slowly or quickly, that's the only choice."

"You sick, disgusting pig!" Longyan shouted back. "That's why we fight you. You have to be taught culture."

"*We* have to be taught culture?" The Major laughed. "It would appear *you* need to be taught how to fight. And that, in fact, is your only hope. If you defect, we'll make you a Chinese bannerman, same rank as you now have. And we'll even allow you to pick five of your soldiers. They too will live and fight on our side."

Longyan heard the hopeful murmuring of his men. He paused for a moment. Then he said firmly, "No! Never! You Manchus have the brains of the donkeys who were your mothers!"

CHAPTER TWELVE

Death
明

The Next Two Years:
Manchuria and Suzhou, 1642–1643

MEIHUA HAD A lot to smile about. It was a warm November, at least so far, with just a hint of winter frost in the air. While Suzhou women often fretted about cold weather, the onset of winter had never bothered Meihua much, not in the Yangtze basin, where soft-coal heaters drove away the drafts and where it almost never snowed. But this year was different. Good conditions were essential for the outdoor training of the Virtuous Army. Bound feet were impossible on ice, and besides, who would believe that a bevy of elite women wanted to dash outdoors in winter storms?

Meihua also had a lot to worry about. She was on her own now, even since Father Gao had left for Beijing in August. He begged her to let him go north, arguing that he had taught her all he knew and that he could offer much better secret intelligence from the capital city. She consented reluctantly, urging him also to let her know how Longyan was really doing; unfortunately Father Gao arrived in Beijing a month after Longyan had left for Shanhaiguan and Manchuria.

The priest wondered if Meihua had guessed the real reason he requested going to Beijing. All priests had received encoded orders from the Jesuit command center in Beijing:

CLEAR–CUT EVIDENCE THAT MING DYNASTY WILL SOON FALL. DO NOT ENDANGER OUR POSITION WITH OVERLY CLOSE TIES TO HIGH MING OFFICIALS OR TO STRONG ADVOCATES OF THE MING LOYALIST CAUSE. THOSE WHO FEEL COMPROMISED IN PROVINCES SHOULD COME TO BEIJING

AT ONCE. ESTABLISH NO NEW ALLIANCES. WE SHALL ALL
WAIT AND SEE.

Father Gao was hardly surprised at the message, but he was surprised at his reaction. Months of training the Virtuous Army left him emotionally on the side of Suzhou's ladies, in spite of the impossible odds against them. "You now have the ability to fight," Father Gao counseled the officers in a farewell comment, "but knowing when to fight—and when *not* to fight—is the real test of military judgment." He hoped they would never fire those weapons in combat, both to prevent what might be terrible carnage to them and to avoid implicating him as their secret instructor. Besides, he worried that the origin of the firearms might be traced: first to the small iron foundry outside Suzhou that manufactured the tripod-mounted muskets (the ironsmith himself was Peach Blossom's uncle and owed the Lin family countless favors) and then to the actual European prototypes, which were kept disassembled and hidden by various Jesuit fathers.

Meihua was left in sole command of the biweekly meetings of the Ladies' Filial Piety Society. As ranking officer—now with the title "Major Lin," using her maiden name rather than that of her husband's family—she directed eight captains, sixteen lieutenants, and over eighty sergeants. It was an army of female officers, many of whom proved adept students, especially on the musket range, which became the test of competence and toughness. No one dared flinch when the powder was ignited; most could hit a straw effigy at forty paces at least seven times out of ten. To avoid arousing suspicion about their military practice sessions, the women renovated a abandoned Lin family guest house as the Filial Piety Society gathering place. The old guest house, where Father Gao had once met the masked ladies, was but a few hundred yards beneath the cave in an uninhabited section of Suzhou's outskirts. And the carefully concealed cave mouth faced away from the city so that the muffled explosions could not be heard.

"We've been lucky so far. But the cold weather will soon be here." Meihua addressed her black-uniformed officers, standing at attention in neat rows in front of her. "And so will the enemy. Intelligence reports indicate that Li Zicheng's rebels are already in northern Jiangsu. And Manchu detachments have raided several towns in Shandong."

Meihua's "intelligence" was derived from the Jesuit network, picked up by Father Gao in Beijing, then relayed by priests down the post road and the Grand Canal. All messages were encoded in the Jesuit "barbarian" system—using Chinese characters (foreign-language messages would surely be confiscated), written with countless mistakes typical of non-Chinese writers (the trick was to count the actual mistakes to find out which characters should actually be read).

"We will suspend training only if the weather turns really bad. But even then we won't waste time. You will all begin recruiting our soldiers. Every sergeant is responsible for enlisting the new fighters. Every recruit must be a woman. And everyone must be absolutely loyal to you and to our cause."

"Major?" One lieutenant raised her voice.

"Yes?"

"What if someone turns out to be disloyal? Maybe threatens to inform on us?"

"Then you will have her killed," Meihua said coldly without hesitation. "And, if you fail to do this, you yourself will be killed."

A quiet chill spread through the women. For the first time, the wide-eyed officers realized that this was in fact war, that the consequences were lethal. Everyone knew about underworld killings in Suzhou, even that sometimes male members of their own families could pay to have someone eliminated. But women never talked of such things.

Meihua stood motionless, moving only her eyes, scrutinizing each officer, searching for signs of weakness. Only five or six seemed to be cracking, their own eyes unable to keep contact, furtively looking at the cave ceiling. She would talk to them individually, making sure they understood the danger of disobedience. She was dead serious. They had to obey.

Where did I find the strength to appear so cold? Meihua wondered. Where was the inner steel coming from? Not her own mother—she was her source of love, of insight, of gentleness, of patience, but not sharp discipline. Nor did it come from her father, who had always offered a distant Confucian sense of love; she knew her father could be tough, but she seldom saw that side. Suddenly Meihua knew where she had found it: the Wu taitai had unintentionally trained a resilient female army officer—only the toughest daughter-in-law could survive in the Wu red chamber.

"Excuse me . . . milady . . ."

Meihua snapped around as she heard an unfamiliar male voice from the cave entrance behind her. Two sergeants grabbed a young Chinese man dressed in black garb, clearly one of those Christian converts who were becoming more common now that the Europeans had come in larger numbers to Suzhou. The man appeared, by his accent and demeanor, to stem from a lower gentry or merchant family, perhaps another failure in the examinations. The local joke had it that if you couldn't become a scholar, then a merchant would do; if not a merchant, then perhaps an actor; if not an actor, then a Chinese Christian so at least you could be slightly better than a real barbarian.

Overcoming his befuddlement at seeing ladies in military dress, the man blurted out his message. "I'm really sorry. It's just that I've got a letter. From Father Gao. In Beijing. He told me to bring it to you. Here."

Meihua gestured to the sergeants, who released their grip, allowing his shaking hands to offer a box from which Meihua drew out a small hand scroll. Twisting toward the cave entrance for better light, she scanned the document, sifting it for the coded meaning:

REBELS ALL OVER NORTH CHINA. SOME LESS THAN FIFTY MILES FROM BEIJING. MANCHUS IN HUGE NUMBERS NORTH OF WALL. MANCHU RAIDS IN HEBEI, SHANXI, SHANDONG. MING SURVIVAL BECOMING MORE DOUBTFUL.

TERRIBLE NEWS. LONGYAN'S UNIT MASSACRED BY MANCHUS. NO SURVIVORS REPORTED.

For a moment, Meihua didn't move at all; the shock seemed to bypass her brain and jolted down her spine into her heart and stomach. But still encased in the ice of command, Meihua couldn't let herself react emotionally. Right now she knew what she had to do.

Spinning around, she said firmly to her officers, all still at attention, "All right. You have your orders. Dismissed."

After her officers had departed, Meihua spoke to the young man. "You're aware, of course, that if anything you have seen is revealed—I mean any of it—your death will be immediate."

"Yes." He trembled.

"And that you will jeopardize all Jesuits in China?"

"Yes."

"All right, now. I will write a return message. And you will make sure that it reaches Father Gao in Beijing. Within one month. It must get there."

She sat down at a writing table and began rendering characters in an awkward, error-ridden fashion that surely looked like the work of a rank beginner. She didn't care if the young convert thought her calligraphy looked silly—appearances didn't count at a moment of crisis. It had to look like the work of some recently arrived Jesuit sending an innocuous message. The code was what was important.

MUST KNOW ABOUT ANY TROOP MOVEMENT TOWARD SUZHOU AREA. ANYTHING SOUTH OF NANJING. PLEASE INFORM IMMEDIATELY.

WHAT OF MING TROOP DEPLOYMENTS? WILL THE DYNASTY BE ABLE TO RESIST AT ALL? WHERE ARE STRONGEST POSITIONS? WHERE WEAKEST? MUST KNOW IN ORDER TO OFFER OUR HELP.

LONGYAN TERRIBLE TRAGEDY. PLEASE CONFIRM DETAILS. I WANT YOUR PERSONAL REPORT. YOUR PERSONAL REPORT.

She watched the young man sprint down the hill with her message. Then Meihua stared through the overcast day at a hill on the other side of Suzhou, a hill she had once climbed during the Dragon Boat Festival. She remembered the words of a ten-year-old boy: "What's it like? What's it like, you know, being a girl?" Then, and only then, did she begin to cry.

For the next eight weeks, Meihua lived in a world of heavy secrets, a clandestine warrior by day and a grieving friend at night. Even after years of separation, Longyan remained her link to an emotional life she had never fully experienced, and now would probably never know. Oh, why had she been so critical of him? Why, in her last letters, had she failed to tell him what she really felt? How could she live without the possibility of such correspondence?

She didn't tell anyone the sad news; otherwise it would be obvious that she was privy to unusual intelligence that would have compromised the Virtuous Army and its Jesuit informants. So it wasn't until late winter, after the Chinese new year and well into February in the Western year of 1643, that the official news reached the Wu family by courier:

IT IS OUR SAD DUTY TO REPORT THAT CAPTAIN WANG LONGYAN, WHO BEARS A RELATIONSHIP TO THE NOBLE WU FAMILY, IS MISSING IN ACTION. HE IS PRESUMED DEAD AFTER A SKIRMISH WITH THE MANCHU BARBARIANS IN WHICH MOST OF HIS COMMAND LOST THEIR LIVES. HE IS POSTHUMOUSLY DECORATED WITH THE IMPERIAL ORDER OF THE WHITE CRANE FOR BRAVE SERVICE IN HIS MAJESTY'S ARMY OF THE GREEN STANDARD.

Longyan's death pierced the Wu family much more deeply than Meihua would ever have imagined. In fact it was the Patriarch's wailing cry, "My son is dead!" that had brought her running, assuming it was the ailing Xinping he was mourning.

"So much talent. So much hidden talent," the Patriarch mumbled sorrowfully, rubbing his head while staring at the imperial letter, family and servants not knowing how to console him. "He made me so angry," the Patriarch said to no one in particular, "but he had a good heart. And I was wrong, you know, to disown him. I so declare, before our ancestors."

The Patriarch walked to a shelf of art objects in the corner of his study and selected a small black vase, roundish in shape, with delicate, irregular white ribs down its sides. "Song dynasty," he said reverently, "a work of unquestionable genius, with a trace of the unconventional about it. This is the object we shall bury, near the tombs of our ancestors, to remember my son. My son, *Wu* Longyan."

To Meihua's amazement, the Patriarch ordered a huge public funeral for Longyan. In early April, at the time of Qing Ming, the Grave-Sweeping Festival, a throng of hundreds walked behind the Patriarch, who carried the lacquered box with the Song vase through the streets of Suzhou. The family marched solemnly; everyone was there but for Xinping, who was too sick to leave his bed. More than fifty professional mourners wailed and tossed paper money before the procession; a band with cymbals, drums, horns, and high-pitched flutes made certain that everyone came out to watch. Even the Taitai seemed genuinely moved, weeping quietly as her older daughters helped her take the few steps from the palanquin to the grave site in Suzhou's hills. Meihua wondered whether the Taitai's tears were calculated to look properly mournful to outsiders or perhaps were a genuine outpouring of some repressed maternal urge. Curious families, who had been busy weeding and sweeping around the remains of their own ancestors, as they did on this special day of mourning every year, were drawn to the Wu funeral.

"We bury this symbol of our son, Wu Longyan," the Patriarch intoned, tossing earth on a newly raised mound next to dozens like it, the tombs of the Wu clan for several centuries. "It is from the Song period to which we trace our roots. But it is to our own dynasty that he gave his service, and his life. He had many talents that never came to full fruition. But he was one thing above all else. . . ." The Patriarch's voice cracked. "He was . . . loyal. True Confucian loyalty. Long live the Ming emperor."

"Long live the Ming emperor!" Meihua's voice joined the huge, spontaneous cry of the throng who surrounded the tumulus. "Long, long life!" they all shouted.

Meihua knew that the Patriarch's grief was real, but now she also knew why so many unrelated people had joined the funeral procession. Longyan was the first son of a leading Suzhou family to perish at the hands of the Manchu invaders.

Longyan was now a symbol, a martyr. His death perpetuated the sacred Confucian virtue of *zhong*—"loyalty"—unwavering support to one's sovereign and to one's values. But Longyan's death was an ominous harbinger for the 1640s: a time of terrible suffering now seemed inevitable.

Of the many sentiments flittering through the hearts of the mourners as they disbanded—respect, sorrow, fear—Meihua's feelings were the most focused. In her eyes, she saw a Manchu, big, sweaty, a pigtail down his back, a club in his hand, his war pony pounding directly toward her. She did not fear him; she loathed him. White-hot anger flushed her veins. "Long live the Ming emperor," she murmured, eliminating any emotion from her breast but one—revenge.

Father Gao crouched by the roadside, hailstones pelting his arms and legs, his body barely protected by a tar-impregnated cotton poncho. Prayerful bowing of head and hands was the only way to protect himself from the sharp ice balls.

"Oh Holy Father, why this torment?" he murmured. "I only seek to serve you. It's a mission of mercy. Why such trials?" Father Gao was too good a Jesuit to expect some sort of miracle, a clearing of the clouds, a heavenly hand to guide him. The prayer was more for himself, to give him the courage to press on.

Father Gao assumed that Saint Ignatius would never understand the reason for his difficult voyage, but maybe God would. The priest had come to love a wayward Chinese man as a son. He refused to believe that Longyan was dead. Like Meihua, Father Gao could not express his feelings for Longyan in words; that would have violated both Christian and Confucian senses of propriety. But also like Meihua, he was ready to kill himself on what most would deem a futile cause: trying to discover Longyan's fate for himself and, if Longyan was alive, somehow to save him.

Father Gao had already been on the road three weeks, meandering his way northward from Beijing, bribing his way through a pass in the Great Wall to the astonishment of the Ming guard force. Only a stupid barbarian priest, perhaps seeking to commit suicide, would want to sneak through the wall going *north*. And now where was he? He was someplace in southern Manchuria, on a road he didn't recognize, near some villages that weren't on any map, looking for a sign of a battle that no one had ever heard of. Worst of all was the mud; thick, murky liquid earth encrusted his clothing and trapped his boots. Days ago he gave up protecting his spare clothing, carried in a canvas pouch from a rope suspended over his shoulder, now sopping with brown goo. His heavy staff was like a blind man's cane, testing the muck ahead of him for rocks and potholes.

"Five miles." That's what the frightened farmer had said. "Five miles to the death camp. Don't tell them I told you."

That was just yesterday, after Father Gao had bribed the farmer with ten copper pieces. Yesterday had been only partly cloudy. Father Gao thought he had glimpsed the plateau to which the farmer pointed through a break in the mist. But today he didn't have a clue—even the moss that grew on the north side of trees was obscured by mud.

Suddenly the rain stopped. The priest suddenly found himself face to face with a sopping wet Manchu soldier who almost died of fright at seeing the massive foreigner. The Manchu, a sentry who had wrongly assumed that no one would try to penetrate their defenses in this weather, grabbed his pike a second too late. Father Gao could easily have killed him, and the Manchu knew it. Yet the priest allowed himself to be bound and blindfolded. The sentry was still baffled when he escorted the priest to the watch commander's tent.

"Who are you?" the interpreter translated the watch commander's sharp question from Manchu to Chinese.

"A foreigner." Father Gao spoke slowly from his prostrate position, two guards pinning him to the ground. "From the West. The Chinese call me a barbarian."

"Hah! A barbarian? That's what the fag Chinese call us. What kind of barbarian are you?"

"A priest. A man of religion. A man who intends no harm."

"No harm? A priest? Who wears a demon-killing totem?" The commander held up the crucifix that had been torn from Father Gao's neck.

"No harm. Really." Father Gao had to think quickly. "I'm not really a priest. Not like the Chinese priests. Not a Buddhist. Not a Taoist. I'm different."

"How are you different?"

"I'm a . . . I'm a shaman."

"A shaman?" The commander gaped in astonishment. How could the strange barbarian be a shaman? How could he have anything in common with the Manchus? "Show me."

Father Gao struggled to his feet as the commander waved away the guards. From his bag he removed a wax candle and a glass-covered painting of Christ with children. And then, in a voice much louder than usual, he began chanting the Mass, nodding his head vigorously and crossing himself energetically. Spotting a small dish with dry tinder, he placed it before the image of Christ and murmured, "Oh Lord, let this work, let it work even though it's wet." With a piece of metal in one hand and a flint in the other, he struck it once, twice, three times—nothing happened. The Manchus laughed. The watch commander beckoned the guards to grab him again. Just then, on the fourth try, a shower of sparks forced the guards back. Father Gao brought his hands close to the dish and struck once again, producing a tiny flame that quickly spread through the tinder, a flame he used to light the candle.

"Ave Maria," the priest exclaimed, then continued to chant the Hail Mary. "Please, Lord, just one more time," he said under his breath, hiding a vial under the sleeve of his gown. *"Benedicat vos omnipotens Deus, Pater, et Filius, et Spiritus Sanctus! Amen!"* he shouted, crossing himself with the right hand, then waving his left across the candle. A tremendous poof of yellow, green, and orange smoke shot forth as he sprinkled the gunpowder laced with chemicals on the candle, leaving the Manchus open-mouthed in awe.

Ten minutes later Father Gao was in a fresh gown sitting on a carpeted tent floor across from an imperious figure on a low stool wearing a silk jacket with long sleeves, a wide skirt that hung almost to his ankles, a black round hat, and a jade archer's ring on his right thumb.

"A shaman?" the Manchu inquired in perfect Chinese. "You're no shaman. Are you?"

Father Gao made an instinctive judgment. "No. I'm not."

"Why did you pretend? Why do some silly magic trick?"

"To save my life."

The Manchu laughed. "It worked. It did save your life. For a moment, anyway. But why shouldn't I kill you right now?"

"Because I could be more helpful to you alive."

"How so?"

"Because I know a lot of other magic tricks. I know tricks that can help you."

"Help us? How?"

"To help you . . ." Father Gao's brain was spinning. There was only one kind of help that made any sense. Dare he suggest it? There wasn't any other way. "To help you win against the Ming," he said with a heavy sigh.

"So what? We're going to win anyway."

"I know," said Father Gao, "but I can help you win faster. Even more, I can help you sew up the victory once you've taken the Dragon Throne." Now the priest was violating every rule of the Jesuit order. He was not only letting friendship overrule his judgment, imperiling himself to help Longyan, but he was also siding with the new dynasty rather than retaining neutrality.

"Yes?"

"You need people you can trust. Once I'm on your side, you can have everything I know." Father Gao was engaging in a desperate gamble. Surely the Ming were about to lose, but it was not as certain that the Manchus would win. Indeed, it was quite possible that the throne would fall to some rebel inside the wall. Father Gao was betting his life, and his faith, that the Manchus would take Beijing. If he was right, perhaps everything would be forgiven. If he was wrong, in all likelihood he would be killed and only God would be his judge (though Saint Ignatius would probably give him quite a tongue-lashing should he make it to heaven).

"We'll see. You're going to have to show us your tricks. Then we'll decide." The Manchus stared at the priest, admiring his quickness, wondering about his motives.

"You'll keep me alive. I know you will."

"Don't sound so arrogant, barbarian. Do you know who you're talking to?"

"No."

"The name is Sose. I'm a prince. Chief adviser to Qing Taizong on language. I could have you killed in a second." What Sose did not say was that he was among the ten or twenty most powerful men in the Manchu cause. In fact, his father had invented the Manchu written language shortly after 1600 as the request of the great tribal unifier, Nurhaci. Sose and his son, Soni, had become the indispensable linguists of the Qing dynasty, fluent in Manchu, Chinese, Mongol, and Korean. Language ability made Sose a natural negotiator, one of the few Manchu leaders who spent many hours talking with captured Chinese. Sose thus became an advocate of conciliatory policies toward the Chinese, often repeating to the Manchus an old Chinese adage, "You can conquer the empire from horseback, but you cannot rule from horseback."

Sose scrutinized the Jesuit, wondering about his motives, pondering what services he might offer. "You're alive because I allow you to live. You know that, don't you?"

"I know," replied Father too, sensing that some divine power, Manchu shaman or Western saint, had intervened to save him." "But *if* it turns out that I'm valuable enough to leave alive, could I ask a favor?" Unless the Manchu granted the request, the whole gamble was lost and he might as well be dead.

"You're hardly in a position to request favors. But what is it?"

"I want to find out if a certain military officer, a Ming captain, is still alive."

"So you're really a loyalist? An enemy of the Manchus?"

"No. Really I'm not. But I do care about some people, whatever side they're on. He's just a—"

"Don't waste my time with such small talk. What's his name?"

"Wang. Captain Wang Longyan."

"I'll see what I can do." Why is he so desperate? Sose wondered. Did someone pay him to do this? Or did he have a sexual relationship with the captain? No matter, maybe there is something in the bargain, he thought. The priest seems sharp enough. If his friend is alive, maybe he's a good soldier, maybe he has important intelligence.

"Of course," Sose continued, "you know that we can accept only bannermen, only those Chinese who agree to serve in our system."

"I know."

"And if there's any trickery . . ."

"Yes?"

"I won't hesitate to kill you. And what's his name—Captain Wang?—I'll kill him too, *if* he's still alive."

Father Gao, shaking with emotion as he climbed down the swaying rope ladder into the prisoner pit, mechanically recited the Paternoster out of hope for Longyan and fear for himself.

"Captain Wang?" he called quietly as he reached the ground, eyes blinded by the darkness. "Longyan? Are you here?" The priest held his breath, listening for a response, holding back the stench of human waste, diseased flesh, dying bodies. "Oh God," he pleaded, falling to his knees, "please let him be here. Longyan, please be here."

Father Gao recoiled as something slithered ratlike across his bended leg. The gray, wet object fell lifeless on the ground. Father

Gao looked closer—the object was an almost fleshless arm wrapped in a scrap of soggy wool, attached to a ghostly body crumpled in the darkest corner of the pit. The seemingly lifeless creature was clothed in the remnants of a gray blanket; an emaciated, scab-ridden face was barely supported by a scrawny neck; a few tufts of hair remained where skin disease had not yet ventured.

"Longyan. Oh my God. You *are* alive." Father Gao cradled Longyan's barely recognizable head and stared into his motionless eyes. "I knew you weren't dead. You couldn't be. Everyone gave up, my son, but I didn't."

"Father Gao," Longyan groaned. "You shouldn't have come. It's hopeless."

"Nonsense," replied the priest. He wanted to minister to Long-yan, to clean his wounds, to bring him back to life. That would have to wait. There was a prior task. The priest shouted to keep him from fading into a deathly sleep. "Longyan," he yelled, "There's a way out. You must defect. You must become a banner-man."

The priest gagged at the stench of several rotting bodies hud-dling closer, awaiting their captain's fateful answer. Longyan's eyes fluttered momentarily. "I cannot," he groaned, "unless they re-lease my men."

"That they will not do," Father Gao replied unhesitatingly. "They will be slaves. That is, if any survive." He glanced around the darkened cavern at unreacting eyes in hollow faces.

"Then I'll become a slave. Or just die. I don't care."

"You *must* care," Father Gao said sharply. "The Manchus have decided you should be a bannerman."

He watched as Longyan slowly shook his head no. What could he possibly say to change Longyan's mind? He could only think of one possible argument. "It is the Manchus' policy," Father Gao tried to sound convincing, "for anyone refusing the offer, that his family shall be exterminated. The entire family. All living genera-tions. So the choice is yours. It's simple. Serve your dynasty. You know it's a lost cause. Or serve your family. Serve your father. You've always wanted to do that."

"Really," Longyan blinked, "this is the Manchus' policy?"

"Yes," Father Gao lied. "Indeed, if you raise any questions about the policy, the execution order will be given."

160

Longyan tried to see Father Gao's eyes, to check whether the priest was telling the truth, but his lids kept shutting from the strain. How else, Father Gao fretted, to make him switch sides without pushing the Manchu overlords for details? The priest wanted to promise God that he had spoken his final lie, but decided that would make further compromises that would be even more painful.

"Come on, lad," the priest urged, "make up your mind. They've only given me a few minutes. Please. For your family's sake. Please."

The stick figure struggled to a seated posture, bony arms holding the floor for support, head resting against the corner of the wall. For a long moment, Longyan breathed heavily from the exertion, trying to focus his brain. "All right," he murmured painfully, "for my family's sake."

"All right what?"

"I shall serve the barbarians."

"Serve the who?" Father Gao asked quietly.

"I shall serve the barb—I mean . . . I shall serve the great Qing dynasty."

CHAPTER THIRTEEN

Loyalism

明

Two to Three Years Later:
Beijing and Suzhou, 1644–1646

LIKE THE PLAGUE victims perishing across the realm, the Ming dynasty was a corpse long before its heart stopped beating. As province after province fell to domestic rebels, principled Ming officials suffered execution or went into hiding; opportunists quickly changed loyalties and declared fealty to rebel pretenders. By early 1644, only Beijing was left. Eunuchs and palace ladies wailed in terror of the advancing rebel forces, knowing that ragtag remnants of the Green Standard Army would offer no protection. In February, after the outer walls of the city fell to the invaders, Li Zicheng's peasant armies were within days of sacking the Forbidden City itself.

In April, Li Zicheng's peasant armies ripped into Beijing like a sword through termite-infested wood. As his dynasty collapsed around him, the last Ming emperor climbed Coal Hill, took a final look at the Forbidden City his ancestors had built, then hanged himself from a tree. The rebel Li Zicheng pronounced himself the emperor of the new Shun dynasty, inaugurating one of the shortest reigns in history.

The one man who might have played a pivotal role, Gen. Wu Sangui, mysteriously kept his troops out of the Beijing fray in early 1644. The general began a march toward the capital in the waning days of the Ming, but quite suddenly reversed his tracks and returned with several thousand troops to Shanhaiguan. Had he concluded that the Ming cause was hopeless? Was he returning to defend the Great Wall against impending Manchu attack?

After Li Zicheng took the Forbidden City, some speculated that the rebel sought a separate truce with General Wu, perhaps urging that the Shun and the Ming join forces to hold off the Manchus. Whether such a message was ever sent and whether General Wu ever communicated his response remains unknown. But any chance of an alliance was undercut when Li Zicheng infuriated the general by arresting members of Wu's family in Beijing and taking Wu's favorite concubine for his own.

And so, in the fateful spring of 1644, General Wu Sangui sat in Shanhaiguan, furious about his personal situation and baffled by his military situation. His sovereign was dead, his dynasty was defunct, rebels held the imperial capital, and barbarians threatened to overrun the empire. Over sixty thousand troops of the Manchu Eight Banners camped in the ten-mile strip north of the border. Fewer than thirty thousand Ming Green Standard soldiers stood in defense. Perhaps the Great Wall might have slowed down the invaders, forcing them to storm the narrow pass and allowing General Wu's troops to hold the gate for a few days, but no one could have doubted that the Manchus would eventually break through the defenses.

The cost of pitched battle between the Manchu Qing and the Chinese Ming would have been immense to both armies. And after victory, the next challenge for the Manchus would have been a move on Beijing, the thinned and exhausted banner ranks regrouping for an assault on the what would surely be a rebel-occupied capital city. Neither side—not the Manchus under the Prince Regent Dorgon nor the Ming under Gen. Wu Sangui—viewed the prospects with much relish.

"General Wu," Longyan tried to quell the trembling in his voice, "I come as an emissary of the Shunzhi emperor of the great Qing dynasty."

Longyan, now Major Wang of the Chinese Bordered Red Banner, wore his Qing military uniform: short jacket with horseshoe sleeves, flowing cotton pants, black boots, flat conical hat. He nervously rolled the jade archer's thumb ring on his right hand, standing anxiously in the same great hall where he had proudly banqueted as a Ming officer just two years earlier; he was addressing the same general who had earlier praised his loyalty to the Ming dynasty. It was his duty to negotiate a possible way to avoid the coming carnage.

"So now it's *Major* Wang," General Wu said snidely, shifting in his seat so that all his senior officers could see the sneer. "An unusual way to get a promotion. Wouldn't you say, Major?"

"Yes, sir." Longyan bowed his head. He had dreaded this moment ever since the Qing emperor Taizong, better known by his Manchu name Abahai, had personally asked him to negotiate on behalf of the new dynasty. "Your father was once grand secretary, yes?" Abahai had asked Longyan weakly on his deathbed. "So of all our Chinese bannermen, your family is the most influential. They will listen to you." Longyan no longer could be a passive defector. He had cast his lot with the Manchus and had to do his emperor's bidding. When a sovereign requested, it took precedence over what one's father would have desired.

"What is it you want, Major?" General Wu asked impatiently.

"I wish to suggest an alternative to battle. A way to avoid bloodshed." Father Gao had tried desperately to convince Longyan that there was honor in such a proposal. How much better, the priest had argued after Longyan had recovered, to save lives than to waste them needlessly. After all, the Ming was doomed, so now the task was to minimize damage and soften the transition. The priest argued that the Wu patriarch would understand, but Longyan knew otherwise.

"Yes? What alternative? Surrender?"

"No, General, not surrender."

Longyan had absolutely rejected the original Manchu idea of forcing the surrender of the Ming dynasty's most famous general. He explained Chinese customs to the Manchus: General Wu would suffer a terrible loss of face, probably bringing about his suicide, then he would become a martyr to the Ming loyalists and that surely would strengthen their resistance. Always give a Chinese a way out, Longyan implored, a way to save face. Having counseled against surrender, Longyan was obliged to concoct a novel option.

"The dynasty proposes that, after you open the Shanhaiguan gate, we join forces to drive the rebels from Beijing." Longyan laid out the offer slowly, hoping the Ming commander would appreciate its merits. "Upon our success, you will be granted a large feudatory in the southwest as your personal domain with your troops.

You will have land and power. You will be an independent lord with fealty to the Qing throne."

"So it's really surrender with an incentive. You expect to purchase my loyalty?" The general tried to sound offended, but it was apparent that he had never expected such a rich bargain. It certainly was an appealing alternative to suicide.

"No. To suggest other ways to channel your loyalty," Longyan said hopefully. "To save lives and enhance power." Of course, Longyan knew the general was correct: It was surrender in a more elegant package.

"And how long do I have to consider this offer?"

"I am sorry, sir, but you must decide now. I am required to take back your answer today. Otherwise the battle will begin tomorrow." Longyan had begged the Manchus for more time, but Prince Regent Dorgon had been adamant. He had exclaimed, "You want to give him a third of our empire? And then you want to give him time to think about whether it's the best he can expect? No! He must decide instantly."

Gen. Wu Sangui sighed deeply and looked about the room at his staff officers and line commanders. His jaw tightened, as it always did before he made life-and-death decisions. "In that case, I accept your offer."

"You do?" Longyan asked with open-eyed astonishment as the room gasped collectively. "I thought you would never give up. I thought you were the ultimate loyalist."

"And that's what I thought of you as well."

"But why you?"

"Because it's the more humane approach." General Wu tried to sound sincere. "Not just for my troops, but for the people of the empire. I have lost the war, perhaps I can help win the peace." The words seemed noble, but they rang hollow on his lips. He could already hear critics crying cowardice. They would surely accuse him of putting personal grievances above defending the Han Chinese people against barbarian invaders.

"Don't you worry that people will call you a traitor?" Longyan asked, saying what was on everyone's mind. "It's a decision that could haunt you."

"And you as well, Major," General Wu replied curtly, fire in his eyes. "You as well."

And so, in one of the most controversial turning points in Chinese military history, General Wu opened the Shanhaiguan gate to the invaders. Manchus poured into China, sweeping across the plain to Beijing in less than a week, routing the rebels. The Ming dynasty, almost three hundred years old, perished in early April. The Shun dynasty, less than a few weeks old, collapsed in early June. The Manchu child-emperor Shunzhi, already having been crowned on April 27, was installed on the throne the Ming had built, beginning the new Qing dynasty's reign over the Chinese empire.

The decision to open the Shanhaiguan gate would haunt everyone: adherents of both dynasties, Gen. Wu Sangui, and Longyan. General Wu received a massive domain in the southwestern Sichuan area, where he rebuilt his armies and accumulated rich treasuries; thirty years later he would use that base in a brutal, but eventually futile, campaign against his Qing overlords.

Although his role in crafting General Wu's feudatory remained confidential, Longyan often awakened in a sweat, torn by a guilt that wrenched his insides. He rationalized that rescuing tens of thousand lives was merely an extension of his original decision to save his family. It was a Confucian approach, he told himself, trying to make the conquest more gentle, tempering the Manchu desire for reprisals. But no matter how he tried to convince himself, Longyan remained profoundly disturbed. Why, he anguished, couldn't he have served the Ming in its prime, perhaps a hundred years earlier? And if not that, why couldn't he have been killed in the ambush two years earlier rather than confront a terrible loss of face?

In the autumn of 1644, after a prolonged stay at Shanhaiguan, Longyan and Father Gao rode smallish, stocky Manchu horses slowly into Beijing. Longyan was totally recovered from his tortured imprisonment, his handsome face and erect posture exuding authority, his body restored to a muscular toughness. His bow and arrows hung from one side of his saddle; his short broadsword slapped in its scabbard on the opposite side. Longyan wore his full Manchu military regalia, while Father Gao chose a simple scholar's gown. Both rode with a nonchalant competence revealing over a year in the service of the hard-riding Manchus north of the Great Wall.

Where was everybody? Why was the city so empty? The Beijing Longyan had left two years earlier was always filled with a noisy din. Today the few pedestrians moved quickly, solemnly, in and out of shops, melting into the *hutong* alleyways. Where were the hawkers, the screaming children, the laughing serving girls, the storytellers? As they approached the eastern wall of the Forbidden City, the crisp October sunshine revealed red walls and golden roofs, now back in good repair, but almost devoid of life. The Dongmen, the Eastern Gate, sported a freshly painted frieze in blues, yellows, and reds, but not a sign of the whining eunuchs who used to sell palace artworks for princely prices. And the East-gate Market was still there with its appalling array of smells, but the shopkeepers seemed to have lost their tongues. Eastgate's once incessant din was now a persistent murmur.

At each street corner, Longyan and Father Gao shared glances. At first they were surprised, then it slowly became obvious why Beijing was so different. It was the change of dynasties. The late Ming had been corrupt and boisterous. The new rulers were setting a different tone: orderly, firm, tough. The Manchus were serious about the commitment to purity, which was the very name of their Qing dynasty.

So that's what a dynastic change feels like, Longyan mused, knowing that the event had not occurred for almost three hundred years. But this was more than dynastic change; it was a foreign conquest of the Dragon Throne. Manchu nomads were the new rulers of the Middle Kingdom. And Longyan couldn't escape the fact that he had thrown in his lot with barbarian conquerors.

The gates were all guarded by Manchu bannermen (the advisers to the new Shunzhi emperor would hardly give Chinese or Mongol bannermen such a critical task). Longyan could feel Manchu eyes scrutinizing him as he rode southward along the wall; he could see their features, tall bodies and high cheekbones, as they stared down from the gates and walkways. Suddenly Longyan felt like an outsider himself, trusted by neither the Manchu overlords nor by the conquered Chinese. Now Longyan knew why so many Beijing residents slunk into the corners as he came by.

As they turned the southeast corner of the Forbidden City and moved toward the Front Gate, which Longyan himself had once guarded, they saw that one kind of store was doing even better business under Manchu rule. Barbershops had long lines outside. The hairstyle had changed, not because of a shift in fashions, but because the Qing demanded that all Chinese adopt the queue, the pigtail, in Manchu style. All Beijing males were required to shave the front part of their heads, letting the hair in the back grow until it could be braided, eventually reaching their waists in length. The shaving had to be done at least every two weeks or men would risk violating the regulations.

While barbers thrived, the Chinese citizenry, though not daring to protest publicly, found the regulation repugnant. Not only did the queue violate any respectable sense of hairstyle, it was also a visible sign of subordination. Anyone evading the queue order was placed in prison, where the new style was forced on the violator. A second offense was punishable by death. Just in case one might think the new overlords weren't serious, the major gates were used as execution grounds; severed heads were posthumously shaved so that they would become ancestors under Manchu dominion. And still yet some defied the regulation to make a deliberate statement of Ming loyalism. "Losing one's head to save one's hair" was an expression describing the fate of extremists.

Longyan and Father Gao already wore the queue. Bannermen and other collaborators had no choice. Would the Manchus force it on all Chinese, Longyan wondered, even in the south, even in Suzhou? He imagined how disgusted his father would be at the prospect. Would the family refuse? Was their loyalism that deep? Would they understand why Longyan had defected to the Manchus? Would they know that he had done it to protect the Wu clan from execution? Would they believe him when he told them he had no choice?

"Bannerman!"

Longyan snapped his head toward the voice coming from a darkened doorway. A man in tattered garb stepped out and stood by the nose of Longyan's horse, holding the bitless bridle. "Remember me? I'm Gu. Remember? Captain Gu. At the Green Standard Officers' School. I taught riding."

"Oh, yes," Longyan said loudly, overcoming his surprise at Gu's beggar's clothing. "Of course. Captain Gu."

"Not so loud," Gu replied, "I don't want *them* to recognize me." He pointed toward some Manchus on the guard walkway.

"Why not?"

"Because I refused to become a bannerman."

"You did? You refused? And you're still alive? Did they kill your family?"

"Who told you all that?" Captain Gu shook his head. "What rumors! They don't kill you if you refuse to become a bannerman. They just kick you out of your job. Now I clean dishes. Kill your family? That's crazy. It's just that I can't do special favors for the family anymore. No more going through the back gate."

"Are you sure? They don't kill you if you refuse? They don't execute your father and your whole clan?"

"Of course not! Now you'd better go. I really don't need them fussing around here."

Father Gao and Longyan rode along the wall in silence. The priest, knowing what was about to happen, decided to speak first.

"I'm sorry, my son."

"I'm not your son! And you lied to me!"

"Please understand. I owed it to your family not to let you die. If I hadn't pulled you out of there—well, you surely would have died. It was the only thing I could think of. The only way I could be sure you would become a bannerman and save your life."

"What gave you the authority?" Longyan seethed. "So you saved me. And my men probably all died."

"They would have died anyway."

"Why? Why did you do it?"

Father Gao didn't dare tell him the real reasons. He didn't reveal Meihua's desperate request to find Longyan alive and keep him that way. Father Gao didn't explain how he himself felt, that he wanted a living son, not a dead memory. It was time to lie again. "It's my religion. I can't let good people, from good families, just die like that. My religion requires that I save them."

"It's a stupid religion." Longyan galloped off, leaving Father Gao in his dust.

The priest let Longyan go. It could have been worse, Father Gao reflected, since he had long worried about how Longyan would react when he found out the truth. He also knew that Longyan's shaky sense of identity would be further tested. Would Longyan's father prefer an alive son, or perhaps a dead loyalist? How was Longyan going to explain his capitulation now that he knew that it had not meant saving his entire family? The remaining shred of dignity was stripped away from a decision that now appeared to be motivated by cowardly self-interest.

Of course, Father Gao also failed to tell Longyan about another lie, one that made the others pale by comparison. He didn't tell him why Sose had agreed to accept Longyan as a bannerman rather than let him rot in the prison pit. Father Gao had made a bargain with Sose, a linguistic deal that appealed to the Manchu's leading exponent of using foreign languages for political and diplomatic power.

Father Gao had agreed to teach the Manchu prince a new language, a Western language. He had agreed to teach him Latin. Learning Latin could be valuable for three very important reasons. First, it gave Sose a special code that he could share with his son, Soni, and eventually his grandson, Songgotu. They would become the Manchu experts on language; in effect, they would serve as the tongues of the conquering Qing dynasty. They were the only Manchus who could handle Latin, thus not only allowing them to babble secretly with no one else understanding, but also allowing them to record some documents confidentially, holding them for later translation into existing East Asian languages.

Second, it gave Sose direct access to the Jesuit scientific and military manuals; Latin was truly the key to Father Gao's real "magic." Sose, in effect, controlled not only knowledge to breakthrough weaponry like gunpowder explosives and mobile cannons, but also knowledge about astronomy, which was deeply prized by the court. Like the Jesuits, Sose could learn how to make astronomical predictions, such as the timing of eclipses, which were essential to the ritual life of the Emperor. Wizards, now including Sose's family as well as several Jesuit priests, had a high place in the Qing court.

And third, most dangerous for Father Gao, Latin was the key not only to the Jesuit's religious texts, but also to their private records. Father Gao had given Sose a potential stranglehold over Jesuit operations throughout the Middle Kingdom. Sose and his offspring were drawn by their newfound knowledge into the Jesuit network, into their commercial operations, into their linkages with other parts of Asia and Europe. In effect, an elite Manchu family was given intimate secrets of the most elite European religious community. It would prove a special alliance—critics would call it an unholy alliance.

Father Gao had not revealed the Latin language simply to protect Longyan. He gambled that the revelation would help the Jesuit cause, that it would ingratiate him to his new masters. Above all, he gambled that they would want to keep him alive, to keep up his flow of new insights, to make him a special adviser to those in high places. So it was a gamble right in the tradition of Ignatius Loyola, a gamble that knowledge was the key to trust, that trust was the key to power, and that power was the way to men's souls.

Meanwhile Longyan could wait no longer. He had to begin facing life as a Manchu turncoat. Perhaps a letter to Meihua would test his ability to rationalize his decision:

> I know this letter may come as a bit of a surprise. Perhaps even a shock. But, if you were informed that I was dead, the report was untrue. I was captured. I almost died. But I'm still alive. Does that surprise you?

Meihua would always remember how she nearly fainted when Peach Blossom brought the letter to her boudoir. Her hand was still shaking a week later, when she finally summoned the strength to compose her own letter. After years of silence, a stream of letters flowed up and down the Grand Canal, an awkward dialogue that conveyed surface truths but hid inner secrets.

> *Longyan? Is it really you? Not a ghost seeking to play at my heart? You're alive? I cannot believe it! Who will believe it? Your father already conducted a giant memorial service. Almost a year ago.*

> Father Gao has been with me, above the wall, for more than a year now. We wanted to tell you, to tell everyone. But the Manchus would not let us write anyone. We were kept under strict watch. I have not been able to communicate until getting back to Beijing.
> What will Father think? Now that he has conducted the service? Will he be disappointed that I am alive?

Meihua didn't know how to answer, so she told Longyan what she thought he wanted to hear:

> *He was very proud of you, Longyan. Proud that you would die for your convictions. Proud that you would die out of loyalty to a dynasty. The service was very moving. Hundreds came. But, of course, everyone will be much happier that you are still alive. They will surely welcome you back. How is it that you survived, anyway? Did you escape?*

Longyan had no trouble reading between the lines. Dead heroes seemed more welcome than live soldiers. Certainly more welcome than those who were traitors. So what could he say? For days he tried to conjure up the best answer. It had to be a lie, of course. But what lie? He finally settled on:

> I don't know how to tell you this. I have been forced to become what they call a Chinese bannerman—that is, a Chinese in the service of the Manchu Qing dynasty. I had no choice. If I refused, they would have executed all my men. My decision saved many lives. I would have willingly gone to my death, faced the end that all you thought had actually happened, but fate forced me to move in another direction.

Meihua was puzzled by Longyan's unconvincing explanation. Did he simply lack the courage to die—and now lacked the courage to tell the truth? Did it really happen as he says? She wondered. Is he covering something else? A Chinese bannerman! A servant of the Manchus! Can you imagine the Patriarch's response?

> *I am sure that you have told me just what happened. But somehow it sounds wrong. Couldn't you say that the Manchus said that, if you refused, they would execute your whole family? So therefore, your act of disloyalty was clearly the ultimate act of filiality? I think your father would understand it better.*

Oh no, Longyan lamented to himself, that's precisely what Father Gao said originally. But I can't say that. Everyone will know that it's not the Manchus' policy. They aren't treating other families that way. The old lie just won't hold up. So this new lie is at least plausible, even if it's not as Confucian. He wrote back: "I must tell the truth."

Oh, forgive me for pushing you so hard. I am delighted you're still alive. I just want to make sure that the family understands. When are you coming back? Can you visit?

Right now, there's no chance of such a visit. I have so much to do here in Beijing. I have made a bargain. You know, for the lives of my men. I must fulfill the bargain.

Please, oh please, if you must stay in Beijing, can you help make this period more humane? Can you stop the queue order? At least stop it in Suzhou?

Longyan knew he didn't have the slightest influence over such a critical policy. He simply decided to ignore her request. Besides, he fretted, she should be more careful in what she writes.

Please speak with care about delicate matters. We have a new dynasty. They are most serious about purification. They understandably will not tolerate dissent. We must obey their orders with respect. However I came to my decision, I am with them fully. Long live the Qing dynasty. Long live the Shunzhi emperor.

Long live the Qing dynasty? Long live the Shunzhi emperor? The words continued to ring in Meihua's ears, especially this night, as she shivered in the pitch-black chill of early December. Was that his real sentiment? Or was he just writing it to appear loyal to the Manchus? Even with a more generous interpretation, Meihua could not believe that Longyan would be such a sycophant.

It was two o'clock in the morning. Three hundred troops and officers of the Virtuous Army were silently hidden on opposing steep hillocks through which ran the major east-west road into Suzhou. All of the women had sneaked out of their households, leaving others in their red chambers covering for them; bound-foot officers had been transported by sedan chairs carried by big-foot enlisted servants.

For a week, rumors spoke of the coming Manchus. The barbarian conquerors were reported moving toward Suzhou, traveling roughly ten miles each night, which should place them on this narrow road, just beyond the city limits, sometime in the early morning hours. Less than a month earlier, a Manchu detachment had swept through Nanjing, a hundred miles to the north. The Manchus brought not only troops armed with bows, swords, and pikes, but also barbers armed with razors. In Nanjing, it was said, not a man over sixteen was left with his hair. Indeed, it was also said, that the Yangtze basin had sprouted a new industry, making pillows for the Manchus filled with the hair of shaved Chinese.

In Yangzhou, less than two hundred miles north, Manchu troops had conducted the most infamous massacre of the conquest. For ten full days, residents were terrorized as soldiers conducted mass executions, looted residences and shops, and torched the inner city. For weeks the Grand Canal reeked of rotting bodies floating in pools of purple blood.

So far, Suzhou had been spared, but now the great city of canals shook in anticipation of the coming terror. No one slept. People moved to and fro all night, often going to the houses of relatives and friends for comfort. The commotion provided an ideal cover for young elite women to congregate in Suzhou's hilly outskirts.

It was two-thirty when the black-garbed women soldiers heard the clopping of horse hooves. The Manchus were moving at a slow walk, the only way to ride a horse at night. The tremendous clatter of hooves indicated that a detachment of several hundred cavalry and foot soldiers was about to enter Suzhou. Meihua knew the precise number: 109 cavalry, 271 foot soldiers, 380 Manchus in all. Her intelligence came from local farmers, all relatives of Suzhou servant girls, who provisioned the Manchus with meat, vegetables, and flour. They had done the counting for her.

By day, Meihua had learned, Manchus tended to ride far enough apart so that they couldn't be attacked en masse, but at night the risk of ambush was much less, so they clustered together. After all, who could see clearly enough to hit a rider in total darkness? Wouldn't you have to be so close that the Manchus could easily counterattack? Those were the questions she had pondered at length, talking with her officers, consulting Sun Zi's *Art of War,* looking over the landscape in daylight. Finally, it had come to her. A plan! At least the plan seemed perfect in theory, but would it work when the real test came?

"Now?" a captain whispered.

Meihua shook her head no.

"Now! You've got to do it now," the captain whispered again. "They're going to escape!"

"Hush. Not yet. Wait." Meihua listened until the leading horses had passed her by a couple hundred yards. And still she waited, counting slowly, her softly spoken numbers reverberating to the heavy beat of her heart. ". . . ninety-nine, one hundred. Now! Now do it!"

The captain ducked into a small cave, retrieved a long stick from a hidden fire, its tip a glowing ember, and touched it to the firing wick on a cannon. A half minute later the cannon roared into action, sending a flaming ball down into the valley that exploded on impact, killing a dozen riders and scattering the rest in terrified retreats, galloping east and west away from the cannon. At just that moment, a series of muffled explosions lit up the sky a quarter mile to the east, blowing up the road at its narrowest point, creating impassable craters. Just to make sure, a detachment of fifty musketeers closed the road with barrages of rifle fire, prompting the Manchus to a mass retreat toward the west.

"Now! Now again!" Meihua shouted. Then under her breath, "Oh please, let this work."

The captain ignited a second cannon, this time spraying shot across the Manchu cavalry. Several fell again, but that wasn't the point. The cannon was a signal. Flaming arrows were fired into piles of dried tinder and oil, all laced with gunpowder, at hundred-yard intervals along the road. Suddenly the darkest night was illuminated with white-hot bonfires shooting flames into the sky. The hundreds of Manchus were all visible; their horses whinnied in panic and bolted in all directions. Then, just as the women had drilled, the musketeers hidden in the steep hillsides on both sides of the road began to fire their weapons methodically. Captains shouted the orders, "Load, ignite, fire!" Lieutenants and sergeants did the shooting, all teams reloading in less than thirty seconds.

It was all over quickly. Although the Manchu ranks were decimated in ten minutes, Meihua continued the barrage for a full twenty minutes, just to make sure. The fires quickly fizzled out, leaving her troops firing toward sounds in the pitch-black night, uncertain whether they were hitting or not. When there was no more movement from the enemy troops, only a few cries and moans, Meihua personally led a torch-lit walk through the battle-field. She ordered a coup de grâce whenever they founded a wounded Manchu.

Her ecstatic officers clustered around Meihua, shouting their congratulations as she reviewed the final death count. "Silence!" she commanded, ignoring the pile of bodies at her feet and staring at a tally sheet. "This is wrong. Very wrong. More than thirty horsemen—thirty-three to be exact—got away. How is that possi-ble?"

"I was t-toward the rear." One shivering private stuttered out her words. "I think maybe the Manchu column was longer than we thought. I heard more horses coming. They weren't quite in gunshot range when we opened fire."

"Did they see you? Did they see who was firing at them?"

"Maybe. When the gunpowder exploded, maybe they saw it was women. I don't know."

It was almost five o'clock when Meihua returned home, accom-panied by five female servants. She was elated, exhausted, and anx-ious. On the one hand, the victory was stunning. Over three hundred Manchus had been slaughtered. And the attack had worked almost as Meihua and her officers designed it. Only four of the Virtuous Army were dead; fortunately they were all junior ser-vants who would simply be reported as "missing," not an uncom-mon occurrence, as peasant women often became homesick and went home.

But Meihua also shook with fear as she realized that her strategy had one serious flaw. She'd figured that the Manchus would never see that their assailants were women, that the darkness would pre-serve anonymity even if some of the troops escaped. She had never imagined that the brilliant flashes of light might reveal their own identity to Manchu horsemen who were hanging back from the main detachment. If they had been recognized, her fear was not only for the women soldiers, but also for their entire families.

But now that the deed was done, the women had to finish their act: to go home, wash up, and pretend that nothing had happened. And if anyone threatened to reveal what had happened, the death order was still operative. Meihua thought it wouldn't be necessary since two servants had already been killed over the past year for trying to divulge secrets.

She had lectured her officers on military history:

"Two emotions are fatal in warfare.

"One is fear. While a certain amount of fear makes soldiers fight harder, too much fear deadens reason and makes soldiers stupid.

"But the bigger danger is pride. Too much pride creates losers who assume they can't lose. Too much pride makes soldiers speak boastfully. So you all know the penalty for prideful boasting."

Meihua's lecture worked. Not one of her soldiers broke rank. The night of December 15, 1645, became one of the most glorious secrets in late-imperial Chinese history. None but the dainty ladies and their red chamber servants knew for certain who had pulled off the greatest ambush against Manchu bannermen in the history of the Qing conquest.

Meihua's greatest anxiety—that the Manchus would describe their attackers—never came to pass. She wrongly assumed that no surviving Manchu ever saw their enemy that cold night. Actually more than a dozen of the escaped Manchus confessed to each other that they had seen women soldiers that night. But as they struggled back toward Beijing, dismayed at losing a battle, the troops agreed to say that it was too dark to see anyone. After all, it was bad enough to be defeated by Chinese loyalists, but imagine the humiliation if anyone suggested that they had been overwhelmed by women. So the Suzhou Midnight Massacre, as it would be called, remained a romantic subject for rumormongers. One night, a drunken Manchu was reported to have blabbered about "little women with muskets" in a Beijing teahouse, but he was never seen again.

The defeat did not change the course of history in the slightest. The Manchus had already won the capital, and slowly they would tighten their noose around the entire empire, including the hotbeds of Ming loyalism in Suzhou and other lower Yangtze River elite communities. But the Suzhou Midnight Massacre was an enormous blow to Manchu prestige and a real lift for the residual supporters of the Ming. The fact that no one knew who did it infuriated the Manchus and intrigued the Chinese.

Of course, there was one person, neither Manchu nor Chinese, who correctly surmised what had happened. "O Holy Father," a large priest quietly intoned in the Beijing Jesuit monastery. "What have I done? Have I trained women so that they can win a battle and lose a war? Oh please, I meant well. Don't let the forces of revenge take the lives of those women and their families. Please give them your blessing."

Father Gao stood, genuflected, and crossed himself. Then he spun about and grinned. He did a little jig and clasped his hands over his head in a victory signal. "O Holy Father, forgive my sin of pride. Forgive my chattering like a silly Franciscan about the Holy Mother. But I think the Dear Virgin should be giggling this day. A bunch of crippled damsels just humiliated the toughest fighting force in Asia."

Longyan lolled in an armchair at the bow of a giant Grand Canal barge, watching the river world unfold in slow motion in rhythm with the rolling green wave pushed sideways by the boat, ponderously churning up plants, dead fish, and miscellaneous flotsam. The great hemp line, strapped to the backs of dozens of coolies on shore, stretched taut to the caller's drumbeat, then slacked as the massive craft slogged a few more feet down the world's greatest man-made waterway. Hawkers hovered along shore, like sharks meandering behind oceangoing vessels, trying to sell everything from bean-paste candies to miniature wooden barges.

"Oh, sir. Excuse me, sir."

"Yes?" Longyan cocked back his head at a man dressed in the characteristic blue pants and long-sleeved shirt of the river navy, the gold braid around his cap indicating that he was an officer.

"I'm the captain. I just wanted to say that it's just such a great honor having you onboard. It's not often we get someone as important as you."

"Thank you," Longyan replied curtly.

"I mean not only a leading Chinese bannerman. But also, am I informed correctly, new prefect of Huaiyin? It's just such an honor. I don't quite know what to say."

"Captain. There's nothing to say. Thank you. Now I'd like to be left alone. All right?"

Longyan shook his head as the captain finally retired. How fleeting is power, he mused, recalling that no one had asked about his welfare four years ago, when he took this same barge northbound. Prefect of Huaiyin? Yes, that was true. But if the captain had only heard how the appointment had been made, he might not have been quite so effusive.

"You know who I am?" an elegantly dressed Manchu prince had asked him back in Beijing less than a month earlier.

"Of course, my lord, you are the Senior Minister of Appointments."

"No, no. Not my title. My name."

"Of course, Mr. Minister, your honorable name is Sose." Longyan always wondered how the Manchus could be happy with a silly system that gave people single names. But at least everyone knew who Sose was: a close supporter of the now deceased founders of the Qing dynasty, Nurhaci and Abahai, and part of the coterie surrounding the young Shunzhi emperor. It was rumored that Sose was opposed to the draconian policies of Dorgon, the imperial regent, who sought absolute obedience from subjugated Chinese. It was also rumored that Sose, who spoke perfect Chinese, was one of the few Manchus to urge that the Qing use their military power sparingly, and instead win Chinese support by appointing prominent Ming bureaucrats to high Qing posts. It was even said that Sose had studied the Confucian classics well enough to quote from them like an examination candidate.

"I've watched you for some time, you know," Sose said matter-of-factly.

"You have?"

"Of course. Didn't Father Gao tell you? Didn't he tell you that you'd probably be dead today if it weren't for me?"

"You?"

"It was I who had you released from the death pit. Father Gao guaranteed that you would serve us loyally. That you have done. And now I must test your loyalty even more deeply."

"How so?"

"I know you've heard of the Suzhou Midnight Massacre. No

one knows who did it. But there's a big split here in Beijing over how to deal with it. Some very powerful figures—you can guess who—want to send down the elite Manchu troops. They want to conduct an inquisition. They want to show who's the boss."

"That's what I feared. I don't know who did it, either. But I hope you can avoid that tough approach. It will just make it harder to consolidate power over time." With Sose, unlike most Manchus, Longyan found it easy to converse. Sose seemed like a Chinese elite with a bigger physique and a firmer face. Longyan admired the way Sose overcame cultural barriers as easily as he mastered language barriers. If anyone could take the harsh edge off the Qing conquest, Longyan knew it was this spokesman for the more conciliatory Manchus.

"Exactly," Sose concurred, "just what I said. I said, don't send Manchus at all. Send loyal Chinese. Make sure the Chinese find out who did it. They should be executed. Not a mass execution. Only the real culprits. Then make sure the Chinese let everyone know that if it happens again, a reign of terror will follow. I think it's the way to prevent awful violence and repression. What do you think?"

"You want Chinese to report on other Chinese?"

"It's certainly better than thousands being arrested and tortured. Isn't it?"

"I suppose so."

"Good. I'm glad you agree. Because you're going to have a chance to make a softer policy work. I'm appointing some loyal Chinese bannermen to key posts. Not in their own districts. That would require them to directly supervise family and friends. But in nearby locations—even in your own province, unlike the Ming regulation. You will be Prefect of Huaiyin. You will help find the criminals and bring them to justice. You will make sure that no more foolishness occurs. And you will do this because your life, and the lives of all dear to you, depends on how you do your job."

So Longyan, along with twenty other Chinese bannermen, received what they privately called "impossible assignments." It was bad enough to be a collaborator with the conquering Manchu barbarians; now they had to become informers against fellow Chinese who were acting more in the good Confucian tradition. They had to ferret out what was clearly a closely guarded secret of Ming loyalism. And they had to convince Chinese to become turncoats like themselves.

Meihua's letter had rejoiced:

> *It's so good you're coming. A prefect, no less? That's the highest rank of anyone in the family, excepting when your father was in Beijing. I'm sure he'll be very proud.*

Meihua wasn't sure of how Patriarch Wu would react at all. In fact, she thought he might see Longyan's new appointment as a combination of disloyalty and opportunism. Which was, in fact, how she herself looked at it. But Meihua did not really dwell on the subject. She was too busy with other matters:

> *It must be serendipity that brings you to Suzhou. Xinping is now sicker than ever. Dr. Long is not sure whether he will survive. He misses you. I know he will be proud of his brother's accomplishments. I also know he wishes he had the strength, in so many ways, to have made great achievements on his own. It may surprise you to learn, my dear brother, that you are probably the only hope for real success in the family.*

CHAPTER FOURTEEN

Traitors

明

Less Than a Year Later:
Suzhou and Huaiyin, 1646

MANEUVERING A GREAT barge into its berth in Suzhou was always a complicated affair, partly because of the swift currents under the bridge, partly because the vessel had to be spun around 180 degrees to be readied for its return voyage to Beijing. Crowds gathered across the bridge and on both embankments, most to gawk, but some hoping to win a copper or two by assisting in the process, heaving on a line here, shifting the heavy woven-hemp fenders there. The barge captain and the drum major directed the whole business, orders barked from the bridge competing with shifting cadences from the red lacquer drum, deckhand rushing from rail to rail, stewards tossing coins to helpful strangers onshore. Inevitably, a few coolies would fall in the water, but luckily, this time, no one was crushed between the barge and the embankment. For restaurateurs and tea-shop proprietors, barge-docking days were wonderful for business; canalside tables were always booked weeks in advance by self-appointed experts who cheered and jeered as the events unfolded.

Longyan was oblivious to Grand Canal hubbub. His eyes remained riveted on the Wu family greeting party—the Patriarch, the Matriarch, Meihua, and several servants—standing in a quiet circle on the wharf. From the moment he saw them, a half mile away and an hour before the ornery barge was docked, Longyan and his family shared restrained waves; elites, of course, never shouted to each other for fear of sounding like noisy street riffraff.

Meihua stood quietest of all, a little apart from the family circle, dressed in what was known as a city gown, fashionably gathered slightly around her waist, but quite somber in its dark blue hue, her hairstyle also understated with polished ebony combs rather than beads and flowers. From a distance, Longyan was entranced by Meihua's elegant form, the light breeze blowing her featherlight silk gown slightly, her hand gracefully waving a greeting. But as he grew closer, Longyan sensed that something seemed very wrong. Why did Meihua keep dabbing her eyes with a handkerchief? Why was the Matriarch directing servants to look after her daughter-in-law? Why did the Patriarch lean on Lao Li for support—he wasn't that old and feeble, was he? Was it that difficult, Longyan wondered, to meet a son who was now a ranking official in the new dynasty?

Instead of the warm words and hugs Longyan hoped for, he was welcomed with an extraordinary greeting, one that raised more questions than it answered. The servants fell to their knees and bowed with their heads touching the ground, three times, all in unison, in time with a ceremony organizer who shouted, *"Kow-wow!"*—"Touch the head." The Patriarch, the Matriarch, and Meihua remained standing, but also bowed deeply three times as well. Then the organizer raised his hands and a small band—flute, two-stringed *erhu,* drums, and clackers—struck up a slow, martial melody, an ancient song to celebrate the installation of new officials.

Throughout the ceremony, Longyan stood dumbstruck by the fanfare; his Qing dynasty imperial robes, blue jacket with dragons on front, conical cap with light green jade ball on top, all quivered in nervous surprise. As a whispery silence fell over the crowds on the bridge and canal embankments, Longyan found himself the central actor in a huge drama, wondering what the play was all about.

On one level, the unexpected ceremony was reassuring. The Patriarch was greeting his son as an official, expressing formal pride at the appointment, seemingly not regretting that he was receiving a living emissary of the Manchus, and apparently not embarrassed that he had previously feted his son as a Ming martyr. The whole ceremony was infused with ritual correctness, making a public statement. But what, Longyan wondered, did the family really feel? Did the lavish welcome express real pride? Or was the formality a cloak for other emotions?

Longyan's questions remained unanswered for the next two

hours as his gondola, flying a prefect's flag, led the procession through Suzhou's canals to the Wu family mansion. Bystanders bowed respectfully. But Longyan heard an unseen woman's cackling laughter as she observed the caravan from a darkened shop window, "Looks like a funeral to me. A funeral in reverse. The corpse comes back from the dead!" The Patriarch, following his son in the next gondola, was embarrassed enough to direct his servants to shut the blabbermouth up.

Surely, Longyan surmised, the rigid ceremonial atmosphere would melt into informality when they entered the family house. So he was surprised when the Patriarch guided him into the meeting room, offering Longyan the position of honor, the central chair facing the door.

"Prefect Wu," the Patriarch spoke impassively, sitting next to his son in the host's chair. "We welcome you back to this humble household. You do us honor by being here. You would do me a great honor if you call yourself by our family name. Please use Wu and not Wang. I wish to express my deep apologies for suggesting otherwise several years ago."

"Father . . ." Longyan would have to choose his words carefully, not only because of the importance of the occasion, but also because of his gaffe as a three-year-old in this very room. "Father, it is you who honor me. I am a wayward son returning home, asking your forgiveness. My elevation to official rank was simply happenstance. I am pleased, but not proud. I would be more honored if you would simply call me Longyan."

"Prefect Wu," the Patriarch replied without considering the alternative. "This humble former official would not have the temerity to impose familial terms on you. All of us hope that you might honor us with your presence from time to time."

"Father?" Longyan waited, hoping that the Patriarch might relax slightly. The Patriarch sat stiffly, eyes fixed someplace off in space. Longyan had his answer; he knew what his father felt about him. At least Longyan was a Wu, he wasn't disowned; but he was serving another dynasty, a disloyal act in Confucian terms, unfilial behavior in his father's estimation, and so he would remain "Prefect Wu."

Longyan gave up trying to change the demeanor of the conversation. "Father. I thank you for your generous welcome. Might I ask after the health of the family?"

"Your mother is well." The Matriarch smiled and nodded her head at the mention of her name. Then she drew her hands together and bowed respectfully. Longyan surveyed her with astonishment; could she really change so radically simply because her son became an official?

"And your sister is as well as possible." Meihua bowed slightly and avoided Longyan's attentive scrutiny. Without eye contact, Longyan was left to examine her soft features, her gently folded long fingers, her thin neck twisted slightly away, her delicately tucked-up hair. Meihua appeared to wear her age well: indeed only the puffiness around her eyes bespoke the trials of life.

"Why do you say she's 'as well as possible'?" Longyan asked the question of his father, since male guests never addressed the women directly unless given permission by the host. Such informality only occurred with a family, not with a visit from a high official.

"You don't know?" the Patriarch asked with surprise.

"Don't know what?"

"Xinping died almost a month ago," the Patriarch let out the words in a rush. "Bad *qi*. That was the cause. I fear it's reaching plague proportions."

Longyan caught his breath for a moment. Then he walked to the Patriarch's chair, knelt before it, and grasped his father's shaking hands. "Oh no, I'm so terribly sorry. What a loss. He had real talent. Such great promise." The Patriarch squeezed Longyan's hands momentarily, choked back a sob, then pushed him away and resumed his rigid posture.

Longyan walked to Meihua's chair and took her face gently between his hands, stroking away the tears, lifting her eyes to his. "Oh, my sister. What can I say? You were so devoted to him. You so wanted him to succeed. I know he would have done so." The bleariness of her tears obscured any direct contact between them.

"Thank you, my brother, and welcome home. Your presence gives us all solace. He had hoped to see you one last time, but he couldn't hold on. It's a blessing that he's gone. Now he's with your ancestors." She hesitated for a moment, pushed down Longyan's hands and straightened her hair. "A prefect?" she continued more brightly. "We're all so proud of your position. We know it will be a difficult task. But we're sure you will do it well. And we're sure you will fulfill your responsibilities with sensitivity."

"I wish there was something I could do," Longyan said softly as he resumed his seat. "I shall certainly offer my respects in the Ancestral Hall. And I shall miss him, both as a brother and as a friend."

"We are honored by your concern, Prefect Wu," the Patriarch said dispassionately.

"Would you please stop calling me this Prefect Wu!" Longyan said sharply. "It was better when you treated me as a wastrel. At least I was a wayward son, rather than some government official. Please, I beg you, call me Longyan."

Longyan waited. No one responded. The Patriarch stared stonily ahead.

"All right," Longyan finally blurted, "call me Prefect Wu if you like. I didn't have any choice in serving the Manchus. It wasn't just my death, but the death of all my men as well. Besides, the Ming dynasty was collapsing of its own corruption. You, Father, of all people, you knew that so well. Can't you accept a live son? Can't you accept a live son who wants to work for a dynasty that believes in order?"

Silence reigned for a long moment. Then the Patriarch spoke with cold clarity. "A dynasty that believes in order? Do you call this order?" The Patriarch stood and slowly removed his black hat, turning in place, revealing his shaved pate and the beginnings of a braided queue down his neck. "Is it not bad enough that barbarians rule Beijing? Is it not bad enough that they force disgusting barbarians' customs on cultured people? That's not bad enough? Just to make it worse, I have a son who serves the barbarians. All right, I respect your rank—that is required by law—but do not ask me to respect your decision."

"Father, I do not defend the queue order. I hate it too, but it's my duty to enforce it. But let's remember that the Ming had lost the dynasty long before the conquest. If it wasn't for the Manchus in Beijing today, it surely would have been a domestic rebel. It's silly to engage in weeping over a romantic past. Everybody criticized the Ming until they were gone. Now you're all playing foolish nostalgic games."

"Nostalgic games?" Meihua stood and hobbled to the center of the room, facing Longyan with hands on hips. "It's not just the queue," she snapped, eyes burning with fire. "Do you know what your beloved Manchus have done? Right here in the Yangtze basin? How about razing entire towns? Pillaging everything of value, killing all old men and boys, enslaving all other males, making whores of all women, even little girls? So, honorable Prefect, this is your policy?"

"I know these things have happened," Longyan replied as calmly as possible. "I do not condone them. I want to make sure that things are done differently. My orders are quite explicit. I am here to see if we can implement Qing rule with greater humanity. I am a middleman between foreigners and Chinese."

"Brother! You are a broker for barbarians. An agent for those without culture. Do not glorify yourself with clever rhetoric."

"Dearest daughter," the Matriarch raised her voice, "you will please sit down." Longyan watched Meihua nod deferentially and resume her place; but, he thought with surprise, now Meihua is "dearest daughter." That's totally new.

"And now . . . my respected number one son . . ."

Longyan almost fell out of his chair. In one phrase, the Matriarch had buried thirty years of hostile history and adopted Longyan as her own, clearly elevating him to Xinping's former exalted status. In slow-motion unison, everyone in the room—Longyan, Patriarch, Meihua, and four servants—twisted heads, opened eyes and mouths, and stared at the Matriarch in astonishment. The Matriarch paused, enjoying the spotlight, preparing for a premiere performance in a new role, one she had considered from the moment that Xinping's illness was declared terminal and Longyan's prefectureship was declared official.

"Respected number one son," she continued, quietly so that others would strain to hear her voice. "We are indeed proud of your position. We think it is important for the government, but also, whatever our bickering, important for the family as well. We are pleased."

Longyan smiled at the first genuine compliment he had received; and for once, the Matriarch's pompous use of the imperial "we" seemed to imply that she could speak for the whole family. Now he understood the Matriarch's ploy. She was taking the initiative in retructuring family relationships; in effect, she was adopting Longyan as her own and forcefully suggesting that he was the family heir. She gambled that the Patriarch would not object, since Longyan's official post brought great prestige. And by linking herself overtly to Longyan, she was also gambling that the Patriarch would not consider installing another taitai. The fact that the Patriarch did not speak implied his formal consent and the withholding of his emotional support. She had won her gamble.

"But we are worried," the Matriarch continued with a glint of victory in her eyes. "There has been so much terror, so much tragedy. So many mistakes on both sides." Longyan smiled again; a diplomat! "Your father, and your sister-in-law, have firm convictions. It will take much to change their views. So you have a double task. You must administer humanely, for the dynasty's sake, and you must convince others you are making humane judgments, for your family's sake as well as your own."

Longyan looked at the Matriarch, searching for words to capture a torrent of conflicting emotions. Even if it lacked spontaneity, she had delivered a powerful little speech. "Yes, Mother, I will do my very best." Not in all his days did Longyan ever think that he would be at a conversational disadvantage with the Matriarch.

"That is all we can expect, my son. And now how shall you call me?"

"Not honorable Matriarch?"

"No. Honorable Mother."

"Thank you, honorable Mother."

"Now," she continued crisply. "I believe our little greeting is completed. You, dear number one son, must be very tired. You shall probably wish to visit the Ancestral Hall first, then surely you shall want to rest a bit. We've put you in the guest quarters. That's appropriate when my son, the Prefect, comes to visit."

The Matriarch tipped her head slightly, her usual punctuation indicating that she had said something she deemed important; then she opened her hands in a gesture that told everyone the gathering was completed, that nothing more need be said.

A few weeks later, Wu Longyan assumed responsibility of the prefectural *yamen* (office) in Huaiyin, almost two hundred miles northwest of Suzhou city. Twenty magistrates, the lowest imperial officials, reported to him, thus making Longyan responsible for approximately two million persons in the affluent Yangtze Delta region, over one percent of the entire population of China. His yamen employed almost a thousand local persons, including a dozen subprefects and their staffs, constables, tax collectors, court officials, secretaries, doorkeepers (very potent figures who literally determined access to officials in Qing China), cooks, stablekeepers, palanquin carriers, and a bevy of yamen runners (those who took documents and memoranda around the prefecture).

The Prefect was the ultimate local authority responsible for such key functions as taxation, police order, subordinate appointments, public works, and justice. Since imperial tradition demanded that prefects, like all other key provincial officials from magistrates to governors, come from another area (to avoid conflicts of interest), the early meetings with the local permanent staff were always crucial tests of who would actually be in charge.

"The first case is Peasant Zhou," announced the bailiff, nodding before the U-shaped table, Prefect Wu in the center, subprefects to his sides, separate tables on the inside for judicial advisers, secretaries, a raised wicket for the defendant. On the wall behind his head, Longyan had hung two calligraphic scrolls, one reading "culture," the other reading "humanity." Both were designed to show the softer side of Qing rule.

"Peasant Zhou is accused," continued the bailiff, "of killing six members of his family. In one night. By sword."

It was obvious that Zhou was both deranged and drunk. Upon entering the wicket, Zhou pretended he was a monkey, jumping about, scratching himself, shrieking jungle calls. Longyan glared at the defendant, trying to look tough, while inside he was churning over several possibilities. How was he going to look firm and humane at the same time? Especially with such an obvious case? After all, everyone knew that madmen were dangerous, that they were prone to such terrible acts, and that the only way to stop rampages was to execute the culprits.

Longyan was frustrated that his first case bore no relationship to the strained relationship between Manchus and Chinese. After all, Huaiyin prefecture, indeed all of Jiangsu province, was a hotbed of Ming loyalism. His assignment, so clearly described by Sose back in Beijing, was bridging the gap between adherents of two dynasties, not putting fools to death.

The bailiff tried to quiet Peasant Zhou, but to no avail. The monkey had become a rabbit, hobbling along the balustrade around the wicket. "I'm sorry, sir," the bailiff said to Longyan, "but I can't calm him down."

When a defendant refused to cooperate, imperial law codes allowed a prefect to make a summary judgment. But that was a rather extreme approach, hardly the best way to begin a new tenure. Suddenly Longyan had an inspiration. Maybe he could turn his first case to political advantage.

"Bailiff, it's all right," Longyan said with authority. "Take him out for a while. I want a private chat with my subprefects. I'll tell you when to bring him back."

The subprefects shared puzzled glances among themselves. Was the new Prefect so incompetent that he couldn't tell that the man was insane? Certainly any idiot could have passed judgment on such a crazy man. Was the new Prefect afraid to have a madman executed?

"Before we discuss Peasant Zhou's case," Longyan said, "we must have a little chat among ourselves. About a much bigger matter. Who knows anything of the Suzhou Midnight Massacre? I want to know the truth. What do you know?"

After an embarrassingly long silence, Senior Subprefect Wu spoke hesitantly. "We have heard of it. We know nothing about it."

"*We* have heard about it, but *we* know nothing about it?" Longyan mocked his words. "Who is *we*?"

"All of us, sir. Everyone in this room."

"It would appear, that for a subject you know nothing about, rather widespread discussions have taken place. Is there no one in room who knows something more than nothing about the massacre?"

Absolute silence. That was just what Longyan expected. After all, he hadn't imagined that anyone would reveal inside information, particularly since it was likely to point to some of the most influential families in the province. Besides, since the event was veiled in secrecy, it was quite possible that no one knew anything definite enough to report.

"All right, since you cannot help me with the Suzhou massacre," Longyan announced, "bring back the prisoner."

This time Peasant Zhou was more subdued. He had been harshly beaten in the interim—that was the practice with recalcitrant prisoners, one that Longyan and every provincial official supported. Zhou was shackled into the wicket and, for good measure, two guards grabbed his arms. The prisoner slumped sullenly, his eyes occasionally darting around the room, staring defiantly at Longyan, then finally looking listlessly at the floor.

"Peasant Zhou. You stand accused of killing your family. We have reports from six witnesses that you killed them all, with a sword. Is this true?"

"Yes, it's true," Peasant Zhou whimpered. "But they . . . they . . ."

"Yes?"

"They were going to have me locked up. Sent away to prison. A prison for crazy people."

"Well. What do you think? Are you crazy?"

"No. They're crazy. Not me. They're crazy!"

"Peasant Zhou! So you killed them all? Don't you think it's natural we would think you are crazy?"

"Well maybe. But—"

"But nothing. You did something terrible. You admit you did it. So there is no alternative."

"No! No! No!" Zhou screamed. "Please, no! You're not going to execute me."

"We have no choice," Longyan replied. "We must execute you."

"Not slicing! Please not slicing?"

"How we will execute you is not yet decided. Indeed, we will let you help make the decision."

Every official in the room stared at the new Prefect in astonishment. Condemned prisoners never had a say in their sentences. Even Peasant Zhou was speechless.

"Slicing, of course, is the right punishment for murder," Longyan continued. "But I could make the penalty less, if I wished, perhaps hanging or drowning. It's up to you."

"Up to me?"

"Yes. I could lighten the method of execution if you told the whole truth."

"But I have—"

"The whole truth about the Suzhou Midnight Massacre," Longyan interrupted. "What was your role in this terrible event? Where were you last December fifteenth?"

"But, sir, I don't know what you're talking about. . . ."

"Bailiff, could you help?" Longyan asked. "Please come here." Longyan whispered in the bailiff's ear. The bailiff smiled slightly, then walked to the prisoner and whispered slowly in Peasant Zhou's ear. Peasant Zhou looked puzzled. The bailiff repeated the message. A dull grin came across the prisoner's face.

"Oh, your great honorableness," Zhou finally said. "You're right. I confess. I was just outside Suzhou. Shooting those Western guns. Right at Manchus. Lots of us were involved."

"Would you be willing to tell us who else was involved?"

"Oh, yes. Of course."

"Thank you, Peasant Zhou. You have committed two terrible crimes. Domestic homicide, that's bad enough, but also murder of soldiers of the Qing dynasty. The only mitigating factor is your willingness to inform this prefecture about others who were involved in the awful events of December fifteenth of last year. We shall determine your punishment accordingly."

Usually verdicts were drafted by the officer of the court, then reviewed by the senior subprefect, finally signed by the Prefect. In this case, Prefect Wu dictated the verdict so that all could hear it:

"Case of Peasant Zhou, Jonghe Village, Huaiyin prefecture, Jiangsu province.

"In a preliminary investigation of Peasant Zhou's alleged murder of his family members, the court found that the evidence was overwhelming that he had committed such an act. Suspicious that Peasant Zhou was hiding other nefarious crimes, Prefect Wu interrogated him about the ambush of Qing dynasty troops outside Suzhou in the winter of last year. Prefect Wu was able to gain his confession. Then, through persistent interrogation and the promise of a lightened form of execution, Prefect Wu forced Peasant Zhou to offer important information about other culprits in the massacre.

"Please let this report be posted throughout Jiangsu province. And let Peasant Zhou's final disposition await the interrogation by the Governors General of Liang Jiang when they arrive this summer."

★   ★   ★

Eight weeks later, a well-rehearsed Peasant Zhou sat in the wicket again, this time confronting the Governors General, the two highest Qing officials in the Yangtze basin area. By early Qing practice of dyarchy, one was a Manchu and one a Chinese, ostensibly to offer cohesive decisions concerning the two ethnic groups, but actually because of profound distrust. As usual, shortly after the conquest, it was the Manchu who had the determining voice, especially given the sensitive nature of this particular case.

"I've read this case," boomed the Manchu Governor General, "but how do I know you're not trying to fool me? How do I know you're not confessing to a crime you didn't commit?"

The prefectural interpreter, a new appointment since the need for Manchu-Chinese translation had arisen only a year earlier, began to relay the question into Chinese.

"No!" shouted the Manchu. "I don't trust you! I've got my own interpreter. Brought him from Beijing. He's not even Chinese, so he's got no reason to distort things in your direction."

Father Gao walked in, as unobtrusively as his great size would permit, sat behind the Governor General and, offering not the slightest greeting to Longyan, translated the Manchu into clear-cut colloquial Chinese.

"Oh, sir, I'm so sorry," Peasant Zhou gave his practiced reply. "I was told that Manchus were coming to kill us all. I just joined a lot of people one night. They gave us lots of guns. . . ."

"You know how to fire guns?"

"Oh, yes, sir."

"What makes it fire?"

"Uh. It's a little thing on top. . . ."

"You mean the *wick*," urged Father Gao in Chinese.

"The wick makes it fire." That was what Father Gao translated.

"And the wick lights what?" the Manchu asked.

"And the wick lights the gunpowder that shoots out the musket ball. Correct?" Father Gao said in Chinese.

"The wick lights the gunpowder that shoots out the musket ball." Again that was what Father Gao translated so quickly that the Manchu did not realize his embellishments.

"So there were lots of you?"

"Yes."

"Who?"

"I don't know their names. They were from lots of villages. Besides, it was too dark to see them clearly."

"They were from villages? Peasants? Like yourself?"

"Oh, yes, sir. Just peasants. Old-hundred-names, you know, commoners. We were all down near Suzhou. Planting the winter wheat. We move around a lot."

"So if you don't know their names, what's the value of your testimony?"

"I could tell where some of them came from. By their local dialects. I told the Prefect here—I mean the honorable Prefect— what those villages were likely to be."

The Manchu grunted his approval and, with the Chinese Governor General, Father Gao, and their entourage, departed Prefect Wu's yamen. Longyan then dictated the official verdict:

"Peasant Zhou, upon recommendation of Prefect Wu, and upon review by the esteemed Governors General of Liang Jiang, is found guilty of treasonous acts against the Qing dynasty. Most specifically, he has confessed his involvement in the infamous Suzhou ambush of December fifteenth, sixteen hundred forty-four. For this crime, as well as domestic homicide, he shall be executed.

"The method of execution for such a crime is usually the lingering death by slicing. But Peasant Zhou has offered helpful testimony to the prefecture and to the province concerning other village areas that may have been involved in the crime. So through the generosity of the Qing emperor, Peasant Zhou will be put to death by hanging. The sentence will be conducted immediately."

Peasant Zhou bowed deeply; whatever sentiments he wanted to express were choked off by the bailiff's hand over the prisoner's mouth. Every official followed the example of the senior subprefect and bowed from the waist, three times, in genuine respect to Prefect Wu.

Henceforth Longyan's decision became known as the Wu Compromise. As soon as the decision was posted, every prefect and magistrate knew that there was an alternative to executing elite Ming loyalists. The execution of already convicted peasants for the further crime of treason offered a more humane alternative. Fifty such executions were carried out in 1646, probably saving thousands of gentry lives, and surely buying considerable time to soften the imposition of Qing rule. The Wu Compromise promised to bridge the Manchu–Chinese gap—as long as no other overt Ming loyalist acts prompted renewed suspicion by conservative Qing officials.

CHAPTER FIFTEEN

The Ming History

明

The Next Two Years:
Suzhou and Huaiyin, 1646–1647

My dear brother, I so totally misjudged you. Everyone speaks so
warmly of the compromise you have fashioned. Not only the Pa-
triarch, but also the Matriarch, are expressing their great pride for
their son. It appears that all else has been forgotten.

My dearest sister, your warm words mean more than all
the public accolades in the world. Perhaps that is since I
know you speak compliments truthfully since, no disre-
spect intended, you also speak criticisms with little hesitation.

Tell me, dearest sister, how is your life now that you are
left without your husband? It must be so trying. Tell me,
frankly, what do you do with your time? How is it at
home? Tell me what you used to tell me.

Meihua read and reread Longyan's letter. Was there a hint of
something personal? No! She couldn't entertain such fantasies. She
was a widow. A young widow, to be sure, but still a widow. Confucian tradition required that widows remain chaste, devoted forever to deceased husbands. Besides what good had ever come from
her attraction to Longyan before? Longyan fantasies had caused
danger when he was at home; then years without contact after he
left home. (Meihua scanned her brain, thinking of words to replace
"fantasies about Longyan," finally deciding on "ruminations about
one's brother-in-law.")

How kind of you to inquire. This silly woman does grieve for her
husband. He had, as you have said, great potential. We all miss
him dearly.

My life in your noble Wu family home is now filled with much
solace and even satisfaction. I mean that. It's not just polite talk.
The Matriarch looks to me for advice. We are now on excellent
terms. The Patriarch even talks to me of events in the outer
world—as if a stupid woman could possibly understand.
What do I do with my time? I read some these days. I never write,
except to you. I would like much more of that now, if it is not
imposing on a busy official's time. There are many ruminations
which it would be pleasant to share with one's brother-in-law.
Then I spend lots of time on women's things. I am the president of
the Ladies' Filial Piety Society.

The Ladies' Filial Piety Society? Longyan had never heard of it.
Was it for widows? Was Meihua taking this chaste widow business
too far? Or perhaps it was just a prissy ladies' organization. Maybe
it was a gathering place for women so that they could share strate-
gies for dealing with menfolk—how to deal with frantic scholar-
officials caught in shifting political tides. Longyan never imagined
that it might be a front organization for direct political and military
involvement. But, whatever the purpose of the society, he wanted
to make certain that Meihua did her part to keep the lid on the
bubbling cauldron of Ming loyalism.

How sweet of you to become involved in a ladies' society.
I am certain it's nice for all of you, and a good distraction
for you after the death of my brother.
I do hope you can let the women know that it's important
to use their influence over the men in their lives. They
should do everything in their power to suggest that the
men keep order. Nothing would be worse than more violence. Then my position would be untenable.

"Why not fight?" a diminutive lady said sharply, teacup rattling
against saucer in her hands.

"Because it's not the right time to fight," Meihua responded.
She sat in the central chair, twenty-plus women surrounding her,
all officers of the Virtuous Army, all today in the guise of charter
members of the Ladies' Filial Piety Society. Since Meihua had
taken over the presidency from widow Zhang, meetings still

occurred at the abandoned Lin family guest house, doors locked and guarded by female servants who were, in other circumstances, sergeants in the Virtuous Army.

"We fought once," Meihua continued firmly, "fought superbly. And we achieved our objective."

"What objective?" came the pointed retort. "The Manchus control most of China. The Ming cause seems almost lost. What did it amount to?"

"Of course, I hope the Ming can make a comeback, but that hope rests with much bigger forces than ours. I've heard, for instance, that the Prince of Fu is gathering an army. But putting the Ming back on the throne was never a realistic goal. Not for our small brigade of women."

"So what was the goal?"

"To make it clear that Chinese values would persist. That Chinese elites would be treated with respect. That we would not simply let the Manchus trample over us. In that we succeeded. . . ."

"We did?" the little lady asked dubiously.

"Of course. The Manchus sent Chinese bannerman, not their own thugs, down to manage us. And besides, those bannermen are now acting like kittens rather than tigers. Has any elite been harmed because of our military operation?"

"You're just partial to your brother-in-law. You don't want us to use force because it might embarrass him."

"You shut your mouth," Meihua snapped, suddenly becoming the commanding officer. "I *am* partial to him. Not because of family. But because what he's done took courage, too. If we use force now, it will undercut any hope for compromise. You'll guarantee a bloodbath. Is that what you want? Is it?"

"I suppose not. . . ."

"Then you listen." Meihua softened her tone, but kept her authority. "We shall maintain our training and our vigilance. We'll be ready if there's a Ming counteroffensive. But meanwhile, we'll use another means to rally support. Another way to keep up public support and broaden our network."

"A new recruiting drive?"

"No. A new writing project."

"A writing project?"

"Precisely. A *True History of the Ming Dynasty*. Each of us will write a chapter. We will edit it together. Then we'll print it and circulate it throughout the lower Yangtze region."

"I see. . . ."

"It will show the Ming cause is still alive. As long as it stays private, the illiterate Manchus won't know a thing about it. And you know who'll be listed as author?"

"Who?"

"The Sons of Sima Qian."

The room exploded in laughter. Sima Qian was the great Han dynasty historian who remained true to his values in spite of running afoul of the government. Sima Qian, now dead for almost two thousand years, was an appropriate inspiration for the Ming loyalist cause. What was humorous was not only that the authors were women (rather than "sons"), but also that poor Sima Qian had been castrated in punishment for his criticisms (thus totally incapable of producing any offspring).

And Meihua, playing her part as the obedient widow, responded to Longyan's comments about the society:

> Do not worry, my dear brother, for I too want to maintain peace. All we foolish ladies can do is to talk to our men. And I have no husband and would not presume to talk to either your father or mine about affairs of the world. But I do chatter with the women-folk. Maybe I can exert a tiny influence, as a grain of sand raises the ocean's water level a minute amount.

The Patriarch coughed in the clouds of dust as he drew back the draperies covering the old study window. Blinking his eyes in the bright shafts of sunlight, he focused on the dingy room that had not been used since Longyan and Xinping had had their daily lessons with Tutor Lu. Between generations, the room was always kept locked, tomblike, awaiting the next Wu children who would sit in fear of their tutor's eyes and his switch.

"You know," the Patriarch said smilingly, "I studied here, too. For twenty hard years." Sucking his cheeks together, making his face look like a fish, he mimicked the tutor. "Gentlemen, what you feel is not important, in fact you're not important at all, only I'm important, because I teach the classics."

"That's perfect!" Longyan laughed, home for a visit after more than a year as Prefect of Huaiyin. Looking around the cobwebbed room, Longyan repressed some bad memories. "Father, I remember what you used to say. That a study is the center of a family." Longyan's finger drew the character *zhong* in the thick dust on the tabletop: an oblong box with a vertical line through it, meaning "the center."

"Yes, that's what I said when you were a child," the Patriarch nodded. "But its meaning changes when you are an adult." The Patriarch added four quick strokes with his finger—three dots and a long curved line with a hook—the symbol for "heart" under the word "center." Longyan knew instantly that the revised character, still pronounced *zhong,* now meant "loyalism."

"Please, Father," Longyan urged, sweeping the desk clean with the sleeve of his gown. "Please don't put yourself at risk."

"But there's no one here."

"They're everywhere. Believe me, I know."

"I'm sorry," said the Patriarch, brushing his chair clean before sitting down. "Old habits die slowly."

"I'm just trying to help," Longyan said quietly, and he whisked the lint off his chair. "It's not easy caught in between the way I am." Longyan felt a sharp spike of pain in his head, reminding him that he had chosen the path of compromise over purity.

"I know it hurts," the Patriarch said gently. "It may surprise you to learn that you have quite a following among some of my friends. They see you as a sort of bright torch in a dark cave."

"But not you?" Longyan asked hopefully.

The Patriarch paused, looking beyond Longyan to a wilted hanging scroll of Confucian aphorisms, preparing his words with care. "I am really old-fashioned. I cannot turn my back on the dynasty I once served."

"But it collapsed of its own weight. It was completely rotten. Like worm-eaten wood. It devoured even you."

"I know. I even know that the Ming cause is totally hopeless. The Qing have won. And you are trying to make things easier. I know all of this."

"But, you're saying, if you had been me, if you'd been captured, you wouldn't have done the same thing?"

"I don't know. It's easy to be the purist down here—in Suzhou and not in Manchuria. But I tell myself I would have died for my beliefs. That's not to say I don't understand your decision. Let's put it this way. *If* I had decided to serve the new dynasty, *then* I surely would have wanted to do it your way."

Longyan felt a stinging shame throughout his body. His father had stated the matter as gently as possible, but Longyan was caught in the classic Confucian morality conflict. Youngsters learned that the classics demanded ethical perfection; men learned that Chinese politics demanded practical compromises. And so, Longyan suffered from China's chronic male disease—unrelenting guilt. The guilt was overpowering even though his decision had saved thousands of lives and helped buffer the traumatic transition of dynasties.

"I wish I could ease your pain," said the Patriarch, knowing he could offer no more comfort. "But pain comes with office. I knew it well. Ultimately you're cut free—from tutors, from family, from home—and you have to make your own choices. Sometimes they hurt."

"It would be easier, I think, if I'd taken office in the usual way. Through succeeding in the examinations. Rather than losing in a war."

"But *you* made the choice not to proceed with your studies."

"Father, I had no choice," Longyan said sadly. "Something is the matter with my mind. I still don't know what it is. I'm not stupid. I tried very hard. You'll never know how hard. I can read and write, but with difficulty, never like a scholar. So I had to find another way to serve. Father, can you possibly understand?"

As the Patriarch felt his son's imploring stare, he dropped his eyes because it was too hurtful to keep looking at him. What irony, the Patriarch thought. Longyan is serving a living dynasty while I am moaning about a dead one. I have no job and *he's* the one who feels pained. As the Patriarch rubbed his face with his hands, he stared briefly at the place where the fingers were missing on his right hand, then quickly shoved his hands into his robe. He breathed in sharply as if to speak, looked up at Longyan, then stopped suddenly before a word was uttered.

"Yes, Father?" Longyan asked expectantly.

"Oh, it's nothing," the Patriarch lied, feeling his own pang of guilt at withholding a secret. Longyan saw the look on his father's face. He was clearly restraining an almost-told inner truth, but

Longyan dared not confront him. Slowly the Patriarch's anguished look disappeared; in its place came a softer face, an easing of tension lines indicating that something was resolved. If he could not tell the whole truth, he could at least start to bridge the gap between them. "We have a lot in common, you know. A lot more than you might think."

"Yes?"

"It's not the right time to tell you," the Patriarch said firmly, promising himself to tell Longyan the real truth someday.

"Tell me what?" Longyan recalled old Jin's ominous words, several years earlier in Beijing, about the *truth* concerning his father. He remembered something even earlier, whispered secrets with the Matriarch on Dragon Boat day. He could not ask any more directly. It would be unfilial to accuse a father of harboring deep secrets.

"Nothing much. But I can tell you something. I've decided I can no longer call you Prefect Wu."

"You can't?" Oh no, thought Longyan, it's back to disowning again.

"No." The Patriarch laughed. "No, I can't speak of you in such formal terms. Not at all, my son. My son, Longyan."

Longyan's eyes opened wide with surprise. Then, faces lit by a dusty shaft of sunlight, Longyan and the Patriarch shared the first long, warm smile since their *weiqi* games of so many years ago. Both suddenly snapped their heads around as they heard the study door creak open slightly.

"Oh, I'm so sorry," Meihua blurted. "It's just that this room has been locked so long. I thought maybe there was a prowler or something."

"It's no matter," the Patriarch declared, beckoning to her. "No, don't leave. We've just had a most interesting chat. About the past. And about the future."

Meihua tripped demurely across the floor, her tiny silk shoes stirring up a fog of dust, her fan fluttering the choking particles away from her face. Whatever was the Patriarch talking about? She surely would not ask him directly. She tipped her head slightly in a look of perplexity; that was all that was permitted. Longyan wondered at Meihua's demeanor. She seemed the perfect widow, accepting her lot without complaint, rumored to be assertive in the red chamber but properly passive elsewhere. He had tried to draw her into conversation, in quiet places like the rock garden, but she always refused the gambit with a polite comment about the weather or a hand-over-mouth laugh. He wasn't going to learn anything from her in person, so it was back to deciphering the real meaning behind letters. Or perhaps he would ask Father Gao, who made a regular trip to Suzhou in his rounds as the Jesuit representative in Jiangsu province. He might have some insights.

"Ah, you don't understand at all," the Patriarch said patronizingly to Meihua. "Of course not. But you remember what the Matriarch said, yes?"

Meihua tipped her head the other way, still perplexed.

"This man that the world knows as Prefect Wu. I am proud to call him my number one son. This does not mean we are in agreement about politics. Neither of us has changed our affiliations. But it does indicate approval of how my son has handled a difficult assignment."

Meihua drew in her breath, ready to shout her surprise and delight. Then she did what was proper. She said nothing, but nodded her smiling face toward the Patriarch and then toward Longyan. She bowed and shuffled backwards slightly, no mean feat given her crippled condition, stepping birdlike out of the room.

"I'm sure she was delighted," the Patriarch surmised, playing the perennial game of projecting what women actually thought since the rules demanded female silence much of the time.

"So am I, Father," Longyan said with genuine gratitude, knowing that the Patriarch had used Meihua to make his announcement. The entire Wu household would hear about their reconciliation in a matter of minutes.

"What's really going on in Suzhou?" Longyan asked Father Gao, both of them slurping away at shark's-fin soup, gelatinous masses of translucent cartilage in a brown broth. They dined in the Prefect's residence in Huaiyin, barely a week after Longyan's return from visiting his family.

"Going on? Nothing much. Things as usual. Your sister seems preoccupied, probably because of your brother's death. But you know all that. You were there recently yourself."

"No one tells me anything. You know what they say: When

falcons soar, squirrels keep out of sight. My father may treat me as a son, but everyone else sees me as Prefect Wu of the Manchu Qing dynasty. So what's really going on?"

Father Gao spooned some vinegar into his soup, keeping his eyes down lest Longyan sense that he was evading the question. As a houseguest of Prefect Wu—in Father Gao's new domain as Jesuit representative for all of Jiangsu province—who knew who might be listening?

Besides, if Father Gao told the truth, everyone would have been in trouble. Even behind the big rock in the Wu garden, presumably out of earshot, Meihua had coyly responded to Father Gao, "The Suzhou Midnight Massacre? Why, yes, I think I've heard of it. But they say that those shooting sticks make a terrible noise and even knock over grown men who fire them. Can you imagine what they would do to ladies?" He could still see the wry grin on her face, telling him precisely what he wanted to know. Then, sensing Father Gao's inner worries about how his new Manchu masters would react if they knew his connections to Ming loyalists, she added, "Of course, we women believe that the best animal is the rabbit. You know—big ears, but a tiny mouth. Hears everything, says nothing."

"You really like vinegar?" Longyan asked with bemusement.

"Oh, yes . . . Excellent." Father Gao responded, covering the fact that he had unwittingly dumped six spoonfuls in his soup. "Tell me," the priest continued, trying to recover his composure, "what will become of your sister? Now that your brother's gone, could you perhaps come to her rescue?"

"Rescue?" Now it was Longyan who almost choked on his soup. "I trust you aren't suggesting anything . . . intimate. It's simply my duty to Xinping, and to my parents, to worry about her. Besides, you know Confucianism wouldn't permit anything else."

"We Christians, you know, are much more permissive."

"What are you suggesting?"

"Widows have alternatives in the West."

"You mean widows can remarry?"

"Of course. In the Christian tradition, a woman's bondage to her husband is severed by his death. So she can have a new life. Even a new husband."

"Really? And parents tolerate this?"

"Parents often find that it makes widowed daughters much happier. So they too are happier."

"And you priests don't feel any conflict in performing wedding rituals twice in the life of a woman?"

"Not at all. As long as the husband is dead. We do not tolerate divorce."

"So you priests can do all these services—and yet you can't have sexual relations? Not even once in a lifetime after becoming a priest?"

"No."

Longyan laughed loudly. "You make the rules, but don't play the game!"

"And you." Father Gao grinned back. "I hear you play the game. But not by the rules. No wife in sight?"

"We play a very different game here," Longyan parried, laughing to cover his discomfiture at a question that came close to home. "New opponents every night. Usually just one at a time. But combinations can make the game more challenging." Longyan tipped his glass toward Father Gao and they shared a mirthful toast.

But the priest knew the deeper truth—and Longyan knew he knew it. Longyan had a secret, one that could cost him his official post and his reputation. So he could enjoy sex all night long, but he could never risk intimacy, never risk the sharing of secrets, never risk the quest for a wife. No one could learn that he was probably the highest-ranking illiterate, at least among the Chinese, in the Qing bureaucracy. He hated that term, *illiterate*, because he knew it wasn't accurate; but he also realized that his critics would not mince words if the truth was known.

"How's your new secretary?" Both knew that Father Gao's seeming non sequitur was on the same topic: preserving Longyan's secret.

"Henry Yan? Absolutely wonderful!"

Father Gao had originally recommended Henry Yan to Longyan shortly after their return from Manchuria to Beijing, when they learned that Secretary Cao had died. "You've got to do what the Manchus are doing," Father Gao had suggested, "find someone you can trust. Someone who will be totally loyal. I know just the man."

And so he did. Henry Yan was a sallow-faced, scholarly fellow in his mid-twenties, an orphan who had been raised in the Beijing Jesuit monastery, now a Christian convert who aspired to the priesthood. Henry was thus the ultimate outsider, someone totally dependent on his superiors for survival. His unimposing demeanor hid a sharp mind and a sensitive personality. Henry was the name the Jesuits gave him because it sounded a little like his Chinese name, Henei.

"Bring Henry," Longyan shouted to a servant, liking to use the Western name because it reinforced the anomalous position of his male secretary. Henry was the perfect private secretary, skilled in the outward responsibilities but totally committed to maintaining Longyan's private truth.

A few moments later, Henry Yan poked his head through the door, his birdlike face perched on a small, bony body barely noticeable under the black silk gown that seemed like a cover carelessly tossed over an irregular sculpture. He walked hesitantly, a gawky uncertainty in his steps, like a shy animal always ready to run for cover. "Yes, honorable Prefect? And Father, you're here as well?"

"Henry, sit down and join us. Have a little something to eat." A single wave of Longyan's arm mobilized three servants to bring a chair, place another setting at the table, and fill his glass with wine. "Now, please, let's have the news." A second wave from Longyan cleared the room so that Henry could speak freely.

It was Henry Yan's special knowledge of the "news," just as much as his influential position as private secretary to Prefect Wu, that made the little man invaluable. Henry read every document that flowed in and out of the prefectural yamen, often comparing his information to the Jesuit network from around China and across Asia, then sharing notes on a very confidential and controlled basis with other private secretaries in key cities in northern and coastal China. Henry Yan was, simply put, the best-informed man in Jiangsu province. And so, just as Henry was totally dependent on his Chinese and Jesuit patrons, they were totally addicted to his data.

"Perhaps we should begin with Beijing," Henry said, clearing his throat and speaking precisely. "Two factions are contending. The first centers on the young Shunzhi emperor and his advisers, most notably your friend Sose. 'Dyarchs'—that's what members of this faction call themselves—equal weight to Manchus and Chinese. 'Worms'—that's what their opponents call them. Soft and ugly, let anybody step on them."

"Just what I thought," Longyan affirmed. "I wish we had more of them. More worms! That Sose fellow is smart. He knows that dynasties cannot survive by force alone. Let's hope for strong worms—if that's not too odd an idea. But what about their opponents?"

"They're centered around Dorgon, the regent whose health is not so good. Mainly hard-nosed Manchus, members of the council of princes and high officials, but also some key Chinese bannermen, seeking to curry favor with hard-liners."

"And the balance?"

"Worms still have the upper hand. But who knows how long? The other faction. Some call them Vultures. The Vultures hover in the sky, waiting for a mistake, a chance to strike." Henry paused, enjoying his metaphor. "So far they are concentrating their efforts on military operations against the Ming loyalist strongholds in the hinterland, especially in Anhui, Hubei, Hunan, Sichuan, Guangdong. But they really want to squash what they see as the secret resistance here in the Yangtze delta region. They are just waiting for something new to happen, some evidence of loyalism, then they'll pounce on it. The Vultures hate what they see as soft snobs—rich scholars and merchants."

"And where do we Jesuits fit?" Father Gao wondered.

"I've heard you foreign priests described as 'Big-nosed Worms,'" Henry allowed himself a furtive smirk. "But you still have the technological advantage. You've won the biggest battle in Beijing. At the Imperial Bureau of Astronomy, the Jesuits make better predictions than the Arabs that the Ming employed. The German Jesuit Adam Schall has just been named as director of the bureau. He's building a new observatory about a mile east of the Forbidden City. With all the latest instruments."

"Marvelous." Father Gao chuckled.

"That's the good news." Henry pursed his lips, hesitating before changing to a more downbeat mood. "The bad news concerns weapons. The Jesuit fathers are advising the Manchus on how to build cannon and how to use muskets. But the Vultures are wondering why some of the Ming loyalists have the same weapons. Particularly why such weapons could have been used in uprisings like the Suzhou Midnight Massacre."

"That's something I'd like to know myself," Longyan intervened. "Why?"

"You ask me? How should I know?" Father Gao worried that he'd spoken too quickly, sounding too defensive. "I can't imagine who revealed the technology. But, of course, once revealed, it's not so hard to make weapons yourself."

"I suppose so," Longyan responded, eyeing the Jesuit quizzically. "But if the Manchus ever discover direct connections between Loyalists and Christians, you'll face a reign of terror. And I won't be able to do a thing."

"No one has proved such links," Henry Yan responded. "In fact, I honestly don't have a scrap of information about who pulled off the massacre."

"You don't?" Father Gao asked, immensely relieved. His admiration for Meihua took another giant leap; she was clearly as skilled in the art of secrecy as in the art of war. If neither Henry nor Longyan knew, then it was truly a remarkable job of keeping confidences.

"But things will surely change soon," Henry continued. "I have it on good authority that an army of censors, Manchus and Chinese alike, will soon spread across Jiangsu province. They want new evidence of loyalism. If they find anything . . . well, heaven forbid—"

"Henry," Longyan interrupted, "I think we'll be wanting to send a letter. I'll dictate it in a moment." Henry nodded and rushed out to get his portable secretary's case. "Father Gao. This will need your special handling as always."

"To a friend in Suzhou?"

"Of course."

It is a time of enormous danger. Please use your private network. Warn our families. Do nothing that would prompt retaliation. I cannot make these words strong enough.

A chill went down Meihua's spine as she read Longyan's letter, but there was a smile on her lips. Is he just expressing concern for his family, she wondered, or does he really worry about me in particular?

> *Of course I shall heed your words. But why does such a high official bother with someone like me?*

Why now? Longyan grimaced. Why play flirtatious games when I'm trying to warn her?

Henry Yan peered up at Longyan from across the table, where he had been reading Meihua's return letter out loud. "Honorable Prefect," Henry said quietly, "I have heard reports that our term *xin* perfectly describes women. With women, there is no separation between 'mind' and 'heart.' "

"Yes?" Longyan asked dumbly.

"You've got to play a little to her emotions if you want her to listen to your advice." How could someone so powerful be so stupid? Henry wondered privately. What a strange man. The Prefect is a rational giant, Henry observed, but is he also an emotional dwarf?

The little chap could be right, Longyan thought to himself. So what to say to Meihua? As he dictated his letter, Longyan felt a curtain falling inside him. He surprised both himself and his secretary as the words flowed forth:

> I care very deeply for you, my sister. More than anyone on earth besides my parents. I want your happiness. I want your safety. I speak from deep devotion. I speak with a brother's care, but also with an admirer's concern. Please take care of everyone, most especially yourself, at this difficult time.

Meihua kept the letter in her sleeve for almost a week, sneaking glances at it whenever she was alone, whenever she wanted reassurance. She even read it to Peach Blossom just to make sure she had given it the proper reading.

How wonderful to hear your inner words. It has been so long since I have felt connected to you. I will be honest. Persecution is no longer my problem. I no longer need a defender. Loneliness is my problem. I need a friend. Possibly more.

Dare I say it? Your closeness to me gives hope to my life. I believe that, given a chance, I could help you realize your dreams as well. I do not know what I am suggesting. Only that, whatever lies ahead, do not lose touch with me again.

I shall do my best to heed your warning about danger. I shall convey it privately to those who could perhaps use the advice.

"It's a great achievement," Meihua said, three months later, holding the first copy of the *True History of the Ming Dynasty* by the Sons of Sima Qian.

The eight-volume set had been produced in record time: the writing all done by the officers of the Virtuous Army, the printing and binding in Ming imperial red by a small band of senior servants who had learned the craft in their spare time. The *Ming History* spoke glowingly of dynastic heroes from the founding fathers right through to the Suzhou Massacre. The date of publication was listed as the Third Year of Ming Fu Wang, the Ming loyalist prince who still rallied forces in the south, and not the Fourth Year of the Qing Shunzhi Emperor.

The *Ming History* was precisely what Meihua had originally desired: an elite Chinese slap in the Manchu face. But now the volumes weighed heavily in her hands. Would this act of bravado ricochet like the musket balls in the cave? Would it bring the wrath of the Manchus for no purpose other than displaying resistance? Would it perhaps endanger Prefect Wu in Huaiyin?

"How many copies do we have?" Meihua asked.

"A thousand."

"Good," Meihua responded. "Let's keep them in our cave until we decide it's the right time to distribute the books."

"What?" asked Widow Zhang. "We shoot Manchus with guns. But we don't dare criticize them with our books which they can't read anyway?"

"That's not the point," Meihua replied, thinking quickly. "It's just that books are weapons, too. We have to know how to aim them accurately, shooting them at the right moment."

"And when will that be?"

"When I tell you."

Meihua tried to sound firm, but she could feel her authority ebbing for the first time since the founding of the Virtuous Army six years earlier. The *Ming History,* after all, was the product not of a military organization, but rather of the civilian Ladies' Filial Piety Society. She had the awful feeling that someone would reveal the new book, letting pride of authorship outweigh discretion.

Less than a month later, a furious Manchu slammed his thumb ring against a table and shouted at Longyan, "Prefect Wu! How do you explain this?" The Manchu governor general had fire in his eyes. An ashen-faced Father Gao interpreted into Chinese for the prefectual bureaucrats who stood ramrod straight, his shaky voice sounding like a disembodied, sotto voce chorus.

Longyan slowly opened the first volume, shaking his head in disbelief, knowing that it was the symbolism of a new publication, the *True History of the Ming Dynasty,* that had infuriated the Manchus. He surmised that they probably had not bothered to translate the contents and probably missed its subtleties. But there was no denying that this was a collaborative effort, surely from Yangtze delta elites, to snipe at Qing rule.

"I know nothing of this," Longyan said as calmly as he could, "it's the first I've seen of it."

"Nothing? Prove it!"

"Prove it? My word is not good enough? I'm the Prefect of Huaiyin. I am the official representative of His Majesty the Emperor of the great Qing dynasty. Why should my word not be good enough?"

"Because you are Chinese."

"With all due respect, honorable Governor General, is being Chinese now a crime?"

"No. Not a crime. But enough to arouse suspicions. Especially when we have such evidence of treason. Now. I offer you a second chance. What do you know of this publication?"

"Nothing. I told you the absolute truth. What more can I say?"

"Who are the authors?"

"I don't know."

"Who are the Sons of Sima Qian?"

Only the tension of the moment kept Longyan from smiling. "It's not the real authors. It's sort of a historical joke."

"So everybody laughs at the new Manchu rulers?"

"No. I didn't say that."

"Well. We've found out who some of the real authors are. Four of them, anyhow. All women. And from where? Suzhou!"

Longyan shut his eyes in disbelief. He knew what he was going to hear next.

". . . all from elite families. Verdicts have already been passed for three of them. Execution. For the authors and their immediate families. Strangulation by silken cord. Too gentle, I think, but it was not my decision. Public executions will be carried out in the next few days. There's still one case undecided. . . ."

"Yes?" Longyan asked limply.

"Your sister-in-law. Lin family. Widow, yes? Name is Meihua, I believe. All correct?"

"Correct. She's still alive?"

"Alive? Yes. But also judged guilty. Sentence not yet determined. That's why I'm here."

"Yes?"

"Unlike the relatives of the other traitors, you *are* indeed an official of the dynasty. I felt you should have a choice. If I do not intervene, your sister-in-law will be executed. As will your family and hers as well." The Manchu paused momentarily, enjoying a sneer at Longyan's expense. "The other alternative: both families will be stripped of wealth and property. But no one will be executed. Your sister-in-law to be exiled to Hainan Island."

Longyan stared blankly. "How does one make the choice?"

"It's simple. All you have to do is admit you were part of the plot. Then we'll simply remove you from office. You'll be recalled to Beijing. You will probably be arrested, but you won't be harmed."

"But it's not true."

"What difference does the truth make? What would your political future be if your entire family was executed for treason?"

Longyan inhaled deeply. He stared at Father Gao. Clearly the Jesuits were just as jeopardized. A grimace passed over the priest's stony face. Longyan read it correctly. Remember back in Manchuria, when I had to lie, Father Gao was saying, to save your life? Now you must do the same.

"All right," Longyan agreed softly, "have it your way."

"What does that mean?" the Manchu governor general snapped. "Speak clearly. Or I shall authorize the executions."

"It means . . . Yes, I admit that I was part of the plot to publish this treasonous book. I regret my actions. I beg the forgiveness of the noble great Qing dynasty."

CHAPTER SIXTEEN

Beggars

The Next Three Years:
Nanjing, Beijing, and Hainan Island, 1648–1650

A MAD BEGGAR danced on a street corner near the old Ming Forbidden City in Nanjing, eight hundred miles to the south of Beijing. He wore a tattered cotton blanket, years of unwashed dirt and daily chafing having rendered its original color undetectable, rope binding it to his waist, his worldly possessions in a hemp sack at his side. He banged his cane loudly on the paved street, chanting a Buddhist mantra, giggling between verses. The beggar's body was a tiny bag of bones; his face was hidden behind a straggly mat of hair and beard. His antics made bystanders laugh, prompting children to imitate him, but no one dared get within smelling distance.

"Thank you. Thank you," he sang joyfully, scraping up copper coins tossed on the pavement, flipping them in the air and plopping them in a jar, which he balanced on his head. "Western paradise for all of you." As the crowd thinned, the beggar scampered to the shade of an old leafy tree, pulling his blanket over himself and his possessions.

Henry Yan found his "mad beggar" disguise most effective. Who would suspect that behind such a public fool was a learned scholar, turned Christian convert, now serving as clandestine messenger? Circus tricks—balancing jars, hiding coins, mimicking birds—not only brought some income, but also protection from the authorities. Regular begging was ruled illegal by the new Qing authorities, but street performers were still tolerated. And Henry was particularly proud of his "mad" touch; although Chinese tended to keep retarded family members at home under wraps,

214

homeless disturbed people were often seen as humorous distractions, like zoo animals. If acting like a trained monkey seemed silly, it was certainly better than rotting in prison for illegal private mail service.

Of course, Henry could not carry any written messages, not in the new inquisition atmosphere. Any documents would destroy his cover as an uneducated beggar; and besides, where to hide the cumbersome document boxes that protected messages from the elements? In an era when Jesuits were under suspicion as potential collaborators with Ming loyalists, few priests dared communicate in writing. Who knew what the Manchus might make of confiscated correspondence? So Henry resorted to the ultimate device of the Chinese scholar—rote memorization.

Thus Henry meandered up and down the coastal areas of eastern China, serving as the mnemonic newsletter for Jesuit missionaries, recalling precisely dozens of letters, notes, and memoranda, reciting them perfectly when he arrived at various monasteries. Maintaining his "memory palace," the late Father Matteo Ricci's term, required a meticulous daily review of all memorized documents; that's what he was doing when passersby shook their heads at the sleeping beggar.

Henry Yan was most challenged by lengthy communications from the two extremes of his journeys: from an exile on Hainan Island off of China's southernmost coast, and from a humiliated official under close scrutiny in Beijing. The trips by boat, foot, barge, and the occasional donkey took at least three months, and sometimes twice that, making it very difficult to keep every word in his head. This was his second round trip in less than two years, and now, but a few weeks from his return to Beijing, he *had* to remember. The spoken communications started flowing back and forth in his brain, like a direct conversation; it was so hard to eliminate remnants of earlier letters. He remembered Meihua's first dictation from Hainan as if it had been yesterday:

> *Oh, my dearest brother, what have I done? It was not my intention to harm anyone. Not on the Chinese side. Certainly not in our family. It was just a book. A way to keep our spirits up. A show of solidarity. Nothing more.*

You were never involved. I surely know that. I will tell that to
anyone. I told them when they sentenced me. Again when they
brought me to Hainan, the end of the earth.
What can I do to make amends?

And then Longyan's reply from Beijing, six months later:

I'm still furious. It's not just that my whole career is ruined.
My family is also ruined.

It was only my back-door pressure that kept all of them
from suffering your fate of exile. My parents, and a few
retainers, are allowed to live a primitive existence in a small
market town. They are cut off from civilization. Can you
imagine their humiliation?

You did this on your own? Just other women? Thinking
you were helping your fathers and husbands? You are silly
women, just as your letters say.

She had that coming, Henry thought, but I'll bet she's too feisty
to let it go at that. Henry recalled the way she had accepted blame,
then struck back, as in a remote *gongfu* match:

What can I do but apologize? I have brought dishonor on every-
one. The family is penniless. You've lost your power. And I
deserve what I have here.

Do I really deserve this? Meihua wondered, looking out at the
oily gray sea and wiping the sweat beads from her face. A small hut,
that's my new mansion? With one servant left to serve my needs?

Slap—that was the sound of Hainan Island—as Meihua struck at
a whining mosquito that had somehow penetrated the gauze cloth
over her head and body. The few aristocratic women on Hainan all
wore gnat hats, large-brimmed straw hats that supported mosquito
netting, rendering the wearers into wispy ghosts. In spite of Meihua's protests, Peach Blossom forced her to drink a bowl of bitter
brown broth, then she wiped the noxious herbal mixture on her
mistress's arms, legs, and face. "Once they get through the netting,
only fungus and swamp-lily tea will keep them away," a Suzhou
chemist had said and shaken his head mournfully as he gave Peach
Blossom the dried herbs.

For millennia, Hainan Island was synonymous with torture by heat, loneliness, and mosquitoes. And since convicted criminals of high rank were first sent here in the Song dynasty six hundred years earlier, everyone knew that the mosquitoes were the worst. Doctors confirmed the link between mosquitoes and malaria as early as the thirteenth century. That was why some officials chose strangulation with the silken cord over Hainan Island. Everyone remembered the agony of Hai Rui, the virtuous late Ming official associated with the Donglin movement, described by some as the death of the thousand needles.

A forgotten outpost of the Chinese empire, Hainan was a huge, desolate way station for pirates plying the South China Sea and the Gulf of Tonkin. Haikou, the most populated town with almost twenty thousand residents, was scarcely twenty miles from the mainland. But Yaxian, the tiny village where Meihua was exiled, was over two hundred miles farther south and protected by rocky mountains, overgrown jungle, and one heavily guarded road. Even the most accomplished mariner would not attempt to land a vessel on the reef-strewn, surf-pounded coast. Hainan exiles were thus relegated to the southernmost extreme of the Middle Kingdom in a natural prison from which no one escaped.

At a distance, Yaxian might have been mistaken for an idyllic seaside resort, but on closer examination, the stark horrors became evident. Meihua and Peach Blossom were assigned a thatch hut— one of several for exiled prisoners. The Corpse Camp, as it was called, was almost empty; most prisoners survived less than a year or two. Suicide was an even more common cause of death than malaria; and servants often performed a ritual known as "kindness choking," strangling their charges by request.

After a few months on Hainan, most exiles gave up the desire to return to civilization. Usually the mind went first in a delirious detachment from any reality, relegating one to intermittent screaming and giggling. Indeed that was why Henry Yan's mad monk imitation worked so well on Hainan; no one gave a second thought to another deranged castoff who was probably a servant to an insane exiled master. As madness progressed, bodies also decayed from a limited rice diet while faces and limbs festered away from insect bites.

A few, like Meihua, were fighters. She would be a lady to the end, dressing as formally as possible every day, making do with the little makeup Peach Blossom had smuggled in her one permitted trunk. She washed and treated any wound on her body, no matter how slight, so it would not become infected. To keep mental acuity, Meihua spent at least two hours a day chanting classical philosophy and poetry to an uncomprehending Peach Blossom (indeed only another scholar could possibly understand the archaic language and allusions). Refusing to let guilt take her down, Meihua sometimes resorted to composing angry letters:

> *Allow a silly woman her moment of irritation as well, my dear brother. Did I not do more than anyone of our generation to fight for the Ming cause? Was that not your father's deepest wish? Why else his commitment to the Donglin Academy and the Fushe Society? Do I not deserve a little credit for trying to preserve filiality? Is this not perhaps equal to what his sons have done?*

"You must admit," Henry had murmured, never daring look at Longyan, "she does have a point." Longyan ranted on about stupid women playing at politics. Henry stuck to his position, insisting, "I still think she's got a point." Longyan gave a last grumble, then retreated a bit.

> You know it's foolish for women to dabble in politics. Look what good it has done you. Look what it's done for the Wu family.
> But yes, I suppose you were trying to be filial. Yes, I understand there was no way to ask Father's permission. He never would have permitted it. And yes, there's a little side of me that recognizes your courage.

"Every chapter of that *Ming History* written by a woman?" Longyan had been astonished by Henry's report. "Who would have known that there were so many literate women in all of China? All from Suzhou? That's incredible!" He wished he could scold Meihua in person—and then congratulate her for doing the impossible. But he had no more mobility than she did. He was confined to a small house outside Beijing, its gate guarded by an armed officer whose job it was to keep Longyan inside the compound, under long-term house arrest. What difference whether man or woman, he fretted, we prisoners are powerless except in our imaginations.

"What's it like . . ." he recalled his question from so long ago, "what's it like being a girl?"

Longyan's mind was drawn not to philosophical reflection, but rather to personal remorse. He remembered a beautiful twelve-year-old's faint smile, the first time he'd discovered the realm of intimate questions. For twenty-five years he'd repressed a child-hood instinct. Now there was no danger in thinking the unthink-able. After all, Meihua was two thousand miles away and Xinping was in his grave. Longyan didn't have to warn Henry Yan about secrecy as he continued his dictation; it was clearly the most per-sonal note Henry had ever absorbed from his master:

> Men can seldom speak their feelings about women with ease. But somehow a letter allows me to wear a mask, to utter real feelings, covering them with graceful phrases. Do you know what I mean?
>
> So what am I trying to say? I'm angry at you, yes. But I'm also proud of you. You did what I was unable to do. You served Father's real wishes. I think he probably cherishes your rebellion. And I think he probably only tolerated my high position.
>
> But what did it do for all of us? Two prisons without bars. Well at least we can still speak freely, albeit in a strange way.
>
> Why can't I say what I want to say?
>
> Would it be too impolite to say that my feelings for you run deeper than brother for sister? Could you imagine how life might have been different? If only I had not been the failed scholar. If only I had been the firstborn. If only the Matriarch spoke of me then as she spoke of me more re-cently.
>
> Can you imagine life without all the "if only"s?

Four months later, sitting on a small porch overlooking an end-less sea, Henry recited Longyan's letter to Meihua without emo-tion, as if he were a scribe reading to an official. But Henry's lively eyes could not be stilled; he saw the emotions—joy and love—race across Meihua's face. Unabashed in Henry's presence, she began her dictation immediately:

> *If I wrote as you do, there would be no difficult sentences which are not questions. Can you imagine life without all the "if onlys" you ask?*
> *Sometimes we women can be a bit more forthright. Let me try.*
> *Not only can I imagine life differently, but I have fantasized it that way for many years now. It was not that I was unhappy with Xinping, but rather that he would not have been my choice. I would have sought someone of more imagination, more inner fiber, more challenge. Xinping's life was set on outer goals, which he never realized, rather than inner goals, which can be ever chang-ing. I have dreamed of such a life, even occasionally alluded to such a life in my letters to you. But sadly, it remains an "if only" dream.*

Scarcely three weeks after dancing in the streets of Nanjing, the mad beggar hobbled down a Beijing *hutong* alleyway, crouching and whining in front of a gray spirit-wall that guarded the gate to a residence (spirits were repelled because they didn't have the good sense to fly around the wall and go through the gate).

"Alms for the Buddhists!" cried the beggar. "Alms for the Da-oists! A little money and I guarantee heaven."

"Go away, you idiot," shouted the gatekeeper, drawn to the street by the racket.

"Lao Gu," whispered Henry, "it's me. Let me in. I want to see Prefect Wu."

"Get out of here!" the gatekeeper screamed. Then he whis-pered, "He's not here. Taken away. Two months ago."

"Where did they take him?"

"I don't know. Ask the Jesuits. At the observatory."

It was dusk by the time Henry had walked the six miles of back streets to a little gray citadel near the East Gate. Silhouetted in the sunset, a parade of strange bronze monsters marched around the citadel's walkway, sixty feet above the street. The monsters had huge round heads with arms and legs pointing toward early night stars and the glowing three-quarter moon. Black-robed Jesuits walked trancelike among the monsters, inspecting the inanimate beasts, then staring into the twinkling sky.

Henry knew that, whatever the politics of the time, the observatory remained a Jesuit stronghold, Father Adam Schall's brilliant creation using Western designs and Chinese technology. He gave the Jesuit knock—"Father, Son, and Holy Ghost" to the rhythm of the Mass—prompting the giant brass-studded wooden door to creak open. A half hour later, Henry Yan, freshly garbed but still with scruffy hair and beard, faced the famous German Jesuit.

"I'm sorry," Schall said softly, "but I fear we've lost your two friends."

"Both of them?"

"Yes, both of them. Father Gao and Prefect Wu were both arrested by hard-line Manchus. . . ."

"But they promised not to harm Prefect Wu. In Huaiyin. I was there. . . ."

"My son, don't be naive. It was a promise of expediency. Not of the heart. . . ."

"I'm sorry, Father, but both of them? They're like family. . . . What can we do? How can we get them released?"

"Released? That's out of the question. They're convicted criminals. No longer under house arrest. Now they're in the real prison. Verdicts will be rendered by the Manchu minister of justice. Next week, I believe. Everyone expects the death sentence."

"What? Father, please get it changed. Use your influence. Please?"

"My son, I have no influence. Our strength comes only when reformers control the throne. The extremists are now in power. It may only be a matter of time until all of us are arrested. If it gets really bad, I don't even have the *guanxi* to save my own life."

"We've got to do something! What should I do?"

"Nothing, my son. Absolutely nothing. Be a beggar. Hide. And if you sense danger, run for your life."

Three days later, completely disregarding Father Adam Schall's instructions, a well-groomed Henry Yan walked as confidently as possible into the great Eastern Gate of the Forbidden City. His tailored scholar's gown bespoke an erudite intellectual; his stack of

Neo-Confucian classic books suggested an influential tutor. He straightened his three-foot queue under his conical hat, giving a good orthodox image to suspicious guards, bowing reverently as he entered the gate to display respect for dynastic officials.

"Who are you?" ordered the gatekeeper.

"Zhao Helang," he replied calmly. "Private tutor to Zhang Dali, *jinshi* scholar from Hunan province, scheduled to take the palace examination this week."

Every candidate for the highest imperial posts had to take these grueling weeklong tests, toughest in the ladder of civil service examinations. Candidates were sequestered several days in advance, in tiny Examination Hall cubicles, which served as both studies and sleeping quarters. Flat boards that made a desk by day were lowered to become beds at night. Minor fortunes were made preparing candidates in the days leading to the testing; tutors could enter at eight in the morning, but had to exit no later than four in the afternoon. Henry had found the name from a privately circulated list of examination candidates—access to such information was essential to tutors' incomes—then he asked around to find out which tutors were assisting which candidates.

"Let's see," said the gatekeeper, scrutinizing a list, "Zhang, Zhang, Zhang. Ah, here it is. Zhang Dali. Correct. But no Zhao listed. His tutor is named Zhu."

"Zhu is sick," Henry said calmly. "I'm the replacement tutor. Please check. Don't you have additional lists?" Henry knew that substitute tutors' names were submitted by the candidates, always with the approval of the Examination Hall proctors. He had also made the rounds of local clinics to find a tutor who was ill.

"Let's see. I've got two Wangs, a Zhou, a Guo, another Wang. Yes, here it is, a Zhao. Zhao Helang, you said? Quite right. But I'll have to check this chop. Right again. And now the signature." Henry held his breath. This was the key test: Would the forgery really work?

"No," said the gatekeeper after scrutinizing the signature. "It's almost right. But not quite. See this little hook. He never signs that way. Except . . . when did you say you submitted it?"

"Yesterday afternoon."

"Of course. That explains it! The afternoon. He signs almost everything in the morning. Then, how to say, he lubricates his brushes very well at lunch. It's almost a totally different signature in the afternoon. Bet I had your worried."

"Worried? Hardly." Henry lied; his heart had almost stopped in panic. "If you didn't let me in, I would have spent the rest of the day lubricating my brushes too."

The gatekeeper laughed and nodded for the guards to pull the great bronze bolt and swing open the inner door. "You know where to go, don't you?' Henry nodded and popped through the portal.

It took almost a minute before Henry Yan breathed again. He had done it—talked his way into China's most sacred space, the Forbidden City. But that was the easy part. Henry knew the odds. It was quite likely that he'd just done the dumbest thing in imperial history and that his body parts would soon be cut into pieces and fed to pigs in the imperial sties. But Henry did have three little advantages: first, he was sure he was doing the right thing; second, he was totally devoted to his two masters; and third, he truly believed that a Christian force called *Tianzhu,* the "Heavenly Master," would see him through.

Henry hid his classical texts in shrubbery surrounding a family of bronze peacocks and began walking purposefully along a wide paved path toward the west. Everyone knew the basic layout of the Forbidden City, since it was the setting for countless popular stories and endless pornographic tales, mostly involving emperors, empresses, and concubines. With blood pounding through his veins in fear for what he was doing, Henry couldn't help absorbing what the real Forbidden City looked like. Perfect symmetry, red walls and yellow roofs, tiny tiled animals marching along roof beams, meticulous little gardens, gray stone paths, large bronze and ceramic urns, marble bridges over creeks and moats, carp pools and rock gardens.

Nothing, but nothing, was out of place. Nothing except— Henry gulped—his own presence. He was an alien commoner in the Forbidden City. Just keep walking west, he told himself, and don't look scared. Look like you know what you're doing. Everything will be fine. . . .

Boom, crash, boom-boom-boom—an earsplitting din, just around the corner ahead, reverberated off the great red walls. Henry jumped off the path and hid under a marble bridge, feet almost in a trickling stream, until the procession, probably for a high-ranking Manchu prince, passed overhead. Oh, dear God. He tried to quiet himself. I don't see a living soul, he thought. Then I run smack into elite Manchu guards and a brass band? Thank you, Lord, for letting me escape. Oh, Holy Father, what am I doing here?

"What are you doing here?"

Henry froze at the stern Manchu voice speaking in accented Chinese.

"Er . . . uh . . ."

"Speak now! What are you doing here?"

"I'm uh . . . relieving myself."

"You're what?"

"You know . . . taking a piss."

"A piss? A Chinese piss?"

"Er . . . yes . . . I guess so."

"A Chinese piss in a Manchu stream?"

"It was just a regular piss. No insult intended."

"Get out here." Henry cowered as he tiptoed cautiously out into the bright sunlight. Several Manchu guards formed a tight circle about him as he emerged.

"A regular piss?" asked the Manchu again, clearly an officer by virtue of his different uniform. "A regular piss in the Forbidden City? Regular pisses are not permitted. Now which was yours? A high-level imperial piss? An exalted Manchu piss? Or perhaps a lowly and illegal Chinese piss?"

"A lowly, illegal Chinese piss," Henry said, realizing that further resistance was counterproductive.

"So guilty as accused! You know the penalty? Immediate loss of the offending organ!"

"No!" screamed Henry, "please, no! I didn't mean anything. I learned my lesson."

"All right."

"All right?"

"Yes, all right." The Manchu laughed. "I was just kidding. Don't take it so seriously. Are you lost?"

"Uh . . . Really just a joke? Oh, of course. Really funny. Yes, I'm, uh, lost."

"You're a tutor type. Want the Exam Hall?"

"Yes, a tutor. But I have a message. For the Forbidden City

Liaison Department of the Grand Secretariat. Do you know where it is?"

"Of course. Inside the Meridian Gate on the west side, just beyond the great courtyard, in the Liaison Section."

"Oh, thanks."

"Not at all. Oh, by the way. Don't piss on grand secretaries. That privilege is reserved for a higher authority. Know what I mean?"

"Yes. I'll watch where I aim."

Henry staggered down the path, cursing the Manchu guardsmen under his breath, but grateful that he finally knew where he was going. The Liaison Section was a very special part of the Forbidden City; it was the linkage between what was called the Outer Court (the regular bureaucracy including the Six Boards, the Censorate, and the Grand Secretariat) and the Inner Court (the immediate advisers to the Emperor). All regular documents requiring imperial approval had to pass through the Liaison Section, receiving a series of official chops, arriving ultimately into the hands of the Emperor's chief advisers, and finally returning through the Liaison Section to the original office from which they came. No fewer than six copies of each document accompanied the process, producing massive files, since every communication had to be copied laboriously into both the Manchu and Chinese languages.

Crossing the massive courtyard north of the Meridian Gate required the utmost bravado. Henry strided as boldly as he could—huge red gate to his left, bristling with Manchu troops; the famous Sanhedian to his right, the sacred imperial halls, five marble bridges leading to them. It was where all the great officials assembled each morning, where all the tribute missions from foreign countries passed, where the emperors ruled the Middle Kingdom.

But Henry's mind was hardly on politics, architecture, or iconography. He suddenly wished he could melt into the massive slate stones beneath his feet. Everyone but Henry was dressed in uniforms: mainly court regalia, embroidered dragons on chest and hat topstones indicating rank, but several men wore military garb with tunics and boots. Henry's plain black gown, even though expensive by his standards, suddenly marked him as out of place, a scholar among influential officials, a sparrow among peacocks.

"Ni nar? Where are you from?" came the inevitable question

from the Liaison Section guard, who was eyeing Henry's plain costume suspiciously.

"I'm just a tutor. A tutor for one of the candidates for the palace examinations. I'm Zhao Helang. He's Zhang Dali."

"So what?"

"I have a petition."

"About what?"

"About one of the cases confronting the Board of Justice that has been submitted to the Grand Secretariat for review."

"Which case?"

"About unfair arrests," Henry spoke quickly, not wanting to share so much with a nosy guard, but there was no alternative.

"Who's it from?"

"Several examination candidates." That opened the guard's eyes. Petitions from the rising intellectuals always attracted attention. Emperors wanted young, talented bureaucrats on their side. No guard wanted to be accused of overlooking possible protests.

"Who's the petition for?"

"Liaison Office of the Grand Secretariat."

"What's it say?"

"I can't tell you that!" Henry said firmly, testing how the guard would react.

"Oh, sorry. It's just that it sounded interesting. Third building, second door, first office."

Two minutes later, Henry tentatively pushed open a heavy wooden door. "Yes?" said the man at the desk, puffing himself up to look influential, delighted that Henry was even shorter than he was. "I'm Hu," the man said, "First secretary to the junior secretary in the Information Review Section of the Liaison Section of the Grand Secretariat. How can I help you?"

"Secretary Hu. I have an important petition. It must be presented in person. To Grand Secretary Sose. I believe he is in charge of the Liaison Section. Correct?"

"We aren't at liberty to reveal such information."

Henry didn't react. Who was in charge of what offices was common knowledge throughout the Forbidden City. Everyone knew of Grand Secretary Sose. But acting secretive was what made little officials feel like big officials. Clearly another approach was required.

"Of course not," Henry said quickly. "Excuse me. It's just that I need your help, your good influence. This petition comes from top examination candidates on a matter concerning life and death. Even more, it concerns civil order in the Yangtze delta region. Since you are so close to the highest officials, I thought you might like to share credit for handling this matter."

Henry bowed very low. A red envelope fell from his sleeve. While his eyes were still down, Secretary Hu snatched it up and slipped it into his own sleeve, hidden fingers counting the paper notes. "All right. Wait here. I'll see what I can do." Henry sat on a wooden bench, eyes closed in a silent prayer, hoping that his entire life savings had not been expended in a useless bribe, hoping that he would still be alive to see another day, hoping that Father Gao and Prefect Wu might be spared the slicing knife, hoping that—

"Come in. I'm Sose. What's this all about?"

Henry was startled back to consciousness. He followed the large Manchu into a private meeting room, looking a bit like a scruffy mutt about to be scolded by an irritated master. Henry took a deep breath as he sat in a wooden chair opposite the upholstered arm-chair occupied by Grand Secretary Sose. This was it. Life or death. No holding back.

"My name is really Yan Henei. I'm in the Forbidden City illegally. . . ."

"What?" exclaimed Sose. "How did you do that?" As Henry explained, Sose grinned. "So much for Qing dynasty security systems. ' 'Foolproof.' That's what the Guard Commandant announced just last week. Ha. So what's this about a petition?"

"That's also a lie. I just needed something that would sound important. So you would see me."

"They let you into talk with me simply because you *said* you had a petition?"

Henry shook his head.

Sose thought for a second, then reached the correct conclusion. "How much did it cost you?"

"Not much. Ten taels."

"No, not much. How much did you have?"

"Nine taels. I borrowed one extra tael to make an even number."

"All right. I know you're telling the truth. No one could lie about such a crazy escapade. What's the problem?" Sose listened intently as Henry relayed his story about Prefect Wu and Father Gao, describing even Meihua's exile.

Sose nodded sympathetically as Henry described the arrests and pending convictions. "I wish there was something I could do," Sose said mournfully. "But they're key targets of the hard-line faction. I've always thought of myself as tough, but they say I'm soft. I suppose mainly because I have some Chinese associates. And because I'm not much in favor of torture and execution. But that seems inevitable here. . . . There's just nothing I can do."

Sose failed to tell Henry that he too had worried about his own life. Only his close connection to the great Manchu founders, Nurhaci and Abahai, kept Sose from prison, torture, and execution. He maintained his titles, but watched his influence ebb away. All he could do was wait—maybe until the demise of Prince Dorgon, perhaps until the Shunzhi emperor took over himself. Unless unusual evidence could be mustered, Sose knew death sentences for Father Gao and Longyan were certain.

"I've got an idea." Henry pulled a small Western leather-bound book from his sleeve, featuring wood-block copies of masterpieces in European religious art from the previous two hundred years including Giotto, Michelangelo, Leonardo, Raphael, Tintoretto. "Look here, Mr. Grand Secretary, what do you think?"

Sose perused each page, eyes straining to comprehend strange images. "This is what you believe in? This is Father Gao's religion? All these people being killed and tortured?"

Henry nodded. "That's Christ on the cross. Saint Peter there, upside-down on the cross. The one with the arrows, that's Saint Sebastian." Sose pointed perplexedly. "Oh that's Saint Agatha. They're cutting off her breasts."

Sose shook his head. "What kind of religion is this? Don't Christians ever laugh? No funny pictures?"

"Never in their paintings. Sometimes the Jesuits tell jokes. But not in pictures. It's very serious."

"Serious? This makes the hard-liners look gentle. So if you're a Christian, you only get really famous if you get killed? Especially in terrible ways?"

"Exactly. Just my point."

Sose looked puzzled. Then a smile rushed across his face. "Aha!

So we don't want to create Christian martyrs? Christians are more dangerous dead than alive? A brilliant strategy! Can I borrow this book? Maybe there is a way out."

"Of course."

"But what about the Prefect? Wu Longyan. He's not a Christian. Is he?"

"No. But I'll testify that he is. If that will help have him exiled. Rather than executed."

"Your testimony will be critical. Especially since he's unlikely to confess to being a Christian on his own. Of course, you're convicting yourself in the process. You know that?"

"I know it. It's my duty. To my masters. To my faith."

"I can't imagine why any sane Chinese would believe in stupid Western worshipers of torture and death. Even you Chinese have got some better religions of your own. Our Manchu shaman rituals are better. Lots of jokes, drinking, dancing, singing. These Christians are obsessed with killing. I've heard the most popular one is where the man is nailed to the wall."

"To a cross."

"Whatever. Absolutely crazy. In any case, whatever happens to Gao and Wu, you're going with them. Death, torture, exile. You get it too."

"The Heavenly Master asked if we were able to be crucified with him."

"What? Your religious leader wants you to volunteer? Please join me, he says, we'll all get nailed to walls together. I mean crosses. Are you brave or just crazy?"

"I don't know. Maybe both. But I do have a request."

"I know," Sose smiled. He reached in his pocket and handed over ten one-tael notes. "It's not right to steal from poor tutors."

"Thanks. But, no. Not that. It's just that. Well . . ."

"Yes?"

"If we're not all killed. Where do you think they'll send us?"

"You think I can determine where you might be exiled? You can be certain they'll send you to the worst place imaginable. You'll probably wish you were dead! Worse than your hell."

"Maybe I've already been there." Henry managed a tight smile.

CHAPTER SEVENTEEN

Exile

明

The Next Year: Hainan Island, 1651

"TWO YEARS, FIVE months, fourteen days," Meihua chanted quietly in rhythm to her little steps along the stone path Peach Blossom had bribed a local farmer to build. The path meandered through sandy grasslands, above surf-pounded beaches, below the single dirt road that skirted the southern shore of Hainan Island.

The farmers called it the Road of Death, for it featured scattered exile huts patroled by local constables who frequently doubled as coroners dragging bodies to mass graves. Somehow the locals, at least those who lived to old age, which was about forty years on Hainan, seemed immune to the mosquitoes. Indeed, not unlike the mosquitoes, the local residents preyed on the exiles, charging very high rates for food and clothing, often demanding protection money as well. Hiding money was a major preoccupation for exiles, who dispersed their limited treasuries of copper and silver coins under rocks, behind trees, in holes. Robberies were certain, so the goal was to lose as little as possible with each occurrence so that one could afford a few basic amenities until the inevitable death arrived.

Meihua had been sick frequently since coming to Hainan, often very sick, but not yet with the dreaded malaria. Even on this bright, peaceful morning, Peach Blossom felt obliged to accompany her mistress, protecting her head with a red bamboo-strutted umbrella. Meihua, usually elegantly slim, had become gaunt and bony, her face with a harsher profile, her movements more labored. Her clothes, now patched and tattered since only one trunk was allowed, hung more loosely, but still conveyed the aura of quality. Her skin still kept a soft glow and her eyes retained radiance. Depending on the moment, her face projected sad pensiveness or fierce determination, the former mood more frequent as she counted the mounting months of solitary confinement.

Today, as always, she stopped in what she called the ancestral shrine, actually two rough benches and a table with a little roof overhead, where she could sit, stare at the ocean, and think about people. She always began with respectful reminiscences of her parents and siblings, then pondered the Wu patriarch and matriarch, pausing to pay respects to Xinping. She saved Longyan until last, sometimes dwelling on him for an hour, depending on her sentiments and the weather. Peach Blossom carried a box of appropriate documents for what she called "weeping time": all of Longyan's letters, including Meihua's written transcriptions of those orally delivered by Henry Yan.

In excellent weather, Peach Blossom set up a writing table outside, so Meihua could compose her own letters or write a bit of poetry. Books were forbidden to exiles, so the ancestral shrine writing time was her only moment of literary relief, when she communicated to ghosts thousands of miles away. Of course, she could not be outside before ten in the morning and after four in the afternoon; otherwise she would literally be eaten alive by insects, which flourished, like the bamboo and green jungle foliage, in the tropical climate. At other times, she retreated to her single-room hut, shared with Peach Blossom. They slept and ate in the same quarters, draping themselves with fine white netting bought from peasants at outrageous prices.

Meihua rubbed a worn ink block in the watery reservoir of an inkstone, stretched a roll of crude rice paper across her makeshift desk, rolled the tip of her brush in the rich black ink, and raised her wrist delicately over the paper. Staring across the sparkling morning sea, she emptied her mind but for the sound of waves and seagull cries, then let the brush flow across the paper, almost as if it was propelled by a force outside her.

> Scholars meditate in mountain retreats, fretful red dust below, impenetrable mists above, only present visible. But when the clouds lift, a mountain has a past, its rocks and rivers tell the tale. And a mountain has a future. It will surely endure longer than the scholar.

Fools meditate by the ocean, no above or below, just water to see.
When clouds lift, there is only present. No past, no future. A
wave reaches the shore, crashes loudly, then is heard no more.

Peach Blossom suddenly screamed.

Meihua dropped her brush with a huge splatter of ink across the paper and twisted around on the bench. Three men, all in scholar's robes, were walking toward them, several hundred yards away.

"Who are they?" Meihua asked anxiously. Visitors usually meant trouble; they would probably be constables or robbers. Scholars never came to Yaxian.

"I don't know, Mistress," Peach Blossom uttered frightfully, envisioning rape or worse.

"It couldn't be . . ." Meihua uttered under her breath, standing up, starting to hobble toward them. "It couldn't be," she said, focusing on the middle-sized scholar, who was flanked by what seemed a giant and a dwarf. "Oh let it be . . ." She hobbled faster, Peach Blossom barely keeping up, red umbrella bouncing over Meihua, who clip-clopped on the stony path as fast as she could. "Oh, I can't believe it! Oh, Buddha be praised! Peach Blossom, can you believe it? It's Longyan!"

A few seconds later Longyan and Meihua met, stared disbelievingly at one another, thought momentarily about sharing proper bows, and then fell into each other's arms. As they sobbed in shocked relief, the others—Father Gao, Henry Yan, and Peach Blossom—formed a protective circle of hugs around them.

Every code of etiquette was violated, but who cared? They were all exiles, tagged with treason, branded as Christians, never to return to civilization. On the outside, a female servant, a strange little scholar, and a gangly barbarian priest linked arms and cried. And in the middle, two tortured souls who had barely intimated their feelings in twenty years of clandestine correspondence, who had never once touched each other, never even dared gaze for long at each other, embraced unabashedly.

But why? Meihua wondered as she summoned up the strength to speak. "I mean how . . . How did you get here?"

"Henry did it," Father Gao said proudly, "saved us both from death." He quickly related the entire story, including their expectation of an agonizing execution, until the Minister of Justice received a strange book of Christian paintings and decided that live heretics were better than dead martyrs.

"Saved you from death?" Meihua sighed as she absorbed the tale. "Only postponed it, I'm sorry to say. And not very long. You'll see."

She gestured up the hill to the road. The two farmers whose cart had brought the newcomers projected gap-toothed grins as they mimicked the embraces of the reunion below. Then they squatted and sneered in silence like vultures already tasting carrion.

"Even so," Longyan shrugged philosophically, "how rare to have the choice of with whom you can die."

One night, scarcely a month later, a tiny hut basked in the orange light of a half dozen oil lamps, windows flickering like July fireflies. The hut, quivering with life above the inert bluffs, glowed lantern-like against the pitchblack sky. Inside the hut, five white figures moved ghostlike, lamps stretching their silhouettes into playful creatures along the ceiling and walls. The buzz of conversation occasionally lapsed into silence; only then did one hear the inevitable nighttime chorus, the whining drone of a million mosquitoes.

"I want to make a confession," Father Gao's softly booming voice broke the silence.

"You always want to make a confession," Longyan parried, a tinge of amicable annoyance in his voice. Actually Longyan admired the fact that Father Gao was surviving the ordeal in better spirits than his Chinese counterparts. Father Gao claimed that that was because of his faith, but Longyan and Meihua knew it was because the priest finally had a living family. Father Gao relished calling them "my son" and "my child," as if he was the architect of their relationship.

"I feel I'm to blame," said Father Gao, "for the fact we're all here." That was *not* how Father Gao actually felt, but he reasoned that if he could shoulder the blame, others could get on with their lives. Not exactly a Jesuitical thought, he admitted, but if priests could be skilled at letting others describe their sins, why could they not also be good at sharing their guilt?

"That's silly," Meihua retorted. "We're here because of my foolish idea about a Ming history."

"That's only partly true," Father Gao parried. "It's the proxi-

mate reason, I suppose. But I'm still guilty. Of—what to call it—
sort of Christian meddling." Hainan had begun to cast some shadows over Father Gao's Jesuit certitude. Please deliver us from this
hell on earth, he prayed at night, doubting that anyone was listening.

"Christian meddling?" Henry exclaimed. "Your Christian meddling saved Prefect Wu's life. Not once, but twice. Once in Manchuria, once in Beijing." Henry never imagined that a priest could
question his faith—was Father Gao in danger of becoming a convert to Confucian humanism?

"Saved my life, yes." Longyan snickered. "But almost killed me
from shock. I can still hear the verdict:

" 'Prefect Wu, guilty of treason, should be executed by slicing.
But he is also a convert to a barbarian religion. He is a Christian. All
barbarians want to die so they can become dead heroes. Thus we
will force the barbarian lover to live. But in exile.'

"So I'm guilty for a book I knew nothing about. And I'm saved
by a religion in which I do not believe."

"Too bad." Father Gao forced a wry smile. In fact, he had long
ago given up hope for converting anyone in the Wu clan, indeed
any Suzhou elite. When he thought about it, he still harbored a
hope that the Jesuits might convert someone in the imperial family,
maybe even the Emperor himself. But he didn't think about it
much—and that worried him, so he diverted his attention by taking care of the Hainan exile flock.

"Well, who knows?" Longyan replied. "Maybe your Christian-
ity does have some use. It's good for coming back from the dead.
You know, like that crazy criminal with the nails in his hands. You
know the one. You used to wear him around your neck. . . ."

"We call him Christ," Father Gao said with bemused solemnity.
"But even if I saved your life, I also risked the lives of many others."

"What do you mean?" Longyan asked.

The time had come for Father Gao to reveal a long-hidden secret. "I was willing to do almost anything to win new converts. We
Jesuits go for the rich and powerful. I wanted influence no matter
what. . . ."

"And so you took pity on a drunken teenager in a rainstorm?

Took him in so that you could win his confidence and thus maybe influence his family? You think that surprises me?"

"No." Father Gao looked hopefully toward Meihua. "It was more than that—"

"A lot more," Meihua interjected, picking up the cue. "Dearest brother. You know the Suzhou Midnight Massacre?"

"Don't tell me," Longyan suddenly became dead serious. "It was Father Gao? And the Jesuits?"

"No."

"No? Who, then?"

"Me."

"What? You?" Longyan looked startled, then realized it had to be a joke. "Of course, quite right. Let's see. You pulled off the biggest anti-Manchu raid. Not alone, of course. With the assistance of . . . Who could it be? Oh, yes, of course, the Ladies' Filial Piety Society?"

"Precisely."

"Precisely what?"

"Precisely me and the Ladies' Filial Piety Society. Only we called ourselves the Virtuous Army. Several hundred women. Secretly trained. A guerrilla force."

"Oh, come now. Impossible. How could you learn to—oh, my goodness. Not—it couldn't be—"

"Of course . . ."

"Father Gao taught you?"

The silence spoke volumes. Longyan, speechless, slowly dropped his mosquito netting and stared disbelievingly at his veiled companions. Meihua and Father Gao both stood up, casting off their netting as well, ready to face Longyan's wrath. Longyan's eyes flashed from one to the other as if he were a madman deciding where to unleash his rage. For a moment, they all froze into a sculpture, a bronze of restrained emotions, shimmering in the oil-lamp light. A fury welled up in Longyan, from his stomach, up his spine, into his face, through his eyes. A shuddering went through his limbs, first seeming utter wrath, then melting into spasms of tearful laughter.

"You . . . both of you?" Longyan gasped hysterically. "Guns?

Cannons? Little ladies. In the middle of the night? Filial Piety Society?"

As Longyan held his stomach in roaring laughter, the mood became contagious. Peach Blossom tossed netting over Longyan, Meihua, and Father Gao, who danced in a circle. Under the white circus tent, suspended over the priest's oversized frame, three exiles clowned and cavorted, burying history with hilarity. Then, as the giggles faded, they sat down again, still covered by a single gauze shroud, now face to face. Henry positioned an oil lamp in their midst. Peach Blossom slipped them tiny cups of rice wine.

"Dearest sister," Longyan said with a residual trace of bemusement. "I am so glad I am no longer an official. I would have had to sentence the prettiest ladies in China to execution. Can you imagine what that would have done for my reputation?"

"Your reputation?" Meihua parried. "Had you tried it, we would have overrun your silly little prefectural yamen."

"Oh, come now. How many were you?"

"If the situation demanded it, a thousand officers and soldiers."

"A thousand? All women?"

"And, honorable Prefect," Meihua switched, "how large was the prefectural garrison?"

"Well . . . a little over forty men. And ten horses."

"Forty? Oh yes, and the horses. But of course, you were all men. Surely you would have won the battle?"

"All right. You win. Luckily, figuratively speaking. I can't believe it. I just can't believe it." Longyan's admiring smile slowly faded to an earnest frown. He paused, sighed deeply, then nodded his head. "It's only right that I tell the truth as well. I have seldom told you falsehoods. But I have not always told you the whole truth." Longyan could not finish this evening without cleansing his soul.

"Yes?" Meihua looked quizzically.

"It's also something Father Gao knows. Something I confessed to him. Or rather he pried out of me. It's just that I'm . . . how to put it? I'm . . ."

"Yes?"

"I can't read or write."

"What? But you wrote me letters. You read my letters. You're

an official. You've got to handle memorials, edicts, all that government stuff. You can't be"—

"Illiterate is the wrong word," Father Gao interjected. "It makes
him sound stupid. That's not true. It's just that he has a problem.
Like some other brilliant people. Just a problem."

"What problem?" Meihua asked.

"Jumping words," Longyan replied. "When I try to read, the
characters move around. When I try to write, the characters fly
apart."

"So how do you read? And write?"

"I don't. At least not much. Someone else usually reads to me.
Someone else always writes for me."

"Someone else?"

As if on cue, Henry stuck his head under the tent, adjusted the
oil lamp slightly, and offered a shy grin.

"Henry?" Meihua asked.

Longyan nodded. "Now it's Henry. It used to be Mr. Cao,
before he died. It's why I had to quit my studies." Longyan wondered how she was taking all this; maybe he should cast it all in a
more positive light. "It's different from being backward or dumb,
you know. I really can keep track of all the ideas." Oh please,
Longyan pleaded to some unseen deity, let her understand this. She
must understand.

"In fact," Father Gao interjected, "he's got an incredible memory, great talent with maps and charts, and superb leadership ability."

"Stop it," Meihua interjected sharply. "He's my brother. Not
someone applying for a position. I know his talents." Meihua
stared at Longyan, speechless for the longest time, trying to make
sense of the revelation. Gradually her dazed incredulity softened
into a bemused tenderness.

"Does it change your view of me?" Longyan asked fearfully.

Meihua shook her head. "No. But it explains some things. Why
didn't you let me know before?"

"I was too afraid."

"Afraid? Afraid of what?"

"Afraid that . . . maybe you'd lose all respect for me. That you
wouldn't want to write anymore."

"You cared so much that you would keep this problem a total secret? Even from me? Even knowing I wouldn't tell anyone?"

"Yes."

Meihua's eyes watered. "You're not . . ."

"Yes?" Longyan asked, puzzled at her reticence to speak.

"You're not the only one," she continued hesitatingly, "to have such a secret, you know."

Longyan and Father Gao stared at her.

"There's someone else with the jumping words problem," she clarified. "You know that? Right?"

"Father Gao said something about a priest in India."

"No. Not in India. You really don't know? Very close to home."

"Who?"

"Your father."

"My father?"

"He can't write, either."

"Of course he can't. Not now," Longyan replied indignantly. "He used to be a great calligrapher. Until he lost his fingers in an accident."

"Not a great calligrapher. Someone else did his calligraphy for him."

"What?"

"And not an accident. He cut off his own fingers. So no one would ever ask him to prove his ability."

"Sister, that's an awful allegation! Who told you such lies?"

"The Matriarch."

"My mother?"

"Yes. Apparently he confessed it to her long ago. Perhaps when they were newly married . . ."

Longyan suddenly remembered the dialogue he'd heard under the scaffolding during the Dragon Boat Festival. Was that what the Matriarch had been threatening to reveal? Of course! It had to be something of that magnitude. So that was the threat that led to Concubine Wang's dismissal. Why didn't he see it before?

"I guess the Matriarch kept it to herself for many years," Meihua continued. "But then, when Xinping died, she feared that the Patriarch would have her removed from the household. After all, she had not produced an heir who survived. She even thought the Patriarch might have her killed."

"Killed?" Longyan asked in startled wonderment.

"Yes. It was crazy fear on her part. She imagined that he would kill her so he could name a new taitai with no one raising any objections. A new taitai who didn't know the secret."

"Oh, I see," Longyan intervened. "So she told you his secret to protect herself."

"Exactly. And she told the Patriarch she had informed *someone else* but she didn't say who. So she had created a sort of anonymous protection system. Of course, the Patriarch was furious because it all implied that he was a terrible villain. But he couldn't do a thing about it."

For a moment Longyan was stunned. Then the rage he had so recently repressed suddenly returned. "Am I to feel sympathy for my father? Just because he's the object of another of my mother's plots?"

"Why not? He simply did just what you yourself did. A total cover-up."

"No, my sister, he did *not* do just what I did. My deceit harmed no one. His deceit was visited upon his children. He created an image—great scholar, great calligrapher, great official—an image which neither I nor my brother could attain. It killed Xinping. It almost killed me."

"He meant well," Meihua suggested.

"No. I think not. He let me live my life believing I was a failure. Always living under his shadow, never sure of my own self, always sure I was less than he desired."

"But wasn't he just saving the family's reputation?" Father Gao commented.

"We could have protected the reputation. We could have kept the secret from outsiders. But to keep it from me? That was just pride."

"Can't you forgive him?" Meihua implored.

"Did he ever forgive me? Only when he thought me a dead Ming loyalist. Not when I returned as an alive Qing official. Even today he treats me with grudging respect. I've got his name, but do not serve his dynasty. Does filiality only work one way? The son is supposed to forgive the father, but the father does not forgive the son."

"Yes," said Father Gao quietly, "that's what Christians would have you do."

"Well, I'm not a Christian," snapped Longyan, tossing aside the netting and stomping off toward his own hut a quarter mile away. "Any more than I am a Confucian. All beliefs are stupid. Especially when you're rotting to death at the end of the earth."

For the next fortnight, Longyan secluded himself in his own hut, numbing his brain by imbibing liberal doses of rice wine and by playing a cracked and scarred *qin*, the liquor and the musical instrument both purchased from local farmers at prices that would turn princes to paupers. Neither Father Gao nor Henry Yan could dissuade him from his hermitage. And Meihua's repeated efforts to see him, conveyed properly through Peach Blossom, were always rebuffed with a "not today, perhaps next week."

> *Dearest brother:*
> *It tears at my heart to have you so close, your little house on the horizon, but not to see you at all. Perhaps I should have said nothing. But that would have violated the honesty of that evening. After all, it was you who revealed your secret. I thought, wrongly it seems, that knowing about your father's secret might help clear things up.*
> *I shall now be bold and take a chance. I do not wish to lose the prospect of close ties with you, especially now that we are in such unusual circumstances. But I must speak my mind.*
> *Yes, you are right, your father should not have concealed the truth from you, especially when he knew you suffered from a similar problem. But surely you can understand his desire to conceal it. You yourself had a similar instinct for many years.*
> *Now here is my point. You have already shown yourself a greater man than your father. You have confessed your hidden problem, while he went to incredible lengths, including severing his fingers, to keep his difficulty a secret. Further, you have followed a career which utilized your many other talents, not pretending, as he did, that you were really a scholar and calligrapher.*
> *If I, silly woman, were to be asked which is the greater man, the*

fake scholar or the honest soldier, I should surely pick the latter.
But then, if I was to be further asked, which would be the sage, the
father who demands the impossible from his son, or the son who
forgives the father for his impossible demands, again I should
surely pick the latter.
Do forgive this prattle from an aging woman. This exile surely
affects my mind as well as my body. And this letter, how stupid,
but perhaps you can use its other side for scrap paper.

Every day for over a week, Meihua prayed at her ancestral shrine, imploring a pantheon of deities for a response from Longyan. And each day, prompted by Peach Blossom's reminder that it was getting dangerously close to mosquito time, she gave a longing look at Longyan's hut before walking slowly back to her own.

But this late afternoon was different: There was no danger of insects because black skies and gusting winds foretold a typhoon. Peach Blossom, her umbrella already shredded by the clawing winds, begged her mistress to seek shelter. Meihua refused, letting the blasts tear at her face and hair, the moisture saturate her silk garments, the rain pellets needle her skin. She imagined herself a Buddhist nun who, having given up human desires, found solace in confronting discomfort. Indeed, mesmerized by the foamy black sea, Meihua was unaware that Peach Blossom had left her alone, having retreated in response to a beckon from Henry Yan.

"Dearest sister."

Meihua barely heard Longyan's soft voice against the howling wind. And as she looked in his direction, only his eyes were visible through his heavy, gray, hooded cape. He sat opposite her, both of them grabbing the table for stability, their clothing snapping like flags in the gusts.

Longyan tried to prevent Meihua's shawl from whipping at her face, succeeding only when he moved to her side of the table, his cape shielding both of them. For a moment, both of them stayed rigid, keeping an awkward physical distance. Then Meihua succumbed, snuggling into the warmth of his body, blessing adversity for bringing them together. Longyan smiled, recalling how it was another storm, so long ago, that had brought him close to his strange barbarian ally.

"Dearest sister!" he shouted loudly enough to be heard. "Your letter . . . you're right, of course. I *was* angry. Vindictive . . ."

"You had a right to be!" she shouted back.

"Maybe a right. But anger doesn't accomplish much." He shook his head, recalling his youthful bouts of fury, always accompanied by drinking escapades. "I've made a decision. I won't let myself be driven by anger. Even out here. I've decided to let other emotions move me."

"Other emotions?"

"Like caring. You know, nurturing. And . . ."

"And what other emotions?" She dared not look at him, but felt him struggle to get out the words.

"Oh, all right. Like love." Longyan tipped her face toward his, their eyes meeting longingly. "You know. We're not supposed to speak such words. Not directly. Never before a matchmaker has done her work."

"Right you are," quipped Meihua, anxious to relieve the tension. "We must definitely find the best local matchmaker. Let's see. We should probably check with the Hainan Island Matchmaker Society. What's the address?"

Longyan kissed her, first gently on the lips, then softly on her face, nose, and neck. They stared at each other, eyes speaking in a realm beyond words, lips trembling between flirtatious smiles and deep solemnness. The wind whipped the cape around them, encasing them in a protective cocoon, prolonging their embraces.

Longyan's mind raced as fast as his pulse. What should I say now? he wondered. What will he say now? she wondered. In a world of structured Confucian order, there was no established protocol for moments of real intimacy. Siblings, matchmakers, parents, someone was always there to broker relationships, to offer an ex post facto legitimacy when sex, or even pregnancy, violated the taboos. Ming-Qing China offered endless outlets for carnal desires, but precious little for deeper emotions between men and women. Intimacy was for women inside the red chamber, where they could share inner feelings, and for men in their social gatherings or in their private studies and studios.

Almost on cue, Father Gao arrived, his burly body clinging to the rickety posts supporting the shrine, his booming voice speaking loudly enough to be heard, not so loud as to frighten. "My children," he smiled, "I hope I don't intrude. Indeed, maybe I might help."

Longyan and Meihua thrust each other away, trying to smooth out wind-whipped clothing, pretending nothing had happened. Father Gao shook his head, walked behind their bench, and enveloped both of them, his back shielding them from the storm. "There's nothing to hide. You've done nothing improper. Unless you're hiding real feelings. What do you want to happen? You know—in your future relationship?"

The priest waited. Hearing no reply, he tried again. "Do you wish marriage?"

"It's not right," Longyan said cautiously, "for us to speak of such things."

"Besides," Meihua intervened, "widows can't remarry."

"Ridiculous," Father Gao said firmly, "what silliness. I have the answer. My faith permits widows to remarry. I can perform the ceremony. And besides, I'm a pretty good matchmaker."

Less than a month later, five exiles gathered on the bluff where once had stood the ancestral shrine, before the typhoon tore it away and uprooted dozens of scraggly sand pines along the shore. Peach Blossom and Henry Yan had fashioned an archway of summer flowers leading to an altar, which supported a heavy wooden cross softened with a spiraling garland of pink and blue azaleas. Father Gao smiled beatifically as he scanned the seascape; after all, it wasn't often that Jesuit missionaries performed ceremonies usually reserved for country priests.

Meihua fretted about her gown, the same red silk she had worn when she'd married Xinping fifteen years earlier, blessing Peach Blossom for bringing it, praying that Longyan wouldn't remember it. Thank heaven for men's blindness, she thought and smiled, when Longyan seemed not to recognize the gown, but only focused on her face.

Longyan was entranced by Meihua's glowing skin, her bright eyes, and her hair interlaced with tiny red desert roses. She looks even better in that old gown than when I first saw it, Longyan thought to himself, being careful not to show that he noticed. How lucky we men are, Longyan thought, to wear clothing like this simple blue robe for such occasions. I don't look that much different, he convinced himself, from my appearance at Xinping's wedding except for a few lines in the forehead and a pigtail down the back.

Meihua and Longyan stood together, a living embodiment of the ancestral shrine that was once here, flanked by Peach Blossom and Henry Yan, all of them facing Father Gao. After a long discussion, it had been determined that the ceremony would not be conducted in the couple's Chinese, nor in the barbarian's German, nor even in the now official Manchu language. Instead the priest chanted in Latin, a neutral tongue that sounded perfect for a wedding ceremony.

For a full hour, Father Gao sang the wedding Mass, checking his prayer book for the right words, sprinkling holy water, waving a pot of smoking incense, always punctuating with signs of the cross. Peach Blossom started to giggle when two dragonflies, glued together in aerial intercourse, came unstuck unceremoniously after alighting on the hot incense pot. Only Henry's swift jab in her ribs stopped a laughing fit.

As the proceeding wore on, Longyan wondered if he'd made the right decision when Father Gao asked him about the length of the service. "The full ritual," Longyan had declared pompously, "anything shorter would not be appropriate." Even Meihua started to wear down after a while, Peach Blossom's vigorous fanning keeping her mistress barely awake. Finally, just when delirious exhaustion was setting in, Father Gao changed his loud conclusion, repeating his words in Chinese so everyone would know it was over:

"By the power vested in me by the Holy Father, and by the sacred influence of the Holy Trinity, I now pronounce you, Wu Longyan and Lin Meihua, bound by the eternal linkage of holy matrimony. In the name of the Father, the Son, and the Holy Ghost."

Meihua looked startled. "What's this about ghosts?"

"Don't worry, Mistress Lin," Henry said, "it's not really a ghost. More like a good spirit. The Son is sort of a good ancestor. And the Father—it really means heaven."

Meihua was relieved. "So we're married?"

Father Gao nodded.

"And now we need a proper procession," Henry announced, raising both hands, the signal to unleash his little plan.

Thirty or more peasants rushed from the bushes brandishing sticks and bells. Strings of firecrackers exploded in the scruffy trees along the sandy path back to the hut. Henry led the procession like a drum major, Longyan and Meihua walking slowly behind, Peach Blossom fussing to keep her mistress pretty, and Father Gao strolling contentedly at the rear.

"So we're married?" Longyan echoed Meihua's words a few hours later as they languished under white netting, safely protected from buzzing mosquitoes seeking to prey on naked bodies. Their eyes moved slowly up and down each other's bodies, promising where hands and lips would follow. It was all delectably slow, filled with anticipation, entirely unrushed. There was, after all, a lifetime ahead—and however short that might be, it was a lifetime with nothing to do, except to enjoy each other fully.

CHAPTER EIGHTEEN

Release

明

The Following Year: Hainan Island, 1652

"PLEASE ACCEPT OUR little gift," a plump farm woman implored Peach Blossom, making sure Meihua overheard her as well. "It's a wedding present. For your mistress. And your new master." She slapped the water buffalo's rump so that he grudgingly walked a few feet ahead, revealing a bullock cart carrying a large oblong mound covered by a white sheet. The woman smiled broadly and beckoned Peach Blossom to the cart.

Peach Blossom gingerly lifted the edge of the sheet. Unable to see much, she pulled back the sheet sharply. Her face whitened and she jumped back toward the protection of her mistress. "Aiya!" the servant screamed. "It's a corpse! Do you want to curse their marriage? Get out of here. Right now!"

"Oh, that's disgusting!" exclaimed Meihua, averting her eyes and covering her nose with a handkerchief. Meihua embraced Peach Blossom, stroking her head to offer comfort.

But as the woman sullenly pulled away the buffalo, shaking her head and murmuring under her breath, Meihua watched her with puzzlement. "Why would you give us a corpse?" Meihua called after her, curiosity overcoming revulsion.

"Oh, milady!" the woman shouted back hopefully. "We meant no harm. It's to prolong your life."

"A dead body?"

"Yes, milady," said the peasant woman, leaving her bullock cart and walking back toward Meihua. "You didn't know? If no one among your huts dies for a long time, the constable becomes suspicious. He starts wondering. Are you getting special food? Or maybe some new medicines? So he makes it real hard on you. Cuts back rations. No more netting. Believe me, he can kill you. Real quick."

"So the corpse?"

"Oh, everybody wants one. You give it to the constable. Explain it's a servant. Then he's very happy to know one of your group is dead. People down here, the exile types, they would pay hundreds of taels for a body like this. It's the best kind. A young woman in her twenties. Malaria rotted her face to nothing. Even though she's local, the constable can't recognize her. You know, not even if he does what he sometimes does, with the women's bodies. . . ."

"That's quite enough," Meihua interrupted. "We thank you for your kind gift." Peach Blossom was about to express her dismay, but Meihua gave her a keep-your-mouth-shut look.

"You're welcome, milady. Don't forget to have a little funeral before you give it to the constable. And never forget—" The woman paused to express herself well, wishing she could use Mandarin rather than her local dialect, which had taken Meihua and Peach Blossom more than a year to master.

"What?"

"Never forget to always be sad. I know things are better now. Since the marriage. Don't worry, none of the farmers will tell. But if the constable ever finds out, he'll ruin everything. Never, never let anyone know you are sometimes happy.

The farm woman's gifts—the corpse, the funeral, and the advice—proved invaluable. Henry supervised such a fine funeral, replete with paid peasant mourners and bushels of paper money, that the constable gave his highest praise—"The best death in over a year."

It was Longyan, moodiest of the lot, who accepted the assignment of projecting continual sadness. His brightest idea, the "wasted bribe," required that Peach Blossom give the constable a ten-tael gift, crying and pleading on her knees, begging him to let her mistress escape. Longyan figured that the constable would pocket the bribe without lifting a finger to help anyone, delighted to discover that the Suzhou group was so desperate. The ploy worked perfectly, literally buying a few months and prompting Father Gao to give Longyan a new title: Master of Tears.

Behind the mournful façade, and in spite of ongoing physical trials, the Suzhou exile community discovered secret satisfactions on Hainan Island. Indeed, discomfiture offered perspectives to new relationships and new discoveries, just as the denial of food and sleep sometimes enhances the faith of the novitiate. No one could disagree with Meihua, who announced one night, "When my death occurs, I shall look upon these months as the most rewarding in my life."

Father Gao picked the most remote and rickety abandoned hut for what he called his *Academia Sinica,* his Chinese Academy. Originally he planned to split his day, half for praying and half for writing. But the secular soon drove out the sacred. Father Gao hit upon a new project: producing a multivolume magnum opus, his visions of how Western technology could be applied to every aspect of the Chinese empire, from shipbuilding to mining. In the absence of any books, Henry Yan's bountiful memory supplied a rich array of local information from all corners of China. *A Barbarian's Humble Offering* was Father Gao's title, hoping that the book might someday be of use, presuming a change in Beijing's political climate.

"Father, do you mind if I make your insights read a little better in Chinese?" Henry asked, jotting down the priest's dictation.

"Do whatever it takes," Father Gao replied with a smile. He knew that Henry never changed the scientific observations, but often made the text more soothing to Chinese eyes. "A bit more humility in my *Humble Offering*?"

"I wouldn't dare suggest it," Henry responded. He was already transposing sentences. Father Gao's opening passage, "In the past two hundred years, Western engineers have mastered the art of building drawbridges . . ." would be rendered differently in Henry's nocturnal revision: "I am aware that over five thousand years the Celestial Empire has invented every form of constructing bridges, so for your amusement, let me simply describe our crude Western methods of drawbridge construction. . . ."

Others found their souls in different ways. Peach Blossom, whose status had been devastated by Xinping's death as much as by the Hainan exile, projected a new sense of self-importance. In spite of her constant cluckings about "being totally overworked," she thrived as the maid to the "Wu taitai," a name she first gave to Meihua shortly after the wedding and continued to use when no one corrected her. Meihua drew the line, however, when Peach

Blossom suggested calling Longyan the "Wu patriarch," observing that the title implied children and that, for whatever reason, no offspring seemed forthcoming. Meihua guessed that her infertility came from the trauma of exile; no one could dispute her theory, given the absence of other married couples of childbearing age among the community. Peach Blossom was secretly delighted about the lack of children; it was so much better to envision herself as a lady-in-waiting rather than a harried nanny.

Peach Blossom and Henry Yan evolved a powerful supply network, reaching across Hainan Island, offering many imported provisions from the mainland's Guangdong province. On New Year's Day, in February 1652, they astonished everyone by presenting moon cakes and spring rolls, treats no one had tasted since leaving the Yangtze River basin. Then as Henry clapped his hands, Peach Blossom unveiled two red new year's scrolls, extolling "long life" and "good health." As if to make his point more clearly, Henry offered his latest effort at a mosquito repellent; he was irritated that his concoction, a bottle of brown ooze, was deemed too sticky and too smelly for human use. All of the materials—foodstuffs, red paper, chemicals—emanated from other parts of China hundreds of miles away.

Longyan and Meihua became inseparable. "Like two halves making more than a whole" was Father Gao's beaming comment. He called them one name—Mei-Long, "Beautiful Dragon"—a word play more intriguing to a Westerner than to Chinese who grew up with such verbal games. Their relationship was completely atypical; indeed it would have been impossible in Suzhou, where sustained interaction between the sexes, with any sense of equality, was unthinkable. Men usually lived in the outer world, women lived in the red chamber. Elite married men and women came together to eat certain meals, to socialize with family and friends, and to create offspring. And even so, a great deal of eating, socializing, and sexual experimentation occurred outside the marriage relationship.

Although neither Longyan nor Meihua disagreed with that established view of manhood and womanhood, Hainan's isolation required a totally different approach. In the absence of a Confucian guidebook for unconventional relationships, Meihua and Longyan explored the ultimate virgin territory of human emotions. Meihua patiently sought to draw out Longyan's venom, to soften his anger. It was a slow process, overcoming years of his depressive cycles, trying to replace his "I'll show you" motivation with a deeper "this I want to do" attitude. Together they talked out feelings, especially about people who had prompted anger and insecurity, most especially about the Wu matriarch and patriarch. While it was usually Longyan who needed Meihua's gentle caring, not infrequently Meihua revisited her harsh memories of coming to the Wu mansion after being torn from her own Lin household.

"I'm not stupid. Really, I'm not," he whispered softly in her ear. He spoke those words at least once a day, each time with a shaky assertiveness.

"I know. Everyone knows. It's only you yourself who needs convincing," Meihua would whisper back.

A few moments passed, then she would complete the catechism: "And I'm not just another woman. Not just makeup and silk. I've got a mind, too."

"I know it. You know it. That's all that counts." He smiled softly, his eyes locking gently on hers.

What amazed everyone was the creative outpourings from the Meihua-Longyan union. Every day, for hours on end, the two pondered and chatted, before Meihua took up her brush and began to write. Her calligraphy, now released from a demure woman's form, tested a variety of styles from quick grass script to ponderous oversized characters. She would watch patiently as Longyan tried to write, then, sensing what he sought to do, transformed his idea into her own holistic images.

From calligraphy, Meihua and Longyan collaborated on bamboo painting, rendering leaves and stalks in every manner, from densely weighty to gracefully fluid, just as they perceived bamboo groves on their daily walks. Sea-shaped rocks emerged from gray and black washes Meihua applied to porous rice paper, often with gulls and terns pecking in the surrounding sand. At Longyan's suggestion, Meihua experimented with variations on landscape painting, beach cliffs substituting for the usual mountains, shipwreck driftwood in the foreground framing a seated scholar in meditation, splashes of red birds and green foliage in the background.

A private code of silly words and strange symbols united Meihua and Longyan. At least once a day, one of them was sure to utter *wu-wang*, literally meaning "hopeless," but which they interpreted as "let us not hope," really meaning "we're not sure whether we want to leave or stay." So whenever Father Gao, Henry Yan, or Peach Blossom expressed a desire to return to civilization, Longyan and Meihua would say "*wu-wang*," then baffling everyone with their laughter. Of course, it was "hopeless," the others acknowledged, but why make a joke of it?

But whatever joy came from the realm of emotions, the persistent topic of conversation on Hainan was illness. Everyone knew that exile was a death sentence, so the unstated question was always how long, how many weeks or months of life were left. But no one ever put it that way.

"Father Gao, your leg seems a little better today," Meihua said, more out of hope than out of fact, observing the priest struggling to sit down, white-knuckled hands clutching a shaking, gnarled cane.

"Not better, dear child," he summoned a smile, "but not worse." Father Gao no longer fretted about such lies. His right leg was withering away, blue and green lumps replacing the once-pink flesh, and his left leg was filled with shooting pains as well. "How lucky you are to be spared."

"Thank you, Father," Meihua replied, taking solace in his untruth. Her once glorious hair was falling out, leaving patches of baldness on her scalp, requiring Peach Blossom to devote a full hour each morning to weaving an intricate covering of baby's breath and falling hair. The red blotches on her face and hands were covered by lumpy Guangzhou base makeup, unsatisfactory alternatives for the more refined Hangzhou tinted powders and Nanjing touch-up sticks.

Longyan's pustules were worrisome as well, spreading from his hands to his neck, causing extreme itching and often emitting a mixture of blood and white liquid. No one knew what caused his malady, but everyone agreed, without knowing for sure, that it did not appear to be malaria.

Only Peach Blossom seemed spared by the Hainan horrors; but that was because she concealed her vicious headaches from everyone, even from Meihua, who was irritated by her servant's frequent disappearances. When the pain struck, Peach Blossom hid herself in a grove of tangerine trees, hot compresses on her face to ease the throbbing pain, a washrag in her mouth to drown out her screams.

By March 1652, everyone knew that Henry Yan had contracted malaria. For a week or so, he pretended that his dizziness and fever were just a cold, that he could sleep it off. But when the dread disease was finally acknowledged by all, Father Gao sat by Henry's bedside, ministering to his cycles of sweating fever and shaking chills, trying unsuccessfully to force him to swallow a little water and food. Slowly Henry lost the ability to communicate; his mouth emitted only moans and his eyes stared blankly into space. Then late one night, the flickering oil lamps showed a blueness moving from Henry's fingertips up his arm as the death's coldness moved inexorably from his extremities toward his heart. Father Gao ordered hot cloths applied to Henry's body, trying to fight back frosty lifelessness, but it was hopeless. The priest reluctantly performed the last rites, closing his purple cloth around Henry's hands. Just before dawn, Henry shuddered, sucked hopelessly a last breath or two, then succumbed.

Henry's body was given to the constable for his records and burial (authorities in Haikou monitored the constable's reports for evidence that exile produced its desired results). In a small forest of scrub pines, protected from the vicious typhoons, Longyan paid peasants to build a memorial mound. White streamers laced the mound, and Longyan's words in Meihua's calligraphy:

Without a father,
But the most filial.

Without a degree,
But the most scholarly.

In front of the mound, Father Gao erected a cross on which he had painstakingly carved: in Chinese: YAN HENEI, CONFUCIAN SCHOLAR, DIED SHUNZHI REIGN, EIGHTH YEAR; in Latin: HENRY YAN, JESUIT FRIEND, DIED YEAR OF OUR LORD MDCLII, I.H.S.

Scarcely a month before he contracted malaria, Henry had relayed a rumor to Father Gao and Longyan, careful not to let the ladies overhear since he did not want to arouse unfulfilled hopes. The ruthless Prince Regent Dorgon had died, bringing the adolescent Shunzhi emperor to the throne, surrounded by a reformist clique of Manchu princes and Chinese banner officers. Henry had been pleased with the way he described the change: "The Worms have eaten their way back into the Throne."

But, Longyan wondered, did that mean they would be released? Henry had shrugged: maybe so, that was in keeping with the new spirit; but maybe not, the current leaders might not want to test their power in such overt ways. "Don't worry," Henry had assured them, "my ears still hear things at court. I'll let you know what's happening almost instantaneously. No more than six months after the events. I'll check especially with the Grand Secretariat and the Board of Justice. That's where any changes in prison sentences would be recorded."

"Don't worry. . . ." The words still echoed in Longyan's ears as he bowed before Henry's memorial mound. Who were Henry's sources? How had he gotten his information? Now no one would ever know. Now one could only speculate and wait.

As long as things were deemed hopeless, as long as there was no future beyond Hainan Island, Longyan had been reconciled to his lot. But now with the hint of returning to civilization, Longyan became intensely frustrated. Meihua was baffled about the change in Longyan's character, about his flights of anger and depressive silences. She attributed his irritability to Henry's death; even though she herself could now perform the necessary secretarial duties to assist her husband, maybe he had been emotionally closer to his former assistant than she thought. Or maybe, she feared, their passion was cooling. Meihua worried that it might be her fault. Was it her hair loss or the red splotches on her face; was she now ugly in his eyes?

Just when Meihua was becoming resigned to a more typical, more aloof relationship with Longyan, a totally unexpected event occurred. One afternoon, shortly after the typhoon season, a Chinese banner detachment thundered into the exile encampment on horseback. The major dismounted and politely asked for "Prefect Wu Longyan and his retinue." When Longyan came forward, the major bowed and presented a document box. Longyan, in a most natural gesture, handed the enclosed scroll to Meihua, who read it slowly:

" 'By order of the Emperor of the great Qing dynasty:
'Let it be known that an injustice has been done to the family

and associates of Wu Longyan, from Suzhou, member of the Chinese Bordered Red Banner, formerly Prefect of Huaiyin. He and his retinue have been seriously punished for alleged treasonous activities. While the Throne does not condone the publication of seditious literature, neither does it exact severe penalties on important scholarly families.

'Wu Longyan and his family are hereby released from their punishments. Former titles and property are all restored. The exiles will be returned to Beijing.' "

Speechless disbelief quickly turned to raucous elation. Peach Blossom expended her remaining connections, and most of the cash reserves, on a farewell party for the peasants who had befriended them over almost three years of exile. Longyan informed the banner major about the constable's malicious treatment of prisoners. All it required was a simple administrative order to strip the constable of his rank and return him to peasant status. Without any land or income, and now surrounded by the peasants and exiles whom he had victimized, the constable's fate could easily be imagined.

It was not until the forty-day voyage by oceangoing junk up China's coastline from Hainan to Qingdao in Shandong province that doubts reemerged. Did "Wu Longyan and his family are hereby released" apply to *all* his family—Patriarch and Matriarch as well as Hainan exiles? "Former titles and property are all restored"—was Longyan still a prefect? And was the Suzhou family estate back in family hands?

But the most frequently asked question was, Why are we being sent to Beijing? Why not Suzhou? Father Gao thought maybe exiles were required to return to the capital city, perhaps to be officially reinstated as subjects of the dynasty. No, Longyan shook his head, there was no such rule. Meihua suggested that it was because Longyan was restored to official status so he had to go to Beijing to receive his new orders. That was possible, Longyan acknowledged, but why send the whole group with him? Longyan suppressed a deeper fear that perhaps the release was a hoax; maybe they were being taken back to Beijing, where they would be executed so they represented no threat at all.

Such worries festered in the hellish last few days at sea. Scarcely ten miles from Qingdao, the busy port already in clear view from deck, the tubby junk was becalmed. Its great lateen sails slapped noisily in the swells, spars and beams creaking, the stench of feces and vomit spreading through the motionless air. The captain and crew were so sick that they couldn't serve the passengers, who clung together on deck ministering to each other's aches, boils, and cramps. Three days later, the bloated craft wallowed its way to an anchorage a mile offshore.

Only Father Gao, a veteran of ocean travel, had the strength to pull himself to the rail as he heard some rhythmic shouting. A black longboat moved sleekly across the harbor, thirty paddles stroking to the beat of a coxwain's voice, breaking to a quick, turning stop beside the junk.

Sose, dressed in his Qing imperial regalia, climbed swiftly up the rope-and-wood ladder, over the gunwale into the vessel. "Are they all right?" Sose asked Father Gao, shocked by the passengers' condition, barely able to keep from retching at the sight and smell. No one was able to do more than nod slightly in a daze.

"We're alive," Father Gao murmured finally. "Except for Henry. The young man you met. Dead. Malaria."

"At least the rest of you are safe," Sose said with relief. "Now we must get you back to health. Clean you up. For the trip to Beijing."

CHAPTER NINETEEN

Filiality

明

Later that Year: Beijing, September 1652

"FROM HAINAN DEATH Camp to the Forbidden City in three months?" Longyan exclaimed. "I thought maybe you were going to execute us."

"Execute you?" Sose laughed. "Hardly! We don't invite condemned prisoners to the imperial guest house." He gestured expansively toward a lavish crimson-and-gold building within the Zhongnanhai section of the Forbidden City, where the three former exiles were treated in royal style. In the artificial lake before them, princesses and concubines paddled little boats, their shouts and giggles a lyrical counterpoint to scolding jackaws and screeching cockatoos. Silk dresses, small buildings, darting kites, provided splashes of gold, blue, and yellow against the green pines and red autumn maple leaves.

Father Gao leaned back against a pillar in the pavilion where they sat, looking bemused at his costume—short jacket with a Mandarin square in the center, broad skirt with cloud embroidery around the rim, circular hat with red stone on top—a Jesuit variation on the fifth-ranking bureaucrat garb (of nine official ranks). The clothing did not imply that Father Gao occupied any office, but rather served as a sort of passport around the Forbidden City, admitting him to most buildings in the Chinese bureaucratic area, though not to the truly forbidden Manchu elite quarters.

Sose described how the Jesuits, after the severe persecutions of the 1640s, had reasserted their authority in the 1650s, not only at the Imperial Bureau of Astronomy, but also within the Forbidden City itself. Father Gao's gamble had paid off handsomely. Sose and his sons, particularly his eldest son, Soni, were now entrusted with approving all imperial translations, using linguistic leverage to influence Qing policies. Public documents were rendered in Manchu, Chinese, and Mongol, supervised by Sose's family. Meanwhile the family advised the Manchu military about new weapons and tactics (drawn from Latin documents in the Jesuit library). All secret communications within Sose's family were circulated using an abbreviated Latin code. As long as Sose and his ilk were in power, Father Gao and the followers of Saint Ignatius could rest easily in Beijing.

Sose shook his head almost imperceptibly. He mused on the incredible fate that had saved their lives. Four stubborn figures—a Chinese gentleman and lady, a barbarian priest, and a Manchu warrior—had rebounded from death. Imagine, Sose thought, if Father Gao had sought support from a hard-lined Manchu, or if Longyan had really refused to serve as a bannerman, or if no official had urged leniency on Meihua's behalf. Even worse, Sose shuddered, imagine if Dorgon still was in power and the young Shunzhi emperor remained powerless; then all four of them would surely have perished.

Surely a miracle had saved them. Father Gao called it divine intervention; Longyan felt it was good Confucian humanism; Meihua thought it was a long-overdue response to decades of invoking the Amida Buddha. Only Sose knew the real truth—he had paid a Manchu shaman to conduct a sacred and expensive ritual exorcising demons from the Forbidden City. While moderation might work in politics, he knew that absolute spiritual powers were required in emergencies. Dorgon promptly died the morning after the exorcism, paving the way for a new coalition of Chinese reformers, flexible Manchus, and a sprinkling of Jesuits.

Meihua smiled contentedly as a late afternoon breeze ruffled her pale green silk gown, its straight cut the latest Beijing fashion. "I still can't believe it," she said to Longyan. She wasn't referring solely to their release, but also to the symbolism of Longyan's splendid uniform, the jadeite stone on his cap indicating second rank, a peacock feather flowing back indicating special imperial commendation. In one swift stroke of a brush, Sose had approved Longyan's promotion (a much higher rank than prefect, but so far no new post to go with it).

Meihua had suddenly become the wife to one of the top thousand officials in all of China. Once again Sose's chop had cut through bureaucratic entanglements, validating their relationship as a "Qing dynasty marriage" (a legal fiction invented for the occasion, releasing Meihua from the usual requirements of Confucian chaste widowhood on the grounds that her ties to Xinping were abrogated by the change of dynasties). Privately, Longyan joked that a fierce Ming loyalist officer now became a willing Qing bride. Meihua did not find the comment amusing.

"My lord, our gratitude is boundless," Longyan addressed Sose genuinely. "I only wish—"

"What? Not satisfied?"

"No! No, it's not that. It's just that there are so many unanswered questions. About my parents. About our property. About our futures."

"I always thought patience was supposed to be a Chinese virtue." Sose smiled. "Such questions will be answered. But you must await the imperial audience."

"The Emperor wishes to see me?"

"Yes." Sose smiled. "All three of you who suffered exile."

"Really? Why are we so important?"

"You don't understand?" Sose wrinkled his brow. "It's not you per se. It's rather a gesture to a prominent Chinese family that has been wronged. You see, the Emperor needs support from his elite Chinese subjects. It's very good for the imperial image."

"Image?" Meihua blurted without thinking. "We're good for the imperial image?"

"My wife shares my desire to serve the Emperor in any way he sees fit," Longyan said strongly, shooting her an unmistakable hush-up look.

Of course, everyone knew what to expect in an imperial audience. Itinerant storytellers always set the scene in detail. The Emperor was never visible, but remained hidden behind a golden screen. All subjects performed the full kowtow—the *ketou*, "hitting the head"—with three kneelings and nine prostrations, tapping the head against the marble floor each time. Petitioners always spoke in archaic Chinese, never doing business directly; the Emperor seldom spoke back, instead his chief advisers made short, formal responses. That was the way the Forbidden City operated during the late Ming period (the additional advantage was that the Ming emperors, often distracted by hobbies like building cabinets or courting concubines, could skip the audience altogether and no one would know the difference).

So what confronted three trembling exiles, each dressed in formal court finery, was a series of shocking surprises. After a long wait in anterooms, secretaries and pages scurrying about, they were escorted to the audience chamber in the Sanhedian, the sacred center of Imperial China. It was shortly after dawn; grayish mist hung over the three elevated palaces, shrouding their vermilion columns and yellow roofs with mystery. For almost three hundred years, this had been the nerve center of the Chinese empire, where emperors, scholars, and eunuchs conspired to rule All Under Heaven. It was here that emperors greeted those who passed the highest palace examination and named the highest officials in the land. It was also here that the worst criminals were sentenced to terrifying punishments.

Upon entering the audience chamber, they sensed something unexpected. You were not supposed to see the sovereign himself. And yet there he was, the Shunzhi emperor himself, seated comfortably on a raised platform, no screen in sight. A slight fifteen-year-old, the Emperor seemed attentive, conversing easily with several officials who stood around his dais, reflecting momentarily before offering judgments on various issues. His pockmarked face, while assuring he would not succumb to the dreaded smallpox, rendered him an unattractive young man who probably would have been a typical Manchu functionary but for an accident of birth.

It was hard to imagine that the Shunzhi emperor's father was the great Abahai, architect of the conquest of China, and that his grandfather was the fearsome warrior Nurhaci, consolidator of the Manchu state. But the young Emperor's decision to show himself directly at the dawn audience evidenced uncommon shrewdness. Probably he was influenced by Manchu preconquest practices, but possibly by Confucian advisers, who told him that the great Tang dynasty emperors dispensed with screens so that they could see into the hearts of their subjects. No matter how soft and young he looked, the Shunzhi emperor had clearly inherited some of the sharp political judgment of his father and grandfather.

"Ah," said the Emperor, shifting his body on a square couch, covered in the same yellow dragon pattern as his tunic, "the exiles. Come in now. Don't fret. I'm not so terrible. No, no, no. Don't do the kowtow. Just sit down. Right there. On the floor. Right in front of me."

"Your August Imperial Presence," Longyan began, bowing from his kneeling position, "we foolish commoners—"

"Now, now. Don't speak such words. I'll wager you went to one of those audience experts. Told you just what to say. Come on now, be honest. Did you see an audience expert?" The Emperor's eyes sparkled, reflecting the wit and the wile of the Manchu leadership. Meihua sensed it immediately; she could no longer envision all the invaders as crass, bloodthirsty barbarians. At least this one had an uncommon sense of humor.

"Yes, Your August—"

"How much?"

"How much what, Oh Far-seeing Great—"

"How much did the expert charge you?"

"Twenty taels."

"Outrageous. Total waste of money. Now to important things. Do you know what everyone forgets to do in here?"

"No. What?"

"They forget to look around the room. When you get out of here, everyone is going to ask, 'What's it like?' And you'll say, 'I don't know. I was too nervous to remember anything.' Now, take a good look."

With boyish pride, the Emperor jabbed his finger around the room, pointing out a golden palanquin, cloisonné peacocks, a Song emperor's calligraphy, a ceiling frieze of the twelve celestial animals with dragons cavorting in the middle. "See the lacquer box up there?" The Emperor giggled, pointing to a black and red container suspended from the ceiling on a string. "It's where the name of my successor is hidden. It's a big secret. Right, Mr. Blackrobe?"

"Correct, Your Majesty," Father Adam Schall answered, bowing from his seated position at the front edge of the imperial dais. "Your Majesty honors me by letting me sit in your presence. And even to call me by a new name." Schall had been given the honor a year earlier; he was not about to compromise the privilege by bantering with the sovereign. Only a few Manchu princes were

260

granted such proximity to the Emperor; not a few others were privately infuriated that a Western barbarian was granted the honor.

"Ha!" laughed the Emperor. "You're just happy I didn't call you Mr. Bignose today." The Emperor was actually quite taken with the Jesuits, not only for their gifts like pendulum-driven chiming clocks, but also because they seemed more genuinely interested in the Chinese and Manchu worlds than other Western barbarians. But he was candid with Schall, having told him, "One mistake in predicting eclipses and you Jesuits are out of favor." Even the Emperor had limited power if critics questioned the accuracy of his astronomical advisers. No wonder that Schall oversaw every calculation himself, often working eighteen-hour days between the Forbidden City and the imperial observatory.

An aide whispered something to the Emperor. "Oh, yes, yes. I'm forgetting myself." He cleared his throat and addressed Longyan, Meihua, and Father Gao. "We deeply regret that evil people caused you harm. You are all exonerated. And, uh . . ." The aide whispered again. "And your titles and property are returned as well."

Was this why they had been summoned to Beijing, Longyan wondered, simply to hear the Emperor repeat what was in his earlier proclamation? "Your Majesty, we are so grateful." Longyan tried to conceal his disappointment. "We do not know what to—" Longyan stopped short.

The Emperor was grinning and pointing behind Longyan's back. Longyan shot a glance over his shoulder. To his surprise, there was his father, kowtowing his deference to the Emperor; the Matriarch was farther back, mirroring her husband's motions. And to Meihua's disbelief, there were her father and mother, both beaming as they knelt to pay imperial respects. No one could read anyone's deeper emotions; the awesome experience of an imperial audience left no room for private feelings. Reunions would have to wait until later.

Most surprising was the presence of so many nonimperial women at an audience; usually only male courtiers and male tribute emissaries were permitted. Once again the Shunzhi emperor was conveying a message, particularly to elite Chinese women who may have harbored Ming loyalist sentiments. The Emperor of the great Qing dynasty was not one to bear grudges. But there were limits to his tolerance, and he was not about to violate one long-standing tradition: women might attend an audience but, with the possible exception of an empress dowager, no woman would be permitted to speak at such a sacred occasion.

"Now, now," said the Emperor to the Wu patriarch. "Your son can tell you. I do not favor too much formality. I understand you were a loyal official of the former dynasty."

"Why yes, August and Wise Imperial Presence. I was once an official. But they dismissed me."

"And so, the previous dynasty pushed you out of office? The current dynasty pushed you out of your home? Tell me, which dynasty do you think is the worst?"

Patriarch Wu looked dumbfounded. Either answer would roast him. The Patriarch bowed deeply, his hands clenched, his head pounding for an appropriate answer. Longyan had never seen his father at a loss for words; he shut his eyes and shook his head in shame. Only Meihua sensed what was happening, that the Emperor was enjoying another little joke.

After a painful silence, the Emperor laughed. "Pretty clever," the Emperor congratulated himself, "wouldn't you say, big-nosed priest?"

"Very clever, Your Majesty." Father Schall offered a stage laugh, prompting polite titters from everyone.

Longyan felt faint from an emotional crisscross. This was, after all, an imperial audience in which an unconventional emperor was toying with an unconventional father whom Longyan had not seen for over two years. While it appeared the Emperor was simply playing games so far, Longyan fretted that this occasion might prove the undoing of the whole Wu clan. Meihua caught Long-yan's eye, injecting him with some of her resilient confidence: keep your poise, she was saying, act in measured ways. Longyan prayed that he wouldn't have to use her advice; maybe the Emperor wouldn't address him again.

"Excuse my little silliness," the Emperor said, "sometimes I find it too much fun to play around with my power. Don't you think so, Grand Secretary Wu?"

"Who?" the Patriarch said involuntarily.

"Grand Secretary Wu."

"That's a very old position for me, Your Majesty, one I haven't held for forty years."

"And I wish we could turn back time. Clearly it's been hard on you to lose that post." Patriarch Wu was indeed a frail figure, stooped from his seventy years of age, face deeply lined from torment, eyes flitting about as if looking for the next attacker. "But we can restore the title. You are again given the rank of grand secretary. And you will receive all of the privileges of that rank. Given your age, you are not expected to fulfill the duties of office."

"Your Majesty, I deserve nothing, I'm honored beyond words."

"Say nothing of it. We owe you that. Wouldn't you agree, Governor Wu?"

No one said anything. The Emperor stared at Longyan. "Wouldn't you agree, Governor?"

"Does the Emperor address me?" Longyan pointed at himself. "I used to be a prefect. But I have no post today. Thanks to your generosity, I have high rank, but no position."

"Nonsense." The Emperor giggled. "Oh, this is so much fun. I just reinstated your father and promoted you at the same time. Governor of Zhejiang. I thought about sending you to Sichuan. But it's so far away. And the peppers could kill you."

"Your Majesty . . ."

"Hush, now. There's more."

Now Meihua was feeling faint. She cast a glance at the Patriarch, who was locked into a prayerful posture, hands together, eyes groundward, body motionless. The old man shook his head slowly, mouthing unspoken words, "I don't believe this. I don't believe this."

Meihua glanced at the Wu matriarch in the back of the room, who didn't seem to mind being relegated to a shadowy corner of the chamber. The Matriarch smiled beatifically, exuding a director's pride at the end of a successful drama, as if the actors had finally followed her cues perfectly. Meihua looked ahead to Longyan, who seemed so small, so vulnerable in the cavernous room. Oh please, she prayed, let the rest of this go right, the way it's supposed to go. She did not realize that Longyan's real mother had uttered the same invocation long ago, bringing totally negative results.

"Governor Wu." The Emperor spoke his lines clearly. "You

have accomplished much in your life. As a soldier. And as an administrator. But we know how much the Chinese people prize scholarship. You have not had the time to become a scholar."

The Emperor paused for effect; this was the heart of his performance. His audience was the Chinese scholar-official class, not only in the room, but those who would hear the rippling rumors of this encounter across the empire. "We now grant you the time for scholarship. You shall have the opportunity to write your Wu family history, including its glorious exploits during the last dynasty. You shall have home leave for three years in Suzhou before taking up your new post."

A network of smiles flashed through the room. A family history, with special emphasis on the Ming period, what a perfect way to rebuild confidence among the Chinese upper classes! What a Confucian gesture from a Manchu monarch! And those who privately knew about Longyan's secret problem also recognized he would have devoted helpers. Wonderful, thought Meihua, a new project for the two of us, back in civilization, in Suzhou. The Wu patriarch couldn't wait to present offerings to his ancestors—this was surely the ultimate achievement in the life of his clan.

Father Gao forced a gratified look as well; at least the new spirit of compromise might stop some of the murmurings about Jesuit attachments to the ousted Ming dynasty. But for how long? Father Gao wondered, a darker feeling creeping up his spine, a chronic cynicism that infected Jesuits who remained in China too long, who had seen too many cycles of Beijing politics. His body fixed in kneeling posture, Father Gao's eyes scanned the dimly lit room, spotting frowning Manchu princes and senior advisers off in the corners. He could read their minds: Is this why we conquered China, they were thinking, to coddle Chinese snobbish intellectuals? Just wait, he could see them thinking, our time will come, these people will find out who really rules the empire. Why, Father Gao wondered, breathing deeply to contain his shiver, do Chinese always seem to see new reformist phases as permanent, seemingly forgetting the sufferings of earlier years?

"Your Majesty," Longyan said solemnly, carefully measuring his every word. "The honor you bestow on me and my family is truly remarkable. We do not deserve it. The broader message you convey will do much to heal wounds. And—"

"Governor, I am so glad that you see our overall purpose." Perfect, thought Meihua, Longyan said just the right thing. This makes all the hurt of Hainan seem tolerable.

"And, Your Majesty," Longyan continued, "that is why it pains me so deeply to decline your suggestion."

"Decline my suggestion?" The words, though spoken by a boy, boomed through the chamber as if emanating from a disembodied oracle. A hundred heads snapped in Longyan's direction. Father Schall, seated next to the Emperor, seemed to lead a silent shocked congregation as his unblinking eyes moved slowly from fearsome sovereign to fearful subject. Father Gao saw some undisguised smirks on Manchu faces in the shadows.

"Yes, Your Majesty," Longyan acknowledged shakily.

"You *cannot* decline my suggestion. My suggestions are never rejected!" The little boy's fists clenched and his eyes became fiery.

"Your Majesty, I have no choice. May I explain?"

"It had better be a good explanation. For your sake."

Longyan sucked in his breath. "Your Majesty faces a massive problem governing China. It is not just a problem of governing All Under Heaven, all lands bounded by the Four Seas. It is a problem of creating harmony between two cultures. . . ."

"So, so, so. This I know. Tell me what I do not know. . . ."

"Your fine prince, Sose, has taught me something of your language. I've learned we have some ideas in common. The Manchu notion of 'honesty,' for instance, derives from a soldier speaking truth before a meeting of warriors. The Chinese character, 'honesty,' is literally a man standing next to his words. I wish to be honest by both our traditions."

"Yes," said the Emperor impatiently. "What are you saying?"

"I must speak with utter honesty. I can neither read nor write, Your Majesty. My memory is good. My decisions are made rationally. But something happens when I deal with words. They come apart. So I have always relied on others to write my thoughts and to read my incoming correspondence. I have long hidden this problem. I can hide it no more. So I cannot do what you wish."

Meihua shared the stunned, deathly silence of everyone in the room. A thousand hopes crashed like a crystal goblet on a stone floor. Why, she fretted, why tell the truth now? She glanced at the Patriarch. The Patriarch's eyes remained fixed ahead of him, but his fingers trembled. What worried him most, she wondered: that Longyan was ruining a wonderful opportunity or that the truth might be told about the father as well as the son?

"Hmm." The Emperor stroked his forehead. "Cannot read or write? But clearly with great talent. Maybe your problem is special. But we have seen others who have similar difficulties. Do they call you stupid?"

"They did, Sire, when I was a child." Longyan shot a look at his father. The Patriarch's heart skipped a beat. Does my son know the truth? Will it all be revealed here? Will all the world know I am a fraud?

"Hmm. Yes. We have heard of this." The Emperor beckoned Sose to his side, whispered a few words. Both of them were painfully aware of learning deficiencies among Manchu princes and high officials. And indeed, most of the imperial family was illiterate by Chinese standards; no one knew whether slow learning was an inherited problem or caused by the absence of a Manchu tradition of schooling. Sose thought for a moment, then nodded. The new rulers could use help, especially from a Chinese courageous enough to admit his weakness.

"Yes," the Emperor continued, emboldened by Sose's assent, "such problems even occur in very high places."

"Your Majesty. I do have an idea."

"Speak."

"I have experience in handling such difficulties. Could I, perhaps with the help of Sose and with the assistance of your Jesuit advisers, offer some different ways of teaching within the Forbidden City?"

The Emperor thought for a moment. "Different ways?"

"Yes. Most tutors educate in the old-fashioned way. It's just preparation for the examinations. Memorize, recite, memorize, write. If you're not taking the examinations, there is no need for such a boring approach. I can teach the ideas, the basic values, and some of the more important quotations. I can also teach how to use those ideas in a practical way."

"But what about the reading and writing? Do you have a new way to teach that?"

"No. But my wife does. She learned to read and write in an

unconventional way. She taught herself. She could also teach here as well, Your Majesty, making learning more interesting."

"A literate woman?" the little Emperor laughed. "I hear you Chinese are fearful of literate women. Right? Well, no problem for us. We Manchus aren't so fearful of our women. If a woman can fight, we say, it's one more soldier and one less baby."

"Now as to your teaching here . . ." The Emperor paused and beckoned Sose, who knelt respectfully next to the throne. Meihua barely overheard Sose's stagewhisper: "Yes, it's ideal . . . new ways to learn . . . the princes will be more like the Chinese . . . also don't forget the women loyalists . . ."

The Emperor was convinced. "Your offer is accepted. We understand each other. As you know better than most, literacy is difficult. We need teachers who respect how hard it is for students to learn. Imagine the problems we have faced. Conquering with swords and bows was the easy part. Ruling with brushes and ink is much more difficult." The Emperor paused and shook his head. "But . . . you leave us with a major problem."

"A problem, August Emperor?"

"Of course. We need to send a message. To our Chinese friends across the empire. You know, about scholarship. That's why I asked you to undertake the history."

Longyan paused and weighed his words very carefully. "I do have another idea."

"Yes?"

"Give the task of writing the Wu family history to my father. He was a great scholar in his day. A great calligrapher, too. Before he lost his fingers in an accident. He could easily do all the research, then dictate the history to a secretary. Once a scholar, always a scholar. Of course, he can still read, analyze the words, and compose the text."

All eyes shifted to the Wu patriarch. Only a few knew what was transpiring in the unspoken communication between father and son. Longyan stared unblinkingly at the Patriarch, conveying without question that his son knew the truth. Longyan's glaring eyes spoke a silent message: The son knew his father suffered the same disability and that the severed fingers were not the result of an accident. The Wu patriarch looked back in frozen fright. A lifetime of concealment was suddenly shattered. There was no time for resentments or recriminations. There was no time for crafted responses.

How would the Patriarch react? Four people knew how important was this moment: Longyan, Meihua, Father Gao, and the Matriarch. They watched the old man in stony silence. Would the Patriarch also tell the truth in the presence of the Emperor and the court? Or would he perpetuate the lie?

An eternity passed. No one said a word. The Emperor was puzzled by the strange silence, wondering whether it was yet another odd Chinese custom. Father and son seemed frozen in a sculpture of stares. For a moment it appeared the father might speak; he moved a little and started to open his mouth. Then the Wu patriarch fell silent, his head falling to his chest.

Finally, when it was apparent that his subjects would remain mute, the Emperor spoke. "Yes, indeed. A most Confucian idea. The son defers to the father. Most Confucian indeed."

The Wu patriarch bowed his head. Most thought his bow expressed humble appreciation; only a few knew it was from the deepest humiliation. In a lifetime of almost successes, this day had promised to be the most glorious, but ultimately it became the most excruciating. The joy that the sovereign had granted, the son had taken away.

Meihua and Longyan shared a loving smile. They would forever bask in the glow of this day. For once, what was right was also what was best. They could live as few Chinese elites could live, with utter honesty and fearlessness. They could also interact as a rare team, a Chinese husband and wife who fully respected each other's creative powers, who became stronger by acknowledging weaknesses to each other.

In later years, Longyan was able to soften toward his father. Only then did the Wu patriarch begin to realize a different truth: it was Hainan Island that had shaped different values for his son and daughter-in-law. Had you been there, Longyan would say to his aging father, you would have been able to act differently as well. You operated properly by Confucian conventions, Longyan would argue, you placed your face, your image as clan head, above all else. Father and son would then learn, as Meihua and Father Gao urged them to learn, the ultimate lesson of Hainan Island: forgiveness is the most important, and the most elusive, virtue in the realm of family relations.

As the imperial audience concluded, Father Gao bowed his head. He knew he should be thankful. His children, who had suffered so much, had now achieved stature in the Chinese empire. He should thank the Heavenly Father who intervened through a humble priest to make this possible. But he couldn't summon up the courage to make the prayer. He feared that a Christian God might perceive that a not-so-humble priest was losing his faith. The Holy Catholic Church seemed very far away on this particular day, as if the Vatican was off in some dusty corner of the luminous Forbidden City. Father Gao felt himself just another man overwhelmed by the power of the Middle Kingdom. Today was a good one, tomorrow might be different; it all depended on the throw of the joss sticks, not on some foreign ideology.

None of these subtleties of family and faith made much of an impression on the Shunzhi emperor. But he knew what was most important to the Dragon Throne. He was unreservedly proud of conducting what everyone saw as a most important dawn audience. As a result, more Manchus would be educated, and more Chinese would be mollified. That was his divine responsibility: to be sovereign of All Under Heaven whether they came from north or south of the Great Wall.

The Emperor wiggled his head and giggled. "Dismissed," he declared, enjoying his prerogative to end the audience. "Don't forget to look at the miniature jade mountain on the way out," he called to the Wu and Lin clans, who were bowing in his direction while trying to walk backwards. "It's unbelievable. One piece of jade. Biggest in the whole world."

As everyone was leaving, the Emperor rubbed his hands together and beamed at his advisers. "What do you think?" the Emperor asked in an undisguised stage whisper. "Maybe we Manchus are getting good at Confucianism after all."

"So clever . . . so thoughtful . . ." The courtiers outdid one another with praise for the Emperor's audience. "The August One sees all. . . ."

Father Gao shuddered at the doorway, the bright early morning sunshine not dispelling the chill in his bones. He took a last glance at the throne. The Emperor, having completely forgotten the audience, was engrossed with a toy pair of acrobats some tribute bearer had presented, flipping them over and over into various grotesque positions.

"So clever . . . so playful . . ." The courtiers, clustered around the golden throne, showered compliments on how the Emperor handled the toy. Bright yellow garments illuminated by shafts of sunlight gave the scene a buzzing glitter, like a contented beehive. Around the edges of the room, in the haze of oil lamps and still chilly from the dawn moisture, grayish figures whispered their discontents. "Just you wait. . . . Our time will come."

Father Gao considered crossing himself, less as a Catholic gesture than as ritual way of warding off evil. But both his arms were fully occupied as he struggled with crutches across the still-slippery smooth stones. His body was forever crippled from the last time dark forces ruled the Forbidden City.